BLIND WILLOW, SLEEPING WOMAN

HARUKI MURAKAMI

TWENTY-FOUR STORIES

BLIND WILLOW, SLEEPING WOMAN

TRANSLATED FROM THE JAPANESE BY PHILIP GABRIEL AND JAY RUBIN

ALFRED A. KNOPF · NEW YORK · 2006

THIS IS A BORZOI BOOK PUBLISHED BY ALFRED A. KNOPF

www.aaknopf.com

Knopf, Borzoi Books, and the colophon are registered trademarks of Random House, Inc.

"The Seventh Man" appeared originally in Granta; "Blind Willow, Sleeping Woman," "Birthday Girl," and "Chance Traveler" in Harper's; "Dabchick" in McSweeney's; "Airplane: Or, How He Talked to Himself as If Reciting Poetry" (originally published as "Airplane"), "The Folklore of My Generation: A Pre-History of Late-Stage Capitalism" (originally published as "The Folklore of Our Times" and translated by Alfred Birnbaum), "Hunting Knife," "The Ice Man" (in a translation by Richard Peterson), "The Kidney-Shaped Stone That Moves Every Day," "Man-Eating Cats," "New York Mining Disaster," "A 'Poor Aunt' Story," "Tony Takitani," "A Shinagawa Monkey," "Where I'm Likely to Find It," and "The Year of Spaghetti" in The New Yorker; "Crabs" in Storie Magazine; and "The Mirror" in The Yale Review. "Firefly" appeared originally in the novel Norwegian Wood, by Haruki Murakami (New York: Vintage, 2000).

Library of Congress Cataloging-in-Publication Data

Murakami, Haruki, [date]

Blind willow, sleeping woman : twenty-four stories / by Haruki Murakami.— 1st ed.

p.   cm.

ISBN 1-4000-4461-8

I. Title.

PL856.U673A23 2006

895.6'35—dc22   2005044544

Manufactured in the United States of America

FIRST EDITION

CONTENTS

To put it in the simplest possible terms, I find writing novels a challenge, writing short stories a joy. If writing novels is like planting a forest, then writing short stories is more like planting a garden. The two processes complement each other, creating a complete landscape that I treasure. The green foliage of the trees casts a pleasant shade over the earth, and the wind rustles the leaves, which are sometimes dyed a brilliant gold. Meanwhile, in the garden, buds appear on flowers, and colorful petals attract bees and butterflies, reminding us of the subtle transition from one season to the next.

Since my debut as a fiction writer in 1979 I've fairly consistently alternated between writing novels and short stories. My pattern's been this: once I finish a novel, I find I want to write some short stories; once a group of stories is done, then I feel like focusing on a novel. I never write any short stories while I'm writing a novel, and never write a novel while I'm working on short stories. The two types of writing may very well engage different parts of the brain, and it takes some time to get off one track and switch to the other.

It was only after I began my career with two short novels, *Hear the Wind Sing* and *Pinball, 1973,* that I started, from 1980 to 1981, to write short stories. The first three I ever wrote were "A Slow Boat to China," "A 'Poor Aunt' Story," and "New York Mining Disaster." I knew little about short story writing then so it was rough going, but I did find the experience very memorable. I felt the possibilities of my fictional world expand by several degrees. And readers seemed to appreciate this other side of me as a writer. "A Slow Boat to China" was collected in my first English short story collection, *The Elephant Vanishes,* while the other two can be found in the present collection. This was my starting point as a short story writer, and also when I developed my system of alternating between novels and short stories.

"The Mirror," "A Perfect Day for Kangaroos," "Dabchick," "The Year of Spaghetti," and "The Rise and Fall of Sharpie Cakes" were all in a collection of "short shorts" I wrote from 1981 to 1982. "The Rise and Fall of Sharpie Cakes," as readers can easily see, reveals my impressions of the literary world at the time of my debut, in the form of a fable. At the time, I couldn't fit in well with the Japanese literary establishment, a situation that continues to the present day.

One of the joys of writing short stories is that they don't take so long to finish. Generally it takes me about a week to get a short story into some kind of decent shape (though revisions can be endless). It's not like the total physical and mental commitment you have to make for the year or two it takes to compose a novel. You merely enter a room, finish your work, and exit. That's it. For me, at least, writing a novel can seem to drag on forever, and I sometimes wonder if I'm going to survive. So I find writing short stories a necessary change of pace.

One more nice thing about short stories is that you can create a story out of the smallest details—an idea that springs up in your mind, a word, an image, whatever. In most cases it's like jazz improvisation, with the story taking me where it wants to. And another good point is that with short stories you don't have to worry about failing. If the idea doesn't work out the way you hoped it would, you just shrug your shoulders and tell yourself that they can't all be winners. Even with masters of the genre like F. Scott Fitzgerald and Raymond Carver—even Anton Chekhov—not every short story is a masterpiece. I find this a great comfort. You can learn from your mistakes (in other words, those you can't call a complete success) and use that in the next story you write. In my case, when I write novels I try very hard to learn from the successes and failures I experience in writing short stories. In that sense, the short story is a kind of experimental laboratory for me as a novelist. It's hard to experiment the way I like inside the framework of a novel, so without short stories I know I'd find the task of writing novels even more difficult and demanding.

Essentially I consider myself a novelist, but a lot of people tell me they prefer my short stories to my novels. That doesn't bother me, and I don't try to convince them otherwise. I'm actually happy to hear them say that. My short stories are like soft shadows I've set out in the world, faint footprints I've left behind. I remember exactly where I set down each and every one of them, and how I felt when I did. Short stories are like guideposts to my heart, and it makes me happy as a writer to be able to share these intimate feelings with my readers.

The Elephant Vanishes came out in 1991 and was subsequently translated into many other languages. Another collection in English, *after the quake*, was published in 2002 (2000 in Japan). This book contained six short tales all dealing in one way or another with the 1995 Kobe earthquake. I'd written it in the hope that all six stories would form a unified image in the reader's mind, so it was more like a concept album than a short story collection. In that sense, then, the present book, *Blind Willow, Sleeping Woman,* is the first real short story collection I've brought out abroad in a long time.

This book naturally contains some stories I wrote after *The Elephant Vanishes* appeared. "Birthday Girl," "Man-Eating Cats," "The Seventh Man," and "Ice Man" are some of these. I wrote "Birthday Girl" at the request of the editor when I was working on an anthology of other writers' stories on the theme of birthdays. It helps to be a writer when you're selecting stories for an anthology, since if you're short one story you can write one yourself. "Ice Man," by the way, is based on a dream my wife had, while "The Seventh Man" is based on an idea that came to me when I was into surfing and was gazing out at the waves.

To tell the truth, though, from the beginning of 1990 to the beginning of 2000 I wrote very few short stories. It wasn't that I'd lost interest in short stories. I was just so involved in writing a number of novels that I couldn't spare the time. I didn't have the time to switch tracks. I did write a short story from time to time when I had to, but I never focused on them. Instead, I wrote novels: *The Wind-Up Bird Chronicle; South of the Border, West of the Sun; Sputnik Sweetheart; Kafka on the Shore.* And in between, I wrote nonfiction, the two works that make up the English version of *Underground.* Each of these took an enormous amount of time and energy. I suppose that back then my main battleground was this—the writing of one novel after another. Perhaps it was just that time of life for me. In between, like an intermezzo, was the collection *after the quake*, but as I said, this really wasn't a short story collection.

In 2005, though, for the first time in a long time I was struck by a strong desire to write a series of short stories. A powerful urge took hold of me, you might say. So I sat down at my desk, wrote about a story a week, and finished five in not much more than a month. I frankly couldn't think of anything else but these stories, and I wrote them almost without stopping. These five stories, published recently in Japan in a volume entitled *Tokyo Kitanshu* (Strange Tales from Tokyo) are collected at the end of this book. Although they all share the theme of being strange tales, each story can be read independently, and they don't form a clear-cut, single unit as did the stories in *after the quake.* Come to think of it, however, everything I write is, more or less, a strange tale.

"Crabs," "A 'Poor Aunt' Story," "Hunting Knife," and "Blind Willow, Sleeping Woman" have all been greatly revised prior to their translation, so the versions here differ significantly from the first versions published in Japan. With some of the other older stories, too, I found spots I wasn't pleased with and made some minor changes.

I should also mention that many times I've rewritten short stories and incorporated them into novels, and the present collection contains several of these prototypes. "The Wind-up Bird and Tuesday's Women" (included in *The Elephant Vanishes*) became the model for the opening section of the novel *The Wind-Up Bird Chronicle,* and likewise both "Firefly" and "Man-Eating Cats," with some changes, were incorporated as parts of, respectively, the novels *Norwegian Wood* and *Sputnik Sweetheart.* There was a period when narratives I'd written as short stories, after I'd published them, kept expanding in my mind, developing into novels. A short story I'd written long ago would barge into my house in the middle of the night, shake me awake, and shout, "Hey, this is no time to be sleeping! You can't forget about me, there's still more to write!" Impelled by that voice, I'd find myself writing a novel. In this sense, too, my short stories and novels connect up inside me in a very natural, organic way.

Many people have encouraged me and led me to write short stories. Every time I see Amanda Urban, my agent at ICM, she repeats this mantra-like exhortation: "Haruki, write more short stories!" Gary Fisketjon at Knopf, editor of *The Elephant Vanishes,* also edited the present collection and was pivotal in seeing *Blind Willow, Sleeping Woman* into print. Both Jay Rubin and Philip Gabriel, my hardworking, skilled translators, have their own unique touch, and it's been a real pleasure to read my stories again in their superb translations. I've also been greatly inspired by Deborah Treisman, and her predecessor, Linda Asher, literary editors at *The New Yorker,* which has published many of my stories. Thanks to all of them, this new collection of short stories is now published and—as a short story writer—I couldn't be more pleased with what we've accomplished.

— H . M .

BLIND WILLOW, SLEEPING WOMAN

When I closed my eyes, the scent of the wind wafted up toward me. A May wind, swelling up like a piece of fruit, with a rough outer skin, slimy flesh, dozens of seeds. The flesh split open in midair, spraying seeds like gentle buckshot into the bare skin of my arms, leaving behind a faint trace of pain.

"What time is it?" my cousin asked me. About eight inches shorter than me, he had to look up when he talked.

I glanced at my watch. "Ten twenty."

"Does that watch tell good time?"

"Yeah, I think so."

My cousin grabbed my wrist to look at the watch. His slim, smooth fingers were surprisingly strong. "Did it cost a lot?"

"No, it's pretty cheap," I said, glancing again at the timetable.

No response.

My cousin looked confused. The white teeth between his parted lips looked like bones that had atrophied.

"It's pretty cheap," I said, looking right at him, carefully repeating the words. *"It's pretty cheap, but it keeps good time."*

My cousin nodded silently.

⊙

My cousin can't hear well out of his right ear. Soon after he went into elementary school he was hit by a baseball and it screwed up his hearing.

3

That doesn't keep him from functioning normally most of the time. He attends a regular school, leads an entirely normal life. In his classroom, he always sits in the front row, on the right, so he can keep his left ear toward the teacher. And his grades aren't so bad. The thing is, though, he goes through periods when he can hear sounds pretty well, and periods when he can't. It's cyclical, like the tides. And sometimes, maybe twice a year, he can barely hear anything out of either ear. It's like the silence in his right ear deepens to the point where it crushes out any sound on the left side. When that happens, ordinary life goes out the window and he has to take some time off from school. The doctors are basically stumped. They've never seen a case like it, so there's nothing they can do.

"Just because a watch is expensive doesn't mean it's accurate," my cousin said, as if trying to convince himself. "I used to have a pretty expensive watch, but it was always off. I got it when I started junior high, but I lost it a year later. Since then I've gone without a watch. They won't buy me a new one."

"Must be tough to get along without one," I said.

"What?" he asked.

"Isn't it hard to get along without a watch?" I repeated, looking right at him.

"No, it isn't," he replied, shaking his head. "It's not like I'm living off in the mountains or something. If I want to know the time I just ask somebody."

"True enough," I said.

We were silent again for a while.

I knew I should say something more, try to be kind to him, try to make him relax a little until we arrived at the hospital. But it had been five years since I saw him last. In the meanwhile he'd grown from nine to fourteen, and I'd gone from twenty to twenty-five. And that span of time had created a translucent barrier between us that was hard to traverse. Even when I had to say something, the right words just wouldn't come out. And every time I hesitated, every time I swallowed back something I was about to say, my cousin looked at me with a slightly confused look on his face. His left ear tilted ever so slightly toward me.

"What time is it now?" he asked me.

"Ten twenty-nine," I replied.

It was ten thirty-two when the bus finally rolled into view.

The bus that came was a new type, not like the one I used to take to high school. The windshield in front of the driver was much bigger, the whole vehicle like some huge bomber minus the wings. And the bus was more crowded than I'd imagined. Nobody was standing in the aisle, but we couldn't sit together. We weren't going very far, so we stood next to the rear door in back. Why the bus should be so crowded at this time of day was a mystery. The bus route started from a private railway station, continued up into a residential area in the hills, then circled back to the station, and there weren't any tourist spots along the way. A few schools along the route made the buses crowded when kids were going to school, but at this time of day the bus should have been empty.

My cousin and I held on to the straps and poles. The bus was brand-new, straight from the factory, the metal surfaces so shiny you could see your face reflected in them. The nap of the seats was all fluffy, and even the tiniest of screws had that proud, expectant feeling that only brand-new machinery possesses.

The new bus, and the way it was unexpectedly crowded, threw me off. Maybe the bus route had changed since I last rode it. I looked carefully around the bus and glanced outside. But it was the same old view of a quiet residential district I remembered well.

"This is the right bus, isn't it?" my cousin asked worriedly. Ever since we got aboard I must have had a perplexed look on my face.

"Not to worry," I said, trying to reassure myself as much as him. "There's only one bus route that goes by here, so this has got to be it."

"Did you used to take this bus when you went to high school?" my cousin asked.

"Yeah, that's right."

"Did you like school?"

"Not particularly," I said. "But I could see my friends there, and it wasn't such a long ride."

My cousin thought about what I'd said.

"Do you still see them?"

"No, not for a long time," I said, choosing my words carefully.

"Why not? Why don't you see them?"

" 'Cause we live so far away from each other." That wasn't the reason, but I couldn't think of any other way to explain it.

Right beside me sat a group of old people. Must have been close to fifteen of them. They were the reason the bus was crowded, I suddenly
realized. They were all suntanned, even the backs of their necks dark.
And every single one of them was skinny. Most of the men had on thick
mountain-climbing types of shirts; the women, simple, unadorned
blouses. All of them had small rucksacks in their laps, the kind you'd use
for short hikes into the hills. It was amazing how much they looked alike.
Like a drawer full of samples of something, all neatly lined up. The
strange thing, though, was that there wasn't any mountain-climbing
route along this bus line. So where in the world could they have been
going? I thought about this as I stood there, clinging to the strap, but no
plausible explanation came to mind.

◎

"I wonder if it's going to hurt this time—the treatments?" my cousin
asked me.

"I don't know," I said. "I didn't hear any of the details."

"Have you ever been to an ear doctor?"

I shook my head. I hadn't been to an ear doctor once in my life.

"Has it hurt before?" I asked.

"Not really," my cousin said glumly. "It wasn't totally painless, of
course; sometimes it hurt a *little*. But nothing terrible."

"Maybe this time it'll be the same. Your mom said they're not going to
do anything much different from usual."

"But if they do the same as always, how's that going to help?"

"Well, you never know. Sometimes the unexpected happens."

"You mean like pulling out a cork?" my cousin said. I glanced at him,
but didn't detect any sarcasm.

"It'll feel different having a new doctor treat you, and sometimes just
a slight change in procedure might make all the difference. I wouldn't
give up so easily."

"I'm not giving up," my cousin said.

"But you are kind of fed up with it?"

"I guess," he said, and sighed. "The fear is the worst thing. The pain I
imagine is worse than the actual pain. Know what I mean?"

"Yeah, I know."

⊙

A lot of things had happened that spring. A situation developed at work and I ended up quitting my job at a little advertising firm in Tokyo where I'd been working for two years. Around the same time I broke up with my girlfriend; we'd been going out since college. A month after that my grandmother died of intestinal cancer, and for the first time in five years I came back to this town, small suitcase in hand. My old room was just as I'd left it. The books I'd read were still on the shelf, my bed was still there, my desk, and all the old records I used to listen to. But everything in the room had dried up, had long ago lost its color and smell. Time alone had stood still.

I'd planned to go back to Tokyo a couple of days after my grandmother's funeral to run down some leads for a new job. I was planning to move to a new apartment, too; I needed a change of scenery. As the days passed, though, it seemed like too much trouble to get off my butt and get going. To put a finer point on it, even if I'd wanted to get up and get going, I couldn't. I spent my time holed up in my old room, listening to those records, rereading old books, occasionally doing a little weeding in the garden. I didn't meet anybody, and the only people I talked to were members of my family.

One day my aunt dropped by and asked me to take my cousin to a new hospital. She should take him herself, she said, but something had come up on the day of the appointment and she couldn't. The hospital was near my old high school, so I knew where it was, and since I had nothing else going on, I couldn't very well refuse. My aunt handed me an envelope with some cash in it for us to use as lunch money.

This switch to a new hospital came about because the treatment he'd been getting at his old hospital hadn't done a thing to help. In fact, he was having more problems than ever. When my aunt complained to the doctor in charge, he suggested that the problem had more to do with the boy's home environment than anything medical, and the two of them went at it. Not that anybody really expected that changing hospitals would lead to a quick improvement in his hearing. Nobody said as much, but they'd pretty much given up hope that his condition would ever improve.

My cousin lived nearby, but I was just over a decade older than him and we had never been what you'd call close. When the relatives got together I might take him someplace or play with him, but that was the extent of it. Still, before long everyone started to look at my cousin and me as a pair, thinking that he was attached to me and that he was my favorite. For the longest time I couldn't figure out why. Now, though, seeing the way he tilted his head, his left ear aimed at me, I found it strangely touching. Like the sound of rain heard long ago, his awkwardness struck a chord with me. And I began to catch a glimpse of why our relatives wanted to bring us together.

The bus had passed by seven or eight bus stops when my cousin anxiously looked up at me again.

"Is it much farther?"

"Yeah, we still have a ways. It's a big hospital, so we won't miss it."

I casually watched as the wind from the open window gently rustled the brims of the old people's hats and the scarves around their necks. Who *were* these people? And where could they possibly be headed?

"Hey, are you going to work in my father's company?" my cousin asked.

I looked at him in surprise. His father, my uncle, ran a large printing company in Kobe. I'd never given the idea a thought, and nobody ever dropped a hint.

"Nobody's said anything about that," I said. "Why do you ask?"

My cousin blushed. "I just thought you might be," he said. "But why don't you? You wouldn't have to leave. And everybody'd be happy."

The taped message announced the next stop, but no one pushed the button to get off. Nobody was waiting to get on at the bus stop either.

"But there's stuff I have to do, so I have to go back to Tokyo," I said. My cousin nodded silently.

There wasn't a single thing I *had* to do. But I couldn't very well *stay here.*

The number of houses thinned out as the bus climbed the mountain slope. Thick branches began to throw a heavy shadow across the road. We passed by some foreign-looking houses, painted, with low walls in front. The cold breeze felt good. Each time the bus rounded a curve the sea down below popped into view, then disappeared. Until the bus pulled up at the hospital my cousin and I just stood there, watching the scenery go by.

"The examination will take some time and I can handle it alone," my cousin said, "so why don't you go and wait for me somewhere?" After a quick hello to the doctor, I exited the exam room and went to the cafeteria. I'd barely had a bite for breakfast and was starving, but nothing on the menu whetted my appetite. I made do with a cup of coffee.

It was a weekday morning and one little family and I had the place to ourselves. The father was in his midforties, wearing a navy-blue-striped pair of pajamas and plastic slippers. The mother and little twin girls had come to pay a visit. The twins had on identical white dresses and were bent over the table, serious looks on their faces, drinking glasses of orange juice. The father's injury, or illness, didn't seem too serious, and both parents and kids looked bored.

Outside the window was a lawn. A sprinkler ticked as it rotated, misting the grass with a silvery spray. A pair of shrill long-tailed birds cut right above the sprinkler and disappeared from sight. Past the lawn there were a few deserted tennis courts, the nets gone. Beyond the tennis courts was a line of zelkovas, and between their branches you could glimpse the ocean. The early summer sun glinted here and there off the small waves. The breeze rustled the new leaves of the zelkovas, ever so slightly bending the spray from the sprinkler.

I felt like I'd seen this scene, many years before. A broad swatch of lawn, twin girls slurping up orange juice, long-tailed birds flying off who knows where, netless tennis courts, the sea beyond . . . But it was an illusion. It was vivid enough, an intense sense of the real, but an illusion nonetheless. I'd never been to this hospital in my life.

I stretched my legs out on the seat opposite, took a deep breath, and closed my eyes. In the darkness I could see a lump of white. Silently it expanded, then contracted, like a microbe under a microscope. Changing form, spreading out, breaking up, re-forming.

It was eight years ago when I went to that other hospital. A small hospital next to the sea. All you could see out the window were some oleanders. It was a hospital, and it smelled of rain. My friend's girlfriend had her chest operated on there, and the two of us went to see how she was doing. The summer of our junior year in high school.

It wasn't much of an operation, really, just done to correct the position of one of her ribs that curved inward a bit. Not an emergency procedure, just the type of thing that would eventually have to be done, so she figured why not take care of it now. The operation itself was over quickly, but they wanted her to take her time recuperating, so she stayed in the hospital for ten days. My friend and I rode there together on a 125cc Yamaha motorcycle. He drove on the way there, I drove on the way back. He'd asked me to come. "No way I'm going to a hospital by myself," he'd said.

My friend stopped at a candy store near the station and bought a box of chocolates. I held on to his belt with one hand, the other hand clutching tightly the box of chocolates. It was a hot day and our shirts kept getting soaked, then drying in the wind. As my friend drove he sang some nothing song in an awful voice. I can still remember the smell of his sweat. Not too long after that he died.

His girlfriend had on blue pajamas and a thin gown sort of thing down to her knees. The three of us sat at a table in the cafeteria, smoked Short Hope cigarettes, drank Cokes, and ate ice cream. She was starving and ate two sugarcoated doughnuts and drank cocoa with tons of cream in it. Still that didn't seem enough for her.

"By the time you get out of here you're going to be a regular blimp," my friend said, somewhat disgustedly.

"It's okay—I'm recovering," she replied, wiping the tips of her fingers, covered in oil from the doughnuts.

As they talked I glanced out the window at the oleanders. They were huge, almost like a forest unto themselves. I could hear the sound of waves too. The railing next to the window was completely rusted from the constant breeze. An antique-looking ceiling fan nudged the hot, sticky air around the room. The cafeteria had the smell of a hospital. Even the food and drinks had that hospital odor to them. The girlfriend's pajamas had two breast pockets, in one of which was a small gold-colored pen. Whenever she leaned forward I could see her small, white breasts peep out of the V-neck collar.

The memories ground to a halt right there. I tried to remember what had happened after that. I drank a Coke, gazed at the oleanders, snuck a peek at her breasts—and then what? I shifted in the plastic chair and, resting my head in my hands, tried to dig down further in the layers of memory. Like gouging out a cork with the tip of a thin-bladed knife.

I looked off to one side and tried to visualize the doctors splitting open the flesh of her chest, sticking their rubber-gloved hands inside to straighten out her crooked rib. But it all seemed too surreal, like some sort of allegory.

That's right—after that we talked about sex. At least my friend did. But what did he say? Something about me, no doubt. How I'd tried, unsuccessfully, to make it with a girl. Not much of a story, but the way he told it, blowing everything out of proportion, made his girlfriend burst out laughing. Made me laugh as well. The guy really knew how to tell a story.

"Please don't make me laugh," she said, a bit painfully. "My chest hurts when I laugh."

"Where does it hurt?" my friend asked.

She pressed a spot on her pajamas above her heart, just to the right of her left breast. He made some joke about that, and she laughed again.

◎

I looked at my watch. It was eleven forty-five but my cousin still wasn't back. It was getting close to lunchtime and the cafeteria was starting to get more crowded. All sorts of sounds and voices mixed together like smoke enveloping the room. I returned once more to the realm of memory. And that small gold pen she had in her breast pocket.

. . . Now I remember—she used that pen to write something on a paper napkin.

She was drawing a picture. The napkin was too soft and the tip of her pen kept getting stuck. Still, she managed to draw a hill. And a small house on top of the hill. A woman was asleep in the house. The house was surrounded by a stand of blind willows. It was the blind willows that had put her to sleep.

"What the heck's a blind willow?" my friend asked.

"There is a kind of tree like that."

"Well, *I* never heard of it."

"That's 'cause I'm the one who created it," she said, smiling. "Blind willows have a lot of pollen, and tiny flies covered with the stuff crawled inside her ear and put the woman to sleep."

She took a new napkin and drew a picture of the blind willow. The blind willow turned out to be a tree the size of an azalea. The tree was in bloom, the flowers surrounded by dark green leaves like a bunch of lizard tails gathered in a bunch. The blind willow didn't resemble a willow at all.

"You got a cigarette?" my friend asked me. I tossed a sweaty pack of Hopes and some matches across the table.

"A blind willow looks small on the outside, but it's got incredibly deep roots," she explained. "Actually, after a certain point it stops growing up and pushes further and further down into the ground. Like the darkness nourishes it."

"And the flies carry that pollen to her ear, burrow inside, and put her to sleep," my friend added, struggling to light his cigarette with the damp matches. "But what happens to the flies?"

"They stay inside the woman and eat her flesh—naturally," his girlfriend said.

"*Gobble* it up," my friend said.

◎

I remembered now how that summer she'd written a long poem about the blind willow and explained it all to us. That was the only homework assignment she did that summer. She made up a story based on a dream she'd had one night, and as she lay in bed for a week she wrote this long poem. My friend said he wanted to read it, but she was still revising it, so she turned him down; instead, she drew those pictures and summarized the plot.

A young man climbed up the hill to rescue the woman the blind-willow pollen had put to sleep.

"That's got to be me," my friend said.

She shook her head. "No, it isn't you."

"You sure?" he asked.

"I'm sure," she said, a fairly serious look on her face. "I don't know why I know that. But I do. You're not angry, are you?"

"You bet I am," my friend frowned, half joking.

Pushing his way through the thick blind willows, the young man slowly made his way up the hill. He was the first one ever to climb the hill once the blind willows took over. Hat pulled down over his eyes, brushing away with one hand the swarms of flies buzzing around him, the young man kept climbing. To see the sleeping woman. To wake her from her long, deep sleep.

"But by the time he reached the top of the hill the woman's body had basically been eaten up already by the flies, right?" my friend said.

"In a sense," his girlfriend replied.

"*In a sense* being eaten by flies makes it a sad story, doesn't it?" my friend said.

"Yes, I guess so," she said after giving it some thought. "What do you think?" she asked me.

"Sounds like a sad story to me," I replied.

It was twelve twenty when my cousin came back. He was carrying a small bag of medicine and had a sort of unfocused look on his face. After he appeared at the entrance to the cafeteria it took some time for him to spot me and come on over. He walked awkwardly, as if he couldn't keep his balance. He sat down across from me and, like he'd been too busy to remember to breathe, took a huge breath.

"How'd it go?" I asked.

"Mmm," he said. I waited for him to say more, but he didn't.

"Are you hungry?" I asked.

He nodded silently.

"You want to eat here? Or do you want to take the bus into town and eat there?"

He looked uncertainly around the room. "Here's fine," he said. I bought lunch tickets and ordered the set lunches for both of us. Until the food was brought over to us my cousin gazed silently out the window at the same scenery I'd been looking at—the sea, the row of zelkovas, the sprinkler.

At the table beside us a nicely decked-out middle-aged couple were eating sandwiches and talking about a friend of theirs who had lung cancer. How he'd quit smoking five years ago but it was too late, how he'd vomit blood when he woke up in the morning. The wife asked the questions, the husband gave the answers. In a certain sense, the husband explained, you can see a person's whole life in the cancer they get.

Our lunches consisted of Salisbury steaks and fried whitefish, salad and rolls. We sat there, across from each other, silently eating. The whole time we were eating the couple next to us droned on and on about how cancer starts, why the cancer rate's gone up, why there isn't any medicine to combat it.

⊙

"Everywhere you go it's the same," my cousin said in a flat tone, gazing at his hands. "The same old questions, the same tests."

We were sitting on a bench in front of the hospital, waiting for the bus. Every once in a while the breeze would rustle the green leaves above us.

"Sometimes you can't hear anything at all?" I asked him.

"That's right," my cousin answered. "I can't hear a thing."

"What does that feel like?"

He tilted his head to one side and thought about it. "All of a sudden you can't hear anything. But it takes a while before you realize what's happened. By then you can't hear a thing. It's like you're at the bottom of the sea wearing earplugs. That continues for a while. All the time you can't hear a thing, but it's not just your ears. Not being able to hear anything is just *part* of it."

"Does it bother you?"

He shook his head, a short, definite shake. "I don't know why, but it doesn't bother me that much. It *is* inconvenient, though. Not being able to hear anything."

I tried to picture it, but the image wouldn't come.

"Did you ever see John Ford's movie *Fort Apache*?" my cousin asked.

"A long time ago," I said.

"It was on TV recently. It's really a good movie."

"Um," I affirmed.

"In the beginning of the movie there's this new colonel who's come to a fort out west. A veteran captain comes out to meet him when he arrives. The captain's played by John Wayne. The colonel doesn't know much about what things are like in the west. And there's an Indian uprising all around the fort."

My cousin took a neatly folded white handkerchief from his pocket and wiped his mouth.

"Once he gets to the fort the colonel turns to John Wayne and says, 'I did see a few Indians on the way over here.' And John Wayne, with this cool look on his face, replies, 'Don't worry. If you were able to spot some Indians, that means there aren't any there.' I don't remember the actual lines, but it went something like that. Do you get what he means?"

I couldn't recall any lines like that from *Fort Apache*. It struck me as a little abstruse for a John Ford movie. But it had been a while since I'd seen the film.

"I think it means that what can be seen by anybody isn't all that important . . . I guess."

My cousin frowned. "I don't really get it either, but every time somebody sympathizes with me about my ears that line comes to me. 'If you were able to spot some Indians, that means there aren't any there.' "

I laughed.

"Is that strange?" my cousin asked.

"Yep," I laughed. And he laughed. It'd been a long time since I'd seen him laugh.

After a while my cousin said, like he was unburdening himself, "Would you look inside my ears for me?"

"Look inside your ears?" I asked, a little surprised.

"Just what you can see from the outside."

"Okay, but why do you want me to do that?"

"I don't know," my cousin blushed. "I just want you to see what they look like."

"Okay," I said. "I'll give it a whirl."

My cousin sat facing away from me, tilting his right ear toward me. He had a really nicely shaped ear. It was on the small side, but the earlobe was all puffy, like a freshly baked madeleine. I'd never looked at anybody's ear so intently before. Once you start observing it closely, the human ear—its structure—is a pretty mysterious thing. With all these absurd twists and turns to it, bumps and depressions. Maybe evolution determined this weird shape was the optimum way to collect sounds, or to protect what's inside. Surrounded by this asymmetrical wall, the hole of the ear gapes open like the entrance to a dark, secret cave.

I pictured my friend's girlfriend, microscopic flies nesting in her ear. Sweet pollen stuck to their tiny legs, they burrow into the warm darkness inside her, sucking up all the juices, laying tiny eggs inside her brain. But you can't see them, or even hear the sound of their wings.

"That's enough," my cousin said.

He spun around to sit facing forward, shifting around on the bench. "So, see anything unusual?"

"Nothing different as far as I could see. From the outside at least."

"Anything's okay—even a feeling you got or something."

"Your ear looks normal to me."

My cousin looked disappointed. Maybe I had said the wrong thing.

"Did the treatment hurt?" I asked.

"No, it didn't. Same as always. They just rummaged around in the same old spot. Feels like they're going to wear it out. Sometimes it doesn't feel like my own ear anymore."

◎

"There's the number twenty-eight," my cousin said after a while, turning to me. "That's our bus, right?"

I'd been lost in thought. I looked up when he said this and saw the bus slowing down as it went round the curve coming up the slope. This wasn't the kind of brand-new bus we'd ridden over on but one of the older buses I remembered. A sign with the number 28 was hanging on the front. I tried to stand up from the bench, but I couldn't. Like I was caught up in the middle of a powerful current, my limbs wouldn't respond.

I'd been thinking of the box of chocolates we'd taken when we went to that hospital on that long-ago summer afternoon. The girl had happily opened the lid to the box only to discover that the dozen little chocolates had completely melted, sticking to the paper between each piece and to the lid itself. On the way to the hospital my friend and I had parked the motorcycle by the seaside, and lay around on the beach just talking and hanging out. The whole while we'd let that box of chocolates lie out in the hot August sun. Our carelessness, our self-centeredness, had wrecked those chocolates, made one fine mess of them all. We should have sensed what was happening. One of us—it didn't matter who—should have said something. But on that afternoon, we didn't sense anything, just exchanged a couple of dumb jokes and said goodbye. And left that hill still overgrown with blind willows.

My cousin grabbed my right arm in a tight grip.

"Are you all right?" he asked me.

His words brought me back to reality, and I stood up from the bench. This time I had no trouble standing. Once more I could feel on my skin the sweet May breeze. For a few seconds I stood there in a strange, dim place. Where the things I could see didn't exist. Where the invisible *did*. Finally, though, the real number 28 bus stopped in front of me, its entirely real door opening. I clambered aboard, heading off to some other place.

I rested my hand on my cousin's shoulder. "I'm all right," I told him.

—TRANSLATED BY PHILIP GABRIEL

BIRTHDAY GIRL

She waited on tables as usual that day, her twentieth birthday. She always worked on Fridays, but if things had gone according to plan that particular Friday, she would have had the night off. The other part-time girl had agreed to switch shifts with her as a matter of course: being screamed at by an angry chef while lugging pumpkin gnocchi and seafood fritto misto to customers' tables was no way to spend one's twentieth birthday. But the other girl had aggravated a cold and gone to bed with unstoppable diarrhea and a fever of 104, so she ended up working after all on short notice.

She found herself trying to comfort the sick girl, who had called to apologize. "Don't worry about it," she said. "I wasn't going to do anything special anyway, even if it is my twentieth birthday."

And in fact she was not all that disappointed. One reason was the terrible argument she had had a few days earlier with the boyfriend who was supposed to be with her that night. They had been going together since high school. The argument had started from nothing much but it had taken an unexpected turn for the worse until it became a long and bitter shouting match—one bad enough, she was pretty sure, to have snapped their long-standing ties once and for all. Something inside her had turned rock-hard and died. He had not called her since the blowup, and she was not about to call him.

Her workplace was one of the better-known Italian restaurants in the tony Roppongi district of Tokyo. It had been in business since the late sixties, and while its cuisine was hardly cutting edge, its high reputation

19

was fully justified. It had many repeat customers and they were never disappointed. The dining room had a calm, relaxed atmosphere without a hint of pushiness. Rather than a young crowd, the restaurant drew an older clientele that included some famous stage people and writers.

The two full-time waiters worked six days a week. She and the other part-time waitress were students who took turns working three days each. In addition there was one floor manager and, at the register, a skinny middle-aged woman who supposedly had been there since the restaurant opened—literally sitting in the one place, it seemed, like some gloomy old character from *Little Dorrit*. She had exactly two functions: to accept payment from the customers and to answer the phone. She spoke only when necessary and always wore the same black dress. There was something cold and hard about her: if you set her afloat on the nighttime sea, she would probably sink any boat that happened to ram her.

The floor manager was perhaps in his late forties. Tall and broad-shouldered, his build suggested that he had been a sportsman in his youth, but excess flesh was now beginning to accumulate on his belly and chin. His short, stiff hair was thinning at the crown, and a special aging bachelor smell clung to him—like newsprint that had been stored in a drawer with cough drops. She had a bachelor uncle who smelled like that.

The manager always wore a black suit, white shirt, and bow tie—not a clip-on bow tie, but the real thing, tied by hand. It was a point of pride for him that he could tie it perfectly without looking in the mirror. He performed his duties adroitly day after day. They consisted of checking the arrival and departure of guests, keeping abreast of the reservation schedule, knowing the names of regular customers, greeting them with a smile, lending a respectful ear to any complaints that might arise, giving expert advice on wines, and overseeing the work of the waiters and waitresses. It was also his special task to deliver dinner to the room of the restaurant's owner.

"The owner had his own room on the sixth floor of the same building where the restaurant was," she said. "An apartment, or office or something."

Somehow she and I had gotten on to the subject of our twentieth birthdays—what sort of day it had been for each of us. Most people remember the day they turned twenty. Hers had happened more than ten years earlier.

"He never, ever showed his face in the restaurant, though. The only one who saw him was the manager. It was strictly *his* job to deliver the owner's dinner to him. None of the other employees knew what he looked like."

"So basically, the owner was getting home delivery from his own restaurant."

"Right," she said. "Every night at eight, the manager had to bring dinner to the owner's room. It was the restaurant's busiest time, so having the manager disappear just then was always a problem for us, but there was no way around it because that was the way it had always been done. They'd load the dinner onto one of those carts that hotels use for room service, the manager would push it into the elevator wearing a respectful look on his face, and fifteen minutes later he'd come back empty-handed. Then, an hour later, he'd go up again and bring down the cart with empty plates and glasses. Every day, like clockwork. I thought it was really weird the first time I saw it happen. It was like some kind of religious ritual, you know? But after a while I got used to it, and never gave it a second thought."

The owner always had chicken. The recipe and the vegetable sides were a little different every day, but the main dish was always chicken. A young chef once told her that he had tried sending up the same exact roast chicken every day for a week just to see what would happen, but there was never any complaint. A chef wants to try different ways of preparing things, of course, and each new chef would challenge himself with every technique for chicken that he could think of. They'd make elegant sauces, they'd try chickens from different suppliers, but none of their efforts had any effect: they might just as well have been throwing pebbles into an empty cave. In the end, every one of them gave up and sent the owner some run-of-the-mill chicken dish every day. That's all that was ever asked of them.

Work started as usual on her twentieth birthday, November 17. It had been raining on and off since the afternoon, and pouring since early evening. At five o'clock the manager gathered the employees together to explain the day's specials. Servers were required to memorize them word for word and not use crib sheets: veal Milanese, pasta topped with sardines and cabbage, chestnut mousse. Sometimes the manager would play the role of a customer and test them with questions. Then came the employees' meal: waiters in *this* restaurant were not going to have growling stomachs as they took their customers' orders!

The restaurant opened its doors at six o'clock, but guests were slow to arrive because of the downpour, and several reservations were simply canceled. Women didn't want their dresses ruined by the rain. The manager walked around tight-lipped, and the waiters killed time polishing the salt and pepper shakers or chatting with the chef about cooking. She surveyed the dining room with its single couple at table and listened to the harpsichord music flowing discreetly from ceiling speakers. A deep smell of late autumn rain worked its way into the restaurant.

It was after seven thirty when the manager started feeling sick. He stumbled over to a chair and sat there for a while pressing his stomach, as if he had just been shot. A greasy sweat clung to his forehead. "I think I'd better go to the hospital," he muttered. For him to be taken ill was a most unusual occurrence: he had never missed a day since he started working in the restaurant over ten years earlier. It was another point of pride for him that he had never been out with illness or injury, but his painful grimace made it clear that he was in very bad shape.

She stepped outside with an umbrella and hailed a cab. One of the waiters held the manager steady and climbed into the car with him to take him to a nearby hospital. Before ducking into the cab, the manager said to her hoarsely, "I want you to take a dinner up to room 604 at eight o'clock. All you have to do is ring the bell, say 'Your dinner is here,' and leave it."

"That's room 604, right?" she said.

"At eight o'clock," he repeated. "On the dot." He grimaced again, climbed in, and the taxi took him away.

The rain showed no signs of letting up after the manager had left, and customers arrived at long intervals. No more than one or two tables were occupied at a time, so if the manager and one waiter had to be absent, this was a good time for it to happen. Things could get so busy that it was not unusual even for the full staff to have trouble coping.

23

When the owner's meal was ready at eight o'clock, she pushed the room service cart into the elevator and rode up to the sixth floor. It was the standard meal for him: a half bottle of red wine with the cork loosened, a thermal pot of coffee, a chicken entree with steamed vegetables, rolls and butter. The heavy aroma of cooked chicken quickly filled the little elevator. It mingled with the smell of the rain. Water droplets dotted the elevator floor, suggesting that someone with a wet umbrella had recently been aboard.

She pushed the cart down the corridor, bringing it to a stop in front of the door marked "604." She double-checked her memory: 604. That was it. She cleared her throat and pressed the doorbell.

There was no answer. She stood there for a good twenty seconds. Just as she was thinking of pressing the bell again, the door opened inward and a skinny old man appeared. He was shorter than she was, by some four or five inches. He had on a dark suit and a necktie. Against his white shirt, the tie stood out distinctly, its brownish yellow coloring like withered leaves. He made a very clean impression, his clothes perfectly pressed, his white hair smoothed down: he looked as though he were about to go out for the night to some sort of gathering. The deep wrinkles that creased his brow made her think of ravines in an aerial photograph.

"Your dinner, sir," she said in a husky voice, then quietly cleared her throat again. Her voice grew husky whenever she was tense.

"Dinner?"

"Yes, sir. The manager suddenly took sick. I had to take his place today. Your meal, sir."

"Oh, I see," the old man said, almost as if talking to himself, his hand still perched on the doorknob. "Took sick, eh? You don't say."

"His stomach started to hurt him all of a sudden. He went to the hospital. He thinks he might have appendicitis."

"Oh, that's not good," the old man said, running his fingers along the wrinkles of his forehead. "Not good at all."

She cleared her throat again. "Shall I bring your meal in, sir?" she asked.

"Ah yes, of course," the old man said. "Yes, of course, if you wish. That's fine with me."

If I wish? she thought. What a strange way to put it. What am I supposed to wish?

The old man opened the door the rest of the way, and she wheeled the cart inside. The floor had short gray carpeting with no area for removing shoes. The first room was a large study, as though the apartment was more a workplace than a residence. The window looked out on the nearby Tokyo Tower, its steel skeleton outlined in lights. A large desk stood by the window, and beside the desk was a compact sofa and love seat. The old man pointed to the plastic laminate coffee table in front of the sofa. She arranged his meal on the table: white napkin and silverware, coffeepot and cup, wine and wineglass, bread and butter, and the plate of chicken and vegetables.

"If you would be kind enough to set the dishes in the hall as usual, sir, I'll come to get them in an hour."

Her words seemed to snap him out of an appreciative contemplation of his dinner. "Oh yes, of course. I'll put them in the hall. On the cart. In an hour. If you wish."

Yes, she replied inwardly, for the moment that is exactly what I wish. "Is there anything else I can do for you, sir?"

"No, I don't think so," he said after a moment's consideration. He was wearing black shoes polished to a high sheen. They were small and chic. He's a stylish dresser, she thought. And he stands very straight for his age.

"Well, then, sir, I'll be getting back to work."

"No, wait just a moment," he said.

"Sir?"

"Do you think it might be possible for you to give me five minutes of your time, miss? I have something I'd like to say to you."

He was so polite in his request that it made her blush. "I . . . think it should be all right," she said. "I mean, if it really is just five minutes." He was her employer, after all. He was paying her by the hour. It was not a question of her giving or his taking her time. And this old man did not look like a person who would do anything bad to her.

"By the way, how old are you?" the old man asked, standing by the table with arms folded and looking directly into her eyes.

"I'm twenty now," she said.

"Twenty *now*," he repeated, narrowing his eyes as if peering through some kind of crack. "Twenty *now*. As of when?"

"Well, I just turned twenty," she said. After a moment's hesitation, she added, "Today is my birthday, sir."

"I *see*," he said, rubbing his chin as if this explained a great deal for him. "Today, is it? Today is your twentieth birthday?"

She nodded.

"Your life in this world began exactly twenty years ago today."

"Yes, sir," she said, "that is true."

"I see, I see," he said. "That's wonderful. Well, then, happy birthday."

"Thank you very much," she said, and then it dawned on her that this was the very first time all day that anyone had wished her a happy birthday. Of course, if her parents had called from Oita, she might find a message from them on her answering machine when she got home from work.

"Well, well, this is certainly a cause for celebration," he said. "How about a little toast? We can drink this red wine."

"Thank you, sir, but I couldn't, I'm working now."

"Oh, what's the harm in a little sip? No one's going to blame you if I say it's all right. Just a token drink to celebrate."

The old man slid the cork from the bottle and dribbled a little wine into his glass for her. Then he took an ordinary drinking glass from a glass-doored cabinet and poured some wine for himself.

"Happy birthday," he said. "May you live a rich and fruitful life, and may there be nothing to cast dark shadows on it."

They clinked glasses.

May there be nothing to cast dark shadows on it: she silently repeated his remark to herself. Why had he chosen such unusual words for her birthday toast?

"Your twentieth birthday comes only once in a lifetime, miss. It's an irreplaceable day."

"Yes, sir, I know," she said, taking one cautious sip of wine.

"And here, on your special day, you have taken the trouble to deliver my dinner to me like a kindhearted fairy."

"Just doing my job, sir."

"But still," the old man said with a few quick shakes of the head. "But still, lovely young miss."

The old man sat down in the leather chair by his desk and motioned her to the sofa. She lowered herself gingerly onto the edge of the seat, with the wineglass still in her hand. Knees aligned, she tugged at her skirt, clearing her throat again. She saw raindrops tracing lines down the windowpane. The room was strangely quiet.

"Today just happens to be your twentieth birthday, and on top of that you have brought me this wonderful warm meal," the old man said as if reconfirming the situation. Then he set his glass on the desktop with a little thump. "This has to be some kind of special convergence, don't you think?"

Not quite convinced, she managed a nod.

"Which is why," he said, touching the knot of his withered-leaf-colored necktie, "I feel it is important for me to give you a birthday present. A special birthday calls for a special commemorative gift."

Flustered, she shook her head and said, "No, please, sir, don't give it a second thought. All I did was bring your meal the way they ordered me to."

The old man raised both hands, palms toward her. "No, miss, don't *you* give it a second thought. The kind of 'present' I have in mind is not something tangible, not something with a price tag. To put it simply"—he placed his hands on the desk and took one long, slow breath—"what I would like to do for a lovely young fairy such as you is to grant a wish you might have, to make your wish come true. Anything. Anything at all that you wish for—assuming that you *do* have such a wish."

"A wish?" she asked, her throat dry.

"Something you would like to have happen, miss. If you have a wish—one wish, I'll make it come true. That is the kind of birthday present I can give you. But you had better think about it very carefully because I can grant you only one." He raised a finger. "Just one. You can't change your mind afterward and take it back."

She was at a loss for words. One wish? Whipped by the wind, raindrops tapped unevenly at the windowpane. As long as she remained silent, the old man looked into her eyes, saying nothing. Time marked its irregular pulse in her ears.

"I have to wish for something, and it will be granted?"

Instead of answering her question, the old man—hands still side by side on the desk—just smiled. He did it in the most natural and amiable way.

"Do you *have* a wish, miss—or not?" he asked gently.

◎

"This really did happen," she said, looking straight at me. "I'm not making it up."

"Of course not," I said. She was not the sort of person to invent some goofy story out of thin air. "So . . . did you make a wish?"

She went on looking at me for a while, then released a tiny sigh. "Don't get me wrong," she said. "I wasn't taking him one hundred percent seriously myself. I mean, at twenty you're not exactly living in a fairy-tale world anymore. If this was his idea of a joke, though, I had to hand it to him for coming up with it on the spot. He was a dapper old fellow with a twinkle in his eye, so I decided to play along with him. It *was* my twentieth birthday, after all: I figured I ought to have *something* not-so-ordinary happen to me that day. It wasn't a question of believing or not believing."

I nodded without saying anything.

"You can understand how I felt, I'm sure. My twentieth birthday was coming to an end without anything special happening, nobody wishing me a happy birthday, and all I'm doing is carrying tortellini with anchovy sauce to people's tables."

I nodded again. "Don't worry," I said. "I understand."

"So I made a wish."

The old man kept his gaze fixed on her, saying nothing, hands still on the desk. Also on the desk were several thick folders that might have been account books, plus writing implements, a calendar, and a lamp with a green shade. Lying among them, his small hands looked like another set of desktop furnishings. The rain continued to beat against the window, the lights of Tokyo Tower filtering through the shattered drops.

The wrinkles on the old man's forehead deepened slightly. "That is your wish?"

"Yes," she said. "That is my wish."

"A bit unusual for a girl your age," he said. "I was expecting something different."

"If it's no good, I'll wish for something else," she said, clearing her throat. "I don't mind. I'll think of something else."

"No, no," the old man said, raising his hands and waving them like flags. "There's nothing wrong with it, not at all. It's just a little surprising, miss. Don't you have something else? Like, say, you want to be prettier, or smarter, or rich: you're OK with not wishing for something like that—something an ordinary girl would ask for?"

She took some moments to search for the right words. The old man just waited, saying nothing, his hands at rest together on the desk again.

"Of course I'd like to be prettier or smarter or rich. But I really can't imagine what would happen to me if any of those things came true. They might be more than I could handle. I still don't really know what life is all about. I don't know how it *works*."

"I see," the old man said, intertwining his fingers and separating them again. "I see."

"So, is my wish OK?"

"Of course," he said. "Of course. It's no trouble at all for me."

The old man suddenly fixed his eyes on a spot in the air. The wrinkles of his forehead deepened: they might have been the wrinkles of his brain itself as it concentrated on his thoughts. He seemed to be staring at something—perhaps all-but-invisible bits of down—floating in the air. He opened his arms wide, lifted himself slightly from his chair, and whipped his palms together with a dry smack. Settling in the chair again, he slowly ran his fingertips along the wrinkles of his brow as if to soften them, and then turned to her with a gentle smile.

"That did it," he said. "Your wish has been granted."

"Already?"

"Yes, it was no trouble at all. Your wish has been granted, lovely miss. Happy birthday. You may go back to work now. Don't worry, I'll put the cart in the hall."

She took the elevator down to the restaurant. Empty-handed now, she felt almost disturbingly light, as though she were walking on some kind of mysterious fluff.

"Are you OK? You look spaced out," the younger waiter said to her.

She gave him an ambiguous smile and shook her head. "Oh, really? No, I'm fine."

"Tell me about the owner. What's he like?"

"I dunno, I didn't get a very good look at him," she said, cutting the conversation short.

An hour later she went to bring the cart down. It was out in the hall, utensils in place. She lifted the lid to find the chicken and vegetables gone. The wine bottle and coffeepot were empty. The door to room 604 stood there, closed and expressionless. She stared at it for a time, feeling it might open at any moment, but it did not open. She brought the cart down in the elevator and wheeled it in to the dishwasher. The chef looked blankly at the plate: empty as always.

◎

"I never saw the owner again," she said. "Not once. The manager turned out to have just an ordinary stomachache and went back to delivering the owner's meal again himself the next day. I quit the job after New Year's, and I've never been back to the place. I don't know, I just felt it was better not to go near there, kind of like a premonition."

She toyed with a paper coaster, thinking her own thoughts. "Sometimes I get the feeling that everything that happened to me on my twentieth birthday was some kind of illusion. It's as though something happened to make me think that things happened that never really happened at all. But I know for sure that they *did* happen. I can still bring back vivid images of every piece of furniture and every knickknack in room 604. What happened to me in there really happened, and it had an important meaning for me, too."

The two of us kept silent, drinking our drinks and thinking our separate thoughts.

"Do you mind if I ask you one thing?" I asked. "Or, more precisely, *two* things."

"Go right ahead," she said. "I imagine you're going to ask me what I wished for that time. That's the first thing you want to know."

"But it looks as though you don't want to talk about that."

"Does it?"

I nodded.

She put the coaster down and narrowed her eyes as if staring at something in the distance. "You're not supposed to tell anybody what you wished for, you know."

"I won't try to drag it out of you," I said. "I *would* like to know whether or not it came true, though. And also—whatever the wish itself might have been—whether or not you later came to regret what it was you chose to wish for. Were you ever sorry you didn't wish for something else?"

"The answer to the first question is yes and also no. I still have a lot of living left to do, probably. I haven't seen how things are going to work out to the end."

"So it was a wish that takes time to come true?"

"You could say that. Time is going to play an important role."

"Like in cooking certain dishes?"

She nodded.

I thought about that for a moment, but the only thing that came to mind was the image of a gigantic pie cooking slowly in an oven at low heat.

"And the answer to my second question?"

"What was that again?"

"Whether you ever regretted your choice of what to wish for."

A moment of silence followed. The eyes she turned on me seemed to lack any depth. The desiccated shadow of a smile flickered at the corners of her mouth, suggesting a kind of hushed sense of resignation.

"I'm married now," she said. "To a CPA three years older than me. And I have two children, a boy and a girl. We have an Irish setter. I drive an Audi, and I play tennis with my girlfriends twice a week. That's the life I'm living now."

"Sounds pretty good to me," I said.

"Even if the Audi's bumper has two dents?"

"Hey, bumpers are *made* for denting."

"That would make a great bumper sticker," she said. " 'Bumpers are for denting.' "

I looked at her mouth when she said that.

"What I'm trying to tell you is this," she said more softly, scratching an earlobe. It was a beautifully shaped earlobe. "No matter what they wish for, no matter how far they go, people can never be anything but themselves. That's all."

"There's another good bumper sticker," I said. " 'No matter how far they go, people can never be anything but themselves.' "

She laughed aloud, with a real show of pleasure, and the shadow was gone.

She rested her elbow on the bar and looked at me. "Tell me," she said. "What would you have wished for if you had been in my position?"

"On the night of my twentieth birthday, you mean?"

"Uh-huh."

I took some time to think about that, but I couldn't come up with a single wish.

"I can't think of anything," I confessed. "I'm too far away now from my twentieth birthday."

"You really can't think of anything?"

I nodded.

"Not one thing?"

"Not one thing."

She looked into my eyes again—straight in—and said, "That's because you've already *made* your wish."

"But you had better think about it very carefully, my lovely young fairy, because I can grant you only one." In the darkness somewhere, an old man wearing a withered-leaf-colored tie raises a finger. "Just one. You can't change your mind afterward and take it back."

—TRANSLATED BY JAY RUBIN

NEW YORK MINING DISASTER

A friend of mine has a habit of going to the zoo whenever there's a typhoon. He's been doing this for ten years. At a time when most people are closing their shutters, running out to stock up on mineral water, or checking to see if their radios and flashlights are working, my friend wraps himself in a Vietnam-era army surplus poncho, stuffs a couple of cans of beer into his pockets, and sets off. He lives about a fifteen-minute walk away.

If he's unlucky, the zoo is closed, "owing to inclement weather," and its gates are locked. When this happens, my friend sits down on the stone statue of a squirrel next to the entrance, drinks his lukewarm beer, and then heads back home.

But when he makes it there in time he pays the entrance fee, lights a soggy cigarette, and surveys the animals, one by one. Most of them have retreated to their shelters. Some stare blankly at the rain. Others are more animated, jumping around in the gale-force winds. Some are frightened by the sudden drop in barometric pressure; others turn vicious.

My friend makes a point of drinking his first beer in front of the Bengal tiger cage. (Bengal tigers always react the most violently to storms.) He drinks his second one outside the gorilla cage. Most of the time the gorillas aren't the least bit disturbed by the typhoon. They stare at him calmly as he sits like a mermaid on the concrete floor sipping his beer, and you'd swear they actually feel sorry for him.

"It's like being in an elevator when it breaks down and you're trapped inside with strangers," my friend tells me.

Typhoons aside, my friend's no different from anyone else. He works for an export company, managing foreign investments. It's not one of your better firms, but it does well enough. He lives alone in a neat little apartment and gets a new girlfriend every six months. Why he insists on having a new one every six months (and it's always exactly six months) I'll never understand. The girls all look the same, like perfect clones of one another. I can't tell them apart.

My friend owns a nice used car, the collected works of Balzac, and a black suit, black tie, and black shoes that are perfect for attending funerals. Every time someone dies, I call him and ask if I can borrow them, even though the shoes are one size too big for me.

"Sorry to bother you again," I said the last time I called. "Another funeral's come up."

"Help yourself. You must be in a hurry," he answered. "Why don't you come over right away?"

When I arrived, the suit and tie were laid out on the table, neatly pressed, the shoes were polished, and the fridge was full of imported beer. That's the kind of guy he is.

"The other day I saw a cat at the zoo," he said, popping open a beer.

"A cat?"

"Yeah, two weeks ago. I was in Hokkaido on business and dropped by a zoo near my hotel. There was a cat asleep in a cage with a sign that said 'Cat.' "

"What kind of cat?"

"Just an ordinary one. Brown stripes, short tail. And unbelievably fat. It just plopped down on its side and lay there."

"Maybe cats aren't so common in Hokkaido."

"You're kidding me, right?" he asked, astonished. "There must be cats in Hokkaido. They can't be that unusual."

"Well, look at it another way: why shouldn't there be cats in a zoo?" I said. "They're animals, too, right?"

"Cats and dogs are your run-of-the-mill-type animals. Nobody's going to pay money to see them," he said. "Just look around you—they're everywhere. Same thing with people."

When we'd finished off the six-pack, I put the suit and tie and shoe box into a large paper bag.

"Sorry to keep doing this to you," I said. "I know I should buy my own suit, but somehow I never get around to it. I feel like if I buy funeral clothes I'm saying that it's OK if somebody dies."

"No problem," he said. "I'm not using them anyway. Better to have someone use them than to have them hanging in the closet, right?"

It was true that in the three years since he'd had the suit he'd hardly worn it.

"It's weird, but since I bought the suit not a single person I know has died," he explained.

"That's the way it goes."

"Yeah, that's the way it goes," he said.

◎

For me, on the other hand, it was the Year of Funerals. Friends and former friends died one after another, like ears of corn withering in a drought. I was twenty-eight. My friends were all about the same age—twenty-seven, twenty-eight, twenty-nine. Not exactly the right age to die.

A poet might die at twenty-one, a revolutionary or a rock star at twenty-four. But after that you assume everything's going to be all right. You've made it past Dead Man's Curve and you're out of the tunnel, cruising straight for your destination down a six-lane highway—whether you want to be or not. You get your hair cut; every morning you shave. You aren't a poet anymore, or a revolutionary or a rock star. You don't pass out drunk in phone booths or blast out the Doors at four in the morning. Instead, you buy life insurance from your friend's company, drink in hotel bars, and hold on to your dental bills for tax deductions. At twenty-eight, that's normal.

But that's exactly when the unexpected massacre began. It was like a surprise attack on a lazy spring day—as if someone, on top of a metaphysical hill, holding a metaphysical machine gun, had sprayed us with bullets. One minute we were changing our clothes, and the next minute they didn't fit anymore: the sleeves were inside out, and we had one leg in one pair of pants, the other in a different pair. A complete mess.

But that's what death is. A rabbit is a rabbit whether it springs out of a hat or a wheat field. A hot oven is a hot oven, and the black smoke rising from a chimney is what it is—black smoke rising from a chimney.

The first person to straddle the divide between reality and unreality (or unreality and reality) was a friend from college who taught English at a junior high school. He'd been married for three years, and his wife had gone back to her parents' house in Shikoku to have their baby.

One unusually warm Sunday afternoon in January, he went to a department store and bought two cans of shaving cream and a German-made knife big enough to lop off an elephant's ear. He went home and ran a bath. He got some ice from the fridge, downed a bottle of Scotch, climbed into the tub, and slit his wrists. His mother found the body two days later. The police came and took a lot of photographs. Blood had dyed the bath the color of tomato juice. The police ruled it a suicide. After all, the doors had been locked and, of course, the deceased had bought the knife himself. But why did he buy two cans of shaving cream that he didn't plan to use? No one knew.

Maybe it hadn't hit him when he was at the department store that in a couple of hours he'd be dead. Or maybe he was afraid that the cashier would guess that he was going to kill himself.

He didn't leave a will or a farewell note. On the kitchen table there was only a glass, the empty whiskey bottle and ice bowl, and the two cans of shaving cream. While he was waiting for the bath to fill, knocking back glass after glass of Haig on the rocks, he must have stared at those cans and thought something along the lines of *I'll never have to shave again.*

A man's death at twenty-eight is as sad as the winter rain.

During the next twelve months, four more people died.

One died in March in an incident at an oil field in Saudi Arabia or Kuwait, and two died in June—a heart attack and a traffic accident. From July to November peace reigned, but then in December another friend died, also in a car crash.

Unlike my first friend, who'd killed himself, these friends never had the time to realize that they were dying. For them it was like climbing up a staircase they'd climbed a million times before and suddenly finding a step missing.

"Would you make up the bed for me?" the friend who died of a heart attack had asked his wife. He was a furniture designer. It was eleven o'clock in the morning. He'd woken up at nine, worked for a while in his room, and then said he felt sleepy. He went to the kitchen, made some coffee, and drank it. But the coffee didn't help. "I think I'll take a nap," he said. "I hear a buzzing sound in the back of my head." Those were his last words. He curled up in bed, went to sleep, and never woke up again.

The friend who died in December was the youngest, and the only woman. She was twenty-four, like a revolutionary or a rock star. One cold rainy night just before Christmas, she was flattened in the tragic yet quite ordinary space between a beer-delivery truck and a concrete telephone pole.

⊙

A few days after the last funeral, I went to my friend's apartment to return the suit, which I'd picked up from the dry cleaner's, and to give him a bottle of whiskey to thank him.

"Much obliged. I really appreciate it," I said.

As usual, his fridge was full of cold beer, and his comfortable sofa reflected a faint ray of sunlight. On the coffee table there was a clean ashtray and a pot of Christmas poinsettias.

He took the suit, in its plastic covering, from me, his movements leisurely—like those of a bear just coming out of hibernation—and quietly put it away.

"I hope the suit doesn't smell like a funeral," I said.

"Clothes aren't important. The real problem is what's *inside* them."

"Um," I murmured.

"One funeral after another for you this year," he said, stretching out on the sofa and pouring beer into a glass. "How many altogether?"

"Five," I said, spreading out the fingers of my left hand. "But I think that's got to be it."

"Are you sure?"

"Enough people have died."

"It's like the Curse of the Pyramids or something," he said. "I remember reading that somewhere. The curse continues until enough people have died. Or else a red star appears in the sky and the moon's shadow covers the sun."

After we finished a six-pack, we started on the whiskey. The winter sunlight sloped gently into the room.

"You look a little glum these days," he said.

"You think so?" I said.

"You must be thinking about things too much in the middle of the night," he said. "I've stopped thinking about things at night."

"How'd you manage that?"

"When I get depressed, I start to clean. Even if it's two or three in the morning. I wash the dishes, wipe off the stove, mop the floor, bleach the dish towels, organize my desk drawers, iron every shirt in sight," he said, stirring his drink with his finger. "I do that till I'm exhausted, then I have a drink and go to sleep. In the morning I get up and by the time I'm putting on my socks I can't even remember what it was I was thinking about."

I looked around again. As always, the room was clean and orderly.

"People think of all kinds of things at three in the morning. We all do. That's why we each have to figure out our own way of fighting it off."

"You're probably right," I said.

"Even animals think things over at three a.m.," he said, as if remembering something. "Have you ever gone to the zoo at three a.m.?"

"No," I answered vaguely. "No, of course not."

"I've only done it once. A friend of mine works at a zoo, and I asked him to let me in when he had the night shift. You're not supposed to, really." He shook his glass. "It was a strange experience. I can't explain it, but I felt as if the ground had silently split open and something was crawling up out of it. And then there was this invisible thing on a rampage in the dark. It was like the cold night had coagulated. I couldn't see it, but I felt it, and the animals felt it, too. It made me think about the fact that the ground we walk on goes all the way to the earth's core, and I suddenly realized that the core has sucked up an incredible amount of time."

I didn't say anything.

"Anyway, I never want to go again—to the zoo in the middle of the night, I mean."

"You prefer a typhoon?"

"Yeah," he said. "Gimme a typhoon any day."

⊚

The phone rang and he went to his bedroom to take the call. It was his girlfriend clone, with another endless clone phone call. I wanted to tell him I was going to call it a day, but he was on the phone forever. I gave up waiting and switched on the TV. It was a twenty-seven-inch color set with the kind of remote control you barely have to touch to change the channel. The TV had six speakers and great sound. I'd never seen such a wonderful TV.

I made two complete rounds of the channels before settling on a news program. A border clash, a fire, exchange rates going up and down, a new limit on car imports, an outdoor winter swim meet, a family suicide. All these bits of news seemed somehow connected, like people in a high school graduation photo.

"Any interesting news?" my friend asked as he came back into the room.

"Not really," I said.

"Do you watch a lot of TV?"

I shook my head. "I don't have a TV."

"There's at least one good thing about TV," he said after a while. "You can shut it off whenever you like. And nobody complains."

He pushed the Off button on the remote. Immediately, the screen went blank. The room was still. Outside the window, lights in other buildings were starting to come on.

We sat there for five minutes, drinking whiskey, with nothing to talk about. The telephone rang again, but he pretended not to hear it. Just as the phone stopped ringing, he hit the On button. The picture returned instantly, and a commentator standing in front of a graph gestured with a pointer as he explained changes in the price of oil.

"See? He didn't even notice that we'd switched him off for five minutes."

"True enough," I said.

"Why is that?"

It was too much trouble to think it through, so I shook my head.

"When you switch it off, one side ceases to exist. It's him or us. You just hit the switch and there's a communications blackout. It's easy."

"That's one way of thinking of it," I said.

"There are millions of ways of thinking. In India they grow coconut trees. In Argentina it rains political prisoners from helicopters." He switched the TV off again. "I don't want to say anything about other people," he said, "but consider the fact that there are ways of dying that don't end in funerals. Types of death you can't smell."

I nodded silently. I felt that I knew what he was getting at. At the same time, I felt that I had no idea what he meant. I was tired and a bit confused. I sat there, fingering one of the poinsettia's green leaves.

"I've got some champagne," he said earnestly. "I brought it back from a business trip to France a while ago. I don't know much about champagne, but this is supposed to be great. Would you like some? Champagne might be just the thing after a string of funerals."

He brought out the chilled champagne bottle and two clean glasses and set them quietly on the table, then smiled slyly. "Champagne's completely useless, you know," he said. "The only good part is the moment you pop the cork."

"I can't argue with you there," I said.

We popped the cork, and talked for a while about the zoo in Paris and the animals that live there. The champagne was excellent.

◎

There was a party at the end of the year, an annual New Year's Eve party at a bar in Roppongi that had been rented for the occasion. A piano trio played, and there was a lot of good food and drink. When I ran across someone I knew, I'd chat for a while. My job required that I put in an appearance every year. Parties aren't my thing, but this one was easy to take. I had nothing else to do on New Year's Eve and could just stand by myself in a corner, relax, have a drink, and enjoy the music. No obnoxious people, no need to be introduced to strangers and listen to them rant for half an hour about how a vegetarian diet cures cancer.

But that evening someone introduced me to a woman. After the usual small talk, I tried to retreat to my corner again. But the woman followed me back to my seat, whiskey glass in hand.

"I asked to be introduced to you," she said amiably.

She wasn't the type to turn heads, though she was certainly attractive. She was wearing an expensive green silk dress. I guessed that she was about thirty-two. She could easily have made herself look younger, but she didn't seem to think it was worth the trouble. Three rings graced her fingers, and a faint smile played on her lips.

"You look exactly like someone I know," she said. "Your facial features, your back, the way you talk, your overall mood—it's an amazing likeness. I've been watching you ever since you came in."

"If he's that much like me, I'd like to meet the guy," I said. I had no idea what else to say.

"You would?"

"I'd like to see what it feels like to meet someone who's exactly like me."

Her smile deepened for an instant, then softened. "But that's impossible," she said. "He died five years ago. When he was about the same age you are now."

"Is that right?" I said.

"I killed him."

The trio was just finishing its second set, and there was a smattering of halfhearted applause.

"Do you like music?" she asked me.

"I do if it's nice music in a nice world," I said.

"In a nice world there is no nice music," she said, as if revealing some deep secret. "In a nice world the air doesn't vibrate."

"I see," I said, not knowing how to respond.

"Have you seen the movie where Warren Beatty plays the piano in a nightclub?"

"No, I haven't."

"Elizabeth Taylor is one of the customers at the club, and she's really poor and miserable."

"Hmm."

"So Warren Beatty asks Elizabeth Taylor if she has any requests."

"And does she?"

"I forget. It's a really old movie." Her rings sparkled as she drank her whiskey. "I hate requests. They make me feel unhappy. It's like when I take a book out of the library. As soon as I start to read it, all I can think about is when I'll finish it."

She put a cigarette between her lips. I struck a match and lit it for her.

"Let's see," she said. "We were talking about the person who looked like you."

"How did you kill him?"

"I threw him into a beehive."

"You're kidding, right?"

"Yes," she said.

Instead of sighing, I took a sip of whiskey. The ice had melted and it barely tasted like whiskey anymore.

"Of course, legally I'm not a murderer," she said. "Or morally, either."

"Neither legally nor morally a murderer." I didn't want to, but I reviewed the points she'd made. "But you did kill someone."

"Right." She nodded happily. "Someone who looked just like you."

Across the room a man let out a loud laugh. And the people around him laughed, too. Glasses clinked. It sounded very far away but extremely clear. I don't know why, but my heart was pounding, as if it were expanding or moving up and down. I felt as if I were walking on ground that was floating on water.

"It took less than five seconds," she said. "To kill him."

We were silent for a while. She was taking her time, savoring the silence.

"Do you ever think about freedom?" she asked.

"Sometimes," I said. "Why do you ask?"

"Can you draw a daisy?"

"I think so. Is this a personality test?"

"Almost." She laughed.

"Well, did I pass?"

"Yes," she answered. "You'll be fine. Nothing to worry about. Intuition tells me you'll live a good long life."

"Thank you," I said.

The band began playing "Auld Lang Syne."

"Eleven fifty-five," she said, glancing at the gold watch on her pendant. "I really like 'Auld Lang Syne.' How about you?"

"I prefer 'Home on the Range.' All those deer and antelope."

She smiled. "You must like animals."

"I do," I said. And I thought of my friend who likes zoos, and of his funeral suit.

"I enjoyed talking to you. Goodbye."

"Goodbye," I said.

◎

They blew out their lamps to save on air, and darkness surrounded them. No one spoke. All they could hear in the dark was the sound of water dripping from the ceiling every five seconds.

"OK, everybody, try not to breathe so much. We don't have much air left," an old miner said. He held his voice to a whisper, but even so the

wooden beams on the ceiling of the tunnel creaked faintly. In the dark, the miners huddled together, straining to hear one sound. The sound of pickaxes. The sound of life.

They waited for hours. Reality began to melt away in the darkness. Everything began to feel as if it were happening a long time ago, in a world far away. Or was it happening in the future, in a different far-off world?

Outside, people were digging a hole, trying to reach them. It was like a scene from a movie.

—TRANSLATED BY PHILIP GABRIEL

AIRPLANE: OR, HOW HE TALKED TO HIMSELF AS IF RECITING POETRY

That afternoon she asked him, "Is that an old habit, the way you talk to yourself?" She raised her eyes from the table and put the question to him as if the thought had just struck her, but it had obviously not just struck her. She must have been thinking about it for a while. Her voice had that hard but slightly husky edge it always took on at times like this. She had held the words back and rolled them around on her tongue again and again before she let them out of her mouth.

The two were sitting opposite each other at the kitchen table. Aside from the occasional commuter train running on a nearby track, the neighborhood was quiet—almost too quiet at times. Tracks without trains passing over them have a mysterious silence all their own. The vinyl tile of the kitchen floor gave his bare feet a pleasant chill. He had pulled his socks off and stuffed them into his pants pocket. The weather was a bit too warm for an April afternoon. She had rolled up the sleeves of her pale checked shirt as far as the elbows, and her slim white fingers toyed with the handle of her coffee spoon. He stared at the moving fingertips, and the workings of his mind went strangely flat. She seemed to have lifted the edge of the world, and now she was loosening its threads little by little—perfunctorily, apathetically, as if she had to do it no matter how long it might take.

He watched and said nothing. He said nothing because he did not know what to say. The few sips of coffee left in his cup were cold now, and muddy-looking.

He had just turned twenty, and she was seven years older, married, and the mother of one. For him she might as well have been the far side of the moon.

Her husband worked for a travel agency that specialized in trips abroad. And so he was away from home nearly half of every month, in places like London or Rome or Singapore. He obviously liked opera. Thick three- and four-record albums lined the shelves, arranged by composer—Verdi, Puccini, Donizetti, Richard Strauss. The long rows seemed less like a record collection than a symbol of a worldview: calm, immovable. He looked at the husband's records whenever he was at a loss for words or for something to do; he would let his eyes wander over the album spines—from right to left, from left to right—and read the titles aloud in his mind: *La Bohème, Tosca, Turandot, Norma, Fidelio . . .* He had never once listened to music like that. Far from knowing whether he liked it or not, he had never had the chance to hear it. Not one person among his family, friends, or acquaintances was an opera fan. He knew that a music called opera existed, and that certain people liked to listen to it, but the husband's records were his first actual glimpse of such a world.

She herself was not particularly fond of opera. "I don't hate it," she said. "It's just too long."

Next to the record shelves stood a very impressive stereo set. Its big, foreign-made tube amp hunched down heavily, waiting for orders like a well-trained crustacean. There was no way to prevent it from standing out among the room's other, more modest furnishings. It had a truly exceptional presence. One's eyes could not help fixing on it. But he had never once heard it producing sound. She had no idea where to find the power switch, and he never thought to touch the thing.

"There's nothing wrong at home," she told him—any number of times. "My husband is good to me, I love my daughter, I think I'm happy." She sounded calm, even serene, as she said this, without a hint that she was making excuses for her life. She spoke of her marriage with complete objectivity, as though discussing traffic regulations or the international date line. "I think I'm happy, there's nothing wrong."

So why the hell is she sleeping with me? he wondered. He gave it lots of thought but couldn't come up with an answer. What did it even *mean* for there to be "something wrong" with a marriage? He sometimes thought of asking her directly, but he didn't know how to start. How should he say it? "If you're so happy, why the hell are you sleeping with me?" Should he just come out with it like that? He was sure it would make her cry, though.

She cried enough as it was. She would cry for a long, long time, making tiny sounds. He almost never knew why she was crying. But once she started, she wouldn't stop. Try and comfort her as he might, she would not stop crying until a certain amount of time had gone by. In fact, he didn't have to do anything at all; once a certain amount of time had gone by, her crying would come to an end. Why were people so different from one another? he wondered. He had been with any number of women, all of whom would cry, or get angry, each in her own special way. They had points of similarity, but those were far outnumbered by the differences. It seemed to have nothing to do with age. This was his first experience with an older woman, but the difference in age didn't bother him as much as he had expected it to. Far more meaningful than age differences, he felt, were the different tendencies that each individual possessed. He couldn't help thinking that this was an important key for unlocking the riddle of life.

After she finished crying, usually, the two of them would make love. Only after crying would she be the one to initiate it. Otherwise, he had to be the one. Sometimes she would refuse him. Without a word, she would shake her head. Then her eyes would look like white moons floating at the edge of a dawn sky—flat, suggestive moons that shimmered at the single cry of a bird at dawn. Whenever he saw her eyes looking like that, he knew there was nothing more he could say to her. Rejected, he felt neither anger nor displeasure. *That's how it goes,* he thought, nothing more. Sometimes it even made him feel relieved deep inside. They would sit at the kitchen table, drinking coffee, chatting quietly. They spoke in fragments most of the time. Neither was a great talker, and they had little in common to talk about. He could never remember what it was that they had been saying, just that it had been in little pieces. And all the while, one commuter train after another would go past the window.

Their lovemaking was always something hushed and tranquil. It had nothing that could properly be called the joys of the flesh. Of course it would be false to say that they knew nothing of the pleasure that obtains when a man and a woman join their bodies. But mixed with this were far too many other thoughts and elements and styles. It was different from any sex he had experienced before. It made him think of a small room—a nice, *neat* room that was a comfortable place to be. It had strings of many colors hanging from the ceiling, strings of different shapes and lengths, and each string, in its own way, sent a thrill of enticement through him. He wanted to pull one, and the strings wanted to be pulled by him. But he didn't know which one to pull. He felt that he might pull a string and have a magnificent spectacle open up before his eyes, but that, just as easily, everything could be ruined in an instant. And so he hesitated, and while he lingered in confusion another day would end.

The strangeness of this situation was almost too much for him. He believed that he had lived his life with his own sense of values. But when he was in this room, hearing the trains go by and holding the silent older woman in his arms, he couldn't help but feel that he was wandering through chaos. Again and again he would ask himself, "Am I in love with her?" But he could never reach an answer with complete conviction. All he could understand were the colored strings hanging from the little room's ceiling. *They were right there.*

When this strange lovemaking ended, she would always glance at the clock. Lying in his arms, she would avert her face slightly and look at the black clock radio by the head of the bed. In those days, clock radios didn't have lighted digital displays but little numbered panels that would flip over with a tiny click. When she looked at the clock, a train would pass the window. It was strange: whenever she looked at the clock, without fail there would be the sound of a train going by. It was like a predestined conditioned reflex: she would look; a train would go by.

She was checking the clock to make sure it was not time for her four-year-old daughter to be coming home from kindergarten. He had happened to catch a glimpse of the girl exactly once. She seemed to be a sweet little child. That was the only impression she left him with. He had never seen the opera-loving husband who worked for a travel bureau. Fortunately.

It was an afternoon in May when she first asked him about his talking to himself. She had cried that day—again. And then they had made love—again. He couldn't recall what had made her cry. She had probably just felt like crying. He sometimes wondered if she had become involved with him just so that she could cry in someone's arms. Maybe she can't cry alone, and that's why she needs me.

That day she locked the door, closed the curtains, and brought the telephone next to the bed. Then they joined their bodies. Gently, quietly, as always. The doorbell rang, but she ignored it. It seemed not to startle her at all. She shook her head as if to say, "Never mind, it's nothing." The bell rang several more times, but soon the person gave up and went away. Just as she had said, it was nothing. Maybe a salesman. But how could she know? he wondered. A train rumbled by now and then. A piano sounded in the distance. He vaguely recognized the melody. He had heard it once, long ago, in music class, but he couldn't recall it exactly. A vegetable seller's truck clattered by out front. She closed her eyes, inhaled deeply, and he came—with the utmost gentleness.

He went to the bathroom for a shower. When he came back drying himself with a bath towel, he found her lying facedown in bed with her eyes closed. He sat down next to her and, as always, caressed her back as he let his eyes wander over the titles of the opera records.

Soon she left the bed, got properly dressed, and went to the kitchen to make coffee. It was a short time later that she asked him, "Is that an old habit, the way you talk to yourself like that?"

"Like what?" She had taken him off guard. "You mean, while we're . . . ?"

"No no. Not then. Just anytime. Like, when you're taking a shower, or when I'm in the kitchen and you're by yourself, reading the newspaper kind of thing."

"I had no idea," he said, shaking his head. "I never noticed. I talk to myself?"

"You do. Really," she said, toying with his lighter.

"It's not that I don't believe you," he said, the discomfort of it affecting his voice. He put a cigarette in his mouth, took the lighter from her hand, and used it to light up. He had started smoking Seven Stars a short time earlier. It was her husband's brand. He had always smoked Hope regulars. Not that she had asked him to switch to her husband's brand; he had thought of taking the precaution himself. It would just make things easier, he had decided. Like on the TV melodramas.

"I used to talk to myself a lot, too," she said. "When I was little."

"Oh, really?"

"But my mother made me stop. 'A young lady does *not* talk to herself,' she used to say. And whenever I did it, she got *so* angry! She'd lock me in a closet—which, for me, was about the scariest place I could imagine—

all dark and moldy-smelling. Sometimes she'd smack me on the knees with a ruler. It worked. And it didn't take very long. I stopped talking to myself—completely. Not a word. After a while, I couldn't have done it if I had wanted to."

He couldn't think of anything to say to this, and so he said nothing. She bit her lip.

"Even now," she said, "if I feel I'm about to say something, I just swallow my words. It's like a reflex. Because I got yelled at so much when I was little. But, I don't know, what's so bad about talking to yourself? It's natural. It's just words coming out of your mouth. If my mother were still alive, I almost think I'd ask her, 'What's so bad about talking to yourself?' "

"She's dead?"

"Uh-huh. But I wish I had gotten it straight with her. I wish I had asked her, 'Why did you do that to me?' "

She was playing with her coffee spoon. She glanced at the clock on the wall. The moment she did that, a train went by outside.

She waited for the train to pass. Then she said, "I sometimes think that people's hearts are like deep wells. Nobody knows what's at the bottom. All you can do is imagine by what comes floating to the surface every once in a while."

Both of them thought about wells for a little while.

"What do I talk about when I talk to myself?" he asked. "For example."

"Hmm," she said, slowly shaking her head a few times, almost as if she were discreetly testing the range of movement of her neck. "Well, there's airplanes . . ."

"Airplanes?"

"Uh-huh. You know. They fly through the sky."

He laughed. "Why would I talk to myself about airplanes, of all things?"

She laughed, too. And then, using her index fingers, she measured the length of an imaginary object in the air. This was a habit of hers. One that he had picked up.

"You pronounce your words so *clearly*, too. Are you sure you don't remember talking to yourself?"

"I don't remember a thing."

She picked up the ballpoint pen lying on the table, and played with it for a few seconds, but then she looked at the clock again. It had done its job: in the five minutes since her last look, it had advanced five minutes' worth.

"You talk to yourself as if you were reciting poetry."

A hint of red came into her face as she said this. He found this odd: why should my talking to myself make her turn red?

He tried out the words in rhythm: "I talk to myself / Almost as if / I were reciting / Po-e-try."

She picked up the pen again. It was a yellow plastic ballpoint pen with a logo marking the tenth anniversary of a certain bank branch.

He pointed at the pen and said, "Next time you hear me talking to myself, take down what I say, will you?"

She stared straight into his eyes. "You really want to know?"

He nodded.

She took a piece of notepaper and started writing something on it. She wrote slowly, but she kept the pen moving, never once resting or getting stuck for a word. Chin in hand, he looked at her long eyelashes the whole time. She would blink once every few seconds at irregular intervals. The longer he looked at them—these lashes which, until a few moments ago, had been wet with tears—the less he understood: what did his sleeping with her really mean? A strange sense of loss overtook him, as if one part of a complex system had been stretched and stretched until it became terribly simple: I might never be able to go anywhere else again. When this thought came to him, the horror of it was almost more than he could bear. His being, his very self, was going to melt away. Yes, it was true: he was as young as newly formed mud, and he talked to himself as if reciting poetry.

She stopped writing and thrust the paper toward him across the table. He reached out and took it from her.

In the kitchen, the afterimage of some great thing was holding its breath. He often felt the presence of this afterimage when he was with her: the afterimage of a thing that had been lost. Something of which he had no memory.

"I know it all by heart," she said. "This is what you said to yourself about airplanes."

He read the words aloud:

Airplane
Airplane flying
I, on the airplane
The airplane
Flying
But still, though it flew
The airplane's
The sky?

"All of this?!" He was stunned.

"Uh-huh, the whole thing," she said.

"Incredible! I can't believe I said all this to myself and don't remember any of it."

She gave her lower lip a little bite and flashed a tiny smile. "You did, though, just like that."

He let out a sigh. "This is too weird. I've never once thought about airplanes. I have absolutely no memory of this. Why, all of a sudden, would an airplane come popping out?"

"I don't know, but that is exactly what you were saying before in the shower. *You* may not have been thinking about airplanes, but somewhere deep in a forest, far away, your *heart* was thinking about them."

"Who knows? Maybe somewhere deep in a forest I was making an airplane."

With a small thunk, she set the ballpoint pen on the table, then raised her eyes and stared at him.

◎

They remained silent for some time. The coffee in their cups clouded up and grew cold. The earth turned on its axis while the moon imperceptibly shifted the force of gravity and turned the tides. Time flowed on in silence, and trains passed over the rails.

He and she were thinking about the very same thing: an airplane. The airplane that his heart was making deep in the forest. How big it was, and its shape, and the color of its paint, and where it was going, and who would board it. They thought about the airplane that was waiting for someone deep in the forest.

She cried again soon after that. This was the very first time that she had cried twice in the same day. It was also the last. It was a special thing for her. He reached across the table and touched her hair. There was something tremendously *real* about the way it felt. Like life itself, it was hard and smooth, and far away.

⊚

Yes, he thought: in those days, I used to talk to myself as if reciting poetry.

— TRANSLATED BY JAY RUBIN

THE MIRROR

All the stories you've been telling tonight seem to fall into two categories. There's the type where you have the world of the living on one side, the world of death on the other, and some force that allows a crossing-over from one side to the other. This would include ghosts and the like. The second type involves paranormal abilities, premonitions, the ability to predict the future. All of your stories belong to one of these two groups.

In fact, your experiences tend to fall almost totally under one of these categories or the other. What I mean is, people who see ghosts just see ghosts and never have premonitions. And those who have premonitions don't see ghosts. I don't know why, but there would appear to be some individual predilection for one or the other. At least that's the impression I get.

Of course some people don't fall into either category. Me, for instance. In my thirty-odd years I've never once seen a ghost, never once had a premonition or prophetic dream. There was one time I was riding an elevator with a couple of friends and they swore they saw a ghost riding with us, but I didn't see a thing. They claimed there was a woman in a gray suit standing right next to me, but there wasn't any woman with us, at least as far as I could make out. The three of us were the only ones in the elevator. No kidding. And these two friends weren't the type to deliberately play tricks on me. The whole thing was really weird, but the fact remains that I've still never seen a ghost.

But there was one time—just the one time—when I had an experience that scared me out of my wits. This happened over ten years ago, and I've never told anybody about it. I was afraid to even talk about it. I felt that if I did, it might happen all over again, so I've never brought it up. But tonight each of you has related his own scary experience, and as the host I can't very well call it a night without contributing something of my own. So I've decided to just come right out and tell you the story. Here goes.

⊙

I graduated from high school at the end of the 1960s, just when the student movement was in full swing. I was part of the hippie generation, and refused to go to college. Instead, I wandered all over Japan working at various manual labor jobs. I was convinced that was the most righteous way to live. Young and impetuous, I guess you'd call me. Looking back on it now, though, I think I had a pretty fun life back then. Whether that was the right choice or not, if I had it to do over again, I'm pretty sure I would.

In the fall of my second year of roaming all over the country, I got a job for a couple of months as a night watchman at a junior high school. This was in a school in a tiny town in Niigata Prefecture. I'd gotten pretty worn out working over the summer and wanted to take it easy for a while. Being a night watchman isn't exactly rocket science. During the day I slept in the janitor's office, and at night all I had to do was go twice around the whole school making sure everything was okay. The rest of the time I listened to records in the music room, read books in the library, played basketball by myself in the gym. Being alone all night in a school isn't so bad, really. Was I afraid? No way. When you're eighteen or nineteen, nothing fazes you.

I don't imagine any of you have ever worked as a night watchman, so maybe I should explain the duties. You're supposed to make two rounds each night, at nine p.m. and three a.m. That's the schedule. The school was a fairly new three-story concrete building, with eighteen to twenty classrooms. Not an especially large school as these things go. In addition to the classrooms you had a music room, a home ec room, an art studio, a staff office, and the principal's office. Plus a separate cafeteria, swimming pool, gym, and auditorium. My job was to make a quick check of all of these.

As I made my rounds, I followed a twenty-point checklist. I'd make a check mark next to each one—staff office, *check*, science lab, *check* . . . I suppose I could have just stayed in bed in the janitor's room, where I slept, and checked these off without going to the trouble of actually walking around. But I wasn't such a haphazard sort of guy. It didn't take much time to make the rounds, and besides, if someone broke in while I was sleeping, I'd be the one who'd get attacked.

Anyway, there I was each night at nine and three, making my rounds, a flashlight in my left hand, a wooden kendo sword in my right. I'd practiced kendo in high school and felt pretty confident in my ability to fend off anyone. If an attacker was an amateur, and even if he had a real sword with him, that wouldn't have scared me. I was young, remember. If it happened now, I'd run like hell.

Anyhow, this took place on a windy night in the beginning of October. It was actually kind of steamy for the time of year. A swarm of mosquitoes buzzed around in the evening, and I remember burning a couple of mosquito-repellent coils to keep them away. The wind was noisy. The gate to the swimming pool was broken and the wind made the gate slap open and shut. I thought of fixing it, but it was too dark out, so it kept banging all night.

My nine p.m. round went by fine, all twenty items on my list neatly checked off. All the doors were locked, everything in its proper place. Nothing out of the ordinary. I went back to the janitor's room, set my alarm for three, and fell fast asleep.

When the alarm went off at three, though, I woke up feeling weird. I can't explain it, but I just felt different. I didn't feel like getting up—it was like something was suppressing my will to get out of bed. I'm the type who usually leaps right out of bed, so I couldn't understand it. I had to force myself to get out of bed and get ready to make my rounds. The gate to the pool was still making its rhythmic banging, but it sounded different from before. Something's definitely weird, I thought, reluctant to get going. But I made up my mind I had to do my job, no matter what. If you skip out on doing your duty once, you'll skip out again and again, and I didn't want to fall into that. So I grabbed my flashlight and wooden sword and off I went.

It was an altogether odd night. The wind grew stronger as the night went on, the air more humid. My skin started itching and I couldn't focus. I decided to go around the gym, auditorium, and pool first. Everything checked out OK. The gate to the pool banged away in the wind like some crazy person who alternately shakes his head and nods. There was no order to it. First a couple of nods—yes, yes—then no, no, no . . . It's a weird thing to compare it to, I know, but that's what it felt like.

Inside the school building it was situation normal. I looked around and checked off the points on my list. Nothing out of the usual had happened, despite the weird feeling I'd had. Relieved, I started back to the janitor's room. The last place on my checklist was the boiler room next to the cafeteria on the east side of the building, the opposite side from the janitor's room. This meant I had to walk down the long hallway on the first floor on my way back. It was pitch black. On nights when the moon was out, there was a little light in the hallway, but when there wasn't, you couldn't see a thing. I had to shine my flashlight ahead of me to see where I was going. This particular night, a typhoon was not too far off, so there was no moon at all. Occasionally there'd be a break in the clouds, but then it plunged into darkness again.

I walked faster than usual down the hallway, the rubber soles of my basketball shoes squeaking against the linoleum floor. It was a green linoleum floor, the color of a hazy bed of moss. I can picture it even now.

The entrance to the school was midway down the hallway, and as I passed it I thought, *What the*—? I thought I'd seen something in the dark. I broke out in a sweat. Regripping the wooden sword, I turned toward what I saw. I shined my flashlight at the wall next to the shelf for storing shoes.

And there I was. A mirror, in other words. It was just my reflection in a mirror. There wasn't a mirror there the night before, so they must have put in one between then and now. Man, was I startled. It was a long, full-length mirror. Relieved that it was just me in a mirror, I felt a bit stupid for having been so surprised. So that's all it is, I told myself. How dumb. I put my flashlight down, took a cigarette from my pocket, and lit it. As I took a puff, I glanced at myself in the mirror. A faint streetlight from outside shone in through the window, reaching the mirror. From behind me, the swimming pool gate was banging in the wind.

After a couple of puffs, I suddenly noticed something odd. My reflection in the mirror wasn't me. It looked exactly like me on the outside, but it definitely wasn't me. No, that's not it. It *was* me, of course, but *another* me. Another me that never should have been. I don't know how to put it. It's hard to explain what it felt like.

The one thing I did understand was that this other figure loathed me. Inside it was a hatred like an iceberg floating in a dark sea. The kind of hatred that no one could ever diminish.

I stood there for a while, dumbfounded. My cigarette slipped from between my fingers and fell to the floor. The cigarette in the mirror fell to the floor, too. We stood there, staring at each other. I felt like I was bound hand and foot, and couldn't move.

Finally his hand moved, the fingertips of his right hand touching his chin, and then slowly, like a bug, crept up his face. I suddenly realized I was doing the same thing. Like I was the reflection of what was in the mirror and he was trying to take control of me.

Wrenching out my last ounce of strength I roared out a growl, and the bonds that held me rooted to the spot broke. I raised my kendo sword and smashed it down on the mirror as hard as I could. I heard glass shattering but didn't look back as I raced back to my room. Once inside, I hurriedly locked the door and leapt under the covers. I was worried about the cigarette I'd dropped on the floor, but there was no way I was going back. The wind was howling the whole time, and the gate to the pool continued to make a racket until dawn. Yes, yes, no, yes, no, no, no . . .

I'm sure you've already guessed the ending to my story. There never was any mirror.

When the sun came up, the typhoon had already passed. The wind had died down and it was a sunny day. I went over to the entrance. The cigarette butt I'd tossed away was there, as was my wooden sword. But no mirror. There never had been any mirror there.

What I saw wasn't a ghost. It was simply—myself. I can never forget how terrified I was that night, and whenever I remember it, this thought always springs to mind: that the most frightening thing in the world is our own self. What do you think?

You may have noticed that I don't have a single mirror here in my house. Learning to shave without one was no easy feat, believe me.

—TRANSLATED BY PHILIP GABRIEL

A FOLKLORE FOR MY GENERATION: A PRE-HISTORY OF LATE-STAGE CAPITALISM

was born in 1949, entered junior high in 1961, and college in 1967. And reached my long-awaited twentieth birthday—my intro into adulthood—during the height of the boisterous slapstick that was the student movement. Which I suppose qualifies me as a typical child of the sixties. So there I was, during the most vulnerable, most immature, and yet most precious period of life, breathing in everything about this live-for-the-moment decade, high on the wildness of it all. There were doors we had to kick in, right in front of us, and you better believe we kicked them in! With Jim Morrison, the Beatles, and Dylan blasting out the sound track to our lives.

There was something special about the sixties. That seems true now, in retrospect, but even when I was caught up in the whirlwind of it happening I was convinced of it. But if you asked me to be more specific, to pinpoint what it was about the sixties that was so special, I don't think I could do more than stammer out some trite reply. We were merely observers, getting totally absorbed in some exciting movie, our palms all sweaty, only to find that, after the houselights came on and we exited the theater, the thrilling afterglow that coursed through us ultimately meant nothing whatsoever. Maybe something prevented us from learning a valuable lesson from all this? I don't know. I'm way too close to the period to say.

I'm not bragging about the times I lived through. I'm simply trying to convey what it felt like to live through that age, and the fact that there really *was* something special about it. Yet if I were to try to unpack those times and point out something in particular that was extraordinary, I don't know if I could. What I'd find if I did such a dissection would be these: the momentum and energy of the times, the tremendous spark of promise. More than anything else, the feeling of inevitable irritation like when you look through the wrong end of a telescope. Heroism and villainy, ecstasy and disillusionment, martyrdom and betrayal, outlines and specialized studies, silence and eloquence, people marking time in the most boring way—they were all there, for sure. Any age has all these. The present does, and so will the future. But in Our Age (to use an exaggerated term) these were more colorful, and you could actually *grasp* them. They were literally lined up on a shelf, right before our very eyes.

Nowadays, if you try to grasp the reality of anything, there's always a whole slew of convoluted extras that come with it: hidden advertising, dubious discount coupons, point cards stores hand out that you know you should throw out but still hold on to, options that are forced on you before you know what's happening. Back in Our Age, nobody plunked down indecipherable three-volume owner's manuals in front of you. Whatever it was, we just clutched it in our hands and took it straight home—like taking a baby chick home from one of those little nighttime stands. Everything was simple, and direct. Cause and effect were good buddies back then; thesis and reality hugged each other like it was the most natural thing in the world. And my guess is that the sixties were the last time that'll ever happen.

A Pre-History of Late-Stage Capitalism—that's my own personal name for that age.

Let me tell you a little bit about the young girls back then. And us guys with our nearly brand-new genitals and the wild, joyous, sad sex we had. That's one of my themes here.

Take virginity, for instance—a word that, for some unfathomable reason, always reminds me of a field on a beautiful sunny spring afternoon. In the sixties, virginity was a much bigger deal than it is today. I'm generalizing, of course—I haven't taken a survey or anything—but my sense of it is that about fifty percent of the girls in my generation had lost their virginity by the time they reached twenty. At least among the girls I knew, that seemed to be the case. Which means that about half of the girls, whether they'd made a conscious choice or not, were still virgins.

It strikes me now that most of the girls in my generation—the moderates, you might dub them—whether virgins or not, agonized over the whole issue of sex. They didn't insist that virginity was such a precious thing, nor did they denounce it as some stupid relic of the past. So what actually happened—sorry, but I'm generalizing again—was that they went with the flow. It all depended on the circumstances and the partner. Makes sense to me.

So on either side of this silent majority, you had your liberals and your conservatives—the entire spectrum, from girls who practiced sex as a kind of indoor sport, to those who were firm believers in remaining pure till they got married. There were guys, too, who were adamant that whoever they married had to be a virgin.

Like every generation, there were all kinds of people, with all kinds of values. But the big difference between the sixties and the decades before and after was that we were convinced that someday all those differences could be overcome.

Peace!

◎

What follows is the story of a guy I know, a high school classmate in Kobe. He was one of those guys who was an all-round star: good grades, good at sports, a natural leader. He was more clean-cut than handsome, I suppose. He had a nice clear voice, and was a good public speaker, even a decent singer. He was always elected as class representative, and when our class met as a group he was the one who did the final wrap-up. He wasn't full of original opinions, but in class discussion who expects any originality? There're tons of situations when originality is not what's called for. Most situations, in fact. All we wanted was to get out of there as quick as we could, and we could count on him to wind up the discussion in the time allotted. In that sense, he was a handy sort of guy to have around.

With him, everything was by the book. If somebody was making a racket in study hall he'd quietly tell them to simmer down. The guy was basically perfect, but it bothered me that I couldn't figure out what was going through his head. Sometimes I felt like yanking his head off his neck and giving it a good shake to see what was rattling around inside. He was very popular with the girls, too. Whenever he popped to his feet in class to say something every girl would gaze at him with a dreamy look of admiration. He was also your go-to guy if you were stuck with a math problem you couldn't solve. We're talking about a guy who was twenty-seven times more popular than me.

If you've ever gone to public high school, you know the type I mean. There's somebody like him in every class, the kind that keeps things running smoothly. Years spent in school absorbing training manuals for life have taught me many things, and one of the lessons I came away with was this: like it or not, every group has somebody like him.

Personally, I'm not too fond of the type. For whatever reason, we just don't click. I much prefer imperfect, more memorable types of people. So with this particular guy, even though we were in the same class for a year, we never hung out. The first time we ever had a semi-decent conversation was after we graduated, during summer vacation when we were freshmen in college. We happened to be taking driving lessons at the same driving school and talked a few times there. We'd have a cup of tea together while we were waiting. Driving school has got to be one of the most boring places on earth, and if you see a familiar face you jump at it. I don't remember what we talked about, but I know I wasn't left with much of an impression one way or the other.

One other thing I did remember about him is his girlfriend. She was in a different class and was one of a handful of girls who were drop-dead gorgeous. Besides her stunning looks, she got good grades, was good at sports, was kind and a natural leader, and was the one who always summed up class discussions. Every class has a girl like her.

To make a long story short, they were perfect for each other. Mister Clean and Miss Clean. Like right out of a toothpaste commercial.

They were inseparable. During lunch break they sat side by side in a corner of the school yard, talking. They went home together, too, riding the same train but getting off at different stops. He was on the soccer club, she was in the English conversation club, and whoever finished earlier than the other would study in the library, waiting so they could go home together. It seemed like they were together every free moment they had. And they were always talking. I don't know how they could keep from running out of things to say, but somehow they managed it.

We—and by "we" I mean the guys I hung out with—didn't dislike this couple. We never made fun of them or said bad things about them. In fact, we hardly thought about them at all. They were like the weather, something that was just out there, that barely registered on our attention meter. We were too much into our own pursuits, the vital thrilling things the times had to offer. For instance? For instance sex, rock and roll, Jean-Luc Godard films, political movements, Kenzaburo Oe's novels. But especially sex.

Of course we were ignorant, conceited kids. We had no idea what life was all about. In the real world there was no such thing as Mister Clean and Miss Clean. They only exist on TV. The kind of illusions we had, then, and the kind of illusions this guy and his girlfriend had, weren't all that different.

This is their story. It's not a very happy one, and looking back on it now it's hard to locate any lesson in it. But anyway, this is their story, and at the same time *our* story. So it's a kind of folklore that I've collected and now, as a sort of bumbling narrator, will pass on to you.

◎

The story he told me came out after we had batted around other topics over some wine, so strictly speaking it might not be entirely true. There are parts I didn't catch, and details I've kind of imagined woven in. And to protect the real people in it, I've changed some of the facts, though this doesn't impact the overall story. Still, I think things took place pretty much as said. I say this because though I might have forgotten some of the details, I distinctly recall the overall tone. When you listen to some-body's story and then try to reproduce it in writing, the tone's the main thing. Get the tone right and you have a true story on your hands. Maybe some of the facts aren't quite correct, but that doesn't matter—it actually might elevate the truth factor of the story. Turn this around, and you could say there're stories that are factually accurate yet aren't true at all. Those are the kind of stories you can count on to be boring, and even, in some instances, dangerous. You can smell those a mile away.

One other thing I need to make clear here is that this former class-mate was a lousy storyteller. God might have generously doled out other attributes to the guy, but the ability to relate a story wasn't one of them. (Not that the storyteller's romantic art serves any real purpose in life.) So as he related his story, I could barely stifle a yawn. He'd get off track, go around in circles, take forever to remember some of the facts. He'd take a fragment of his story in his hand, frown at it for a while, and once he was convinced he had it right he'd line his facts up one by one on the table. But often this order was wrong. So as a novelist—a story specialist, if you will—I've rearranged these fragments, carefully gluing them together to form what I hope is a coherent narrative.

We happened to run across each other in Lucca, a town in central Italy. I was renting an apartment in Rome at the time. My wife had to go back to Japan, so I was enjoying a leisurely, solitary train trip, first from Venice to Verona, then on to Mantua and Pisa, with a stopover in Lucca. It was my second time there. Lucca's a quiet, pleasant town, and there's a wonderful restaurant on the outskirts of town where they have superb mushroom dishes.

He'd come to Lucca on business, and we just happened to be staying in the same hotel. Small world.

We had dinner together at a restaurant that night. Both of us were traveling alone, and were bored. The older you get, the more boring traveling alone becomes. It's different when you're younger—whether you're alone or not, traveling can be a blast. But as you age, the fun factor declines. Only the first couple of days are enjoyable. After that, the scenery becomes annoying, and people's voices start to grate. There's no escape, for if you close your eyes to block these out, all kinds of unpleasant memories pop up. It gets to be too much trouble to eat in a restaurant, and you find yourself checking your watch over and over as you wait for streetcars that never seem to arrive. Trying to make yourself understood in a foreign language becomes a total pain.

That's why, when we spotted each other, we breathed a sigh of relief, just like that time we ran across each other at driving school. We sat down at a table near the fireplace, ordered a pricey bottle of red wine, had a full-course mushroom dinner: mushroom hors d'oeuvres, mushroom pasta, and arrosto con funghi.

It turned out he owned a furniture company that imported European furniture, and was in Europe on a buying trip. You could tell his business was doing well. He didn't boast about it or put on any airs—when he handed me his business card he just said he was running a small company—yet he'd clearly done well for himself. His clothes, the way he spoke, his expression, manner, everything about him made this obvious. He was entirely at home with his worldly success, in a pleasant sort of way.

He told me he'd read all my novels. "Our way of thinking and goals are very different," he said, "but I think it's a wonderful thing to be able to tell stories to other people."

That made sense. "If you can do a good job of telling the story," I added.

At first we mainly talked about our impressions of Italy. How the trains never ran on time, how meals took forever. I don't remember how it came about, exactly, but by the time we were into our second bottle of wine he'd already started telling his story. And I was listening, making the appropriate signs to show I was following along. I think he must have wanted to get this off his chest for a long time, but for some reason hadn't. If we hadn't been in a nice little restaurant in a pleasant little town in central Italy, sitting before a fireplace, sipping a mellow 1983 Coltibuono, I seriously doubt he would have told me the tale. But tell it he did.

"I've always thought I was a boring person," he began. "I've never been the type who could just cut loose and have a good time. It was like I could always sense a boundary around me and I did my best not to step across the line. Like I was following a well-laid-out highway with signs telling me where to exit, warning me that a curve was coming up, not to pass. Follow the directions, I figured, and life would turn out okay. People praised me for toeing the line, and when I was little I was sure everybody else was doing the same thing as me. But I soon found out that wasn't the case."

He held his wineglass up to the fire and gazed at it for a time.

"In that sense, my life, at least the beginning stages, went smoothly. But I had no idea what my life meant, and that kind of vague thought only grew stronger the older I got. What did I want out of life? I had no idea! I was good at math, at English, sports, you name it. My parents always praised me, my teachers always said I was doing fine, and I knew I could get into a good college with no problem. But I had no idea at all what I was aiming at, what I wanted to do. As far as a major in college, I was clueless. Should I go for law, engineering, or medicine? I knew I could have done well in any one of them, but nothing excited me. So I went along with my parents' and teachers' recommendations and entered the law department at Tokyo University. There was no principle guiding me, really—it's just that everybody said that was the best choice."

He took another sip of wine. "Do you remember my girlfriend in high school?"

"Was her name Fujisawa?" I said, somehow able to call up the name. I wasn't entirely sure that was right, but it turned out it was.

He nodded. "Right. Yoshiko Fujisawa. Things were good with her, too. I liked her a lot, liked being with her and talking about all kinds of things. I could tell her everything I felt, and she understood me. I could go on forever when I was with her. It was wonderful. I mean, before her, I never had a friend I could really talk to."

He and Yoshiko were spiritual twins. It was almost uncanny how similar their backgrounds were. As I've said, they were both attractive, smart, natural-born leaders. Class superstars. Both of them were from affluent families, with parents who didn't get along. Both had mothers who were older than their fathers, and fathers who kept a mistress and stayed away from home as much as they could. Fear of public opinion kept their parents from divorcing. At home, then, their mothers ruled the roost, and expected their children to be the tops in whatever they did. He and Yoshiko were both popular enough, but never had any real friends. They weren't sure why. Maybe it was because ordinary, imperfect people always choose similarly imperfect people as friends. At any rate, the two of them were always lonely, always a bit on edge.

Somehow, though, they hooked up and started going out. They ate lunch together every day, walked home from school together. Spent every spare moment with each other, talking. There was always so much to talk about. On Sundays they studied together. When it was just the two of them they could relax the most. Each knew exactly how the other was feeling. They could talk forever about the loneliness they'd experienced, the sense of loss, their fears, their dreams.

They made out once a week, usually in one of the rooms of their respective houses. It wasn't hard to be alone, what with their fathers always gone and their mothers running errands half the time, their homes were practically deserted. They followed two rules during their make-out sessions: their clothes had to stay on, and they'd only use their fingers. They'd passionately make out for ten or fifteen minutes, then sit down together at a desk and study together.

"That's enough. Why don't we study now?" she'd say, smoothing down the hem of her skirt. Both of them got almost identical grades, so they made a game out of studying, competing, for instance, to see who could solve math problems the quickest. Studying was never a burden; it was like second nature to them. It was a lot of fun, he told me. You might think this is stupid, but we really enjoyed studying. Maybe only people like the two of us could ever understand how much fun it was.

Not that he was totally happy with their relationship. Something was missing. Actual sex, in other words. "A sense of being one, physically," is how he put it. I felt we had to take the next step, he said. I thought if we did, we'd be freer in our relationship, and understand each other better. For me that would have been a completely natural development.

But she saw things differently. Her mouth set, she shook her head slightly. "I love you so much," she quietly explained, "but I want to stay a virgin until I get married." No matter how much he tried to persuade her, she wouldn't listen.

"I love you, I really do," she said. "But those are two different things. I'm not going to change my mind. I'm sorry, but you'll just have to put up with it. You will, if you really love me."

When she put it that way, he told me, I had to respect her wishes. It was a question of how she wanted to live her life and there wasn't anything I could say about that. To me, whether a girl's a virgin or not didn't matter that much. If I got married and found out my bride wasn't a virgin, I wouldn't care. I'm not a very radical type of person, or a dreamy, romantic sort. But I'm not all that conservative, either. I'm more of a realist, I guess. A girl's virginity just isn't that big a deal. It's much more important that a couple really know each other. But that's just my opinion, and I'm not about to force others to agree. She had her own vision of how her life should be, so I just had to grin and bear it, and make do with touching her under her clothes. I'm sure you could imagine what this involved.

I can imagine, I said. I have similar memories.

His face reddened a bit and he smiled.

That wasn't so bad, don't get me wrong, but since we never went any further, I never felt relaxed. To me we were always stopping halfway. What I wanted was to be one with her, with nothing coming between us.

To possess her, to be possessed. I needed a sign to prove that. Sexual desire figured into it, of course, but that wasn't the main thing. I'm talking about a sense of being one, physically. I'd never once experienced that sense of oneness with a person. I'd always been alone, always feeling tense, stuck behind a wall. I was positive that once we were one, my wall would come crumbling down, and I'd discover who I was, the self I'd only had vague glimpses of.

"But it didn't work out?" I asked him.

"No, it didn't," he said, and stared for a time at the blazing logs in the fireplace, his eyes strangely dull. "It never did work out," he said.

He was seriously thinking of marrying her, and told her so. After we graduate from college we can get married right away, he told her. We could even get engaged earlier. His words made her very happy, and she beamed a charming smile at him. At the same time, her smile revealed a hint of weariness, of a wiser, more mature person listening to a young person's immature ideas. I can't marry you, she said. I'm going to marry someone a few years older than me, and you're going to marry someone a few years younger. That's the way things are done. Women mature faster than men, and age more quickly. You don't know anything about the world yet. Even if we were to marry right out of college, it wouldn't work out. We'd never stay as happy as we are now. Of course I love you—I've never loved anyone else. But those are two different things. ("Those are two different things" being her pet saying.) We're still in high school, and we've lived sheltered lives. But the world outside isn't like that. It's a big world out there, and we have to get ready for it.

He understood what she was getting at. Compared to other boys his age, he had his feet firmly on the ground. If someone else had been arguing the same point he probably would have agreed. But this was no abstract generalization. This was his life they were talking about.

I just don't get it, he told her. I love you so much. I want us to be one. This couldn't be clearer to me, or more important. I don't care if it's unrealistic. That's how much I love you.

She shook her head again, as if to tell him it was out of the question. She stroked his hair and said, "I wonder what either of us knows about love. Our love has never been tested. We've never had to take responsibility for anything. We're still children."

He couldn't say a thing. It just made him sad he couldn't smash down the wall around him now. Until then he'd always seen that wall as pro-

tecting him, but now it was a barrier, barring his way. A wave of impo-
tence swept over him. I can't do anything anymore, he thought. I'm
going to be surrounded by this thick wall forever, never allowed to venture outside. The rest of my insipid, pointless life.

◎

Their relationship remained the same until the two of them graduated
from high school. They'd meet up at the library as always, study together,
make out with their clothes on. She didn't seem to mind that they never
went all the way. She actually seemed to like things left that way, uncon-
summated. Everybody else imagined that Mister and Miss Clean were
both enjoying an uncomplicated youth. But he continued to struggle
with his unresolved feelings.

In the spring of 1967, he entered Tokyo University, while she went to
a women's college in Kobe. It was definitely a first-rate school, but with
her grades she could have gotten into someplace much better, even
Tokyo University if she'd wanted to. But she didn't think it was necessary, and didn't take the entrance exam. I don't particularly want to
study, or get into the Ministry of Finance, she explained. I'm a girl. I'm
different from you. You're going to go far. But I want to take a break, and
spend the next four years enjoying myself. After I get married, I won't be
able to do that again.

He was frankly disappointed. He'd been hoping they'd both go to
Tokyo and start their relationship afresh. He pleaded with her to join
him, but again she merely shook her head.

He came back from Tokyo for summer vacation after his freshman
year, and they went on dates almost every day. (That's the summer he
and I ran across each other at driving school.) She drove them all around
and they continued the same make-out sessions as before. He started,
though, to sense that something in their relationship was changing. Reality was silently starting to worm its way between them.

It wasn't like there was some obvious change. Actually, the problem
was more a *lack* of change. Nothing about her had changed—the way
she spoke, her clothes, the topics she chose to talk about, her opinions—
they were all the same as before. Their relationship was like a pendulum
gradually grinding to a halt, and he felt out of synch.

Life in Tokyo was lonely. The city was filthy, the food awful, the people uncouth. He thought about her all the time. At night he'd hole up in his room and write letter after letter to her. She wrote back, though not as often. She wrote all the details about her life, and he devoured her letters. Her letters were what kept him sane. He started smoking and drinking, and cutting classes.

When summer vacation finally rolled around, though, and he rushed back to Kobe, a lot of things disappointed him. He'd only been away for three months, yet strangely enough his hometown now struck him as dusty and lifeless. Talking with his mother was a total bore. The scenery back home he'd waxed nostalgic over while he was in Tokyo now looked insipid. Kobe, he discovered, was just a self-satisfied backwater town. He didn't want to talk to anybody, and even going to the barbershop he'd gone to since he was a child depressed him. When he took his dog for a walk, the seashore was empty and littered with trash.

You'd think going on dates with Yoshiko would have excited him, but it didn't. Every time they said goodbye, he'd go home and brood. He was still in love with her—that was a given. But it wasn't enough. I have to *do* something, he felt. Passion will get by on its own steam for a time, but it doesn't last forever. If we don't do something drastic our relationship will reach an impasse, and all the passion will be suffocated out of us.

One day, he decided to raise again the issue of sex that they'd frozen out of their conversations. This will be the last time I bring it up, he decided.

"These last three months in Tokyo I've been thinking about you all the time," he told her. "I love you, and my feelings won't change, even if we're away from each other. But being apart so long, all kinds of dark thoughts start to take over. You probably don't understand this, but people are weak when they're alone. I've never been so alone like this in my life. It's awful. So I want something that can bring us closer together. I want to know for sure that we're bound together, even if we're apart."

But his girlfriend turned him down. She sighed and gently kissed him.

"I'm sorry," she said, "but I can't give you my virginity. These are two different things. I'll do anything for you, except that. If you love me, please don't bring that up again."

He raised the idea of their getting married.

"There are girls in my class who are engaged already," she said. "Just two of them, actually. But their fiancés have jobs. That's what getting engaged involves. Marriage involves responsibility. You become independent and accept another person into your life. If you don't take responsibility you can't gain anything."

"I can take responsibility," he declared. "Listen—I'm going to a top university, and I'm getting good grades. I can get a job later in any company or government office I want. You name the company and I'll get into it as the top candidate. I can do anything, if I put my mind to it. So what's the problem?"

She closed her eyes, leaned back against the car seat, and didn't say anything for a while. "I'm scared," she said. She covered her face with her hands and began to cry. "I'm so very very scared. Life is frightening. In a few years, I'll have to go out in the real world and it scares me. Why don't you understand that? Why can't you try to understand what I'm feeling? Why do you have to torment me like this?"

He held her close. "As long as I'm here you don't need to be afraid," he said. "I'm scared, too—as much as you are. But if I'm with you, I'm not afraid. As long as we pull together, there's nothing to be afraid of."

She shook her head again. "You don't understand. I'm not like you. I'm a woman. You don't get it at all."

It was pointless for him to say anything more. She cried for a long time, and when she was finished she said the following, rather astonishing thing:

"If . . . we ever broke up, I want you to know I'll always think about you. It's true. I'll never forget you, because I really love you. You're the first person I've ever loved and just being with you makes me happy. You know that. But these are two different things. If you need me to promise you, I will. I *will* sleep with you someday. But not right now. After I marry somebody else, I'll sleep with you. I promise."

"At the time I had no idea what she was trying to tell me," he said, staring at the burning logs in the fireplace. The waiter brought over our entrees and laid a few logs on the fire while he was at it. Sparks crackled up. The middle-aged couple at the table next to us was puzzling over which desserts to order. "What she said was like a riddle. After I got home I gave a lot of thought to what she'd said, but I just couldn't grasp it at all. Do you understand what she meant?"

"Well, I guess she meant she wanted to stay a virgin until she got married, and since after she was married there was no reason to be a virgin anymore, she wouldn't mind having an affair with you. She was just telling you to wait till then."

"I suppose that's it. That's the only thing I can think of."

"It's a unique way of thinking," I said. "Logical, though."

A gentle smile played at his lips. "You're right. It is logical."

"She gets married a virgin. And once she's somebody's wife she has an affair. Sounds like some classic French novel. Minus any fancy-dress ball or maids running around."

"But that's the only practical solution she was able to come up with," he said.

"A damn shame," I said.

He looked at me for a while, and then slowly nodded. "You got that right. I'm glad you understand." He nodded again. "Now I can see it that way—now that I'm older. Back then, though, I couldn't. I was just a kid. I couldn't grasp all the minute fluctuations of the human heart. So pure shock was my only reaction. Honestly, I was completely floored."

"I could see that," I said.

We didn't say anything for a while as we ate.

"As I'm sure you can imagine," he continued, "we broke up. Neither of us announced we were breaking up, it just ended naturally. A very quiet breakup. I think we were too worn out to continue the relationship. From my perspective, her approach to life was—how should I put it?— not very sincere. No, that's not it. . . . What I wanted was for her to have a better life. It disappointed me a little. I didn't want her to get so hung up on virginity or marriage or whatever, but live a more natural, full sort of life."

"But I don't think she could have acted otherwise," I said.

He nodded. "You might be right," he said, taking a bite of a thick piece of mushroom. "After a while, you become inflexible. You can't bounce back anymore. It could have happened to me, too. Ever since we were little, people had been pushing us, expecting us to succeed. And we met their expectations, because we were bright enough to. But your maturity level can't keep pace, and one day you find there's no going back. At least as far as morals go."

"That didn't happen to you?" I asked.

"Somehow I was able to overcome it," he said after giving it some thought. He put down his knife and fork and wiped his mouth with the napkin. "After we broke up, I started going out with another girl in Tokyo. We lived together for a while. Honestly, she didn't move me as much as Yoshiko did, but I did love her. We really understood each other, and were always up-front with each other. She taught me about human beings—how beautiful they can be, the kind of faults they have. I finally made some friends, too, and got interested in politics. I'm not saying my personality completely changed or anything. I was a very practical person, and I still am. I don't write novels, and you don't import furniture. You know what I mean. In college I learned there were lots of realities in the world. It's a huge world, there are lots of different values co-existing, and there's no need to always be the top student. And then I went out into the world."

"And you've done very well for yourself."

"I suppose," he said, and gave a sheepish sigh. He gazed at me like we were a pair of accomplices. "Compared to other people of my generation, I make a good living. So on a practical level, yes, I've been successful."

He fell silent. Knowing he wanted to say more, I sat there, patiently waiting for him to go on.

"I didn't see Yoshiko for a long time after that," he continued. "For a long time. I'd graduated and started work at a trading company. I worked there for five years, part of which took me overseas. I was busy every day. Two years after I graduated, I heard that Yoshiko had gotten married. My mother gave me the news. I didn't ask who she'd married. When I heard the news, the first thought that struck me was whether she'd been able to keep her virginity until marriage. After that I felt a little sad. The next day I felt even sadder. I felt like something important was finally over, like a door behind me had closed forever. That's only to be expected, since I loved her. We'd gone out for four years, and I guess I was still clinging to the hope that we might get married someday. She'd been a huge part of my youth, so it was only natural that I felt sad. But I decided that as long as she was happy, I was OK with it. I honestly felt that way. I was a little—worried about her. There was a part of her that was very fragile."

The waiter came, removed our plates, and brought over the dessert wagon. We both turned down dessert and ordered coffee.

"I got married late, when I was thirty-two. So when Yoshiko called me, I was still single. I was twenty-eight then, which makes it more than a decade ago. I'd just quit the company I'd been working for and had gone out on my own. I was convinced that the imported furniture market was about to take off, so I borrowed money from my father and started up my own little firm. Despite my confidence, though, things didn't go so well at first. Orders were late, goods went unsold, warehouse fees piled up, there were loans to repay. I was frankly worn out, and starting to lose confidence. This was the hardest time I've ever gone through in my life. And it was exactly during that rough spell that Yoshiko phoned me one day. I don't know how she got my number, but one evening around eight, she called. I knew it was her right away. How could I ever forget that voice? It brought back so many memories. I was feeling pretty down then, and it felt wonderful to hear my old girlfriend's voice again."

He stared at the blazing logs in the fireplace as if trying to summon up a memory. By this time the restaurant was completely full, loud with the sound of people's voices, laughter, plates clinking. Almost all the guests were locals, it seemed, and they called out to the waiters by first name: *Giuseppe! Paolo!*

"I don't know who she heard it from, but she knew everything about me. How I was still single and had worked abroad. How I'd quit my job a year before and started up my own company. She knew it all. Don't worry, she told me, you'll do fine. Just have confidence in yourself. I know you'll be successful. How could you not be? It made me so happy to hear her say that. Her voice was so kind. I can do this, I thought, I can make a go of it. Hearing her voice made me regain the confidence I used to have. As long as things stay real, I thought, I know I'm going to make it. I felt like the world was out there just for me." He smiled.

"It was my turn then to ask about her life. What kind of person she'd married, whether she had children, where she lived. She didn't have any children. Her husband was four years older than her and worked at a TV station. He was a director, she said. He must be very busy, I commented. So busy he doesn't have time to make any children, she replied, and laughed. She lived in Tokyo, in a condo in Shinagawa. I was living in Shiroganedai at the time, so we weren't exactly neighbors but lived pretty close to each other. What a coincidence, I told her. Anyway, that's what we talked about—all the typical things two people who used to go out in high school might talk about. Sometimes it felt a bit awkward, but I enjoyed talking with her again. We talked like two old friends who'd said goodbye long ago and who were now walking down two separate paths in life. It had been a long time since I'd spoken so openly, so honestly, to anybody, and we talked for a long, long time. Once we'd said everything there was to say, we were silent. It was a—how should I put it?—a very deep silence. The kind of silence where, if you close your eyes, all sorts of images start to well up in your mind." He stared for a while at his hands on the table, then raised his head and looked at me. "I wanted to hang up then, if I could have. Thank her for calling, tell her how much I enjoyed talking with her. You know what I mean?"

"From a practical standpoint that would have been the most realistic thing to do," I agreed.

"But she didn't hang up. And she invited me to her place. Can you come over? she asked. My husband's on a business trip and I'm by myself and bored. I didn't know what to say, so I was silent. And so was she. There was just that silence for a while, and then she said this: I haven't forgotten the promise I made to you."

◎

"I haven't forgotten the promise I made to you," she said. At first he didn't know what she meant. And then it all came back—her promise to sleep with him after she got married. He'd never considered this a real promise, just a stray thought she'd let slip out in a moment of confusion.

But it hadn't been the result of any confusion on her part. For her it was a binding promise, a firm agreement she'd entered into.

For a moment he didn't know what to think, no idea what he should do. He glanced around him, completely at a loss, but discovered no signposts to show him the way. Of course he wanted to sleep with her—that goes without saying. After they broke up, he often imagined what it would be like making love to her. Even when he was with other girls, in the dark he pictured holding her. Not that he'd seen her naked—all he knew about her body was what he'd been able to feel with his hand up her clothes.

He knew full well how dangerous it would be for him to sleep with her at this juncture. How destructive it could wind up being. He also didn't feel like reawakening what he'd already abandoned back there in the dark. This isn't the right thing for me to do, he knew. There's something unreal about it, something incompatible with who I am.

But of course he agreed to see her. This was, after all, a beautiful fairy tale he might experience only once in life. His gorgeous ex-girlfriend, the one he'd spent his precious youth with, was telling him she wanted to sleep with him, asking him to come over to her house right away— and she lived close by. Plus there was that secret, legendary promise exchanged a long, long time ago in a deep woods.

He sat there for a while, eyes closed, not speaking. He felt like he'd lost the power of speech.

"Are you still there?" she asked.

"I'm here," he said. "Okay. I'll be over soon. I should be there in less than a half hour. Tell me your address."

He wrote down the name of her condo and the apartment number, and her phone number. He quickly shaved, changed clothes, and went out to flag down a cab.

⊚

"If it'd been you, what would you have done?" he asked me.

I shook my head. I had no idea what to say.

He laughed and stared at his coffee cup. "I wish I could have gotten by without answering, too. But I couldn't. I had to make a decision right then and there. To go or not to go, one or the other. There's no in-between. I ended up going to her place. As I knocked on her door, I was thinking how nice it would be if she wasn't at home. But she was there, as beautiful as she used to be. Smelling just as wonderful as I remembered. We had a few drinks and talked, listened to some old records. And then what do you think happened?"

I have no idea, I told him.

"A long time ago, when I was a child, there was a fairy tale I read," he said, staring at the opposite wall the whole time. "I don't remember how the story went, but the last line has stayed with me. Probably because this was the first time I'd ever read a fairy tale that had such a strange ending. This is how it ended: 'And when it was all over, the king and his retainers burst out laughing.' Don't you think that's sort of a strange ending?"

"I do," I said.

"I wish I could remember the plot, but I can't. All I can remember is that strange last line. 'And when it was all over, the king and his retainers burst out laughing.' What kind of story could it have been?"

We'd finished our coffee by this point.

"We held each other," he went on, "but didn't have sex. I didn't take her clothes off. I just touched her with my fingers, just like the old days. I decided that was the best thing to do, and she'd apparently come to the same conclusion. For a long time we sat there, touching each other. That was the only way we could grasp what we were supposed to understand at that time. If this had been long ago, that wouldn't have been the case—we would have had sex, and grown even closer. We might have ended up happy. But we'd already passed that point. That possibility was sealed up, frozen solid. And it would never open up again."

He turned his empty coffee cup around and around. He did this so long the waiter came over to see if he wanted anything. Finally he let go of the cup, called the waiter back over, and ordered another espresso.

"I must have stayed at her apartment for about an hour. I don't remember exactly. Any longer and I might have gone a little nuts," he said and smiled. "I said goodbye to her and left. This was our final farewell. I knew it, and so did she. The last time I saw her, she was standing in the doorway, arms folded. She seemed about to say something, but didn't. She didn't have to say it out loud—I knew what she was going to say. I felt so empty. So hollow. Sounds struck me as weird, everything looked distorted. I wandered around in a daze, thinking how my life had been totally pointless. I wanted to turn around, go back to her place, and have her. But I couldn't. There was no way I could do that."

He closed his eyes and shook his head. He drank his second espresso.

"It's kind of embarrassing to say this, but that night I went out and slept with a prostitute. It was the first time in my life I'd paid for sex. And probably the last."

I stared at my own coffee cup for a while. And thought of how full of myself I used to be. I wanted to try to explain this to him, but didn't think I could.

"When I tell it like this, it sounds like something that happened to somebody else," he laughed. He was silent for a time, lost in thought. I didn't say anything, either.

" 'And when it was all over, the king and his retainers burst out laughing,' " he finally said. "That line always comes to me whenever I remember what happened. It's like a conditioned reflex. It seems to me that very sad things always contain an element of the comical."

As I said at the beginning, there's no real moral or lesson to be learned from all this. But this is something that actually happened to him. Something that happened to all of us. That's why when he told me his story, I couldn't laugh. And even now I can't.

—TRANSLATED BY PHILIP GABRIEL

HUNTING KNIFE

Two rafts were anchored offshore like twin islands. They were the perfect distance to swim to from the beach—exactly fifty strokes out to one of them, then thirty strokes from one to the other. About fourteen feet square, each raft had a metal ladder, and a carpet of artificial grass covering its surface. The water, ten or twelve feet deep at this point, was so transparent you could follow the chains attached to the rafts all the way down to the concrete anchors at the bottom. The swimming area was enclosed by a coral reef, and there were hardly any waves, so the rafts barely bobbed in the water. They seemed resigned to being anchored to that spot with the intense sun beating down on them day after day.

I liked to stand out there and look back at the shore, at the long white beach, the red lifeguard tower, the green row of palm trees—it was a gorgeous scene, maybe a little too picture-postcard perfect. Off to the right, the beach ended in a line of dark craggy rocks that led to the hotel cottages where my wife and I were staying. It was the end of June, still early in the tourist season, and there weren't many people in the hotel or on the beach.

There was an American military base nearby, and the rafts lay right in the flight path of the helicopters returning to it. The helicopters would appear offshore, bisect the space between the two rafts, then zoom over the palm trees and disappear. They flew so low you could almost make out the expressions on the faces of the pilots. Still, except for those helicopters swooping overhead, the beach was a sleepy, quiet place—the perfect spot to be left alone on vacation.

Each cottage was a white two-story building divided into four units, two on the first floor, two on the second. Our room was on the first floor, with an ocean view. Right outside our window was a stand of white plumeria, and beyond that a garden with a neatly trimmed lawn. Morning and night, the sprinklers made a drowsy clatter on the grass. Past the garden was a swimming pool and a row of tall palm trees, whose huge fronds waved gently in the trade winds.

A mother and her son, Americans, were staying in the unit next door to my wife and me. They seemed to have settled in long before we arrived. The mother was around sixty, the son close to our age, twenty-eight or twenty-nine. They resembled each other more than any mother and son I'd ever seen—both with identical long, narrow faces, broad foreheads, tightly set lips. The mother was tall, her posture erect, her movements always alert and brisk. The son seemed tall, too, but you really couldn't say for sure, as he was confined to a wheelchair. Invariably, his mother was behind him, pushing the chair.

They were incredibly quiet, their room like a museum. They never had the TV on, though twice I did hear music from their place—Mozart's clarinet quintet the first time, the second time some orchestral music I didn't recognize. Richard Strauss was my guess. Other than that, no sound at all. They didn't use the air conditioner—they left their front door open instead, so the cool sea breeze could blow in. But, even with the door open, I never heard them talking. Any conversation they had—I'm assuming they had to talk sometime—must have been more or less an exchange of whispers. This seemed to rub off on my wife and me, and whenever we were in our room we found ourselves speaking in low voices.

We often came across the mother and son in the restaurant, or in the lobby, or on one of the walkways through the garden. The hotel was a small, cozy place, so I guess we were bound to cross paths, whether we wanted to or not. We'd nod to one another as we passed. The mother and son had different ways of nodding hello. The mother would give a strong, affirmative nod; the son barely tilted his head. The impression that these two variant nods gave off, though, was pretty much the same: both greetings began and ended there, and nothing lay beyond. We never tried to speak to them. My wife and I had more than enough to talk about between ourselves—whether we should move to a new apartment when we got home, what we should do about jobs, whether or not to have kids. This was the last summer of our twenties.

After breakfast, the mother and son always sat in the lobby and read the newspapers—each methodically proceeding from one page to the next, top to bottom, as if they were locked in a fierce contest to see who could take the longest to read the whole thing. Some days it wasn't newspapers but massive hardcover books. They seemed less like a mother and son than an old married couple who had long ago grown bored with each other.

◎

At around ten every morning, my wife and I would take a cooler down to the beach. We'd lather up well with sunblock, then sprawl out on mats on the sand. I'd listen to the Stones or Marvin Gaye on a Walkman, while my wife plowed through a paperback of *Gone with the Wind*. She claimed that she'd learned a lot about life from that book. I'd never read it, so I had no idea what she meant. Every day, the sun would pop up inland, trace a slow path between the rafts—in the opposite direction from the helicopters—then sink leisurely beneath the horizon.

At two every afternoon, the mother and son would appear at the beach. The mother always wore a plain light-colored dress with a broad-brimmed straw hat. The son never wore a hat; he had on sunglasses instead. They'd sit in the shade below the palm trees, the breeze rustling around them, and stare off at the ocean, not really doing anything. The mother sat in a folding beach chair, but the son never got out of his wheelchair. Every now and then they'd shift slightly in order to stay in the shade. The mother had a silver thermos with her, and occasionally she poured herself a drink in a paper cup or munched on a cracker.

Some days they'd leave after a half hour; other days they stayed as late as three. When I was swimming, I could feel them watching me. It was quite a long way from the rafts to the line of palm trees, so I may have been imagining it. Or perhaps I was just oversensitive, but whenever I clambered up onto one of the rafts I got the distinct feeling that their eyes were trained in my direction. Sometimes the silver thermos would glint like a knife in the sunlight.

One listless day followed another, with nothing to distinguish one from the next. You could have changed the order and no one would have noticed. The sun rose in the east, set in the west, the olive-green helicopters zoomed in low, and I downed gallons of beer and swam to my heart's content.

◎

On the afternoon of our last full day at the hotel, I went out for one last swim. My wife was taking a nap, so I left for the beach alone. It was a Saturday, so there were more people there than usual. Tanned young soldiers with buzz cuts and tattooed arms were playing volleyball. Kids were splashing around at the edge of the water, building sand castles and shrieking in delight at each big wave. But there was almost no one in the water; the rafts were deserted. The sky was cloudless, the sun high overhead, the sand hot. It was after two, but the mother and son still hadn't made their appearance.

I walked out until the water came up to my chest, then did the crawl, heading for the raft on the left. Slowly, testing the resistance of the water with my palms, I swam on, counting the number of strokes. The water was chilly, and it felt good on my suntanned skin. Swimming in such clear water, I could see my own shadow on the sandy bottom, as if I were a bird gliding through the sky. After I had counted forty strokes, I looked up and, sure enough, there was the raft right ahead of me. Exactly ten strokes later, my left hand touched its side. I floated there for a minute, catching my breath, then grabbed hold of the ladder and scrambled aboard.

I was surprised to find someone else already there—an overweight blond woman. I hadn't seen anyone on the raft when I set out from the beach, so she must have got there while I was swimming toward it. The woman was wearing a tiny bikini—one of those fluttery red things, like the banners Japanese farmers fly in their fields to warn that they've just sprayed chemicals—and she was lying facedown. The woman was so obese that the swimsuit looked even smaller than it was. She seemed to have arrived recently—her skin was still pale, without a trace of a tan.

She glanced up for a second and then closed her eyes again. I sat down at the opposite end of the raft, dangled my feet in the water, and looked off at the shore. The mother and son still weren't under their palm trees. They were nowhere else, either. There was no way I could have missed them; the metal wheelchair, glistening in the sunlight, was a dead giveaway. I felt let down. Without them, a piece of the picture was missing. Perhaps they had checked out of the hotel and gone back to where they came from—wherever that was. When I'd seen them a little earlier, in the hotel restaurant, I hadn't got the impression that they were preparing to leave. They had taken their time eating the daily special and had quietly drunk a cup of coffee afterward—the same routine as always.

I lay facedown like the blond woman and tanned myself for ten minutes or so, listening to the tiny waves slap against the side of the raft. The drops of water in my ear warmed in the intense sun.

"Boy, it's hot," the woman said from the other end of the raft. She had a high-pitched, saccharine kind of voice.

"It sure is," I replied.

"Do you know what time it is?"

"I don't have a watch, but it must be around two thirty. Two forty, maybe?"

"Really?" she said, and let out something close to a sigh, as if that might not be the time she was hoping for. Perhaps she didn't care one way or another about the time.

She sat up. Sweat was beaded on her like flies on food. The rolls of fat started just below her ears and sloped gently down to her shoulders, then in one continuous series down her chubby arms. Even her wrists and ankles seemed to disappear inside those fleshy folds. I couldn't help thinking of the Michelin Man. As heavy as she was, though, the woman didn't strike me as unhealthy. She wasn't bad-looking, either. She simply had too much meat on her bones. I guessed that she was in her late thirties.

"You must have been here a while, you're so tanned."

"Nine days."

"What an amazing tan," she said. Instead of responding, I cleared my throat. The water in my ears gurgled as I coughed.

"I'm staying at the military hotel," she said.

I knew the place. It was just down the road from the beach.

"My brother's a navy officer, and he invited me to come. The navy's not so bad, you know? The pay's OK. They've got everything you want, right there on the base, plus perks like this resort. It was different when I was in college. That was during the Vietnam War. Having a career military person in your family then was kind of embarrassing. You had to slink around. But the world's really changed since then."

I nodded vaguely.

"My ex used to be in the navy, too," she went on. "A fighter pilot. He had a tour of duty in Vietnam for two years, then he became a pilot for United. I was a stewardess for United then, and that's how we met. I'm trying to remember what year we got married . . . Nineteen seventy-something. Anyhow, about six years ago. It happens all the time."

"What does?"

"You know—airline crews work crazy hours, so they tend to date each other. The working hours and lifestyle are totally off the wall. Anyhow, we get married, I quit my job, and then he takes up with another stewardess and winds up marrying her. That happens all the time, too."

I tried changing the subject. "Where do you live now?"

"Los Angeles," she said. "You ever been there?"

"No," I said.

"I was born there. Then my father was transferred to Salt Lake City. Have you been there?"

"No."

"I wouldn't recommend it," she said, shaking her head. She palmed the sweat from her face.

It was strange to think she'd been a stewardess. I'd seen plenty of brawny stewardesses who could have been wrestlers. I'd seen some with beefy arms and downy upper lips. But I'd never seen one as big as her. Maybe United didn't care how heavy their stewardesses were. Or maybe she hadn't been this fat when she had that job.

"Where are you staying?" she asked me.

I pointed out the hotel.

"By yourself?"

I explained how my wife and I were on vacation.

"A honeymoon?"

No, I replied. We've been married six years.

"Really?" she said, surprised. "You don't look that old."

I scanned the beach. No sign yet of the mother and son. The soldiers were still tossing a volleyball around. The lifeguard up on his tower was staring intently at something with his oversize binoculars. Two military helicopters finally appeared offshore and, like messengers in a Greek tragedy delivering inauspicious news, they thundered solemnly overhead and disappeared inland. Silently, we watched the green machines vanish into the distance.

"I bet from up there we look like we're having a great time," the woman said. "Sunning ourselves out here on this raft, not a care in the world."

"You may be right."

"Most things look beautiful when you're way up high," she said. She rolled over onto her stomach again and closed her eyes.

Time passed by in silence. Sensing that it was the right moment to leave, I stood up and told her that I had to be getting back. I dived into the water and swam off. Halfway there, I stopped, treading water, and turned back toward the raft. She was watching me and waved. I gave a slight wave back. From far away, she looked like a dolphin. All she needed was a pair of flippers and she could leap back into the sea.

In my room I took a nap, then as evening came on my wife and I went down to the restaurant as always and ate dinner. The mother and son weren't there. And when we walked back to our room from the restaurant their door was closed. Light filtered out through the small frosted-glass pane in the door, but I couldn't tell if the room was still occupied.

"I wonder if they've already checked out," I said to my wife. "They weren't at the beach or at dinner."

"Everybody checks out eventually," my wife said. "You can't live like this forever."

"I guess so," I agreed, but I wasn't convinced. I couldn't picture that mother and son anywhere but right here.

We started packing. Once we'd filled our suitcases and stowed them at the foot of our bed, the room suddenly seemed cold and alien. Our vacation was coming to an end.

◎

I woke up and glanced at my watch on the table next to my bed. It was one twenty. My heart was beating furiously. I slid off the bed down onto the carpet, sat cross-legged, and took some deep breaths. Then I held my breath, relaxed my shoulders, sat up straight, and tried to focus. I must have swum too much, I decided, or got too much sun. I stood and looked around the room. At the foot of the bed, our two suitcases crouched like stealthy animals. That's right, I remembered—tomorrow we won't be here anymore.

In the pale moonlight shining in through the window, my wife was fast asleep. I couldn't hear her breathing at all, and it was almost as if she were dead. Sometimes she sleeps that way. When we first got married, it kind of scared me; every now and then, I thought maybe she really *was* dead. But it was just that silent, bottomless sleep. I stripped off my sweaty pajamas and changed into a clean shirt and pair of shorts. Slipping a miniature bottle of Wild Turkey that was on the table into my pocket, I opened the door quietly and went outside. The night air was chilly and it carried with it the damp odor of all the surrounding plants. The moon was full, bathing the world in a strange hue you never see in the daytime. It was like looking through a special color filter, one that made some things more colorful than they really are, and left others as drab and drained as a corpse.

I wasn't sleepy at all. It was as if sleep had never existed, my mind was so totally clear and focused. Silence reigned. No wind, no insects, no night birds calling out. Only the far-off sound of waves, and I had to listen carefully to hear even them.

I made one slow circuit of the cottage, then cut across the lawn. In the moonlight, the lawn, which was circular, looked more like an iced-over pond. I stepped carefully, trying not to crack the ice. Beyond the lawn was a narrow set of stone steps, and at the top a bar decorated in a tropical theme. Every evening, just before dinner, I had a vodka and tonic at this bar. This late at night, of course, the place was closed, the bar shuttered, and the parasols at each table all neatly folded up like slumbering pterodactyls.

The young man in the wheelchair was there, resting an elbow on one of the tables, gazing out at the water. From a distance, his metal wheelchair in the moonlight looked like some precision instrument made especially for the deepest, darkest hours of the night.

I had never seen the man alone before. In my mind, he and his mother were always a single unit—he in his chair, his mother pushing it. It felt odd—rude, even—to see him like this. He was wearing an orange Hawaiian shirt I'd seen before, and white cotton trousers. He was just sitting without moving, staring at the ocean.

I stood there for a while, wondering whether I should signal to him that I was there. But, before I could decide what to do, he sensed my presence and turned around. When he saw me, he gave his usual minimalist nod.

"Good evening," I said.

"Good evening," he answered in a small voice. This was the first time I'd heard him speak. His voice sounded a little sleepy but otherwise perfectly normal. Not too high, not too low.

"A midnight stroll?" he asked.

"I couldn't sleep," I said.

He looked me over from top to bottom, and a faint smile came to his lips. "Same here," he said. "Have a seat, if you'd like."

I hesitated for a moment, nodded, then walked over to his table. I pulled out one of the plastic chairs and sat down opposite him. I turned to look in the same direction that he was looking. At the end of the beach were the jagged rocks, like muffins sliced in half, with waves slapping at them at regular intervals. Neat, graceful little waves—as if they'd been measured off with a ruler. Beyond that, there wasn't much to look at.

"I didn't see you at the beach today," I said.

"I was resting in my room the whole day," the young man replied. "My mother wasn't feeling well."

"I'm sorry to hear it."

"It's not a physical thing. More of an emotional, nervous condition." He rubbed his cheek with the middle finger of his right hand. Despite the late hour, his cheeks were as smooth as porcelain, not a trace of stubble. "She's OK now. She's sound asleep. It's different from my legs—one good night's sleep and she's better. Not completely cured or anything, but at least she's her usual self again. Come morning, she'll be fine."

He was silent for thirty seconds, maybe a minute. I uncrossed my legs under the table and wondered if this was the right moment to leave. It was as if my whole life revolved around trying to judge the right point in a conversation to say goodbye. But I missed my chance: just as I was going to tell him I had to go, he spoke up.

"There are all kinds of nervous disorders. Even if they have the same cause, there are a million different symptoms. It's like an earthquake—the underlying energy is the same, but, depending on where it happens, the results are different. In one case, an island might sink; in another a new island is formed."

He yawned. A long, formal kind of yawn. Elegant, almost. "Excuse me," he said afterward. He looked exhausted; his eyes were blurry, as if he might fall asleep at any second. I glanced at my watch and realized that I wasn't wearing one—just a band of white skin where my watch had been.

"Don't worry about me," he said, "I might look sleepy but I'm not. Four hours a night is enough for me, and I usually get that just before dawn. So at this time of night I'm mostly here, just hanging out."

He picked up the Cinzano ashtray on the table, gazed at it for a while as if it were some rare find, then put it back.

"Whenever my mother has her nervous condition, the left side of her face gets frozen. She can't move her eye or her mouth. If you look at that side of her face, it looks like a cracked vase. It's weird, but it's nothing fatal or anything. One night's sleep and she's good to go."

I had no idea how to respond, so I just gave a noncommittal nod. A cracked vase?

"Don't tell my mother I told you about this, okay? She's hates if anybody talks about her condition."

"Sure," I said. "Besides, we're leaving here tomorrow, so I doubt I'll have a chance to talk with her."

"That's too bad," he said, as if he really meant it.

"It is, but I've got to get back to work, so what can I do?" I said.

"Where are you from?"

"Tokyo."

"*Tokyo,*" he repeated. He narrowed his eyes again and stared out at the ocean, as if he'd be able, if he stared hard enough, to see the city lights of Tokyo out beyond the horizon.

"Are you going to be here much longer?" I asked.

"Hard to say," he replied, tracing the handgrip on his wheelchair with his fingers. "Another month, maybe two. It all depends. My sister's husband owns stock in this hotel, so we can stay here for next to nothing. My father runs a big tile company in Cleveland, and my brother-in-law's basically taken it over. I don't like the guy very much, but I guess you can't choose your family, can you? I don't know, maybe he's not as terrible as I make out. Unhealthy people like me tend to be a little narrow-minded." He took a handkerchief from his pocket and slowly, delicately, blew his nose, then repocketed the handkerchief. "Anyhow, he owns stock in a lot of companies. A lot of investment property, too. A shrewd guy, just like my father. So we're all—my family, I mean—divided into two types of people: the healthy ones and the sick ones. The functional and the dysfunctional. The healthy ones are busy making tile, increasing their wealth, and evading taxes—but don't tell anybody I said that, OK?—and they take care of the sick ones. It's a neat division of labor."

He stopped speaking and took a deep breath. He tapped his fingernails against the tabletop for a while. I was silent, waiting for him to go on.

"They all decide everything for us. Tell us to stay a month here, a month there. We're like the rain, my mother and I. We rain here, and the next thing you know we're raining somewhere else."

The waves lapped at the rocks, leaving white foam behind; by the time the foam vanished, new waves had appeared. I watched this process vacantly. The moonlight cast irregular shadows among the rocks.

"Of course, since it's a division of labor," he went on, "my mother and I have our roles to play, too. It's a two-way street. It's hard to describe, but I think we complement their excesses by doing nothing. That's our raison d'être. Do you know what I mean?"

"Yeah, sort of," I replied, "but I'm not entirely sure I do."

He laughed quietly. "A family's a strange thing," he said. "A family has to exist as its own premise, or else the system won't function. In that sense, my useless legs are a kind of a banner that my family rallies around. My dead legs are the pivot around which things revolve."

He was tapping the tabletop again. Not in irritation—merely moving his fingers and quietly contemplating things in his own time zone.

"One of the main characteristics of this system is that lack gravitates toward greater lack, excess toward greater excess. When Debussy was seeming to get nowhere with an opera he was composing, he put it this way: 'I spent my days pursuing the nothingness—*rien*—it creates.' *My* job is to create that void, that *rien*."

He sank back into an insomniac silence, his mind wandering to some distant region. Perhaps to the void inside him. Eventually, his attention returned to the here and now, the point he came back to a few degrees out of alignment with where he'd departed from. I tried rubbing my own cheek. The scratch of stubble told me that, yes, time was still moving. I took the miniature bottle of whiskey from my pocket and laid it on the table.

"Care for a drink? I don't have a glass, I'm afraid."

He shook his head. "Thanks, but I don't drink. I'm not sure how I'd react if I did, so I don't. But I don't mind other people drinking—be my guest."

I tipped the bottle back and let the whiskey slide slowly down my throat. I closed my eyes, savoring the warmth. He watched the whole process from across the table.

"This might be a strange question," he said, "but do you know anything about knives?"

"Knives?"

"Knives. You know, like hunting knives."

I'd used knives when camping, I told him, but I didn't know much about them. That seemed to disappoint him. But not for long.

"Never mind," he said. "I just happen to have a knife I wanted you to take a look at. I bought it about a month ago from a catalogue. But I don't know the first thing about knives. I don't know if it's any good or if I wasted my money. So I wanted to have somebody else take a look and tell me what they think. If you don't mind."

"No, I don't mind," I told him.

Gingerly he withdrew a five-inch-long, beautifully curved object from his pocket and placed it on the table.

"Don't worry. I'm not planning to hurt anybody with it, or hurt myself. It's just that one day I felt like I had to own a sharp knife. I was just dying to get a knife, that's all. So I looked through some catalogues and ordered one. Nobody knows that I'm always carrying this knife around with me—not even my mother. You're the only person who knows."

"And I'm leaving for Tokyo tomorrow."

"That's right," he said, and smiled. He picked up the knife and let it rest in his palm for a moment, testing its weight as if it held some great significance. Then he passed it to me across the table. The knife did have a strange heft—it was as if I were holding a living creature with a will of its own. Wood inlay was set into the brass handle, and the metal was cool, even though it had been in his pocket all this time.

"Go ahead and open the blade."

I pushed a depression on the upper part of the hilt and flipped out the heavy blade. Fully extended, it was about three inches long. With the blade out, the knife felt even heavier. It wasn't just the weight that struck me; it was the way the knife fit perfectly in my palm. I tried swinging it around a couple of times, up and down, side to side, and with that perfect balance I never had to grip harder to keep it from slipping. The steel blade, with its sharply etched blood groove, carved out a crisp arc as I slashed with it.

"Like I said, I don't know that much about knives," I told him, "but this is one great knife. It's got such a great feel to it."

"But isn't it kind of small for a hunting knife?"

"I don't know," I said. "I guess it depends on what you use it for."

"True enough," he said, and nodded a few times as if to convince himself.

I folded the blade into the handle and handed it back to him. The young man opened it up again and deftly twirled the knife once in his hand. Then, as if he were sighting down a rifle, he shut one eye and aimed the knife directly at the full moon. Moonlight reflected off the blade and for an instant flashed on the side of his face.

"I wonder if you could do me a favor," he said. "Could you cut something with it?"

"Cut something? Like what?"

"Anything. Whatever's around. I just want you to cut something. I'm stuck in this chair, so there isn't much I can cut. I'd really like it if you'd cut something up for me."

I couldn't think of any reason to refuse, so I picked up the knife and took a couple of stabs at the trunk of a nearby palm tree. I sliced down diagonally, lopping off the bark. Then I picked up one of those Styrofoam kickboards lying near the pool and sliced it in half lengthwise. The knife was even sharper than I'd imagined.

"This knife's fantastic," I said.

"It's handcrafted," the young man said. "And pretty expensive, too."

I aimed the knife out at the moon as he'd done, and stared hard at it. In the light, it looked like the stem of some ferocious plant just breaking through the surface of the soil. Something that connected nothingness and excess.

"Cut some more things," he urged me.

I slashed out at everything I could lay my hands on. At coconuts that had fallen on the ground, at the massive leaves of a tropical plant, the menu posted at the entrance to the bar. I even hacked away at a couple of pieces of driftwood on the beach. When I ran out of things to cut, I started moving slowly, deliberately, as if I were doing Tai Chi, silently slicing the knife through the night air. Nothing stood in my way. The night was deep, and time was pliable. The light of the full moon only added to that depth, that pliancy.

As I stabbed the air, I suddenly thought of the fat woman, the ex–United Airlines stewardess. I could see her pale, bloated flesh hovering in the air around me, formless, like mist. Everything was there inside that mist. The rafts, the sea, the sky, the helicopters, the pilots. I tried slashing them in two, but the perspective was off, and it all stayed just out of reach of the tip of my blade. Was it all an illusion? Or was *I* the illusion? Maybe it didn't matter. Come tomorrow, I wouldn't be here anymore.

"Sometimes I have this dream," the young man in the wheelchair said. His voice had a strange echo to it, as if it were rising up from the bottom of a cavernous hole. "There's a sharp knife stabbed into the soft part of my head, where the memories lie. It's stuck deep down inside. It doesn't hurt or weigh me down—it's just stuck there. And I'm standing off to one side, looking at this like it's happening to someone else. I want someone to pull the knife out, but no one knows it's stuck inside my head. I think about yanking it out myself, but I can't reach my hands inside my head. It's the strangest thing. I can stab myself, but I can't reach the knife to pull it out. And then everything starts to disappear. I start to fade away, too. Only the knife is always there—to the very end. Like the bone of some prehistoric animal on the beach. That's the kind of dream I have," he said.

—TRANSLATED BY PHILIP GABRIEL

A PERFECT DAY FOR KANGAROOS

There were four kangaroos in the cage—one male, two females, and a newborn baby kangaroo.

My girlfriend and I were standing in front of the cage. This zoo wasn't so popular to begin with, and what with it being Monday morning, the animals outnumbered the visitors. No exaggeration. Cross my heart.

The whole point for us was to see the baby kangaroo. I mean, why else would we be at the zoo?

A month before in the local section of the newspaper we'd spotted an announcement of the baby kangaroo's birth, and ever since then we'd been patiently waiting for the perfect morning to pay the baby kangaroo a visit. But somehow the right day just wouldn't come. One morning it was raining, and sure enough, more rain the next day. Of course it was too muddy the day after that, and then the wind blew like crazy for two days straight. One morning my girlfriend had a toothache, and another morning I had some business to take care of down at city hall. I'm not trying to make some profound statement here, but I would venture to say this:

That's life.

So anyhow, a month zipped on by.

A month can go by just like that. I could barely remember anything I'd done the whole month. Sometimes it felt like I'd done a lot, sometimes like I hadn't accomplished a thing. It was only when the guy came at the end of the month to collect money for the newspaper delivery that I realized a whole month had flown by.

Yep, that's life all right.

Finally, though, the morning we were going to see the baby kangaroo arrived. We woke up at six, drew back the curtains, and determined it was a perfect day for kangaroos. We quickly washed up, had breakfast, fed the cat, did some quick laundry, put on hats to protect us from the sun, and set off.

"Do you think the baby kangaroo is still alive?" she asked me in the train.

"I'm sure it is. There wasn't any article about it dying. If it had died, I'm sure we would have read about it."

"Maybe it's not dead, but sick and in some hospital."

"Well, I think there would have been an article about that, too."

"But what if it had a nervous breakdown and is hiding off in a corner?"

"A baby having a breakdown?"

"Not the baby. The *mother*! Maybe it suffered some sort of trauma and is holed up with the baby in a dark back room."

Women really think of every possible scenario, I thought, impressed. A trauma? What kind of trauma could affect a kangaroo?

"If I don't see the baby kangaroo now I don't think I'll have another chance to. Ever," she said.

"I suppose not."

"I mean, have you ever seen one?"

"Nope, not me," I said.

"Are you so sure you'll ever have another chance to?"

"I don't know."

"*That's* why I'm worried."

"Yeah, but look," I shot back, "I've never seen a giraffe give birth, or even whales swimming, so why make such a big deal about a baby kangaroo?"

"Because it's a baby kangaroo," she said. "That's why."

I gave up and started leafing through the newspaper. I'd never once won an argument with a girl.

◎

The kangaroo was, naturally, still alive and well, and he (or was it a *she*?) looked a lot bigger than in the photo in the paper, as it leapt all around the kangaroo enclosure. It was less a baby than a kind of mini-kangaroo. My girlfriend was disappointed.

"It isn't a baby anymore," she said.

"Sure it is," I said, trying to cheer her up.

I wrapped an arm around her waist and gently stroked her. She shook her head. I wanted to do something to console her, but anything I might have said would not have changed one essential fact: the baby kangaroo had indeed grown up. So I kept quiet.

I went over to the concession stand and bought two chocolate ice cream cones, and when I got back she was still leaning against the cage, staring at the kangaroos.

"It isn't a baby anymore," she repeated.

"You sure?" I asked, handing her one of the ice creams.

"A baby would be inside its mother's pouch."

I nodded and licked my ice cream.

"But it isn't in her pouch."

We tried to locate the mother kangaroo. The father was easy to spot— he was the biggest and quietest of the foursome. Looking like a composer whose talent has run dry, he just stood stock-still, staring at the leaves inside their feed trough. The other kangaroos were female, identical in shape, color, and expression. Either one could have been the baby's mother.

"One of them's got to be the mother, and one of them isn't," I commented.

"Um."

"So what is the one who isn't the mother?"

"You got me," she said.

Oblivious to all this, the baby kangaroo leapt around the enclosure, occasionally pausing to scratch in the dirt for no apparent reason. He/She certainly found a lot to keep him/her occupied. The baby kangaroo leapt around where the father stood, chewed at a bit of leaves, dug in the dirt, bothered the females, lay down on the ground, then got up and hopped around some more.

"How come kangaroos hop so fast?" my girlfriend asked.

"To get away from their enemies."

"What enemies?"

"Human beings," I said. "Humans kill them with boomerangs and eat them."

"Why do baby kangaroos climb into their mother's pouch?"

"So they can run away with her. Babies can't run so fast."

"So they're protected?"

"Yeah," I said. "They protect all their young."

"How long do they protect them like that?"

I knew I should have read up on kangaroos in an encyclopedia before we made this little excursion. A barrage of questions like this was entirely predictable.

"A month or two, I imagine."

"Well, that baby's only a month old," she said, pointing to the baby kangaroo. "So it still must climb into its mother's pouch."

"Hmm," I said. "I guess so."

"Don't you think it'd feel great to be inside that pouch?"

"Yeah, it would."

The sun was high in the sky by this time, and we could hear the shouts of children at a swimming pool nearby. Sharply etched white summer clouds drifted by.

"Would you like something to eat?" I asked her.

"A hot dog," she said. "And a Coke."

A college student was working the hot dog stand, which was shaped like a minivan. He had a boom box on and Stevie Wonder and Billy Joel serenaded me as I waited for the hot dogs to cook.

When I got back to the kangaroo cage she said, "Look!" and pointed to one of the female kangaroos. "You see? It's inside her pouch!"

And sure enough the baby kangaroo had snuggled up inside his mother's pouch. (Assuming this was the mother.) The pouch had filled out, and a pair of pointed little ears and the tip of a tail peeked out. It was a wonderful sight, and definitely made our trip worth the effort.

"It must be pretty heavy with the baby inside," she said.

"Don't worry—kangaroos are strong."

"Really?"

"Of course they are. That's how they've survived."

Even with the hot sun the mother kangaroo wasn't sweating. She looked like someone who'd just finished her afternoon shopping at a supermarket on the main drag in upscale Aoyama and was taking a break in a nearby coffee shop.

"She's protecting her baby, right?"

"Yep."

"I wonder if the baby's asleep."

"Probably."

We ate our hot dogs, drank our Cokes, and left the kangaroo cage.

When we left, the father kangaroo was still staring into the feed trough in search of lost notes. The mother kangaroo and her baby had become one unit, resting in the flow of time, while the mysterious other female was hopping around the enclosure as if taking her tail out on a test run.

It looked like it was going to be a steamy day, the first hot one we'd had in a while.

"Hey, you want to grab a beer somewhere?" she asked.

"Sounds great," I said.

—TRANSLATED BY PHILIP GABRIEL

DABCHICK

When I reached the bottom of a narrow concrete stairway, I found myself in a corridor that stretched on forever straight ahead—a *long* corridor with ceilings so high the passageway felt more like a dried-up drainage canal than a corridor. It had no decoration of any kind. It was an authentic corridor that was all corridor and nothing but corridor. The lighting was feeble and uneven, as if the light itself had finally reached its destination after a series of terrible mishaps. It had to pass through a layer of thick black dust that caked the fluorescent tubes installed at irregular intervals along the ceiling. And of those tubes, one in three was burnt out. I could hardly see my hand before my eyes. The place was silent. The only sound in the gloomy hallway was the curiously flat slapping of my tennis shoes against the concrete floor.

I kept walking: two hundred yards, three hundred yards, maybe half a mile, not thinking, just walking, no time, no distance, no sense that I was moving forward in any way. But I must have been. All of a sudden I was standing in a T-shaped intersection.

A T-shaped intersection?

◎

I fished a crumpled postcard from my jacket pocket and let my eyes wander over its message: "Walk straight down the corridor. Where it intersects at right angles with another corridor, you will find a door." I

101

searched the wall in front of me, but there was no sign of a door, no sign there had ever been a door, no indication there would ever be a door installed in this wall. It was a plain, simple concrete wall with no distinguishing features other than those shared by other concrete walls. No metaphysical doors, no symbolic doors, no metaphorical doors, no nothing. I ran my palm over long stretches of the wall, but it was just a wall, smooth and blank.

There must be some mistake, I was sure.

Leaning against the wall, I smoked a cigarette. Now what? Was I to forge onward or go back?

Not that the answer was ever seriously in doubt. I had no choice. I had to go on. I was sick of being poor. Sick of monthly payments, of alimony, of my cramped apartment, of the cockroaches in the tub, of the rush-hour subway, sick of everything. Now, at last, I had found a decent job. The work would be easy, the pay astoundingly good. Bonuses twice a year. Long summer vacations. I wasn't about to give up now—just because I was having trouble finding one lousy door. If I couldn't find the door here, I would simply go on until I did find it.

I pulled a ten-yen coin from my pocket and flipped it. Heads. I took the corridor to the right.

The passageway turned twice to the right, once to the left, down ten steps, and turned right again. The air here made me think of coffee Jell-O: it was chilly and strangely thick. I thought about the prospect of a salary, about the refreshing cool of an air-conditioned office. Having a job was a wonderful thing. I quickened my steps and went on down the corridor.

At last there was a door ahead. From this distance, it looked like a ragged, old postage stamp, but the closer I came the more it took on the look of a door—until there could no longer be any doubt.

I cleared my throat and, after a light knock on the door, I took a step back and waited for a response. Fifteen seconds went by. Nothing. Again I knocked, this time a little harder, then stepped back to wait. Again, nothing.

All around me, the air was gradually congealing.

Urged on by my own apprehension, I was taking a step forward to knock for a third time when the door opened soundlessly, naturally, as if a breeze had sprung up to swing it on its hinges, though, to be sure, nature had nothing to do with it. The click of a switch came first, and then a man appeared before me.

He was in his middle twenties and perhaps two inches shorter than I. Water dripped from his freshly washed hair, and the only clothing on his body was a maroon bathrobe. His legs were abnormally white, and his feet as tiny as a child's. His features were as blank as a handwriting practice pad, but his mouth wore a faintly apologetic smile. He was probably not a bad man.

"Sorry. You caught me in the bath," he said, drying his hair with a towel.

"The bath?" I glanced at my watch by reflex.

"It's a rule. We have to bathe after lunch."

"I see."

"May I ask the nature of your business?"

I drew the postcard from my jacket pocket and handed it to the man. He took it in his fingertips so as to avoid wetting it and read it over several times.

"I guess I'm five minutes late," I said. "Sorry."

He nodded and returned the card to me. "Hmmm. You'll be starting to work here, then?"

"That's right."

"Funny, I haven't heard about any new hires. I'll have to announce you to my superior. That's my job, you know. All I do is answer the door and announce people to my superior."

"Well, good. Would you please announce me?"

"Of course. If you'll just tell me the password."

"The password?"

"You didn't know there was a password?"

I shook my head. "No one told me about a password."

"Then I can't help you. My superior is very strict about that. I am not to let in anyone who does not know the password."

This was all news to me. I pulled the postcard from my pocket again and studied it to no avail. It said nothing about a password.

"They probably forgot to write it," I said. "The directions for getting here were a little off, too. If you'll just announce me to your superior, I'm sure everything will be fine. I've been hired to start work here today. I'm sure your superior knows all about it. If you'll just announce my arrival . . ."

"That's what I need the password for," he said and began groping for a cigarette only to find that his bathrobe had no pockets. I gave him one of my cigarettes and lit it for him with my lighter.

"Thanks, that's very nice of you," he said. "Now, are you sure you can't recall anything that might have been a password?"

I could only shake my head.

"I don't like this picky business any better than you do, but my superior must have his reasons. See what I mean? I don't know what kind of person he is. I've never met him. But you know how people like that are—they get these brainstorms. Please don't take it personally."

"No, of course not."

"The guy before me announced somebody he felt sorry for because the person claimed he 'just forgot' the password. He was fired on the spot. And you of all people know how hard it is to find work these days."

I nodded. "How about it, then?" I said. "Can you give me a hint? Just a little one."

Leaning against the door, the man exhaled a cloud of smoke. "Sorry. It's against the rules."

"Oh, come on. What harm can a little hint do?"

"Yeah, but if it ever got out, I'd be in deep trouble."

"I won't tell a soul. You won't tell a soul. How'll they ever know?" This was a deadly serious business for me. I wasn't about to give up.

After some indecision, the man bent close to my ear and whispered, "Are you ready for this? All right, now, it's a simple word and it has something to do with water. It fits in your hand, but you can't eat it."

Now it was my turn to mull things over.

"What's the first letter?"

"D," he said.

"Driftwood," I ventured.

"Wrong," he said. "Two more."

"Two more what?"

"Two more tries. If you miss those, you've had it. I'm sorry, but I'm risking a lot here, breaking the rules like this. I can't just let you keep on guessing."

"Look, I really appreciate you giving me a chance like this, but how about a few more hints? Like how many letters in the word."

He frowned. "Next you're gonna ask me to tell you the whole damned thing."

"No, I would never do that. Never. Just tell me how many letters there are in the word."

"OK. Eight," he said with a sigh. "My father always told me: Give somebody a hand and he'll take an arm."

"I'm sorry. Really."

"Anyhow, it's eight letters."

"Something to do with water, it fits in your hand but you can't eat it."

"That's right."

"It starts with a D and it has eight letters."

"Right."

I concentrated on the riddle. "Dabchick," I said finally.

"Nope. Anyway, you can eat a dabchick."

"You sure?"

"Probably. It might not taste good," he added with less than total conviction. "And it wouldn't fit in your hand."

"Have you ever seen a dabchick?"

"No," he said. "I don't know anything about birds. Especially waterbirds. I grew up in the middle of Tokyo. I can tell you all the stations on the Yamanote Line in order, but I've never seen a dabchick."

Neither had I, of course. I didn't even know I knew the word until I heard myself saying it. But "dabchick" was the only eight-letter word I could think of that fit the clues.

"It's got to be 'dabchick,'" I insisted. "The little palm-sized dabchicks taste so bad you couldn't get a dog to eat one."

"Hey, wait a minute," he said. "It doesn't matter what you say: 'dabchick' is not the password. You can argue all you want, but you've got the wrong word."

"But it fits all the clues—connected with water, fits in your hand, you can't eat it, eight letters. It's perfect."

"There's just one thing wrong."

"What's that?"

" 'Dabchick' is not the password."

"Well, then, what is?"

He had to catch himself. "I can't tell you."

"Because it doesn't exist," I declared in the coldest tone I could manage. "There is no other eight-letter word for a thing connected with water that fits in your hand but you can't eat it."

"But there is," he pleaded, close to tears.

"Is not."

"Is."

"You can't prove it. And 'dabchick' meets all the criteria."

"I know, but still, there might be a dog somewhere that likes to eat palm-sized dabchicks."

"All right, if you're so smart, tell me where you can find a dog like that. What kind of dog? I want concrete evidence."

He moaned and rolled his eyes.

I went on: "I know everything there is to know about dogs, but I have never—ever—seen a dog that likes to eat palm-sized dabchicks."

"Do they taste *that* bad?" he whimpered.

"Awful. Just awful. Yech!"

"Have you ever tasted one?"

"Never. Do you expect me to put something so gross in my mouth?"

"Well, no, I guess not."

"In any case, I want you to announce me to your superior," I demanded. " 'Dabchick.' "

"I give up," he said, wiping his hair once again with his towel. "I'll give it a try. But I'm pretty sure it won't do you any good."

"Thanks," I said. "I owe you one."

"But tell me," he said. "Are there really such things as palm-sized dabchicks?"

"Yes. Without a doubt. They exist somewhere," I said, though for the life of me I couldn't tell how the word had popped into my head.

◎

The palm-sized dabchick wiped his glasses with a velvet square and let out another sigh. His lower right molar throbbed with pain. Another trip to the dentist? he thought. I can't take it anymore. The world is such a drag: dentists, tax returns, car payments, broken-down air conditioners . . . He let his head settle back against the leather-covered armchair, closed his eyes, and thought about death. Death was as silent as the ocean bottom, as sweet as a rose in May. The dabchick had been thinking about death a lot these days. In his mind, he saw himself enjoying his eternal rest.

"Here lies the palm-sized dabchick," said the words engraved on the tombstone.

Just then his intercom buzzed.

He aimed one angry shout at the device: "What!"

"Someone to see you, sir," came the voice of the doorman. "Says he's supposed to start work here today. He knows the password."

The palm-sized dabchick scowled and looked at his watch.

"Fifteen minutes late."

—TRANSLATED BY JAY RUBIN

MAN-EATING CATS

bought a newspaper at the harbor and came across an article about an old woman who had been eaten by cats. She was seventy years old and lived alone in a small suburb of Athens—a quiet sort of life, just her and her three cats in a small one-room apartment. One day, she suddenly keeled over facedown on the sofa—a heart attack, most likely. Nobody knew how long it had taken for her to die after she collapsed. The old woman didn't have any relatives or friends who visited her regularly, and it was a week before her body was discovered. The windows and the door were closed, and the cats were trapped. There wasn't any food in the apartment. Granted, there was probably something in the fridge, but cats haven't evolved to the point where they can open refrigerators. On the verge of starvation, they ended up devouring their owner's flesh.

I read this article to Izumi, who was sitting across from me. On sunny days, we'd walk to the harbor, buy a copy of the Athens English-language paper, order coffee at the café next door to the tax office, and I'd summarize in Japanese anything interesting I might come across. That was the extent of our daily schedule on the island. If something in a particular article caught our interest, we'd bat around opinions for a while. Izumi's English was pretty fluent, and she could easily have read the articles herself. But I never once saw her pick up a paper.

"I like to have someone read to me," she explained. "It's been my dream ever since I was a child—to sit in a sunny place, gaze at the sky or the sea, and have someone read aloud to me. I don't care what they read—a newspaper, a textbook, a novel. It doesn't matter. But no one's ever read to me before. So I suppose that means you're making up for all those lost opportunities. And besides, I love your voice."

We had the sky and the sea there, all right. And I enjoyed reading aloud. When I lived in Japan I used to read picture books aloud to my son. Reading aloud is different from just following sentences with your eyes. Something quite unexpected wells up in your mind, a kind of indefinable resonance that I find impossible to resist.

Taking the occasional sip of bitter coffee, I slowly read the article. I'd read a few lines to myself, mull over how to put it into Japanese, then translate aloud. A few bees popped up from somewhere to lick the jam that a previous customer had spilled on the table. They spent a moment lapping it up, then, as if suddenly remembering something, flew into the air with a ceremonious buzz, circled the table a couple of times, and then—again as if something had jogged their memory—settled once more on the tabletop. After I had finished reading the whole article, Izumi sat there, unmoving, elbows resting on the table. She tented the tips of the fingers of her right hand with the tips of her fingers of her left. I rested the paper on my lap and gazed at her slim fingers. She looked at me through the spaces between her fingers.

"Then what happened?" she asked.

"That's it," I replied, and folded up the paper. I took a handkerchief out of my pocket and wiped the flecks of coffee grounds from my lips. "At least, that's all it says."

"But what happened to the cats?"

I stuffed the handkerchief back in my pocket. "I have no idea. It doesn't say."

Izumi pursed her lips to one side, her own little habit. Whenever she was about to give an opinion—which always took the form of a mini-declaration—she pursed her lips like that, as if she were yanking a bedsheet to smooth out a stray wrinkle. When I first met her, I found this habit quite charming.

"Newspapers are all the same, no matter where you go," she finally announced. "They never tell you what you really want to know."

She took a Salem out of its box, put it in her mouth, and struck a match. Every day, she smoked one pack of Salems—no more, no less. She'd open a new pack in the morning and smoke it up by the end of the day. I didn't smoke. My wife made me quit, five years earlier, when she was pregnant.

"What I really want to know," Izumi began, the smoke from her cigarette silently curling up into the air, "is what happened to the cats afterward. Did the authorities kill them because they'd eaten human flesh? Or did they say, 'You guys have had a tough time of it,' give them a pat on the head, and send them on their way? What do you think?"

I gazed at the bees hovering over the table and thought about it. For a fleeting instant, the restless little bees licking up the jam and the three cats devouring the old woman's flesh became one in my mind. A distant seagull's shrill squawk overlapped the buzz of the bees, and for a second or two my consciousness strayed on the border between reality and the unreal. Where was I? What was I doing here? I couldn't get a purchase on the situation. I took a deep breath, gazed up at the sky, and turned to Izumi.

"I have no idea."

"Think about it. If you were that town's mayor or chief of police, what would you do with those cats?"

"How about putting them in an institution to reform them?" I said. "Turn them into vegetarians."

Izumi didn't laugh. She took a drag on her cigarette and ever so slowly let out a stream of smoke. "That story reminds me of a lecture I heard just after I started at my Catholic junior high school. Did I tell you I went to a very strict Catholic school? Just after the entrance ceremony, one of the head nuns had us all assemble in an auditorium, and then she went up to the podium and gave a talk about Catholic doctrine. She told us a lot of things, but what I remember most—actually, the only thing I *do* remember—is this story she told us about being shipwrecked on a deserted island with a cat."

"Sounds interesting," I said.

" 'You're in a shipwreck,' she told us. 'The only ones who make it to the lifeboat are you and a cat. You land on some nameless desert island, and there's nothing there to eat. All you have is enough water and dry biscuits to sustain one person for about ten days.' She said, 'All right, everyone, I'd like all of you to imagine yourselves in this situation. Close your eyes and try to picture it. You're alone on the desert island, just you and the cat. You have almost no food at all. Do you understand? You're hungry, thirsty, and eventually you'll die. What should you do? Should you share your meager store of food with the cat? No, you should not. That would be a mistake. You are all precious beings, chosen by God, and the cat is not. That's why you should eat all the food yourself.' The nun gave us this deadly serious look. I was a bit shocked. What could possibly be the point of telling a story like that to kids who'd just started at the school? I thought, Whoa, what kind of place have I got myself into?"

◎

Izumi and I were living in an efficiency apartment on a small Greek island. It was the off-season, and the island wasn't exactly much of tourist spot, so the rent was cheap. Neither of us had heard of the island before we got there. It lay near the border of Turkey, and on clear days you could just make out the greenish Turkish mountains. On windy days, the locals joked, you could smell the shish kebab. All joking aside, the island was closer to the Turkish shore than to the next-closest Greek island, and there—looming right before our eyes—was Asia Minor.

In the town square there was a statue of a hero of Greek independence. He had led an insurrection on the Greek mainland and planned an uprising against the Turks, who controlled the island then. But the Turks captured him and put him to death. They set up a sharpened stake in the square beside the harbor, stripped the hapless hero naked, and lowered him onto it. The weight of his body drove the stake through his anus and then the rest of his body until it finally came out of his mouth— an incredibly slow, excruciating way to die. The statue was erected on the spot where this was supposed to have happened. When it was first built, it must have been impressive, but now, what with the sea wind, dust, and seagull droppings, you could barely make out the man's features. The locals hardly gave the shabby statue a passing glance, and for his part the hero looked as if he'd turned his back on the people, the island, the world.

When Izumi and I sat at our outdoor café, drinking coffee or beer, aimlessly gazing at the boats in the harbor, the seagulls, and the far-off Turkish hills, we were sitting at the edge of Europe. The wind was the wind at the edge of the world. An inescapable retro color filled the place. It made me feel as if I were being quietly swallowed up by an alien reality, something foreign and just out of reach, vague yet strangely gentle. And the shadow of that substance colored the faces, the eyes, the skin of the people gathered in the harbor.

At times I couldn't grasp the fact that I was part of this scene. No matter how much I took in the scenery around me, no matter how much I breathed in the air, there was no organic connection between me and all of this.

Two months before, I had been living with my wife and our four-year-old son in a three-bedroom apartment in Unoki, in Tokyo. Not a spacious place, just your basic, functional apartment. My wife and I had our own bedroom, so did our son, and the remaining room served as my study. The apartment was quiet, with a nice view. On weekends, the three of us would take walks along the banks of the Tama River. In spring, the cherry trees along the banks would blossom, and I'd put my son on the back of my bike and we'd go off to watch the Giants' Triple A team in spring training.

I worked at a medium-size design company that specialized in book and magazine layouts. Calling me a designer makes it sound more interesting than it was, since the work was fairly cut-and-dried. Nothing flamboyant or imaginative. Most of the time, our schedule was a bit too hectic, and several times a month I had to pull an all-nighter at the office. Some of the work bored me to tears. Still, I didn't mind the job, and the company was a relaxed place. Because I had seniority, I was able to pick and choose my assignments, and say pretty much whatever I wanted to. My boss was OK, and I got along with my co-workers. And the salary wasn't half bad. So if nothing had happened, I probably would have stayed with the company for the foreseeable future. And my life, like the Moldau River—more precisely the nameless water that makes up the Moldau River—would have continued to flow, ever so swiftly, into the sea.

But along the way I met Izumi.

◎

Izumi was ten years younger than I was. We met at a business meeting. Something clicked between us the first time we laid eyes on each other. Not the kind of thing that happens all that often. We met a couple of times after that, to go over the details of our joint project. I'd go to her office, or she'd drop by mine. Our meetings were always short, other people were involved, and it was basically all business. When our project was finished, though, a terrible loneliness swept over me, as if something absolutely vital had been forcibly snatched from my grasp. I hadn't felt that in years. And I think she felt the same way.

A week later she phoned my office about some minor matter and we chatted for a bit. I told a joke, and she laughed. "Want to go out for a drink?" I asked. We went to a small bar and had a few drinks. I can't recall exactly what we talked about, but we found a million topics and could have talked forever. With a laserlike clarity I could grasp everything she wanted to say. And things I couldn't explain well to anyone else came across to her with an exactness that took me by surprise. We were both married, with no major complaints about our married lives. We loved our spouses and respected them. Still, this was on the order of a minor miracle—running across someone you express your feelings to so clearly, so completely. Most people go their entire lives without meeting a person like that. It would have been a mistake to label this "love." It was more like total empathy.

We started going out regularly for drinks. Her husband's job kept him out late, so she was free to come and go as she pleased. When we got together, though, the time just flew by. We'd look at our watches and discover that we could barely make the last train. It was always hard for me to say goodbye. There was so much more we wanted to tell each other.

Neither of us lured the other to bed, but we did start sleeping together. We'd both been faithful to our spouses up to that point, but somehow we didn't feel guilty, for the simple reason that we had to do it. Undressing her, caressing her skin, holding her close, slipping inside her, coming—it was all just a natural extension of our conversations. So natural that our lovemaking was not a source of heartrending physical pleasure; it was just a calm, pleasant act, stripped of all pretense. Best of all were our quiet talks in bed after sex. I held her naked body close, and she'd curl up in my arms and we'd whisper secrets in our own private language.

We met whenever we could. Strangely enough, or perhaps not so strangely, we were absolutely convinced that our relationship could go on forever, our married lives on one side of the equation, our own relationship on the other, with no problems arising. We were convinced that our affair would never come to light. Sure we had sex, but how was that hurting anyone? On nights when I slept with Izumi, I'd get home late and have to make up some lie to tell my wife, and I did feel a pang of conscience, but it never seemed to be an actual betrayal. Izumi and I had a strictly compartmentalized yet totally intimate relationship.

And, if nothing had happened, maybe we would have continued like that forever, sipping our vodka and tonics, slipping between the sheets whenever we could. Or maybe we would have got tired of lying to our spouses and decided to let the affair die a natural death so that we could return to our comfortable little lifestyles. Either way, I don't think things would have turned out badly. I can't prove it; I just have that feeling. But a twist of fate—inevitable, in retrospect—intervened, and Izumi's husband got wind of our affair. After grilling her, he barged into my home, totally out of control. As luck would have it, my wife was alone at the time, and the whole thing turned ugly. When I got home, she demanded that I explain what was going on. Izumi had already admitted everything, so I couldn't very well make up some story. I told my wife exactly what had happened. "It's not like I'm in love," I explained. "It's a special relationship, but completely different from what I have with you. Like night and day. You haven't detected anything going on, right? That proves it's not the kind of affair you're imagining."

But my wife refused to listen. It was a shock, and she froze, and literally wouldn't speak another word to me. The next day, she packed all her things in the car and drove to her parents' place, in Chigasaki, taking our son with her. I called a couple of times, but she wouldn't come to the phone. Her father came on instead. "I don't want to hear any of your lame excuses," he warned, "and there's no way I'm going to let my daughter go back to a bastard like you." He'd been dead set against our marriage from the start, and his tone of voice said he'd finally been proved right.

At a complete loss, I took a few days off and just lay alone forlornly in bed. Izumi phoned me. She was alone, too. Her husband had left her, as well, but not before smacking her around a bit. He had taken a pair of scissors to every stitch of clothing she owned. From her overcoat to her underwear, it all lay in tatters. She had no idea where he had gone. "I'm exhausted," she said. "I don't know what to do. Everything is ruined, and it'll never be the same again. He's never coming back." She sobbed over the phone. She and her husband had been high school sweethearts. I wanted to comfort her, but what could I possibly say?

"Let's go somewhere and have a drink," she finally suggested. We went to Shibuya and drank till dawn at an all-night bar. Vodka gimlets for me, daiquiris for her. I lost track of how much we drank. For the first time since we'd met we didn't have much to say. At dawn we worked off the liquor walking over to Harajuku, where we had coffee and breakfast at a Denny's. That's when she brought up the notion of going to Greece.

"Greece?" I asked.

"We can't very well stay in Japan," she said, looking deep into my eyes.

I turned the idea around in my mind. Greece? My alcohol-soaked brain couldn't follow the logic.

"I've always wanted to go to Greece," she said. "It's been my dream. I wanted to go on my honeymoon, but we didn't have enough money. So, let's go—the two of us. And just live there, you know, with no worries about anything. Staying in Japan's just going to depress us, and nothing good will come of it."

I didn't have any particular interest in Greece, but I had to agree with her. We calculated how much money we had between us. She had two and a half million yen in savings, while I could come up with one and a half million. Four million yen altogether—about forty thousand dollars.

"Forty thousand dollars should last a few years in the Greek countryside," Izumi said. "Discount plane tickets would set us back around four thousand. That leaves thirty-six. Figure a thousand a month, and that's enough for three years. Two and a half, to be on the safe side. What do you say? Let's go. We'll let things sort themselves out later on."

I looked around me. The early morning Denny's was crowded with young couples. We were the only couple over thirty. And surely the only couple discussing taking all our money and fleeing to Greece after a disastrous affair. What a mess, I thought. I gazed at the palm of my hand for the longest time. Was this really what my life had come to?

"All right," I said finally. "Let's do it."

At work the next day I handed in my letter of resignation. My boss had heard rumors and decided that it would be best to put me on extended leave for the time being. My colleagues were startled to hear that I wanted to quit, but no one tried very hard to talk me out of it. Quitting a job is not so difficult after all, I discovered. Once you make up your mind to get rid of something, there's very little you can't discard. No—not very little. Once you put your mind to it, there's nothing you can't get rid of. And once you start tossing things out, you find yourself wanting to get rid of everything. It's as if you'd gambled away almost all your money and decided, What the hell, I'll bet what's left. Too much trouble to cling to the rest.

I packed everything I thought I'd need into one medium-size blue Samsonite suitcase. Izumi took about the same amount of baggage.

As we were flying over Egypt, I was suddenly gripped by a terrible fear that someone else had taken my bag by mistake. There had to be tens of thousands of identical blue Samsonite bags in the world. Maybe I'd get to Greece, open up the suitcase, and find it stuffed with someone else's possessions. A severe anxiety attack swept over me. If the suitcase got lost, there would be nothing left to link me to my own life— just Izumi. I suddenly felt as if I had vanished. It was the weirdest sensation. The person sitting on that plane was no longer me. My brain had mistakenly attached itself to some convenient packaging that looked like me. My mind was in utter chaos. I had to go back to Japan and get back inside my real body. But here I was in a jet, flying over Egypt, and there was no turning back. This flesh I was temporarily occupying felt as if it were made out of plaster. If I scratched myself, pieces would flake off. I began to shiver uncontrollably. I knew that if these shakes continued much longer the body I was in would crack apart and turn to dust. Despite the air-conditioning in the plane, I broke out in a sweat. My shirt stuck to my skin. An awful smell arose from me. All the while, Izumi held my hand tightly and gave me the occasional hug. She didn't say a word, but she knew how I was feeling. These shakes went on for a good half hour. I wanted to die—to stick the barrel of a revolver in my ear and pull the trigger, so that both my mind and my flesh would be blown to dust.

After the shakes subsided, though, I suddenly felt lighter. I relaxed my tense shoulders and gave myself up to the flow of time. I fell into a deep sleep, and, when I opened my eyes, there below me lay the azure waters of the Aegean.

The biggest problem facing us on the island was an almost total lack of things to do. We didn't work, we had no friends. The island had no movie theaters or tennis courts or books to read. We'd left Japan so abruptly that I had completely forgotten to bring any books. I read two novels I'd picked up at the airport, and a copy of Aeschylus' tragedies Izumi had brought along. I read them all twice. To cater to tourists, the kiosk at the harbor stocked a few English paperbacks, but nothing caught my eye. Reading was my passion, and I'd always imagined that if I had free time I'd wallow in books, but, ironically, here I was—with all the time in the world and nothing to read.

Izumi started studying Greek. She'd brought along a Greek-language textbook, and made a chart of verb conjugations that she carried around, reciting the verbs aloud like a spell. She got to the point where she was able to talk to the shopkeepers in her broken Greek, and to waiters when we stopped by the café, so we managed to make a few acquaintances. Not to be outdone, I dusted off my French. I figured it would come in handy someday, but on this seedy little island I never ran across a soul who spoke French. In town, we were able to get by with English. Some of the old people knew Italian or German. French, though, was useless.

With nothing much to do, we walked everywhere. We tried fishing in the harbor but didn't catch a thing. Lack of fish wasn't the problem; it was that the water was too clear. Fish could see all the way from the hook up to the face of the person trying to catch them. You'd have to be a pretty dumb fish to get caught that way. I bought a sketchbook and a set of watercolors at a local shop and tramped around the island sketching the scenery and the people. Izumi would sit beside me, looking at my paintings, memorizing her Greek conjugations. Local people often came to watch me sketch. To kill time, I'd draw their portraits, which seemed to be a big hit. If I gave them the picture, they'd often treat us to a beer. Once, a fisherman gave us a whole octopus.

"You could make a living doing portraits," Izumi said. "You're good, and you could make a nice little business out of it. Play up the fact that you're a Japanese artist. Can't be many of them around here."

I laughed, but her expression was serious. I pictured myself trekking around the Greek isles, picking up spare change drawing portraits, enjoying the occasional free beer. Not such a bad idea, I concluded.

"And I'll be a tour coordinator for Japanese tourists," Izumi continued. "There should be more of them as time goes by, and that will help make ends meet. Of course that means I'll have to get serious about learning Greek."

"Do you really think we can spend two and a half years doing nothing?" I asked.

"As long as we don't get robbed or sick or something. Barring the unforeseen, we should be able to get by. Still, it's always good to prepare for the unexpected."

Until then I'd almost never been to a doctor, I told her.

Izumi stared straight at me, pursed her lips, and moved them to one side.

"Say I got pregnant," she began. "What would you do? You protect yourself best you can, but people make mistakes. If that happened, our money would run out pretty quick."

"If it comes to that, we should probably go back to Japan," I said.

"You don't get it, do you?" she said quietly. "We can never go back to Japan."

Izumi continued her study of Greek, I my sketching. This was the most peaceful time in my whole life. We ate simply and carefully sipped the cheapest of wines. Every day, we'd climb a nearby hill. There was a small village on top, and from there we could see other islands far away. With all the fresh air and exercise, I was soon in good shape. After the sun set on the island, you couldn't hear a sound. And in that silence Izumi and I would quietly make love and talk about all kinds of things. No more worrying about making the last train, or coming up with lies to tell our spouses. It was wonderful beyond belief. Autumn deepened bit by bit, and early winter came on. The wind picked up, and there were whitecaps in the sea.

It was around this time that we read the story in the paper about the man-eating cats. In the same paper, there was a report about the Japanese emperor's condition worsening, but we'd bought it only to check on exchange rates. The yen was continuing to gain against the drachma. This was vital for us; the stronger the yen, the more money we had.

"Speaking of cats," I said a few days after we'd read the article, "when I was a child I had a cat who disappeared in the strangest way."

Izumi seemed to want to hear more. She lifted her face from her conjugation chart and looked at me. "How so?"

"I was in second, maybe third grade. We lived in a company house that had a big garden. There was this ancient pine tree in the garden, so tall you could barely see the top of it. One day, I was sitting on the back porch reading a book, while our tortoiseshell cat was playing in the garden. The cat was leaping about by itself, the way cats do sometimes. It was all worked up about something, completely oblivious to the fact that I was watching it. The longer I watched, the more frightened I became.

The cat seemed possessed, jumping around, its fur standing on end. It was as if it saw something that I couldn't. Finally, it started racing around and around the pine tree, just like the tiger in 'Little Black Sambo.' Then it screeched to an abrupt halt and scrambled up the tree to the highest branches. I could just make out its little face way up in the topmost branches. The cat was still excited and tense. It was hiding in the branches, staring out at something. I called its name, but it acted like it didn't hear me."

"What was the cat's name?" Izumi asked.

"I forget," I told her. "Gradually, evening came on, and it grew darker. I was worried and waited for a long time for the cat to climb down. Finally it got pitch dark. And we never saw the cat again."

"That's not so unusual," Izumi said. "Cats often disappear like that. Especially when they're in heat. They get overexcited and then can't remember how to get home. Your cat must have come down from the pine tree and gone off somewhere when you weren't watching."

"I suppose," I said. "But I was still a kid then, and I was positive that the cat had decided to live up in the tree. There had to be some reason it couldn't come down. Every day, I'd sit on the porch and look up at the pine tree, hoping to see the cat peeking out from between the branches."

Izumi seemed to have lost interest. She lit her second Salem, then raised her head and looked at me.

"Do you think about your child sometimes?" she asked.

I had no idea how to respond. "Sometimes," I said honestly. "But not all the time. Occasionally something will remind me."

"Don't you want to see him?"

"Sometimes I do," I said. But that was a lie. I just thought that that was the way I was supposed to feel. When I was living with my son, I thought he was the cutest thing I'd ever seen. Whenever I got home late, I'd always go to my son's room first, to see his sleeping face. Sometimes I was seized by a desire to squeeze him so hard he might break. Now everything about him—his face, his voice, his actions—existed in a distant land. All I could recall with any clarity was the smell of his soap. I liked to take baths with him and scrub him. He had sensitive skin, so my wife always kept a special bar of soap just for him. All I could recall about my own son was the smell of that soap.

"If you want to go back to Japan, don't let me stop you," Izumi said. "Don't worry about me. I'd manage somehow."

I nodded. But I knew that it wasn't going to happen.

"I wonder if your child will think of you that way when he's grown up," Izumi said. "Like you were a cat who disappeared up a pine tree."

I laughed. "Maybe so," I said.

Izumi crushed out her cigarette in the ashtray and sighed. "Let's go home and make love, all right?" she said.

"It's still morning," I said.

"What's wrong with that?"

"Not a thing," I said.

Later, when I woke up in the middle of the night, Izumi wasn't there. I looked at my watch next to the bed. Twelve thirty. I fumbled for the lamp, switched it on, and gazed around the room. Everything was as quiet as if someone had stolen in while I slept and sprinkled silent dust all around. Two bent Salem butts were in the ashtray, a balled-up empty cigarette pack beside them. I got out of bed and walked to the living room. Izumi wasn't there. She wasn't in the kitchen or the bathroom. I opened the door and looked out at the front yard. Just a pair of vinyl lounge chairs, bathed in the brilliant moonlight. "Izumi," I called out in a small voice. Nothing. I called out again, this time more loudly. My heart pounded. Was this my voice? It sounded too loud, unnatural. Still no reply. A faint breeze from the sea rustled the tips of the pampas grass. I shut the door, went back to the kitchen, and poured myself half a glass of wine, to calm down.

Radiant moonlight poured in the kitchen window, throwing weird shadows on the walls and floor. The whole thing looked like the symbolic set of some avant-garde play. I suddenly remembered: the night the cat had disappeared up the pine tree had been exactly like this one, a full moon with not a wisp of cloud. After dinner that night, I'd gone out to the porch again to look for the cat. As the night had deepened, the moonlight had brightened. For some inexplicable reason, I couldn't take my eyes off the pine tree. From time to time I was sure that I could make out the cat's eyes, sparkling between the branches. But it was just an illusion.

I tugged on a thick sweater and a pair of jeans, snatched up the coins on the table, put them in my pocket, and went outside. Izumi must have had trouble sleeping and gone out for a walk. That had to be it. The wind had completely died down. All I could hear was the sound of my tennis shoes crunching along the gravel, like in an exaggerated movie sound track. Izumi must have gone to the harbor, I decided. There was nowhere else for her to go. There was only one road to the harbor, so I couldn't miss her. The lights in the houses along the road were all off, the moonlight dyeing the ground silver. It looked like the bottom of the sea.

About halfway to the harbor, I heard the faint sound of music and came to a halt. At first I thought it was a hallucination—like when the air pressure changes and you hear a ringing in your ears. But, listening carefully, I was able to make out a melody. I held my breath and listened as hard as I could. Like steeping my mind in the darkness within my own body. No doubt about it, it was music. Somebody playing an instrument. Live, unamplified music. But what kind of instrument was it? The mandolin-like instrument that Anthony Quinn played in *Zorba the Greek*? A bouzouki? But who would be playing a bouzouki in the middle of the night? And where?

The music seemed to be coming from the village at the top of the hill we climbed every day for exercise. I stood at the crossroads, wondering what to do, which direction to take. Izumi must have heard the same music at this very spot. And I had a distinct feeling that if she had she would have headed toward it.

I took the plunge and turned right at the crossroads, heading up the slope I knew so well. There were no trees lining the path, just knee-high thorny bushes hidden away in the shadows of the cliffs. The further I walked the louder and more distinct the music grew. I could make out the melody more clearly, too. There was a festive flashiness to it. I imagined some sort of banquet being held in the village on top of the hill. Then I remembered that earlier that day, at the harbor, we had seen a lively wedding procession. This must be the wedding banquet, going on into the night.

Just then—without warning—I disappeared.

Maybe it was the moonlight, or that midnight music. With each step I took, I felt myself sinking deeper into a quicksand where my identity vanished; it was the same emotion I had in the plane, flying over Egypt.

This wasn't me walking in the moonlight. It wasn't me, but a stand-in, fashioned out of plaster. I rubbed my hand against my face. But it wasn't my face. And it wasn't my hand. My heart pounded in my chest, sending the blood coursing through my body at a crazy speed. This body was a plaster puppet, a voodoo doll into which a sorcerer had breathed a fleeting life. The glow of real life was missing. My makeshift, phony muscles were just going through the motions. I was a puppet, to be used in some sacrifice.

So where is the real me? I wondered.

Suddenly, Izumi's voice came out of nowhere. *The real you has been eaten by the cats. While you've been standing here, those hungry cats have devoured you—eaten you all up. All that's left are bones.*

I looked around me. It was an illusion, of course. All I could see was the rock-strewn ground, the low bushes, and their tiny shadows. The voice had been in my head.

Stop thinking such dark thoughts, I told myself. As if trying to avoid a huge wave, I clung to a rock at the bottom of the sea and held my breath. The wave would surely pass by. You're just tired, I told myself, and overwrought. Grab on to what's real. It doesn't matter what—just grab something real. I reached into my pocket for the coins. They grew sweaty in my hand.

I tried hard to think of something else. My sunny apartment back in Unoki. The record collection I'd left behind. My nice little jazz collection. My specialty was white jazz pianists of the fifties and sixties. Lennie Tristano, Al Haig, Claude Williamson, Lou Levy, Russ Freeman. Most of the albums were out of print, and it had taken a lot of time and money to collect them. I had diligently made the rounds of record shops, making trades with other collectors, slowly building up my archives. Most of the performances weren't what you'd call "first-rate." But I loved the unique, intimate atmosphere those musty old records conveyed. The world would be a pretty dull place if it were made up of only the first-rate, right? Every detail of those record jackets came back to me—the weight and heft of the albums in my hands.

But now they were all gone forever. And I'd obliterated them myself. Never again in this lifetime would I hear those records.

I remembered the smell of tobacco when I kissed Izumi. The feel of her lips and tongue. I closed my eyes. I wanted her beside me. I wanted her to hold my hand, as she did when we flew over Egypt, and never let go.

The wave finally passed over me and away, and with it, too, the music.

Had they stopped playing? Certainly that was a possibility. After all, it was nearly one o'clock. Or maybe there never had been any music to begin with. That, too, was entirely possible. I no longer trusted my hearing. I closed my eyes again and sank down into my consciousness—dropped a thin, weighted line down into that darkness. But I couldn't hear a thing. Not even an echo.

I looked at my watch. And realized I wasn't wearing one. Sighing, I stuck both hands in my pockets. I didn't really care about the time. I looked up at the sky. The moon was a cold rock, its skin eaten away by the violence of the years. The shadows on its surface were like cancer reaching out its awful feelers. The moonlight plays tricks with people's minds. And makes cats disappear. It had made Izumi disappear. Maybe it had all been carefully choreographed, beginning with that one night long ago.

I stretched, bent my arms, my fingers. Should I continue, or go back the way I came? Where had Izumi gone? Without her, how was I supposed to go on living, all by myself on this backwater island? She was the only thing that held together the fragile, provisional me.

I continued to climb uphill. I'd come this far and might as well reach the top. Had there really been music there? I had to see for myself, even if only the faintest of clues remained. In five minutes, I had reached the summit. To the south, the hill sloped down to the sea, the harbor, and the sleeping town. A scattering of streetlights lit the coast road. The other side of the mountain was wrapped in darkness. There was no indication whatsoever that a lively celebration had taken place here only a short while before.

I returned to the apartment and downed a glass of brandy. I tried to go to sleep, but I couldn't. Until the eastern sky grew light, I was held in the grip of the moon. Then, suddenly, I pictured those cats, starving to death in a locked apartment. I—the real me—was dead, and they were alive, eating my flesh, biting into my heart, sucking my blood, devouring my penis. Far away, I could hear them lapping up my brains. Like Macbeth's witches, the three lithe cats surrounded my broken head, slurping up that thick soup inside. The tips of their rough tongues licked the soft folds of my mind. And with each lick my consciousness flickered like a flame and faded away.

—TRANSLATED BY PHILIP GABRIEL

A "POOR AUNT" STORY

1

t started on a perfectly beautiful Sunday afternoon in July—the very first Sunday afternoon in July. Two or three chunks of cloud floated white and tiny in a distant corner of the sky, like well-formed punctuation marks placed with exceptional care. Unobstructed by anything at all, the light of the sun poured down on the world to its heart's content. In this kingdom of July, even the crumpled silver sphere of a chocolate wrapper discarded on the lawn gave off a proud sparkle, like a legendary crystal at the bottom of a lake. If you stared at the scene long enough, you could tell that the sunlight enfolded yet another kind of light, like one Chinese box inside another. The inner light looked like countless grains of pollen—grains that were soft and opaque and that hung in the sky, almost motionless, until, at long last, they settled down upon the surface of the earth.

On the way home from a Sunday stroll, I had stopped by the plaza outside the Picture Gallery. Sitting at the edge of the pond, my companion and I looked across the water toward the two bronze unicorns on the other shore. The long rainy season had finally ended, and a new summer breeze stirred the leaves of the oak trees, raising tiny ripples now and then on the surface of the shallow pond. Time moved like the breeze: starting and stopping, stopping and starting. Soft-drink cans shone through the clear water of the pond. To me, they looked like the sunken ruins of an ancient lost city. Before us passed a softball team in uniform, a boy on a bicycle, an old man walking his dog, a young foreigner in jogging shorts. The breeze carried snatches of music from a large portable radio on the grass: a sugary song of love either lost or about to be. I seemed to recognize the tune, but I couldn't be sure. It may have just sounded like one I knew. Half-listening, I could feel my bare arms soaking up the sunlight—soundlessly, softly, gently. Every once in a while, I would bring my arms up to face level and stretch them straight out. Summer was here.

Why a poor aunt, of all things, should have grabbed my heart on a Sunday afternoon like this, I have no idea. There was no poor aunt to be seen in the vicinity, nothing to make me imagine her existence. She came to me, nonetheless, and then she was gone. If only for some hundredth part of a second, she had been in my heart. And when she moved on, she left a strange, human-shaped emptiness in her place. It felt as if someone had zipped past a window and disappeared. You run to the window and stick your head out, but no one is there.

A poor aunt?

I scanned the area, then looked up at the sky. Come and gone. Like the transparent path of a bullet, the words had been absorbed into the early Sunday afternoon. Beginnings are always like this. One minute everything exists, the next minute everything is lost.

I tried the words out on my companion. "I'd like to write something about a poor aunt." I'm one of those people who try to write stories.

"A poor aunt?"

She seemed a bit surprised. For a moment, she looked at me with eyes that were attempting to gauge something. "Why? Why a poor aunt?"

Not even I knew the answer to that. For some reason, things that grabbed me were always things I didn't understand.

I said nothing for a time, just ran my fingertip along the edge of the human-shaped emptiness that had been left inside me.

"I wonder if anybody would want to read a story like that?" she said.

"True," I said, "it might not be what you'd call a good read."

"Then why write about such a thing?"

"I can't put it into words very well," I said. "In order to explain why I want to write a story about a poor aunt, I'd have to write the story, but once the story was finished, there wouldn't be any reason to explain the reason for writing the story—or would there?"

She smiled and lit a crumpled cigarette that she took from her pocket. She always crumpled her cigarettes, sometimes so badly they wouldn't light. This one lit.

"By the way," she said. "Do you have any poor aunts among your relatives?"

"Not a one," I said.

"Well, I do. Exactly one. The genuine article. I even lived with her for a few years."

I watched her eyes. They were as calm as ever.

"But I don't want to write about her," she added. "I don't want to write a single word about that aunt of mine."

The portable radio started playing a different tune, much like the first one, but this I didn't recognize at all.

"You don't have a single poor aunt in your family, but still you want to write a 'poor aunt' story. Meanwhile, I do have a real, live poor aunt, but I don't want to write about her. Sort of strange, don't you think?"

I nodded. "I wonder why."

She just tipped her head a little and said nothing. With her back to me, she allowed her slender fingers to trail in the water. It seemed as if my question were coursing through her fingers to be conducted to the ruined city beneath the water. It's still down there, I'm sure, the question mark glittering at the bottom of the pond like a polished metal fragment. For all I know, it's showering the cola cans around it with that same question.

I wonder why. I wonder why. I wonder why.

From the tip of her crumpled cigarette, she dropped her crumpled ashes on the ground. "To tell you the truth," she said, "I do have some things I'd like to say about my poor aunt. But it's impossible for me to come up with the right words. I just can't do it—because I know a real poor aunt." She bit her lip. "It's hard—a lot harder than you seem to realize."

I looked up at the bronze unicorns again, their front hooves thrust out in angry protest against the flow of time for abandoning them in its wake. She wiped the pond water from her fingers on the hem of her shirt, wiped them again, and then she turned to face me. "You're going to try to write about a poor aunt," she said. "You're going to take on this responsibility. And the way I see it, taking on the responsibility for something means offering it salvation. I wonder, though, whether you are capable of that just now. You don't even have a real poor aunt."

I released a long, deep sigh.

"Sorry," she said.

"That's OK," I replied. "You're probably right."

And she was. I didn't even have / A poor aunt of my own.

Huh. Like lines from a song.

2

Chances are, you don't have a poor aunt among your relatives, either. In which case, you and I have something in common. It's an odd thing to have in common—like sharing a puddle on a quiet morning.

But still, you must have at least seen a poor aunt at someone's wedding. Just as every bookshelf has a long-unread book and every closet has a long-unworn shirt, every wedding reception has a poor aunt.

Almost no one bothers to introduce her. Almost no one even talks to her. No one asks her to give a speech. She sits at the table where she belongs, but she's just there—like an empty milk bottle. With sad, little slurps, she spoons in her consommé. She eats her salad with her fish fork. She can't manage to scoop up all her green beans. And she's the only one without a spoon when the ice cream comes. With luck, the present she gives the young couple will be lost in the back of the closet. And if luck goes the other way, hers will be the present thrown out at moving time along with that dusty, unidentifiable trophy and all that goes with it.

Oh, her picture is there all right, whenever they pull out the album of wedding photos, but her image is as cheering as a freshly drowned corpse.

Honey, who's this woman here, in the second row, with glasses?

Never mind, that's nobody, says the young husband. Just a poor aunt of mine.

No name. Just a poor aunt.

◎

All names fade away, of course. We can say that much for sure.

But there are many ways for this to happen. First there are those whose names fade the moment they die. They're the easy ones. We mourn their deaths: "The river ran dry and the fish died out," or "Flames covered the forest, roasting every bird within it." Next there are those who go out like an old television, leaving white flickers that play over the face of the tube until suddenly, one day, it burns out completely. These aren't bad, either: sort of like the footprints of an Indian elephant that's lost its way. No, definitely not bad. And finally there's the type whose names fade even before they die—the poor aunts.

I myself fall into this poor aunt state of namelessness now and then. Suddenly, in the bustle of a terminal, my destination, my name, my address will no longer be there in my brain. But this never lasts long: five or ten seconds at most.

And then you have this:

"For the life of me, I can't remember your name," someone says.

"Never mind. Don't let it bother you. It's not much of a name, anyway."

Over and over, he points to his mouth. "It's right here, on the tip of my tongue, I swear . . ."

I feel as if I've been buried in the earth with half my left foot sticking out. People trip over it and start to apologize. "I swear, it's right here, on the tip of my tongue . . ."

⊚

All right, then, where do the lost names go? The probability of their surviving in this maze of a city must be extremely low. Some are flattened on the road by enormous trucks, some die in the gutter for simple lack of spare change that would get them on a streetcar, while others sink to the bottom of the river, with a pocketful of pride to weigh them down.

Still, there might be some who have survived and found their way to the town of lost names where they have built a quiet, little community. A tiny town, at the entrance to which there would have to be a sign:

NO ADMITTANCE EXCEPT ON BUSINESS

Those who dare to enter without business, of course, receive an appropriately tiny punishment.

⊚

Perhaps it was the tiny punishment that had been prepared for me. A poor aunt—a little one—was stuck to my back.

I first realized she was there in the middle of August. Not that anything in particular happened to alert me to her presence. I simply felt it one day: I had a poor aunt there on my back.

It was not an unpleasant sensation. She wasn't especially heavy. She didn't puff bad breath across my shoulder. She was just stuck there, on my back, like a bleached shadow. People had to look hard even to realize she was there. True, the cats I shared my apartment with gave her suspicious looks for the first few days, but as soon as they understood that she had no designs on their territory, they got used to her.

She made some of my friends nervous. We'd be sitting at a table with drinks when she'd peek over my shoulder at them.

"Gives me the creeps," said one friend.

"Don't let her bother you. She minds her own business. She's harmless enough."

"I know, I know. But, I don't know why, she's depressing."

"So try not to look."

"Yeah, I guess." Then a sigh. "Where'd you have to go to get something like that on your back?"

"It's not that I *went* anywhere. I just kept thinking about some things. That's all."

He nodded and sighed again. "I think I get it. It's your personality. You've always been like this."

"Uh-huh."

We downed several whiskeys over the next hour without much enthusiasm.

"Tell me," I said. "What's so depressing about her?"

"I don't know, it's like my mother's keeping an eye on me."

"I wonder why?"

"You wonder why?! Hey, that's probably my mother glued up there on your back."

⊙

Judging from the impressions of a number of people (since I myself was unable to see her), what I had on my back was not a poor aunt with a single fixed form: she was apparently a kind of ether that changed shape in accordance with the mental images of each observer.

For one friend, it was a dog of his, an Akita, that had died the previous fall from cancer of the esophagus.

"She was on her last legs anyway, I guess. Fifteen years old. But what an awful way to die, poor thing."

"Cancer of the esophagus?"

"Yeah. It's really painful. I'd rather have anything else. All she did was cry—though she had pretty much lost her voice by then. I wanted to put her to sleep, but my mother wouldn't let me."

"Why not?"

"Who the hell knows? Probably would have felt guilty. We kept her alive two months on a feeding tube. Out in the shed. God, what a stink!"

He stayed silent for a while.

"She wasn't much of a dog. Scared of her own shadow. Barked at everybody who came by. A really useless animal. Noisy, covered with scabs . . ."

I nodded.

"She'd have been better off born a cicada. Could have screamed her head off and nobody'd give a damn. No cancer of the esophagus, either."

But there she was, up on my back still, a dog with a plastic tube sticking out of her mouth.

For one real estate agent, it was his old elementary school teacher.

"Must have been 1950, first year of the Korean War," he said, using a thick towel to wipe the sweat from his face. "I had her two years in a row. It's like old times seeing her again. Not that I missed her, exactly. I'd kind of forgotten that she even existed."

The way he offered me a cup of ice-cold barley tea, he seemed to think I must be some kind of relative of his old elementary school teacher.

"She was a sad case, though, come to think of it. Husband got drafted the year they were married. He was on a transport ship and boom! Must have been '43. She stayed on teaching school after that. Got bad burns in the air raids of '44. Left side of her face, down to her arm." He drew an arc from his cheek to his left arm. Then he drained his cup of barley tea and wiped his face again. "Poor thing. She must have been pretty before that happened. Changed her personality, too, they say. Must be near sixty if she's still alive. Hmmm . . . 1950, huh . . . ?"

◎

And so there took shape all kinds of wedding reception seating charts and neighborhood maps. My back was at the center of the poor aunt's gradually widening circle.

At the same time, though, one friend and then another and another began to drop away from me, the way a comb loses teeth.

"He's not a bad guy," they would say about me, "but I don't want to have to look at my depressing old mother (or old dog that died of esophageal cancer or the teacher with her burn scars) whenever I see him."

I was beginning to feel like a dentist's chair—hated by no one but avoided by everyone. If I bumped into friends on the street they'd find some reason to disappear as soon as possible. "I don't know," one girl confessed to me with difficulty—and honesty, "it's kind of hard to be around you these days. I wouldn't mind so much if you had an umbrella stand on your back or something . . ."

An umbrella stand.

Oh, what the hell, I'd tell myself, I was never much of a social animal anyway. And I certainly didn't want to have to live with an umbrella stand on my back.

While friends avoided me, the media couldn't get enough of me. Especially the weekly magazines. Reporters would show up every couple of days, take photos of me and the aunt, complain when her image didn't come out clearly, and shower me with pointless questions. I kept hoping that my cooperation with the magazines would lead to some new discovery or development with regard to the poor aunt, but instead all I got was exhaustion.

Once, I appeared on the *Morning Show*. They dragged me out of bed at six o'clock, drove me to the TV studio, and filled me full of godawful coffee. Incomprehensible people ran all around me doing incomprehensible things. I thought about getting the hell out of there, but before I could bring myself to do it, they said it was my turn. When the cameras weren't on, the show's host was a grumpy, arrogant bastard who did nothing but bawl people out, but the second the camera's red lamp lit, he was all smiles and intelligence: your regulation middle-aged nice guy.

"And now it's time for our daily feature, 'Look What Else Is Out There,' " he announced to the camera. "Today's guest is Mr. ——, who suddenly found he had a poor aunt on his back. Not many people have this particular problem, and what I'd like to do today is ask our guest how it happened to him, and what kind of difficulties he's had to face." Turning to me, he continued, "Do you find having a poor aunt on your back in any way inconvenient?"

"Well, no," I said. "I wouldn't exactly call it inconvenient or difficult. She's not heavy, and I don't have to feed her."

"No lower back pain?"

"No, none at all."

"When did you find her stuck there?"

I briefly summarized my afternoon by the pond with the bronze unicorns, but he seemed unable to grasp my point.

"In other words," he said, clearing his throat, "she was lurking in the pond near where you were sitting, and she possessed your back. Is that it?"

No, I said, shaking my head, that was not it. Oh, no! How had I let myself in for this? All they wanted was jokes or horror stories. I couldn't take much more of this.

"The poor aunt is not a ghost," I tried to explain. "She doesn't 'lurk' anywhere, and she doesn't 'possess' anybody. The poor aunt is just words," I said. "Just words."

No one said a thing. I would have to be more specific.

"A word is like an electrode connected to the mind. If you keep sending the same stimulus through it, there is bound to be some kind of response created, some effect that comes into being. Each individual's response will be entirely different, of course, and in my case the response is something like a sense of independent existence. It's the way you'd feel if your tongue swelled into some huge thing inside your mouth. What I have stuck to my back, finally, is the phrase 'poor aunt'— those very words, without meaning, without form. If I had to give it a label, I'd call it a 'conceptual sign' or something like that."

The host looked confused. "You say it has no meaning or form,". he observed, "but we can clearly see . . . something . . . some real image there on your back. And it gives rise to some sort of meaning in each of us . . ."

I shrugged. "Of course," I said. "That's what signs do."

"So," interjected the host's young female assistant, in hopes of breaking up the barren atmosphere that was beginning to congeal around the show, "you could erase this image or this being or whatever it is, by your own free will if you wanted to."

"No, that I can't do," I said. "Once something has come into being, it continues to exist independent of my will. It's like a memory. You know how a memory can be—especially a memory you wish you could forget but you can't. It's just like that."

She went on, seemingly unconvinced: "This process you mentioned of turning a word into a conceptual sign: is that something even I could do?"

"I can't say how well it would work, but in principle, at least, you could," I answered.

Now the host got into the act. "Say if I were to keep repeating the word 'conceptual' over and over every day, the image of 'conceptual' might appear on my back at some point, is that it?"

"In principle, at least, that could happen," I repeated myself mechanically.

"So the word 'conceptual' will be turned into a conceptual sign."

"Exactly," I replied, but the strong lights and bad-smelling air of the studio were beginning to give me a headache. The piercing voices of the other speakers were intensifying the pain as well.

"What would a 'conceptual' look like?" ventured the host, drawing laughter from some of the other guests.

I said I didn't know. It was not something I wanted to think about. My hands were full already with only one poor aunt that had taken on a separate existence. None of them really gave a damn about any of this. All they were concerned about was keeping the patter alive until the next commercial.

◎

The whole world is a farce, needless to say. Who can escape that? From the glare of a TV studio to the gloom of a hermit's cabin in the woods, it all comes from the same root. Walking through this clownish world with the poor aunt on my back, I was of course the biggest clown of all. Maybe the girl had been right: maybe I'd have been better off with an umbrella stand up there. Maybe then people would have let me into their cliques. I could've painted the umbrella stand a new color twice a month and gone with it to all the parties.

"All riiight! Your umbrella stand is pink this week!" somebody says.

"Sure thing," I answer. "Next week I'm going for British green."

And maybe there are girls out there eager to get into bed with a guy wearing a pink umbrella stand on his back.

Unfortunately, though, what I had on my back was not an umbrella stand but a poor aunt. As time passed, people's interest in me and in the poor aunt on my back faded away. My companion had been right: nobody was interested in poor aunts. Once the initial mild curiosity had run its course, all that was left was a silence as deep as at the bottom of the sea, as deep as if the poor aunt and I had become a single entity.

3

"I saw you on TV," said my companion.

We were sitting by the pond again. I hadn't seen her for three months. It was now early autumn. The time had shot by. We had never gone so long without seeing each other.

"You looked a little tired."

"I was wiped out."

"You weren't yourself."

I nodded. It was true: I hadn't been myself.

She kept folding and unfolding a sweatshirt on her knees. Folding and unfolding. As if she were turning time backward or urging it ahead.

"I guess you finally succeeded in getting your own separate poor aunt."

"I guess."

"How do you feel?"

"Like a watermelon at the bottom of a well."

She smiled, caressing the soft but tightly folded sweatshirt on her knees as if it were a cat.

"Do you understand her better now?"

"A little," I said. "I think. Maybe."

"And has it helped you to write something?"

"Nope." I gave my head a little shake. "Not a thing. The urge to write just isn't there. Maybe I'll never be able to do it."

"Quitter."

"You yourself once told me I couldn't save anything at all with my writing. If that's the case, what's the point of writing about the poor aunt?"

She bit her lower lip and said nothing for a while.

"I've got an idea. Ask me some questions. Maybe I can help out a little."

"As the poor aunt authority?"

"Uh-huh." She smiled. "So fire away. This mood might never hit me again, when I feel like answering poor aunt questions."

It took me a while to know where to start.

"I sometimes wonder what kind of a person becomes a poor aunt. Are they born that way? Or does it take special 'poor aunt' conditions—like some kind of huge bug that laps up everybody passing by a certain street corner and turns them into poor aunts?"

She nodded several times as if to say that my questions were very good.

"Both," she said. "They're the same thing."

"The same thing?"

"Uh-huh. Well, look. A poor aunt might have a 'poor aunt' childhood or youth. Or she might not. It really doesn't matter. There are millions of reasons floating around the world for millions of results. Millions of reasons to live, and millions of reasons to die. Millions of reasons for giving reasons. Reasons like that are easy to come by—just a phone call to find out how much a bunch. But what you're looking for is not one of those, is it?"

"Well," I said, "I guess not."

"She exists. That's all. You have to recognize that fact and accept it. Reasons, causes: these just don't matter. The poor aunt is there. She exists. And that's what a poor aunt is. Her existence *is* her reason. Just like us. We exist here and now, without any particular reason or cause."

We sat by the pond for a long time, neither of us moving or speaking. The clear autumn sunlight cast little shadows on her profile.

"Well?" she said. "Aren't you going to ask me what I see on your back?"

"What do you see on my back?"

"Nothing at all," she said with a smile. "I see only you."

"Thanks," I said.

◉

Time, of course, topples everyone in its path equally—the way that driver beat his old horse until it died on the road. But the thrashing we receive is one of frightful gentleness. Few of us even realize that we are being beaten.

In a poor aunt, however, we can see the tyranny of time before our eyes, as if through an aquarium window. In the cramped glass case, time has been squeezing the poor aunt like an orange, until there's not a single drop of juice left to spill. What draws me to her is that completeness of hers, that utter perfection within her.

It's true—there's not a drop left to spill!

◉

Yes, perfection. It rests its full weight upon the core of the poor aunt's being, like a corpse sealed inside a glacier—a magnificent glacier made of ice like stainless steel. Only ten thousand years of sunshine could melt such a glacier. But no poor aunt can live for ten thousand years, of course, and so she will have to live with her perfection, die with her perfection, and be buried with her perfection.

Perfection and the aunt beneath the ground.

Ten thousand years go by. Then, perhaps, the glacier melts in darkness and perfection thrusts its way out of the grave to reveal itself on the earth's surface. Everything on the earth is completely changed by then, but if by any chance the ceremony known as "wedding" still exists, the perfection left behind by the poor aunt might be invited to one, there to eat an entire dinner with impeccable table manners and be called upon to deliver heartfelt words of congratulation.

But never mind. These events would not take place until the year 11,980.

4

It was late in autumn when the poor aunt left my back. Recalling some work I had to complete before the onset of winter, my poor aunt and I boarded a suburban train. Like any suburban train in the afternoon, it was practically empty. This was my first trip out of the city for quite some time, and I enjoyed watching the scenery go by. The air was crisp and clear, the hills almost unnaturally green, and here and there along the tracks stood trees with bright red berries.

Sitting across the aisle from me on the return trip were a skinny woman in her midthirties and her two children. The older child, a girl, sat on her mother's left wearing a navy serge dress—a kindergarten uniform. On her head she wore a brand-new gray felt hat with a red ribbon—a nice hat with a round, narrow brim. On the mother's right sat a boy perhaps three years old. Nothing about the mother or her children was particularly noteworthy. Their faces, their clothing were ordinary in the extreme. The mother held a large package. She looked tired—but then, most mothers look tired. I had hardly noticed them board the train, perhaps glanced over at them once when they took their seats across from me, after which I continued to look down at the paperback I was reading.

Not long afterward, however, sounds from the little girl began to reach me across the aisle. There was an edge to her voice, an urgency that suggested pleading.

Then I heard the mother say, "I told you to keep still on the train!" She had a magazine spread open on top of her bundle and seemed reluctant to tear her eyes from it.

"But Mama, look what he's doing to my hat," said the little girl.

"Just shut up!"

The girl made as if to speak, but then she swallowed her words. Separated from her by the mother, the little boy held the hat that she had been wearing earlier, and he kept pawing and pulling on it. The girl reached out and tried to grab it, but he twisted himself away, determined to keep it out of her grasp.

"He's going to ruin my hat," the girl said, on the verge of tears.

The mother glanced up from her magazine with a look of annoyance and went through the motions of reaching for the hat, but the boy clamped both his hands on the brim and refused to give it up. So much for the mother's attempt to retrieve it. "Let him play with it a while," she said to the girl. "He'll get bored soon enough." The girl did not look convinced, but she didn't try to argue. She pursed her lips and glared at the hat in her brother's hands. The mother went on reading. Encouraged by his mother's indifference, the boy started yanking at the red ribbon. He was obviously doing it out of sheer nastiness. He knew it would drive his sister crazy—and it had its effect on me as well. I was ready to stomp across the aisle and snatch the thing out of his hands.

The girl stared at her brother in silence, but you could see that she had a plan. Then, all of a sudden, she got to her feet and slapped him hard on the cheek. In the stunned moment that followed, she grabbed the hat and returned to her seat. The little girl did this with such speed and dispatch, it took the interval of one deep breath before the mother and brother could realize what had happened. As the brother let out a wail, the mother slapped the girl's bare knee. She then turned to stroke the boy's cheek and tried to comfort him, but he kept on wailing.

"But Mama, he was ruining my hat," said the little girl.

"Don't talk to me," said the mother. "You don't belong to me anymore."

The girl bit her lip and looked down, staring at her hat.

"Get away from me," the mother said. "Go over there." She pointed at the empty seat next to mine.

The girl looked away, trying to ignore her mother's outstretched finger, but it continued pointing at my left, as if it had been frozen in midair.

"Go on," the mother insisted. "You're not part of this family anymore."

Resigned to her fate, the girl stood up with her hat and schoolbag, trudged across the aisle, and sat down next to me, head bowed. Hat on her lap, she tried smoothing its brim with her little fingers. It's *his* fault, she was clearly thinking; he was going to tear the ribbon off my hat. Her cheeks were streaked with tears.

It was almost evening now. Dull yellow light seemed to filter down from the car lamps like dust from the wings of a doleful moth. It hovered in space to be silently inhaled through the passengers' mouths and noses. I closed my book. Resting my hands on my knees, I stared at my upturned palms for the longest time. When had I last studied my hands like this? In the smoky light, they seemed grimy, even dirty—not like my hands at all. The sight of them filled me with sadness: these were hands that would never make anyone happy, never save anyone. I wanted to place a comforting hand on the shoulder of the little girl sobbing next to me, to tell her that she had been right, that she had done a great job taking the hat that way. But of course I never touched her, never spoke to her. It would only have confused and frightened her all the more. And besides, those hands of mine were so black and dirty.

By the time I left the train, a cold winter wind was blowing. Soon the sweater season would be over, the time for thick winter coats upon us. I thought about coats for a while, trying to decide whether or not to buy myself a new one. I was down the stairs and out the gate before I became aware that the poor aunt had vanished from my back.

I had no idea when it happened. Just as she had come, she had gone before anyone noticed. She had gone back to wherever it was that she had originally existed, and I was my original self again.

But what *was* my original self? I couldn't be sure anymore. I couldn't help feeling that it was another me, another self that strongly resembled my original self. So now what was I to do? I was all alone, like a blank signpost in the middle of the desert. I had lost all sense of direction. I shoved my hand in my pocket and fed every piece of change I found there into a pay phone. Eight rings. Nine. And then she answered.

"I was sleeping," she said with a yawn.

"At six o'clock in the evening?"

"I was up all last night working. Just finished two hours ago."

"Sorry, I didn't mean to wake you," I said. "This may sound strange, but I called just to make sure you're still alive. That's all. Really."

I could feel her smiling into the phone.

"Thanks, that was nice of you," she said. "Don't worry, though, I'm still alive. And I'm working my tail off to *stay* alive. Which is why I'm dead tired. OK? Are you relieved?"

"I'm relieved."

"You know," she said, as if she was about to share a secret with me, "life is pretty damn hard."

"I know," I said. And she was right. "So how would you like to have dinner with me now?"

"Sorry, I'm not hungry. The only thing I want to do right now is turn my head off and go to sleep."

"I'm not really hungry, either," I said. "I just wanted to talk to you. About things."

In the silence at her end, I could sense her biting her lip and touching her little finger to her eyebrow.

"Not right now," she said, emphasizing each syllable. "We'll talk later. You have to let me sleep now. Not a lot. Everything will be fine if I can just sleep a little. I'll call you when I wake up. OK?"

"OK," I said. "Good night."

"You, too. Good night."

She hesitated a moment. "Was it some kind of emergency—what you wanted to talk about?"

"No, no emergency," I said. "We can talk about it later." True, we had plenty of time. Ten thousand years, twenty thousand. I could wait.

"Good night," she said again and hung up. For a while, I looked at the yellow receiver in my hand, then hung it in its cradle. The moment it left my hand, I felt an incredible hunger. I'd go mad if I didn't get something to eat. Anything. Anything at all. If they'd give me something to put in my mouth, I'd crawl to them on all fours. I might even suck their fingers clean.

Yes, I would, I would suck your fingers clean. And then I'd sleep like a weathered crosstie. The meanest kick wouldn't wake me. For ten thousand years I'd be sound asleep.

I leaned against the telephone, emptied my mind out, and closed my eyes. Then I heard footsteps, thousands of footsteps. They washed over me like a wave. They kept walking, on and on, tramping in time. Where was the poor aunt now? I wondered. Where had she gone back to? And where had I come back to?

If, ten thousand years from now, a society came into being that was peopled exclusively by poor aunts, would they open the gates of their town for me? In that town would be a government and town hall run by poor aunts who had been elected by poor aunts, a streetcar line for poor aunts driven by poor aunts, novels for poor aunts written by poor aunts.

Or, then again, they might not need any of those things—the government or the streetcars or the novels.

They might prefer instead to live quietly in giant vinegar bottles of their own making. From the air you could see tens—hundreds—of thousands of vinegar bottles lined up, covering the earth as far as the eye could see. And it would be a sight so beautiful it would take your breath away.

Yes, that's it. And if, by any chance, that world had space to admit a single poem, I would gladly be the one to write it: the first honored poet laureate of the world of poor aunts.

Not bad. Not bad.

And I would sing in praise of the brilliant glow of the sun in the green bottles, sing in praise of the broad sea of grass below, sparkling with the morning dew.

But this is looking far ahead, to the year 11,980, and ten thousand years is too long for me to wait. I have many winters to survive until then.

—TRANSLATED BY JAY RUBIN

NAUSEA 1979

Thanks to his rare talent for keeping a diary over an extended period of time without missing a single day, he was able to cite the exact date his vomiting started and the exact date it stopped. It had started on June 4, 1979 (clear), and stopped on July 14, 1979 (cloudy). I knew this young illustrator from the time he did a drawing for a story I published in a certain magazine.

He was a few years younger than I, but we shared an interest in collecting old jazz LPs. Another thing he liked to do was sleep with his friends' girlfriends and wives. There had been quite a number of them over the years, and often he would fill me in on his exploits. He had even done it a few times while the friend was out buying beer or was taking a shower during one of his visits.

"You do it as fast as you can, with most of your clothes on," he said. "Ordinary sex can drag on and on, right? So once in a while you take exactly the opposite approach. It gives you a whole new perspective. It's fun."

This kind of tour de force was not the only kind of sex that interested him, of course. He could enjoy it the slow, old-fashioned way, too. But it was the act of sleeping with his friends' girlfriends and wives that really turned him on.

"I have absolutely no interest in tricking my friends—in turning them into cuckolds, that sort of thing. Sleeping with their women makes me feel closer to them. It's a *family* thing. And it's just sex, after all. It's not hurting anybody as long as it doesn't come out in the open."

"That never happened?"

"No, never." He seemed a little surprised by my question. "As long as you don't have some kind of subconscious desire to expose what you're doing, these things don't come out. True, you have to be careful not to do or say anything that's going to give the guy ideas. And you have to set very clear ground rules right at the beginning, make sure the woman knows that this is just a friendly game, that you're not going to get involved or hurt anybody. Of course, you don't say it quite so *directly*."

I found it hard to believe that such things could be carried off so easily, but he didn't seem the type to spout a lot of nonsense just to make himself look good, so I began to think he might be right.

"And finally, most of the women have been *looking* for something like this. Their husbands or lovers—which is to say, my friends—are usually way better than me: they're better looking, say, or smarter, or they've got bigger penises. But the women don't care about things like that. They're OK as long as their men are reasonably normal and kind and they've achieved some level of understanding. What they want is for somebody to be interested in them beyond the—in a sense—*static* framework of 'girlfriend' or 'wife.' That's the most fundamental rule in all this. Of course, on a more superficial level, their motives are all over the map."

"For example?"

"For example, getting even with a husband for fooling around, or boredom, or the sheer satisfaction of attracting another man. That kind of thing. I just have to look at them to know. It's not a question of learning a technique. This is strictly an inborn talent. You either have it or you don't."

He did not have a steady girlfriend himself.

As I said, we were both record collectors, and we'd get together now and then to trade. We collected jazz from the fifties and early sixties, but our interests were different enough so that we could always find stuff to exchange. I concentrated on some of the lesser known West Coast musicians, and he liked the later recordings of more nearly middlebrow people like Coleman Hawkins or Lionel Hampton. So if he had a Pete Jolly Trio on Victor and I had Vic Dickenson's *Mainstream*, we'd be happy to call it an even swap. We'd spend the day drinking beer and checking out performances and examining our disks for flaws and striking deals.

⊙

It was after one of our LP-trading sessions that he told me about his vomiting. We were in his apartment, drinking whiskey. Our conversation had moved from music to whiskey to experiences of getting drunk.

"I once vomited every day for forty days. Every single day without a break. Not from drinking, though. And I wasn't sick, either. I'd just throw up for no reason at all. Forty straight days it went on like that. Forty days. It was really something."

His first round of nausea and vomiting came on June 4. This particular episode was not a complete surprise because he had slugged down a good deal of whiskey and beer the night before. He had also, as usual, slept with a friend's wife that night—the night of June 3.

So when he vomited the entire contents of his stomach into his toilet bowl at eight o'clock in the morning on June 4, general common sense could hardly have pronounced this an unnatural occurrence. Neither could it be said of the sheer fact that this was the first time he had vomited from drinking since college. Pressing the flush handle, he sent the unpleasant products of his stomach down the sewer, sat at his desk, and set to work. He did not feel sick at all. If anything, he approached his drawing that day with a special vigor. His work went well, and by noon he had developed a healthy appetite.

He made himself a ham and cucumber sandwich, which he washed down with a can of beer. Half an hour later, the second wave of nausea hit him, and he disgorged the whole sandwich in the toilet. Soppy chunks of bread and ham floated to the surface of the water in the bowl. Still, he did not feel unwell. He had simply vomited. He had felt as if something might be stuck at the back of his throat, and he had knelt down at the toilet more or less out of curiosity when everything in his stomach came gushing out the way a magician pulls pigeons or rabbits or the flags of the world from a hat.

"I had experienced nausea any number of times—in college, when I drank like crazy, or sometimes on buses and things, but this was something completely different. I didn't even have the usual knotting in the stomach. It was as if my stomach was pushing up the food with no particular feeling at all, and absolutely no resistance. I didn't feel bad, and there was none of that suffocating smell. So then I started to feel very strange. I mean, it had happened not once but twice. It was beginning to worry me, so I decided to lay off alcohol for a while."

His third round of vomiting hit him, though, right on schedule the next morning. The eel he had eaten the night before and that morning's marmalade-smeared English muffin emerged from his stomach all but unscathed.

He was brushing his teeth afterward when the telephone rang. He lifted the receiver to hear a man's voice speak his name, and the connection was cut, nothing more.

"It must have been the husband or boyfriend of one of the women you slept with, don't you think?" I asked.

"No way," he said. "I knew all their voices. This was definitely a voice I had never heard before. And it had a nasty ring to it. I started getting calls like this every day. From June 5 to July 14. This coincided almost exactly with the period of my vomiting, you realize."

"OK, but I don't see any way there could be a connection between these prank calls and your vomiting."

"Neither do I," he said. "Which is why I'm still kind of upset by the whole thing. Anyhow, every call was the same. The phone would ring, he'd say my name and hang up. Once a day, every day, but I never knew when—morning, evening, the middle of the night. Of course, I could have just not answered the phone, but that's the way I get jobs, and girls call me sometimes, too."

"Well, sure . . . ," I said.

"And right along with the calls the nausea continued without a single day's break. I think I threw up almost everything I ate. Then I'd get starved and eat again, and then throw up every bit of *that*. It was a vicious circle. Still, I managed to keep down, say, one meal in three—probably just enough to stay alive. If I had been vomiting three meals out of three, I would have needed intravenous feeding or something."

"Didn't you see a doctor?"

"Of course I did. I went to a hospital in my neighborhood, a pretty good-sized one. They took X-rays and tested my urine. Cancer was a real possibility, so they looked me over pretty well. But they couldn't find a thing wrong with me. I was the picture of health. They ended up prescribing me medicine for 'chronic stomach fatigue' or maybe stress. They gave me the old 'early to bed, early to rise,' said to cut back on liquor, and not to let little things bother me. But who did they think they were kidding? *I* know about chronic stomach fatigue: you'd have to be an idiot not to know you have it. You get this heavy feeling in your stomach, and heartburn, and no appetite, and like that. If you *do* get nauseated, it's only *after* you get all those other symptoms. You don't just start throwing up out of nowhere. Which is what happened to me. I might have been hungry all the time, but otherwise, I felt great, and my mind was perfectly clear.

"And as far as 'stress' goes—it's just not something I have. True, I had quite a backlog of work, but not enough to let it get to me, and girls were no problem at all. Plus, I was going to the pool for a good swim two or three times a week. I was doing everything right, wouldn't you say?"

"Sounds like it to me," I said.

"I was just throwing up, that was all," he said.

It went on like this for two weeks, the vomiting and the phone calls. By the fifteenth day, he decided that he had had more than enough of both and took off from work. He might not be able to stop the vomiting, but at least he wanted to get away from the calls, so he went to a hotel and spent the day watching TV and reading. At first, the change of scene appeared to be working. He managed to digest the roast beef sandwich and asparagus salad he ordered for lunch. At 3:30 he met a friend's girl-friend in the hotel tearoom, where he sent his stomach a piece of cherry pie and black coffee, which also stayed down. Then he and the woman went to bed. This also worked without a hitch. After he had sent her home, he ate dinner alone at a nearby restaurant: Kyoto-style broiled mackerel with tofu, vinegared vegetables, miso soup, and a bowl of white rice. As usual, he kept away from alcohol. This was 6:30 p.m.

He went back to his room, watched the news, and started reading a new Ed McBain 87th Precinct novel. When nine o'clock rolled around and he still felt no nausea, he breathed a sigh of relief. Finally, after two long weeks, he was able to enjoy the simple pleasure of a full stomach. Things would probably go back to normal now, he felt. He closed his book, switched on the TV again, and after flicking through the channels with the remote, decided to watch an old western. The movie ended at eleven, and the late news came on. When that ended, he turned off the TV. What he wanted more than anything now was a good whiskey, and he came close to going to the bar upstairs for a nightcap, but he was able to stop himself. Why mess up one perfectly clean day? He turned out the reading lamp and snuggled under the covers.

It was the middle of the night when the phone rang. He opened his eyes to find the clock reading 2:15. At first he was too groggy to grasp why a bell might be ringing nearby, but he shook his head and, almost unconsciously, picked up the receiver and held it to his ear.

"Hello."

The now familiar voice pronounced his name again and, a second later, the connection was cut.

"But you didn't tell anyone you were staying in the hotel, did you?" I asked.

"Of course not—except for the woman I slept with."

"Maybe she leaked it to someone else."

"What possible reason could she have for doing that?"

He had a point there.

"After the call, I threw up every last bit of food in my stomach. The fish, the rice—everything. It was as if the phone call had opened a door and made a passageway for the nausea to get inside me.

"When I was done throwing up, I sat on the edge of the tub and tried to put things in order inside my head. My first thought was that the telephone call had been someone's clever joke or malicious mischief. I didn't know how they knew I was in the hotel, but setting that aside, I figured it might be a trick that someone was playing on me. The second possibility was that I was imagining the phone call. This seemed ridiculous to me at first, but analyzing the situation more coolly, I couldn't dismiss it out of hand. Maybe I had *thought* I heard the phone ring, and when I picked up the receiver I had *thought* I heard the voice saying my name, but in fact there had been nothing at all. Theoretically, at least, such a thing was conceivable, don't you think?"

"Well, I suppose so . . ."

"I rang the front desk and asked them to see if a call had just come in to my room, but they couldn't help me. Their system kept track of all *outgoing* calls, but no record at all of *incoming* calls. That left me with nothing to go by.

"That night in the hotel was a kind of turning point for me. It's when I started thinking about these things more seriously—the nausea and the phone calls—and the idea that they might be linked—whether wholly or partially, I didn't know. But I was beginning to see that I couldn't go on taking either of them as lightly as I had been doing.

"I spent two nights in the hotel, but even after I went home to my apartment, the vomiting and phone calls went on the same as before. I had friends put me up a few times to see what would happen, but the phone calls always found me—and always when I was alone in their houses. Needless to say, it started to give me the creeps, like I had some invisible thing standing behind me and watching every move I made: it knew exactly when to call me and when to jam its finger down my throat. When you start having thoughts like this, it's the first sign of schizophrenia, you know."

"Maybe so," I said, "but there aren't too many schizophrenics who worry about getting schizophrenia, are there?"

"No, you're right. And there are no known cases of a link between schizophrenia and vomiting. At least, that's what the psychiatrists told me at the university hospital. They wouldn't even look at me. They only want patients with unmistakable symptoms. Every carload of commuters on the Yamanote Line contains anywhere from 2.5 to 3 people with symptoms like mine, they said: they simply don't have the facilities to treat each and every one of those. I should take my vomiting to an internist and the phone calls to the police.

"But as you may know, there are two kinds of crimes the police won't bother with: crank calls and stolen bicycles. There are too many cases, and as crimes they're too petty. Police operations would be paralyzed if they got involved in every one. They wouldn't listen to me. Crank calls? What does the person say to you? Your name? That's all? OK, fill out this form and contact us if something worse happens. That's as far as they were willing to go. OK, I said, but how come the guy knows exactly where I am every time? They wouldn't take me seriously. And I knew they'd think I was crazy if I insisted too much.

"Obviously, I wasn't going to get any help from the doctors or the police or anybody else. I would have to take care of it myself. This became clear to me on the twentieth day from the beginning of the 'nausea phone calls.' I think of myself as pretty tough, both physically and mentally, but by this point it was beginning to get to me."

"Everything was OK with that one friend's girlfriend, though?"

"Pretty much. My friend happened to go to the Philippines for two weeks on business, so the two of us enjoyed each other a lot."

"Didn't you get any calls while you were with her?"

"Not one. I could check my diary, but I don't think it ever happened. The calls only came when I was alone. Same with the vomiting. So then I began to wonder: how come I'm alone so much? In fact, I probably average a little over twenty-three hours a day alone. I live alone, I hardly ever see anybody in connection with my work, I take care of most of my business by phone, my girlfriends belong to other people, I eat out ninety percent of the time, the only sport I ever practice is long, lonely swims, my only hobby is listening to these more or less antique records by myself, and the only way I can ever get my kind of work done is to concentrate on it alone. I *do* have a few friends, but when you get to this age, everybody's busy, and it's impossible to get together all the time. You know what this life is like, I'm sure."

"Sure, more or less," I said.

He poured more whiskey over the ice in his glass, stirred it with a finger, and took a sip. "So then I started thinking seriously. What was I going to do from now on? Was I going to go on suffering with crank calls and vomiting?"

"You could have gotten a girlfriend. One of your own."

"I thought about that, of course. I was twenty-seven at the time, not a bad age to settle down. But I'm not that type of guy. I couldn't give up so easily. I couldn't let myself be defeated by something so stupid and meaningless as nausea and phone calls, to change my whole way of life like that. So I decided to fight back. I'd fight until every last ounce of physical and mental strength was squeezed out of me."

"Wow."

"Tell me, Mr. Murakami, what would you have done?"

"I wonder," I said. "I have no idea." Which was true: I had no idea.

"The calls and the vomiting kept up for a long time after that. I lost a tremendous amount of weight. Wait a minute—here it is: On June 4, I weighed 141 pounds. June 21, 134 pounds. July 10, whoa, 128 pounds. *128 pounds!* For my height, that's almost unthinkable! None of my clothes fit anymore. I had to hold my pants up when I walked."

"Let me ask one question: why didn't you just install an answering machine, or something like that?"

"Because I didn't want to run away, of course. If I had done that, it would have been like admitting defeat to the enemy. This was a war of wills! Either he was going to run out of steam or I was going to kick the bucket. I took the same approach with the vomiting. I decided to think of it as an ideal way to diet. Fortunately, I didn't have any extreme loss of muscle strength, and I could keep up my work and daily chores. So I started drinking again. I'd have beer for breakfast and drink plenty of whiskey after the sun went down. I threw up whether I drank or not, so what the hell, why not? It felt better to drink, and it all made more sense.

"So then I took some cash out of my savings account and had a suit and two pairs of pants made to fit my new body shape. Looking at myself so thin in the tailor's mirror, I rather liked what I saw. Come to think of it, throwing up was no big deal. It was a lot less painful than hemorrhoids or tooth decay, and more refined than diarrhea. This was relative, of course. With the problem of nutrition solved and the problem of cancer gone, throwing up was essentially harmless. I mean, in America they go so far as to sell emetics for weight loss."

"So then," I said, "the vomiting and phone calls continued through July 14, was that it?"

"Strictly speaking—wait a second—strictly speaking, my last round of vomiting occurred on July 14 at nine thirty in the morning when I brought up my toast, tomato salad, and milk. The last phone call came at ten twenty-five p.m. that night when I was listening to Erroll Garner's *Concert by the Sea* and drinking Seagram's VO. Handy, isn't it, keeping a diary like this?"

"It really is," I agreed. "But you're saying that, after July 14, both things came to a sudden stop?"

"Just like that," he said. "It was like Hitchcock's *The Birds.* You open the door the next morning and everything's gone. The nausea, the prank calls: I never had either of them again. I went right back up to 140 pounds, and the new suit and pants are still hanging in my closet. They're like souvenirs."

"And the guy on the phone—he just kept saying the same thing, the same way, right up to the end?"

He gave his head a slight shake and looked at me a little vaguely. "Not quite," he said. "His very last call was different. First, he said my name. That was nothing new. But then he added, 'Do you know who I am?' After that, he just waited without saying anything. I kept quiet, too. It must have lasted ten or fifteen seconds, without either of us saying a word. Then he hung up, and the only sound was the dial tone."

"Really, that's all he said? 'Do you know who I am?' "

"That's it, exactly. He pronounced the words slowly: 'Do you know who I am?' I had absolutely no recollection of that voice. At least among the people I had dealt with over the previous five or six years, there was nobody with a voice like that. I suppose it *could* have been someone from my childhood, or someone I had barely spoken with, but I couldn't think of anything I might have done to make someone like that hate me, and I'm not in such demand that some other illustrator would have had it in for me. Of course, as I've told you, my conscience was not entirely clear where my love life was concerned, I grant you that. I was no innocent babe after twenty-seven years of living. But I *knew* all the voices of those guys. I would have recognized them in a second."

"Still," I said, "you have to admit it's not exactly normal to specialize in sleeping with your friends' partners."

"So, what you're telling me, Mr. Murakami, is that my own guilt feelings—feelings of which I myself was unaware—could have taken on the form of nausea or made me hear things that were not there?"

"No, *I'm* not saying that," I corrected him. "*You* are."

"Hmm," he said, taking a mouthful of whiskey and looking up at the ceiling.

"And there are other possibilities," I said. "One of the friends you deceived could have hired a private detective to tail you and make phone calls to you to teach you a lesson or warn you to back off. And the nausea could have been just a temporary condition that happened to coincide with the calls."

"Hmm," he said again. "Both of those make sense. I guess that's why you're a writer and I'm not. But still, where the detective theory is concerned, I didn't stop sleeping with the women, but the calls suddenly stopped coming. Why would that be? It doesn't fit."

"Maybe the guy got fed up, or he ran out of money to keep hiring the detective. Anyhow, it's just a theory. I can give you hundreds of those. The problem is which theory you're willing to accept. And what you learn from it."

"Learn from it?" he shot back. He pressed the base of his whiskey glass to his forehead for a few seconds. "What do you mean, 'learn from it'?"

"What to do if it happens again, of course. Next time it might not end in forty days. Things that start for no reason end for no reason. And the opposite can be true."

"What a nasty thing to say," he said with a chuckle. Turning serious again, he went on, "But it's strange. Until you just said that, it never occurred to me. That it might happen again. Do you think it *will*?"

"How should I know?"

Giving his glass an occasional swirl, he took a few sips of his whiskey. When the glass was empty, he set it on the table and blew his nose into a tissue.

"Maybe next time," he said, "it might happen to somebody else. To *you*, for example, Mr. Murakami. You're probably not all that innocent either, I suspect."

He and I have gotten together a few times since then to trade our far-from-avant-garde records and enjoy a drink, maybe two or three times a year. I'm not the diary-keeping type, so I can't say for sure. Fortunately, neither he nor I have been visited by nausea or phone calls so far.

—TRANSLATED BY JAY RUBIN

THE SEVENTH MAN

A huge wave nearly swept me away," said the seventh man, almost whispering. "It happened one September afternoon when I was ten years old."

The man was the last one to tell his story that night. The hands of the clock had moved past ten. The small group that huddled in a circle could hear the wind tearing through the darkness outside, heading west. It shook the trees, set the windows to rattling, and moved past the house with one final whistle.

"It was the biggest wave I had ever seen in my life," he said. "A strange wave. An absolute giant."

He paused.

"It just barely missed me, but in my place it swallowed everything that mattered most to me and swept it off to another world. I took years to find it again and to recover from the experience—precious years that can never be replaced."

The seventh man appeared to be in his midfifties. He was a thin man, tall, with a mustache, and next to his right eye he had a short but deep-looking scar that could have been made by the stab of a small blade. Stiff, bristly patches of white marked his short hair. His face had the look you see on people when they can't quite find the words they need. In his case, though, the expression seemed to have been there from long before, as though it were part of him. The man wore a simple blue shirt under a gray tweed coat, and every now and then he would bring his hand to his collar. None of those assembled there knew his name or what he did for a living.

He cleared his throat, and for a moment or two his words were lost in silence. The others waited for him to go on.

"In my case, it was a wave," he said. "There's no way for me to tell, of course, what it will be for each of you. But in my case it just happened to take the form of a gigantic wave. It presented itself to me all of a sudden one day, without warning, in the shape of a giant wave. And it was devastating."

I grew up in a seaside town in S—— Prefecture. It was such a small town, I doubt that any of you would recognize the name if I were to mention it. My father was the local doctor, and so I had a rather comfortable childhood. Ever since I could remember, my best friend was a boy I'll call K. His house was close to ours, and he was a grade behind me in school. We were like brothers, walking to and from school together, and always playing together when we got home. We never once fought during our long friendship. I did have a brother, six years older, but what with the age difference and differences in our personalities, we were never very close. My real brotherly affection went to my friend K.

K was a frail, skinny little thing, with a pale complexion and a face almost pretty enough to be a girl's. He had some kind of speech impediment, though, which might have made him seem retarded to anyone who didn't know him. And because he was so frail, I always played his protector, whether at school or at home. I was kind of big and athletic, and the other kids all looked up to me. But the main reason I enjoyed spending time with K was that he was such a sweet, pure-hearted boy. He was not the least bit retarded, but because of his impediment, he didn't do too well at school. In most subjects, he could barely keep up. In art class, though, he was great. Just give him a pencil or paints and he would make pictures that were so full of life that even the teacher was amazed. He won prizes in one contest after another, and I'm sure he would have become a famous painter if he had continued with his art into adulthood. He liked to do seascapes. He'd go out to the shore for hours, painting. I would often sit beside him, watching the swift, precise movements of his brush, wondering how, in a few seconds, he could possibly create such lively shapes and colors where, until then, there had been only blank white paper. I realize now that it was a matter of pure talent.

One year, in September, a huge typhoon hit our area. The radio said it was going to be the worst in ten years. The schools were closed, and all the shops in town lowered their shutters in preparation for the storm. Starting early in the morning, my father and brother went around the house nailing shut all the storm doors, while my mother spent the day in the kitchen cooking emergency provisions. We filled bottles and canteens with water, and packed our most important possessions in rucksacks for possible evacuation. To the adults, typhoons were an annoyance and a threat they had to face almost annually, but to the kids, removed as we were from such practical concerns, it was just a great big circus, a wonderful source of excitement.

Just after noon the color of the sky began to change all of a sudden. There was something strange and unreal about it. I stayed outside on the porch, watching the sky, until the wind began to howl and the rain began to beat against the house with a weird dry sound, like handfuls of sand. Then we closed the last storm door and gathered together in one room of the darkened house, listening to the radio. This particular storm did not have a great deal of rain, it said, but the winds were doing a lot of damage, blowing roofs off houses and capsizing ships. Many people had been killed or injured by flying debris. Over and over again, they warned people against leaving their homes. Every once in a while, the house would creak and shudder as if a huge hand were shaking it, and sometimes there would be a great crash of some heavy-sounding object against a storm door. My father guessed that these were tiles blowing off the neighbors' houses. For lunch we ate the rice and omelets my mother had cooked, listening to the radio and waiting for the typhoon to blow past.

But the typhoon gave no sign of blowing past. The radio said it had lost momentum almost as soon as it came ashore at S—— Prefecture, and now it was moving northeast at the pace of a slow runner. The wind kept up its savage howling as it tried to uproot everything that stood on land and carry it to the far ends of the earth.

Perhaps an hour had gone by with the wind at its worst like this when a hush fell over everything. All of a sudden it was so quiet, we could hear a bird crying in the distance. My father opened the storm door a crack and looked outside. The wind had stopped, and the rain had ceased to fall. Thick, gray clouds edged across the sky, and patches of blue showed here and there. The trees in the yard were still dripping their heavy burden of rainwater.

"We're in the eye of the storm," my father told me. "It'll stay quiet like this for a while, maybe fifteen, twenty minutes, kind of like an intermission. Then the wind'll come back the way it was before."

I asked him if I could go outside. He said I could walk around a little if I didn't go far. "But I want you to come right back here at the first sign of wind."

I went out and started to explore. It was hard to believe that a wild storm had been blowing there until a few minutes before. I looked up at the sky: I felt the storm's great "eye" up there, fixing its cold stare on all of us below. No such "eye" existed, of course: we were just in that momentary quiet spot at the center of the pool of whirling air.

While the grown-ups checked for damage to the house, I went down to the beach. The road was littered with broken tree branches, some of them thick pine boughs that would have been too heavy for an adult to lift alone. There were shattered roof tiles everywhere, cars with cracked windshields, and even a doghouse that had tumbled into the middle of the street. A big hand might have swung down from the sky and flattened everything in its path.

K saw me walking down the road and came outside.

"Where are you going?" he asked.

"Just down to look at the beach," I said.

Without a word, he came along with me. He had a little white dog that followed after us.

"The minute we get any wind, though, we're going straight back home," I said, and K gave me a silent nod.

The shore was a two-hundred-yard walk from my house. It was lined with a concrete breakwater—a big dike that stood as high as I was tall in those days. We had to climb a short stairway to reach the water's edge. This was where we came to play almost every day, so there was no part of it we didn't know well. In the eye of the typhoon, though, it all looked different: the color of the sky and of the sea, the sound of the waves, the smell of the tide, the whole expanse of the shore. We sat atop the breakwater for a time, taking in the view without a word to each other. We were supposedly in the middle of a great typhoon, and yet the waves were strangely hushed. And the point where they washed against the beach was much farther away than usual, even at low tide. The white sand stretched out before us as far as we could see. The whole, huge space felt like a room without furniture, except for the band of flotsam that lined the beach.

We stepped down to the other side of the breakwater and walked along the broad beach, examining the things that had come to rest there. Plastic toys, sandals, chunks of wood that had probably once been parts of furniture, pieces of clothing, unusual bottles, broken crates with foreign writing on them, and other, less recognizable items: it was like a big candy store. The storm must have carried these things from very far away. Whenever something unusual caught our attention, we would pick it up and look at it every which way, and when we were done, K's dog would come over and give it a good sniff.

We couldn't have been doing this more than five minutes when I realized that the waves had come up right next to me. Without any sound or other warning, the sea had suddenly stretched its long, smooth tongue out to where I stood on the beach. I had never seen anything like it before. Child though I was, I had grown up on the shore and knew how frightening the ocean could be—the savagery with which it could strike unannounced. And so I had taken care to keep well back from the waterline. In spite of that, the waves had slid up to within inches of where I stood. And then, just as soundlessly, the water drew back—and stayed back. The waves that had approached me were as unthreatening as waves can be—a gentle washing of the sandy beach. But something ominous about them—something like the touch of a reptile's skin—had sent a chill down my spine. My fear was totally groundless—and totally real. I knew instinctively that they were alive. The waves were alive. They knew I was here and they were planning to grab me. I felt as if some huge man-eating beast were lying somewhere on a grassy plain, dreaming of the moment it would pounce and tear me to pieces with its sharp teeth. I had to run away.

"I'm getting out of here!" I yelled to K. He was maybe ten yards down the beach, squatting with his back to me, and looking at something. I was sure I had yelled loud enough, but my voice did not seem to have reached him. He might have been so absorbed in whatever it was he had found that my call made no impression on him. K was like that. He would get involved with things to the point of forgetting everything else.

Or possibly I had not yelled as loudly as I thought. I do recall that my voice sounded strange to me, as though it belonged to someone else.

Then I heard a deep rumbling sound. It seemed to shake the earth. Actually, before I heard the rumble I heard another sound, a weird gurgling as though a lot of water was surging up through a hole in the ground. It continued for a while, then stopped, after which I heard the strange rumbling. Even that was not enough to make K look up. He was still squatting, looking down at something at his feet, in deep concentration. He probably did not hear the rumbling. How he could have missed such an earthshaking sound, I don't know. This may seem odd, but it might have been a sound that only I could hear—some special kind of sound. Not even K's dog seemed to notice it, and you know how sensitive dogs are to sound.

I told myself to run over to K, grab hold of him, and get out of there. It was the only thing to do. I *knew* that the wave was coming, and K didn't know. As clearly as I knew what I ought to be doing, I found myself running the other way—running full speed toward the dike, alone. What made me do this, I'm sure, was fear, a fear so overpowering it took my voice away and set my legs to running on their own. I ran stumbling along the soft sand beach to the breakwater, where I turned and shouted to K.

"Hurry, K! Get out of there! The wave is coming!" This time my voice worked fine. The rumbling had stopped, I realized, and now, finally, K heard my shouting and looked up. But it was too late. A wave like a huge snake with its head held high, poised to strike, was racing toward the shore. I had never seen anything like it in my life. It had to be as tall as a three-story building. Soundlessly (in my memory, at least, the image is soundless), it rose up behind K to block out the sky. K looked at me for a few seconds, uncomprehending. Then, as if sensing something, he turned toward the wave. He tried to run, but now there was no time to run. In the next instant, the wave had swallowed him. It hit him full on, like a locomotive at full speed.

The wave crashed onto the beach, shattering into a million leaping waves that flew through the air and plunged over the dike where I stood. I was able to dodge its impact by ducking behind the breakwater. The spray wet my clothes, nothing more. I scrambled back up onto the wall and scanned the shore. By then the wave had turned and, with a wild cry, it was rushing back out to sea. It looked like part of a gigantic rug that had been yanked by someone at the other end of the earth. Nowhere on the shore could I find any trace of K, or of his dog. There was only the empty beach. The receding wave had now pulled so much water out from the shore it seemed to expose the entire ocean bottom. I stood alone on the breakwater, frozen in place.

The silence came over everything again—a desperate silence, as though sound itself had been ripped from the earth. The wave had swallowed K and disappeared into the far distance. I stood there, wondering what to do. Should I go down to the beach? K might be down there somewhere, buried in the sand. . . . But I decided not to leave the dike. I knew from experience that big waves often came in twos and threes.

I'm not sure how much time went by—maybe ten or twenty seconds of eerie emptiness—when, just as I had guessed, the next wave came. Another gigantic roar shook the beach, and again, after the sound had faded, another huge wave raised its head to strike. It towered before me, blocking out the sky, like a deadly cliff. This time, though, I didn't run. I stood rooted to the seawall, entranced, waiting for it to attack. What good would it do to run, I thought, now that K had been taken? Or perhaps I simply froze, overcome with fear. I can't be sure what it was that kept me standing there.

The second wave was just as big as the first—maybe even bigger. From far above my head it began to fall, losing its shape, like a brick wall slowly crumbling. It was so huge that it no longer looked like a real wave. It seemed to be some other thing, something from another, far-off world, that just happened to assume the shape of a wave. I readied myself for the moment the darkness would take me. I didn't even close my eyes. I remember hearing my heart pound with incredible clarity.

The moment the wave came before me, however, it stopped. All at once it seemed to run out of energy, to lose its forward motion and simply hover there, in space, crumbling in stillness. And in its crest, inside its cruel, transparent tongue, what I saw was K.

Some of you may find this impossible to believe, and if so, I don't blame you. I myself have trouble accepting it even now. I can't explain what I saw any better than you can, but I know it was no illusion, no hallucination. I am telling you as honestly as I can what happened at that moment—what really happened. In the tip of the wave, as if enclosed in some kind of transparent capsule, floated K's body, reclining on its side. But that is not all. K was looking straight at me, smiling. There, right in front of me, close enough so that I could have reached out and touched him, was my friend, my friend K who, only moments before, had been swallowed by the wave. And he was smiling at me. Not with an ordinary smile—it was a big, wide-open grin that literally stretched from ear to ear. His cold, frozen eyes were locked on mine. He was no longer the K I knew. And his right arm was stretched out in my direction, as if he were trying to grab my hand and pull me into that other world where he was now. A little closer, and his hand would have caught mine. But, having missed, K then smiled at me one more time, his grin wider than ever.

I seem to have lost consciousness at that point. The next thing I knew, I was in bed in my father's clinic. As soon as I awoke, the nurse went to call my father, who came running. He took my pulse, studied my pupils, and put his hand on my forehead. I tried to move my arm, but I couldn't lift it. I was burning with fever, and my mind was clouded. I had been wrestling with a high fever for some time, apparently. "You've been asleep for three days," my father said to me. A neighbor who had seen the whole thing had picked me up and carried me home. They had not been able to find K. I wanted to say something to my father. I *had* to say something to him. But my numb and swollen tongue could not form words. I felt as if some kind of creature had taken up residence in my mouth. My father asked me to tell him my name, but before I could remember what it was, I lost consciousness again, sinking into darkness.

Altogether, I stayed in bed for a week on a liquid diet. I vomited several times, and had bouts of delirium. My father told me afterward I was so bad that he had been afraid that I might suffer permanent neurological damage from the shock and high fever. One way or another, though, I managed to recover—physically, at least. But my life would never be the same again.

They never found K's body. They never found his dog, either. Usually when someone drowned in that area, the body would wash up a few days later on the shore of a small inlet to the east. K's body never did. The big waves probably carried it far out to sea—too far for it to reach the shore. It must have sunk to the ocean bottom to be eaten by the fish. The search went on for a very long time, thanks to the cooperation of the local fishermen, but eventually it petered out. Without a body, there was never any funeral. Half-crazed, K's parents would wander up and down the beach every day, or they would shut themselves up at home, chanting sutras.

As great a blow as this had been for them, though, K's parents never chided me for having taken their son down to the shore in the midst of a typhoon. They knew how I had always loved and protected K as if he had been my own little brother. My parents, too, made a point of never mentioning the incident in my presence. But I knew the truth. I knew that I could have saved K if I had tried. I probably could have run over and dragged him out of the reach of the wave. It would have been close, but as I went over the timing of the events in memory, it always seemed to me that I could have made it. As I said before, though, overcome with fear, I abandoned him there and saved only myself. It pained me all the more that K's parents failed to blame me and that everyone else was so careful never to say anything to me about what had happened. It took me a long time to recover from the emotional shock. I stayed away from school for weeks. I hardly ate a thing, and spent each day in bed, staring at the ceiling.

K was always there, lying in the wave tip, grinning at me, his hand outstretched, beckoning. I couldn't get that searing image out of my mind. And when I managed to sleep, it was there in my dreams—except that, in my dreams, K would hop out of his capsule in the wave and grab my wrist to drag me back inside with him.

And then there was another dream I had. I'm swimming in the ocean. It's a beautiful summer afternoon, and I'm doing an easy breaststroke far from shore. The sun is beating down on my back, and the water feels good. Then, all of a sudden, someone grabs my right leg. I feel an ice-cold grip on my ankle. It's strong, too strong to shake off. I'm being dragged down under the surface. I see K's face there. He has the same huge grin, split from ear to ear, his eyes locked on mine. I try to scream, but my voice will not come. I swallow water, and my lungs start to fill.

I wake up in the darkness, screaming, breathless, drenched in sweat.

At the end of the year, I pleaded with my parents to let me move to another town. I couldn't go on living in sight of the beach where K had been swept away, and my nightmares wouldn't stop. If I didn't get out of there, I'd go crazy. My parents understood and made arrangements for me to live elsewhere. I moved to Nagano Prefecture in January to live with my father's family in a mountain village near Komoro. I finished elementary school in Nagano and stayed on through junior and senior high school there. I never went home, even for holidays. My parents came to visit me now and then.

I live in Nagano to this day. I graduated from a college of engineering in the city of Nagano and went to work for a precision toolmaker in the area. I still work for them. I live like anybody else. As you can see, there's nothing unusual about me. I'm not very sociable, but I have a few friends I go mountain climbing with. Once I got away from my hometown, I stopped having nightmares all the time. They remained a part of my life, though. They would come to me now and then, like bill collectors at the door. It happened whenever I was on the verge of forgetting. And it was always the same dream, down to the smallest detail. I would wake up screaming, my sheets soaked with sweat.

This is probably why I never married. I didn't want to wake someone sleeping next to me with my screams in the middle of the night. I've been in love with several women over the years, but I never spent a night with any of them. The terror was in my bones. It was something I could never share with another person.

I stayed away from my hometown for over forty years. I never went near that seashore—or any other. I was afraid that, if I did, my dream might happen in reality. I had always enjoyed swimming, but after that day I never even went to a pool. I wouldn't go near deep rivers or lakes. I avoided boats and wouldn't take a plane to go abroad. Despite all these precautions, I couldn't get rid of the image of myself drowning. Like K's cold hand, this dark premonition caught hold of my mind and refused to let go.

Then, last spring, I finally revisited the beach where K had been taken by the wave.

My father had died of cancer the year before, and my brother had sold the old house. In going through the storage shed, he had found a cardboard carton crammed with childhood things of mine, which he sent to me in Nagano. Most of it was useless junk, but there was one bundle of pictures that K had painted and given to me. My parents had probably put them away for me as a keepsake of K, but the pictures did nothing but reawaken the old terror. They made me feel as if K's spirit would spring back to life from them, and so I quickly returned them to their paper wrapping, intending to throw them away. I couldn't make myself do it, though. After several days of indecision, I opened the bundle again and forced myself to take a long, hard look at K's watercolors.

Most of them were landscapes, pictures of the familiar stretch of ocean and sand beach and pine woods and the town, and all done with that special clarity and coloration I knew so well from K's hand. They were still amazingly vivid despite the years, and had been executed with even greater skill than I recalled. As I leafed through the bundle, I found myself steeped in warm memories. The deep feelings of the boy K were there in his pictures—the way his eyes were opened on the world. The things we did together, the places we went together began to come back to me with great intensity. And I realized that his eyes were my eyes, that I myself had looked upon the world back then with the same lively, unclouded vision as the boy who had walked by my side.

I made a habit after that of studying one of K's pictures at my desk each day when I got home from work. I could sit there for hours with one painting. In each I found another of those soft landscapes of child-hood that I had shut out of my memory for so long. I had a sense, when-ever I looked at one of K's works, that something was permeating my very flesh.

Perhaps a week had gone by like this when the thought suddenly struck me one evening: I might have been making a terrible mistake all those years. As he lay there in the tip of the wave, surely, K had not been looking at me with hatred or resentment; he had not been trying to take me away with him. And that terrible grin he had fixed me with: that, too, could have been an accident of angle or light and shadow, not a con-scious act on K's part. He had probably already lost consciousness, or perhaps he had been giving me a gentle smile of eternal parting. The intense look of hatred I had thought I saw on his face had been nothing but a reflection of the profound terror that had taken control of me for the moment.

The more I studied K's watercolor that evening, the greater the con-viction with which I began to believe these new thoughts of mine. For no matter how long I continued to look at the picture, I could find noth-ing in it but a boy's gentle, innocent spirit.

I went on sitting at my desk for a very long time. There was nothing else I could do. The sun went down, and the pale darkness of evening began to envelop the room. Then came the deep silence of night, which seemed to go on forever. At last, the scales tipped, and dark gave way to dawn. The new day's sun tinged the sky with pink, and the birds awoke to sing.

It was then I knew I must go back.

I threw a few things in a bag, called the company to say I would not be in, and boarded a train for my old hometown.

I did not find the same quiet little seaside town that I remembered. An industrial city had sprung up nearby during the rapid development of the sixties, bringing great changes to the landscape. The one little gift shop by the station had grown into a mall, and the town's only movie theater had been turned into a supermarket. My house was no longer there. It had been demolished some months before, leaving only a scrape on the earth. The trees in the yard had all been cut down, and patches of weeds dotted the black stretch of ground. K's old house had disappeared as well, having been replaced by a concrete parking lot full of commuters' cars and vans. Not that I was overcome by sentiment. The town had ceased to be mine long before.

I walked down to the shore and climbed the steps of the breakwater. On the other side, as always, the ocean stretched off into the distance, unobstructed, huge, the horizon a single straight line. The shoreline, too, looked the same as it had before: the long beach, the lapping waves, people strolling at the water's edge. The time was after four o'clock, and the soft sun of late afternoon embraced everything below as it began its long, almost meditative, descent to the west. I lowered my bag to the sand and sat down next to it in silent appreciation of the gentle seascape. Looking at this scene, it was impossible to imagine that a great typhoon had once raged here, that a massive wave had swallowed my best friend in all the world. There was almost no one left now, surely, who remembered those terrible events. It began to seem as if the whole thing were an illusion that I had dreamed up in vivid detail.

And then I realized that the deep darkness inside me had vanished. Suddenly. As suddenly as it had come. I raised myself from the sand and, without bothering either to take off my shoes or roll up my cuffs, walked into the surf to let the waves lap at my ankles. Almost in reconciliation, it seemed, the same waves that had washed up on the beach when I was a boy were now fondly washing my feet, soaking black my shoes and pant cuffs. There would be one slow-moving wave, then a long pause, and then another wave would come and go. The people passing by gave me odd looks, but I didn't care. I had found my way back again, at last.

I looked up at the sky. A few gray cotton chunks of cloud hung there, motionless. They seemed to be there for me, though I'm not sure why I felt that way. I remembered having looked up at the sky like this in search of the "eye" of the typhoon. And then, inside me, the axis of time gave one great heave. Forty long years collapsed like a dilapidated house, mixing old time and new time together in a single swirling mass. All sounds faded, and the light around me shuddered. I lost my balance and fell into the waves. My heart throbbed at the back of my throat, and my arms and legs lost all sensation. I lay that way for a long time, face in the water, unable to stand. But I was not afraid. No, not at all. There was no longer anything for me to fear. Those days were gone.

I stopped having my terrible nightmares. I no longer wake up screaming in the middle of the night. And I am trying now to start life over again. No, I know it's probably too late to start again. I may not have much time left to live. But even if it comes too late, I am grateful that, in the end, I was able to attain a kind of salvation, to effect some sort of recovery. Yes, grateful: I could have come to the end of my life unsaved, still screaming in the dark, afraid.

◎

The seventh man fell silent and turned his gaze upon each of the others. No one spoke or moved or even seemed to breathe. All were waiting for the rest of his story. Outside, the wind had fallen, and nothing stirred. The seventh man brought his hand to his collar once again, as if in search of words.

"They tell us that the only thing we have to fear is fear itself, but I don't believe that," he said. Then, a moment later, he added: "Oh, the fear is there, all right. It comes to us in many different forms, at different times, and overwhelms us. But the most frightening thing we can do at such times is to turn our backs on it, to close our eyes. For then we take the most precious thing inside us and surrender it to something else. In my case, that something was the wave."

— TRANSLATED BY JAY RUBIN

THE YEAR OF SPAGHETTI

1971 was the Year of Spaghetti.

In 1971 I cooked spaghetti to live, and lived to cook spaghetti. Steam rising from the aluminum pot was my pride and joy, tomato sauce bubbling up in the saucepan my one great hope in life.

I'd gone to a cooking specialty store and bought a kitchen timer and a huge aluminum cooking pot, big enough to bathe a German shepherd in, then went round all the supermarkets that cater to foreigners, gathering an assortment of odd-sounding spices. I picked up a pasta cookbook at the bookstore, and bought tomatoes by the dozen. I purchased every brand of spaghetti I could lay my hands on, simmered every kind of sauce known to man. Fine particles of garlic, onion, and olive oil swirled in the air, forming a harmonious cloud that penetrated every corner of my tiny apartment, permeating the floor and ceiling and walls, my clothes, my books, my records, my tennis racket, my bundles of old letters. It was a fragrance one might have smelled on ancient Roman aqueducts.

This is a story from the Year of Spaghetti, 1971 A.D.

As a rule I cooked spaghetti, and ate it, alone. I was convinced that spaghetti was a dish best enjoyed alone. I can't really explain why I felt that way, but there it is.

I always drank tea with my spaghetti and ate a simple lettuce-and-cucumber salad. I'd make sure I had plenty of both. I laid everything out neatly on the table, and enjoyed a leisurely meal, glancing at the paper as I ate. From Sunday to Saturday, one Spaghetti Day followed another. And each new Sunday started a brand-new Spaghetti Week.

Every time I sat down to a plate of spaghetti—especially on a rainy afternoon—I had the distinct feeling that somebody was about to knock on my door. The person who I imagined was about to visit me was different each time. Sometimes it was a stranger, sometimes someone I knew. Once, it was a girl with slim legs whom I'd dated in high school, and once it was myself, from a few years back, come to pay a visit. Another time, it was none other than William Holden, with Jennifer Jones on his arm.

William Holden?

Not one of these people, though, actually ventured into my apartment. They hovered just outside the door, without knocking, like fragments of memory, and then slipped away.

◎

Spring, summer, and fall, I cooked away, as if cooking spaghetti were an act of revenge. Like a lonely, jilted girl throwing old love letters into the fireplace, I tossed one handful of spaghetti after another into the pot.

I'd gather up the trampled-down shadows of time, knead them into the shape of a German shepherd, toss them into the roiling water, and sprinkle them with salt. Then I'd hover over the pot, oversize chopsticks in hand, until the timer dinged its plaintive tone.

Spaghetti strands are a crafty bunch, and I couldn't let them out of my sight. If I were to turn my back, they might well slip over the edge of the pot and vanish into the night. Like the tropical jungle waits to swallow up colorful butterflies into the eternity of time, the night lay in silence, hoping to waylay the prodigal strands.

> Spaghetti alla parmigiana
> Spaghetti alla napoletana
> Spaghetti al cartoccio
> Spaghetti aglio e olio
> Spaghetti alla carbonara
> Spaghetti della pina

And then there was the pitiful, nameless leftover spaghetti carelessly tossed into the fridge.

Born in heat, the strands of spaghetti washed down the river of 1971 and vanished.

And I mourn them all—all the spaghetti of the year 1971.

When the phone rang at three twenty I was sprawled out on the tatami, staring at the ceiling. A pool of winter sunlight had formed in the place where I lay. Like a dead fly I lay there, vacant, in a December 1971 spotlight.

At first, I didn't recognize it as the phone ringing. It was more like an unfamiliar memory that had hesitantly slipped in between the layers of air. Finally, though, it began to take shape, and, in the end, a ringing phone was unmistakably what it was. It was one hundred percent a phone ring in one-hundred-percent-real air. Still sprawled out, I reached over and picked up the receiver.

On the other end was a girl, a girl so indistinct that, by four thirty, she might very well have disappeared altogether. She was the ex-girlfriend of a friend of mine. Something had brought them together, this guy and this indistinct girl, and something had led them to break up. I had, I admit, reluctantly played a role in getting them together in the first place.

"Sorry to bother you," she said, "but do you know where he is now?"

I looked at the phone, running my eyes along the length of the cord. The cord was, sure enough, attached to the phone. I managed a vague reply. There was something ominous in the girl's voice, and whatever trouble was brewing I knew I didn't want to get involved.

"Nobody will tell me where he is," she said in a chilly tone. "Everybody's pretending they don't know. But there's something important I have to tell him, so *please*—tell me where he is. I promise I won't drag you into this. Where is he?"

"I honestly don't know," I told her. "I haven't seen him in a long time." My voice didn't sound like my own. I was telling the truth about not having seen him for a long time, but not about the other part—I did know his address and phone number. Whenever I tell a lie, something weird happens to my voice.

No comment from her.

The phone was like a pillar of ice.

Then all the objects around me turned into pillars of ice, as if I were in a J. G. Ballard science fiction story.

"I really don't know," I repeated. "He went away a long time ago, without saying a word."

The girl laughed. "Give me a break. He's not that clever. We're talking about a guy who has to raise a noise no matter what he does."

She was right. The guy really was a bit of a dim bulb.

But I wasn't about to tell her where he was. Do that, and next I'd have *him* on the phone, giving me an earful. I was through with getting caught up in other people's messes. I'd already dug a hole in the backyard and buried everything that needed to be buried in it. Nobody could ever dig it up again.

"I'm sorry," I said.

"You don't like me, do you?" she suddenly said.

I had no idea what to say. I didn't particularly dislike her. I had no real impression of her at all. And it's hard to have a bad impression of somebody you have no impression of.

"I'm sorry," I said again. "But I'm cooking spaghetti right now."

"What?"

"I said I'm cooking spaghetti," I lied. I had no idea why I said that. But that lie was already a part of me—so much so that, at that moment at least, it didn't feel like a lie at all.

I went ahead and filled an imaginary pot with water, lit an imaginary stove with an imaginary match.

"So?" she asked.

I sprinkled imaginary salt into the boiling water, gently lowered a handful of imaginary spaghetti into the imaginary pot, set the imaginary kitchen timer for twelve minutes.

"So I can't talk. The spaghetti will be ruined."

She didn't say anything.

"I'm really sorry, but cooking spaghetti's a delicate operation."

The girl was silent. The phone in my hand began to freeze again.

"So could you call me back?" I added hurriedly.

"Because you're in the middle of making spaghetti?" she asked.

"Yeah."

"Are you making it for someone, or are you going to eat alone?"

"I'll eat it by myself," I said.

She held her breath for a long time, then slowly breathed out. "There's no way you could know this, but I'm really in trouble. I don't know what to do."

"I'm sorry I can't help you," I said.

"There's some money involved, too."

"I see."

"He owes me money," she said. "I lent him some money. I shouldn't have, but I had to."

I was quiet for a minute, my thoughts drifting toward spaghetti. "I'm sorry," I said. "But I've got the spaghetti going, so . . ."

She gave a listless laugh. "Goodbye," she said. "Say hi to your spaghetti for me. I hope it turns out OK."

"Bye," I said.

When I hung up the phone, the circle of light on the floor had shifted an inch or two. I lay down again in that pool of light and resumed staring at the ceiling.

◎

Thinking about spaghetti that boils eternally but is never done is a sad, sad thing.

Now I regret, a little, that I didn't tell the girl anything. Perhaps I should have. I mean, her ex-boyfriend wasn't much to start with—an empty shell of a guy with artistic pretensions, a great talker whom nobody trusted. She sounded as if she really were strapped for money, and, no matter what the situation, you've got to pay back what you borrow.

Sometimes I wonder what happened to the girl—the thought usually pops into my mind when I'm facing a steaming-hot plate of spaghetti. After she hung up, did she disappear forever, sucked into the four thirty p.m. shadows? Was I partly to blame?

I want you to understand my position, though. At the time, I didn't want to get involved with anyone. That's why I kept on cooking spaghetti, all by myself. In that huge pot, big enough to hold a German shepherd.

◎

Durum semolina, golden wheat wafting in Italian fields.

Can you imagine how astonished the Italians would be if they knew that what they were exporting in 1971 was really *loneliness*?

—TRANSLATED BY PHILIP GABRIEL

TONY TAKITANI

Tony Takitani's real name was really that: Tony Takitani.

Because of his name and his curly hair and his somewhat deeply sculpted features, he was often assumed to be a mixed-blood child. This was just after the war, when there were lots of children around whose blood was half American GI. But Tony Takitani's mother and father were both one hundred percent genuine Japanese. His father, Shozaburo Takitani, had been a fairly well-known jazz trombonist, but four years before the Second World War broke out, he was forced to leave Tokyo because of a problem involving a woman. If he had to leave town, he figured, he might as well *really* leave, so he crossed over to China with nothing but his trombone in hand. In those days, Shanghai was an easy one-day's boat ride from Nagasaki. Shozaburo owned nothing in Tokyo—or anywhere else in Japan—that he would hate to lose. He left without regrets. If anything, he suspected, Shanghai, with its well-crafted enticements, would be better suited to his personality than Tokyo. He was standing on the deck of a boat plowing its way up the Yangtze River the first time he saw Shanghai's elegant avenues glowing in the morning sun, and that did it. He fell in love with the town. The light seemed to promise him a future of tremendous brightness. He was twenty-one years old.

And so he took it easy all through the upheaval of the war—from the Japanese invasion of China to the attack on Pearl Harbor to the dropping of two atomic bombs—playing his trombone in Shanghai nightclubs. The war was happening somewhere far away. Shozaburo Takitani was a man who possessed not the slightest hint of will or introspection with regard to history. He wanted nothing more than to be able to play his trombone, eat three meals a day, and have a few women nearby. He was simultaneously modest and arrogant. Deeply self-centered, he nevertheless treated those around him with great kindness and good feeling. Which is why most people liked him. Young, handsome, and good on his horn, he stood out like a crow on a snowy day wherever he went. He slept with more women than he could count. Japanese, Chinese, White Russians, whores, married women, gorgeous girls, and girls who were not so gorgeous: he did it with anyone he could get his hands on. Before long, his super-sweet trombone and his super-active giant penis made him a Shanghai sensation.

Shozaburo Takitani was also blessed—though he himself did not realize it—with a talent for making "useful" friends. He was on great terms with high-ranking Japanese Army officers, Chinese millionaires, and all kinds of influential types who were sucking up gigantic profits from the war through obscure channels. A lot of them carried pistols under their jackets and never walked out of a building without giving the street a quick scan right and left. He and they just "clicked" for some strange reason. And they took special care of him. They were always glad to open doors for him whenever problems came up. Life was a breeze for Shozaburo Takitani in those years.

Fine talents can sometimes work against you, though. When the war ended, his dubious connections won him the attention of the Chinese Army, and he was locked up for a long time. Day after day, the others who had been imprisoned like Shozaburo Takitani were taken out of their cells and executed without trial. Guards would just show up, drag them into the prison yard, and blow their brains out with automatic pistols. It always happened at two o'clock in the afternoon. The tight, hard crack of a pistol would echo through the yard.

This was the greatest crisis that Shozaburo Takitani had ever faced. A literal hair's breadth separated life from death. He assumed he would be dying in this place. But the prospect of death did not frighten him greatly. They'd put a bullet through his brain, and it would be all over. A split second of pain. I've lived the way I wanted to all these years, he thought, and I've slept with tons of women. I've eaten a lot of good food, and had a lot of good times. There's not that much in life I'm sorry I missed. Besides, I'm not in any position to complain about being killed.

It's just the way it goes. What more could I ask for? Millions of Japanese have died in this war, and lots of them in far more terrible ways than what is going to happen to me. He resigned himself to his fate and whistled away the hours in his cell. Day after day he watched the clouds drift by the bars of his tiny window and painted mental pictures on the cell's filthy walls of the faces and bodies of the many women he had slept with. In the end, though, Shozaburo Takitani turned out to be one of only two Japanese prisoners to leave the prison alive and go home to Japan. By that time the other man, a high-ranking officer, had nearly lost his mind. Shozaburo Takitani stood on the deck of the boat repatriating him, and as he watched the avenues of Shanghai shrinking away in the distance, he thought, Life: I'll never understand it.

Emaciated and bereft of possessions, Shozaburo Takitani came back to Japan in the spring of 1946, nine months after the war ended. He discovered that his parents had died when their home burned to the ground in the great Tokyo air raid of March '45. His only brother had disappeared without a trace on the Burmese front. In other words, Shozaburo Takitani was now alone in the world. This was no great shock to him, however, nor did it make him feel particularly sad or miserable. He did, of course, experience some sense of absence, but he felt that, eventually, life had to turn out more or less like this. Everyone ended up alone sooner or later. He was thirty at the time, beyond the age for complaining about loneliness. He felt as if he had put on several years all at once. But that was all. No further emotion welled up inside him.

Yes, Shozaburo Takitani had managed to survive one way or another, and as long as he had managed to survive, he would have to start thinking of ways to go on living.

Because he knew only one line of work, he hunted up some of his old buddies and put together a little jazz band that started playing at the American military bases. His talent for making contacts won him the friendship of a jazz-loving American army major, an Italian American from New Jersey who played a pretty mean clarinet himself. An officer in the Quartermaster Corps, the major could get all the jazz records Shozaburo Takitani needed straight from the U.S. The two of them often jammed together in their spare time. Shozaburo Takitani would go to the major's quarters, break open a beer, and listen to the happy jazz of Bobby Hackett, Jack Teagarden, or Benny Goodman, teaching himself as many of their good licks as he could. The major supplied him with all kinds of food and milk and liquor, which were hard to get ahold of in those days. Not bad, he thought: not a bad time to be alive.

Shozaburo Takitani got married in 1947. His new wife was a distant cousin on his mother's side. They happened to run into each other one day on the street and, over tea, shared news of their relatives and talked about the old days. They started seeing each other after that, and before long ended up living together—because she had gotten pregnant would be a safe guess.

At least that was the way Tony Takitani had heard it from his father. Tony Takitani had no idea how much his father, Shozaburo Takitani, had loved his mother. She was a pretty girl, and quiet, but not too healthy according to his father.

She gave birth to a boy the year after they were married, and three days later she died. Just like that. And just like that she was cremated, all quick and quiet. She experienced no great complications and no suffering to speak of. She just faded into nothingness, as if someone had gone backstage and flicked a switch.

Shozaburo Takitani had no idea how he was supposed to feel about this. He was a stranger to such emotions. He could not seem to grasp with any precision what "death" was all about, nor could he come to any conclusion regarding what this particular death had meant for him. All he could do was swallow it whole as an accomplished fact. And so he came to feel that some kind of flat, disc-like thing had lodged itself in his chest. What it was, or why it was there, he couldn't say. The object simply stayed in place and blocked him from thinking any more deeply about what had happened to him. He thought about nothing at all for a full week after his wife died. He even forgot about the baby he had left in the hospital.

The major took Shozaburo Takitani under his wing and did all he could to console him. They drank together in the base bar nearly every day. You've got to get ahold of yourself, the major would tell him. The one thing you absolutely have to do is bring that boy up right. The words meant nothing to Shozaburo Takitani, who merely nodded in silence. Even to him, though, it was clear that the major was trying to help him. Hey, I know, the major added suddenly one day. Why don't you let me be the boy's godfather? I'll give him a name. Oh, thought Shozaburo Takitani, he had forgotten to give the baby a name.

The major suggested his own first name, Tony. "Tony" was no name for a Japanese child, of course, but such a thought never crossed the major's mind. When he got home, Shozaburo Takitani wrote the name "Tony Takitani" on a piece of paper, stuck it to the wall, and stared at it for the next several days. Hmm, "Tony Takitani." Not bad. Not bad. The American occupation of Japan was probably going to last a while yet, and an American-style name just might come in handy for the kid at some point.

For the child himself, though, living with a name like that was hard. The other kids at school teased him as a half-breed, and whenever he told people his name, they responded with a look of puzzlement or distaste. Some people thought it was a bad joke, and others reacted with anger. For certain people, coming face-to-face with a child called "Tony Takitani" was all it took to reopen old wounds.

Such experiences served only to close the boy off from the world. He never made any real friends, but this did not cause him pain. He found it natural to be by himself: it was a kind of premise for living. By the time he reached some self-awareness, his father was always traveling with the band. When he was little a housekeeper would come to take care of him during the day, but once he was in his last years of elementary school, he could manage without her. He cooked for himself, locked up at night, and slept alone. Not that he ever felt lonely: he was simply more comfortable this way than with someone fussing over him all the time. Having lost his wife, Shozaburo Takitani, for some reason, never married again. He had plenty of girlfriends, of course, but he never brought any of them to the house. Like his son, he was used to taking care of himself. Father and son were not as distant from each other as one might imagine from their lifestyles. But being the kind of people they were, imbued to an equal degree with a habitual solitude, neither took the initiative to open his heart to the other. Neither felt a need to do so. Shozaburo Takitani was not well suited to being a father, and Tony Takitani was not well suited to being a son.

Tony Takitani loved to draw, and he spent hours each day shut up in his room, doing just that. He especially loved to draw pictures of machines. Keeping his pencil point needle-sharp, he would produce clear, accurate drawings of bicycles, radios, engines and such down to the tiniest details. If he drew a flower, he would capture every vein in every leaf. No matter what anyone said to him, it was the only way he knew how to draw. His grades in art, unlike those in other subjects, were always outstanding, and he usually took first prize in school art contests.

And so it was perfectly natural for Tony Takitani to go from high school to an art college (at which point, without either of them suggesting it, father and son began living separately as a matter of course) to a career as an illustrator. In fact, there was no need for him to consider other possibilities. While the young people around him were anguishing over the paths they should follow in life, he went on doing his precise mechanical drawings without a thought for anything else. And because it was a time when young people were acting out against authority and the Establishment with passion and violence, none of his contemporaries saw anything of value in his utilitarian art. His art college professors viewed his work with twisted smiles. His classmates criticized it as lacking in ideological content. Tony Takitani himself could not see what was so great about *their* work *with* ideological content. To him, their pictures all looked immature, ugly, and inaccurate.

Once he graduated from college, though, everything changed for him. Thanks to the extreme practicality and usefulness of his realistic technique, Tony Takitani never had a problem finding work. No one could match the precision with which he drew complicated machines and architecture. "They look realer than the real thing," everyone said. His pictures were more accurate than photographs, and they had a clarity that made any explanation a waste of words. All of a sudden, he was the one illustrator that everybody had to have. And he took on everything, from the covers of automobile magazines to ad illustrations, anything that involved mechanisms. He enjoyed the work, and he made good money.

Shozaburo Takitani, meanwhile, went on playing his horn. Along came modern jazz, then free jazz, then electric jazz, but Shozaburo Takitani never changed: he kept performing in the same old style. He was not a musician of the first rank, but his name could still draw crowds, and he always had work. He had all the tasty treats he wanted, and he always had a woman. In terms of sheer personal satisfaction, his life was one of the more successful ones.

Tony Takitani used every spare minute for work. Without any hobbies to drain his resources, he managed by the time he was thirty-five to amass a small fortune. He let people talk him into buying a big house in an affluent Setagaya suburb, and he owned several apartments that brought him rental income. His accountant took care of all the details.

By this point in his life, Tony Takitani had been involved with several different women. He had even lived with one of them for a short while in his youth. But he never considered marriage, never saw the need of it. The cooking, the cleaning, the laundry he could manage for himself, and when work interfered with those things, he hired a housekeeper. He never felt a desire to have children. He had no close friends of the kind who would come to him for advice or to confess secrets, not even one to drink with. Not that he was a hermit, either. He lacked his father's special charm, but he had perfectly normal relationships with people he saw on a daily basis. There was nothing arrogant or boastful about him. He never made excuses for himself or spoke slightingly of others. Rather than talk about himself, what he enjoyed most was to listen to what others had to say. And so just about everybody who knew him liked him. Still, it was impossible for him to form relationships with people that went beyond the level of sheer everyday reality. His father he would see no more than once in two or three years on some matter of business. And when the business was over, neither man had much of anything to say to the other. Thus, Tony Takitani's life went by, quietly and calmly. I'll probably never marry, he thought to himself.

But then one day, without the slightest warning, Tony Takitani fell in love. It happened with incredible suddenness. She was a publishing company part-timer who came to his office to pick up an illustration. Twenty-two years old, she was a quiet girl who wore a gentle smile the whole time she was in his office. Her features were pleasant enough, but objectively speaking, she was no great beauty. Still, there was something about her that gave Tony Takitani's heart a violent punch. The first moment he saw her, his chest tightened, and he could hardly breathe. Not even he could tell what it was about her that had struck him with such force. And even if it had become clear to him, it was not something he could have explained in words.

The next thing that caught his attention was the way she dressed. He had no particular interest in what people wore, nor was he the kind of man who would mentally register each article of clothing that a woman had on, but there was something so wonderful about the way this girl dressed herself that it made a deep impression on him: indeed, one could even say it moved him. There were plenty of women around who dressed smartly, and plenty more who dressed to impress, but this girl was different. Totally different. She wore her clothing with such utter naturalness and grace that she could have been a bird that had wrapped itself in a special wind as it made ready to fly off to another world. He had never seen a woman who wore her clothes with such apparent joy. And the clothes themselves looked as if, in being draped on her body, they had won new life for themselves.

"Thank you very much," she said as she took the illustration and walked out of his office, leaving him speechless for a time. He sat at his desk, dazed, doing nothing until evening came and the room turned completely dark.

The next day he phoned the publisher and found some pretext to have her come to his office again. When their business was finished, he invited her to lunch. They made small talk as they ate. Though fifteen years apart in age, they had much in common to talk about, almost strangely so. They clicked on every topic. He had never had such an experience before, and neither had she. Though somewhat nervous at first, she gradually relaxed until she was laughing and talking freely. You really know how to dress, said Tony Takitani when they parted. I like clothes, she said with a bashful smile. Most of my pay goes into clothing.

They dated a few times after that. They didn't go anywhere in particular, just found quiet places to sit and talk for hours—about their backgrounds, about their work, about the way they thought or felt about this or that. They never seemed to tire of talking with each other, as if they were filling up each other's emptiness. The fifth time they met, he asked her to marry him. But she had a boyfriend she had been dating since high school. Their relationship had become less than ideal with the passage of time, and now they seemed to fight about the stupidest things whenever they met. In fact, seeing him was nowhere nearly as free and fun as seeing Tony Takitani, but still, that didn't mean she could simply break it off. She had her reasons, whatever they were. And besides, there was that fifteen-year difference in age. She was still young and inexperienced. She wondered what that fifteen-year gap would mean to them in the future. She said she wanted time to think.

Each day that she spent thinking was another day in hell for Tony Takitani. He couldn't work. He drank, alone. Suddenly his solitude became a crushing weight, a source of agony, a prison. I just never noticed it before, he thought. With despairing eyes, he stared at the thickness and coldness of the walls surrounding him and thought, If she says she doesn't want to marry me, I might just kill myself.

He went to see her and told her exactly how he felt. How lonely his life had been until then. How much he had lost over the years. How she had made him realize all that.

She was an intelligent young woman. She had come to like this Tony Takitani. She had liked him from the start, and each meeting had only made her like him more. Whether she could call this love or not, she did not know. But she felt that he had something wonderful inside, and that she would be happy if she made her life with him. And so they married.

◎

By marrying her, Tony Takitani brought the lonely period of his life to an end. When he awoke in the morning, the first thing he did was look for her. When he found her sleeping next to him, he felt relief. When she was not there, he felt anxious and searched the house for her. There was something slightly odd for him about not being lonely. The very fact of having ceased to be lonely caused him to fear the possibility of becoming lonely again. The question haunted him: what would he do? Sometimes the fear would make him break out in a cold sweat. It went on like this for the first three months of their marriage. As he became used to his new life, though, and the possibility of her suddenly disappearing seemed to lessen, the fear gradually eased. In the end he settled down and steeped himself in his new and peaceful happiness.

One time the couple went to hear Shozaburo Takitani play. She wanted to know what kind of music her father-in-law was making. Do you think your father would mind if we went to hear him? she asked. Probably not, he said.

They went to a Ginza nightclub where Shozaburo Takitani was performing. This was the first time Tony Takitani had gone to hear his father play since childhood. Shozaburo Takitani was playing exactly the same music he had played in the old days, the same songs that Tony Takitani had heard so often on records when he was a boy. His father's style was smooth, elegant, sweet. It was not art. But it was music made by the skillful hand of a pro that could put a crowd in a good mood. Tony Takitani sat and listened to it, drinking much more than was usual for him.

Soon, however, as he lent his ear to the performance, something in the music began to make him feel like a narrow pipe filling quietly, but inexorably, with sludge. He found it increasingly difficult to breathe, or even to go on sitting there. He couldn't help feeling that the music he was hearing now was just slightly different from the music he remembered his father playing. That had been years ago, of course, and he had been listening with the ears of a child, after all, but the difference, it seemed to him, was terribly important. It was infinitesimal but crucial, and it was perfectly clear to him. He wanted to go up onto the stage, take his father by the arm, and ask, What is it, Father? Why is it so different? But of course he did nothing of the sort. For one thing, he could never have explained what was in his mind. And so he said nothing. Instead, he went on listening all the way to the end of his father's set, drinking whiskey and water. When it was over, he and his wife applauded and went home.

The couple's married life was free of shadows. The two never fought, and his work continued as successfully as ever. They spent many happy hours together, taking walks, going to movies, traveling. For someone so young, she was a remarkably capable housewife. She understood the virtue of moderation, she was quick and efficient with the household chores, and she never gave her husband anything to worry about. There was, however, one thing that did concern him somewhat, and that was her tendency to buy too many clothes. Confronted with a piece of clothing, she seemed incapable of restraint. In a flash, a strange look would come over her, and even her voice would change. The first time he saw this happen, Tony Takitani thought she had suddenly taken ill. True, he had noticed it before they married, but it started getting serious on their European honeymoon. She bought a shocking number of items during their travels. In Milan and Paris, she made the rounds of the boutiques from morning to night like one possessed. They did no touring at all. They never saw the Duomo or the Louvre. All he remembered from their trip was clothing stores. Valentino, Missoni, Yves Saint Laurent, Givenchy, Ferragamo, Armani, Cerruti, Gianfranco Ferré: with a mesmerized look in her eyes, she swept up everything she could get her hands on, and he followed after her, paying the bills. He almost worried that the raised numbers on his credit card might be worn down.

Her fever did not abate after they returned to Japan. She kept on buying new clothes almost every day. The number of articles of clothing in her possession skyrocketed. To hold them, he had several large armoires made to order. He also had a cabinet built for her shoes. Still there was not enough space for everything. In the end, he had an entire room made over as a walk-in closet. In their large house, they had rooms to spare, and money was no problem. Besides, she did such a marvelous job of wearing what she bought, and she looked so happy whenever she had new clothes, that Tony Takitani decided not to complain to her. Oh, well, he told himself, nobody's perfect.

When the volume of her clothing became too great to fit into the special room, though, even Tony Takitani began to have some misgivings. Once, when she was out, he counted her dresses. He calculated that she could change outfits twice a day and still not repeat herself for almost two years. Any way you looked at it, she had too many dresses. He could not understand why she had to keep buying herself clothing like this, one piece after the other. She was so busy buying them, she had no time to wear them. He wondered if she might have a psychological problem. If so, he would have to apply the brakes to her habit at some point.

He took the plunge one night after dinner. I wish you would consider cutting back somewhat on the way you buy clothing, he said. It's not a question of money, I'm not talking about that. I have absolutely no objection to your buying what you need, and it makes me happy to see you looking so pretty, but do you really need so many expensive dresses?

His wife lowered her gaze and thought about this for a time. Then she looked at him and said, You're right, of course, I don't need so many dresses, I know that. But even if I know it, I can't help myself. When I see a beautiful dress, I have to buy it. Whether I need it or not, or whether I have too many or not: that's beside the point. I just can't stop myself.

I will, though, try to cure myself, she said (adding that it was like a drug addiction). If I keep on going this way, the house is going to fill up with my clothing before too long. And so she locked herself in the house for a week, and managed to keep away from clothing stores. This was a time of great suffering for her. She felt as if she were walking on the surface of a planet with little air. She spent each day in her roomful of clothing, taking down one piece after another to gaze at it. She would caress the material, inhale its fragrance, slip the piece on, and look at herself in the mirror, never tiring of the sight. And the more she looked, the more she wanted something new. The desire for new clothing became unbearable.

She simply couldn't stand it.

She did, however, love her husband deeply. And she respected him. She knew that he was right. I don't need this much clothing. I have only one body to wear it on. She called one of her favorite boutiques and asked the proprietor if she might be allowed to return a coat and dress that she had bought ten days earlier but had never worn. That would be fine, madame, she was told; if you will bring them in, we will be glad to take them back. She was one of their very best customers, of course; they could do that much for her. She put the coat and dress in her blue Renault Cinque and drove to the fashionable Aoyama district. There she returned the clothes and received a credit on her card. She thanked them and hurried to her car, trying not to look at anything else, then drove straight down the highway to home. She had a certain feeling of lightness at having returned the pieces. Yes, she told herself, it was true: I did not need those things. I have enough coats and dresses for the rest of my life. But as she waited at the head of the line for a red light to change, the coat and dress were all she could think about. Colors, cut, and texture: she remembered them in vivid detail. She could picture them as clearly as if she had them in front of her. A film of sweat broke out on her forehead. Forearms pressed against the steering wheel, she drew in a long, deep breath and closed her eyes. When she opened them again, she saw the light change to green. Instinctively, she stepped down on the accelerator.

A large truck that was trying to make it across the intersection on a yellow light slammed into the side of her Renault at full speed. She never felt a thing.

Tony Takitani was left with a room full of size 7 dresses and 112 pairs of shoes. He had no idea what to do with them. He was not going to keep everything his wife had worn for the rest of his life, so he called a dealer and had him take away at least the hats and other accessories for the first price the man offered. Stockings and underthings he bunched together and burned in the garden incinerator. There were simply too many dresses and shoes to deal with, so he left them where they were. After the funeral, he shut himself in the huge walk-in closet, staring all day at the rows of dresses that filled every available bit of space.

Ten days later, Tony Takitani put an ad in the newspaper for a female assistant, dress size 7, height approximately 161 centimeters, shoe size 22 centimeters, good pay, favorable working conditions. Because the salary he quoted was abnormally high, thirteen women showed up to be interviewed in his studio-cum-office in Minami-Aoyama. Five of them were obviously lying about their dress size. From the remaining eight, he chose the one whose build was closest to his wife's, a woman in her mid-twenties with an unremarkable face. She wore a plain white blouse and tight blue skirt. Her clothes and shoes were neat and clean, but they were definitely showing signs of age.

Tony Takitani said to the woman, The work itself is not very difficult. You just come to the office every day from nine to five, answer the telephone, deliver illustrations, pick up materials for me, make copies. That sort of thing. There is only one condition attached. I've recently lost my wife, and I have a huge amount of her clothing at home. Most of what she left is new or almost new. I would like you to wear her things as a kind of uniform while you work here, which is why I specified dress size and shoe size and height as conditions for employment. I know this must sound strange to you, but believe me, I have no ulterior motive. It's just to give me time to get used to the idea that my wife is gone. I'll have to make small adjustments to the atmospheric pressure or whatever it is. I need a period of time like that. And during that period, I'd like to have you nearby wearing her clothing. That way, I'm pretty sure, it will finally come home to me that my wife is dead and gone.

Biting her lip, the young woman immediately set her mind to work. It was, as he said, a very strange request—so strange, in fact, that she could not fully comprehend it. She understood the part about his wife's having died recently. And she understood the part about the wife's having left behind a lot of clothing. But she could not quite grasp why she herself should have to work in the wife's clothes in his presence. Normally, she would have had to assume that there was more to it than met the eye. But, she thought, this man did not seem to be a bad person. You had only to listen to the way he talked to know that. Maybe losing his wife had done something to his mind, but he didn't look like the type of man who would let that kind of thing cause him to harm another person. And finally, whatever the case, she needed work. She had been searching for a job for a very long time, and her unemployment insurance would run out the following month. Then she wouldn't be able to pay the rent. And probably, too, she would never again find a job that paid as well as this one did.

I think I understand, she said. Though not exactly. And I think I can do what you are asking me to do. But first I wonder if you can show me the clothes I will have to wear. I had better check to see if they really are my size. Of course, said Tony Takitani, and he took the woman to his house and showed her the room. She had never seen so many dresses gathered together in a single place outside of a department store, and each dress was obviously a quality piece that had cost a lot of money. The taste, too, was flawless. The sight was almost blinding. The woman could hardly catch her breath. Her heart started pounding for no reason at all. It felt like sexual arousal, she realized.

Suggesting that she check the fit, Tony Takitani left the woman alone in the room. She pulled herself together and tried on a few dresses hanging nearby. She tried on some shoes as well. Everything fit as though it had been made for her. She took one dress after another in hand and looked at it. She ran her fingertips over the material and breathed in its fragrance. Hundreds of beautiful dresses were hanging there in rows. Before long, tears welled up in her eyes. She could not stop herself from crying. The tears poured out of her. There was no way to hold them back. Her body swathed in a dress of the woman who had died, she stood utterly still, sobbing, struggling to keep the sound from escaping her throat. Soon Tony Takitani came to see how she was doing. Why are you crying? he asked. I don't know, she answered, shaking her head. I've never seen so many beautiful dresses before. I think it must have upset me. I'm sorry. She dried her tears with a handkerchief.

If it's all right with you, I'd like to have you start at the office tomorrow, Tony Takitani said in a businesslike manner. Pick out a week's worth of dresses and shoes and take them home with you.

The woman devoted much time to choosing six days' worth of dresses. Then she chose matching shoes. She packed everything into suitcases. Take a coat, too, said Tony Takitani, you don't want to be cold. She chose a warm-looking gray cashmere coat. It was so light, it could have been made of feathers. She had never held such a lightweight coat in her life.

When the woman was gone, Tony Takitani went back into his wife's clothing room, closed the door, and let his eyes wander vacantly over her dresses. He could not understand why the woman had cried when she saw them. To him, they looked like shadows that his wife had left behind.

Size 7 shadows of his wife hung there in long rows, layer upon layer, as if someone had gathered and hung up samples of the infinite possibilities (or at least the theoretically infinite possibilities) implied in the existence of a human being.

These shadows had once clung to his wife's body, which had endowed them with the warm breath of life, and made them move. Now, however, what hung before him were mere scruffy shadows cut off from the roots of life and steadily withering away. What were they now but worn-out old dresses devoid of any meaning whatsoever? Their rich colors danced in space like pollen rising from flowers, lodging in his eyes and ears and nostrils. The frills and buttons and epaulettes and lace and pockets and belts sucked greedily at the room's air, thinning it out until he could hardly breathe. Liberal numbers of mothballs gave off a smell that might as well have been the soundless sound of a million tiny winged insects. He hated these dresses now, it suddenly occurred to him. Slumping against the wall, he folded his arms and closed his eyes. Loneliness seeped into him once again like a lukewarm broth of darkness. It's all over now, he told himself. No matter what I do, it's over.

He called the woman and told her to forget about the job. There was no longer any work for her to do, he said, apologizing. But how can that be? the woman asked, stunned. I'm sorry, but the situation has changed, he said. You can have the clothes and shoes you took home. I'll give them to you, and the suitcases, too. I just want you to forget this ever happened, and please don't tell anyone about it, either. The woman could make nothing of this, and the more she pressed for answers the more pointless it seemed. I see, she said finally, and hung up.

For some minutes, the woman felt angry at Tony Takitani. But soon she came to feel that things had probably worked out for the best. The whole business had been peculiar from the start. She was sorry to have lost the job, but she figured she would manage somehow or other.

She unpacked the dresses she had brought home from Tony Takitani's house, smoothed them out, and hung them in her wardrobe. The shoes she put into the shoe cabinet by the front door. Compared with these new arrivals, her own clothes and shoes looked horrendously shabby. She felt as if they were a totally different type of matter, fashioned of materials in another dimension. She took off the blouse and skirt she had worn to the interview, hung them up, and changed into jeans and a sweatshirt. Then she sat on the floor, drinking a cold beer. Recalling the mountain of dresses she had seen in Tony Takitani's house, she heaved a sigh. So many beautiful dresses, she thought. And that "closet": it was bigger than my whole apartment. Imagine the time and money that must have gone into buying all those clothes! But now the woman who did it is dead. And she left a roomful of size 7 dresses. I wonder what it must feel like to die and leave so many gorgeous dresses behind.

The woman's friends were well aware that she was poor, so they were amazed to see her wearing a new dress every time they got together— and each one a sophisticated, expensive brand. Where did you ever get a dress like that? they would ask her. I promised not to tell, she would say, shaking her head. And besides, even if I told you, you wouldn't believe me.

◎

In the end, Tony Takitani had a used-clothing dealer take away every piece of clothing his wife had left behind. The dealer gave him less than a twentieth of what he had paid, but that didn't matter to him. He could have let them all go for nothing, as long as someone took them away. Away to a place where he could never see them again.

Once it was emptied out, Tony Takitani left the room empty for a long, long time.

Every once in a while, he would go to the room and stay there for an hour or two doing nothing in particular, just letting his mind go blank. He would sit on the floor and stare at the bare walls, at the shadows of his dead wife's shadows. But as the months went by he lost the ability to recall the things that used to be in the room. The memory of their colors and smells faded away almost before he knew it. Even the vivid emotions he had once cherished drew back, as if retreating from the province of his memory. Like a mist in the breeze, his memories changed shape, and with each change they grew fainter. Each memory was now the shadow of a shadow of a shadow. The only thing that remained tangible to him was the sense of absence. Sometimes he could barely recall his wife's face. What he often did recall, though, was the woman, a total stranger, shedding tears in the room at the sight of the dresses that his wife had left behind. He recalled her unremarkable face and her worn-out patent leather shoes. With that, her quiet sobbing rekindled in his memory. He did not want to remember such things, but they came back to life before he knew it was happening. Long after he had forgotten all kinds of things, including the woman's name, her image remained strangely unforgettable.

Two years after his wife died, Tony Takitani's father died of liver cancer. Shozaburo Takitani suffered little for someone with cancer, and his time in the hospital was short. He died almost as if falling asleep. In that sense he lived a charmed life to the end. Aside from a little cash and some stock certificates, Shozaburo Takitani left nothing that could be called property. There was only his instrument, and a gigantic collection of old jazz records. Tony Takitani left the records in the cartons supplied by the moving company, and stacked them up on the floor of the empty room. Because the records smelled of mold, Tony Takitani had to open the windows in the room at regular intervals to change the air. Otherwise, he never set foot in the place.

A year went by this way, but having the mountain of records in the house began to bother him more and more. Often the mere thought of them sitting in there made it difficult for him to breathe. Sometimes, too, he would wake in the middle of the night and be unable to get back to sleep. His memories had grown indistinct, but they were still there, where they had always been, with all the weight that memories can have.

◎

He called a used-record dealer and had him make an offer for the collection. Because it contained many valuable discs that had long been out of print, he received a remarkably high payment—enough to buy a small car. To him, however, the money meant nothing.

Once the mountain of records had disappeared from his house, Tony Takitani was really alone.

—TRANSLATED BY JAY RUBIN

THE RISE AND FALL OF
SHARPIE CAKES

Half awake, I was reading the morning paper when an ad down in one corner caught my eye: "Celebrated Sharpie Cakes, Manufacturer Seeking New Products. Major Informational Seminar." I had never heard of Sharpie Cakes before; they were obviously some kind of cake. I am especially demanding where confections are concerned, and I had plenty of time on my hands. I decided to go see what this "major informational seminar" was all about.

It took place in a hotel ballroom, and tea and cakes were served. The cakes, of course, were Sharpies. I tried one, but I couldn't say I liked it very much. It had a sticky-sweet texture, and the crust was too dry. I couldn't believe that hip young people would enjoy a sweet like this.

Still, everyone attending the informational meeting was either my age or younger. I was given ticket number 952, and at least a hundred people came after me, which meant there were upward of a thousand people at this meeting. Pretty impressive.

Sitting next to me was a girl around twenty wearing thick glasses. She was no beauty, but she seemed to have a nice personality.

"Say, have you ever eaten these Sharpie things before?" I asked her.

"Of course," she said. "They're famous."

"Yeah, but they're not very—" I started to say, when she gave me a kick in the foot. The people around us were throwing angry glances my way. The mood turned nasty, but I got through it with my most innocent Winnie-the-Pooh look.

"Are you crazy?" the girl whispered to me afterward. "Coming to a place like this and bad-mouthing Sharpies? The Sharpie Crows could get you. You'd never make it home alive."

"The Sharpie Crows?" I exclaimed. "What the—"

"Shhhh!" the girl stopped me. The meeting was about to start.

The president of the Sharpie Cake Company opened the proceedings with a brief history of Sharpies. It was one of those dubious "factual" accounts about how somebody-or-other way back in the eighth century whipped together some ingredients to make the very first Sharpie. He claimed there was a poem about Sharpies in the Kokinshu imperial anthology of 905. I was ready to laugh out loud at that one, but everybody was listening so intently, I stopped myself. Besides, I was worried about the Sharpie Crows.

The president's speech went on for an hour. It was incredibly boring. All he wanted to say was that Sharpies are a confection with a long tradition behind it, which he could have just said in so many words.

The managing director appeared next to explain the call for new Sharpie Cake products. Sharpies were a great national confection boasting a long history, he said, but even an outstanding product such as this needed new blood to go on growing and developing dialectically in ways suited to each new age. This may have sounded good, but basically he was just saying that the taste of Sharpies was too old-fashioned now and sales were dropping, so they needed new ideas from young people. He could have said *that* in so many words.

On the way out I got a copy of the Rules for Submission. You had to make a confection based on Sharpies and deliver it to the company one month later. Prize money: two million yen. If I had two million yen I could marry my girlfriend and move into a new apartment. I decided to make a new Sharpie Cake.

As I said before, I can be rather demanding where confections are concerned. And I can make just about anything myself in just about any style: bean jam, cream fillings, pie crusts. It would be easy for me to create a contemporary version of Sharpies in a month. On the due date, I baked two dozen new Sharpie Cakes and brought them to the reception desk at the Sharpie Cake Company.

"They look *good*," said the girl at the counter.

"They *are* good," I said.

One month later I received a call from the Sharpie company asking me to come to their offices the following day. I went there with a tie on and was met in the reception room by the managing director.

"The new Sharpie Cake you submitted has been very well received by the staff," he said. "Especially the, uh, younger members of the staff."

"I'm very glad to hear that," I said.

"On the other hand, however, there are those among the older employees who—how shall I put this?—who say that what you have made is not a Sharpie Cake. We have a real debate going."

"I see," I said, wondering what he was getting at.

"And so, the, uh, board of directors has decided to leave the decision up to Their Holinesses the Sharpie Crows."

"The Sharpie Crows?" I exclaimed. "What are the Sharpie Crows?"

The managing director gave me a confused look. "Do you mean to say you entered this competition without knowing anything about the Sharpie Crows?"

"I'm sorry. I lead a kind of sheltered life."

"This is terrible," he said. "If you don't know about the Sharpie Crows, then . . ." He stopped himself. "Oh, well, never mind. Please come with me."

I followed the director out of the room, down the hall, up an elevator to the sixth floor, then down another hall, at the end of which was a large iron door. The director pushed a buzzer, and a heavyset guard appeared. Once he had confirmed that it was the managing director, he opened the massive door. Security was tight.

"Their Holinesses the Sharpie Crows live in here," said the director. "They are a special family of birds. For centuries they have eaten nothing but Sharpie Cakes to stay alive."

No further explanation was necessary. There were over a hundred crows in the cavernous room, which was like a storehouse with fifteen-foot ceilings and long poles stretching from wall to wall. In tightly packed rows on each pole were perched the Sharpie Crows. They were far larger than ordinary crows, a good three feet in length. Even the smaller ones were at least two feet long. They had no eyes, I realized. Where their eyes should have been, they had globs of white fat. Their bodies were swollen to the point of bursting.

When the crows heard us come in, they started flapping their wings and raising a cry. At first, it sounded like a formless roar to me, but as my ears became accustomed to it, I realized they seemed to be screaming, "Sharpies! Sharpies!" They were horrifying creatures to behold.

From a box in his hands, the director scattered Sharpie Cakes on the floor, in response to which all hundred-plus birds leaped down upon the cakes. In their fever to reach the Sharpie Cakes, the crows pecked at each other's feet and eyes. No wonder they had lost their eyes!

Next the director took something resembling Sharpie Cakes from another box, and scattered those on the floor. "Watch this," he said to me. "This is a recipe that was eliminated from the competition."

The birds thronged down as they had earlier, but as soon as they realized the cakes were not true Sharpies, they spit them out and raised angry squawks:

Sharpies!

Sharpies!

Sharpies!

Their cries echoed off the ceiling until my ears began to hurt.

"You see? They will only eat genuine Sharpies," smirked the director. "They won't touch an imitation."

Sharpies!

Sharpies!

Sharpies!

"Now, let's try it with your new Sharpie Cakes. If they eat them, you win. If not, you lose."

Uh-oh, something told me this was not going to work. They should never have let a bunch of stupid birds decide the results of the competition. Unaware of my misgivings, the director vigorously scattered my "New Sharpies" on the floor. Again the crows pounced, and then all hell broke loose. Some of the birds ate my Sharpies with gusto, but others spit them out and screamed, "Sharpies! Sharpies!" And still others, unable to reach the cakes, went into a frenzy and started pecking at the throats of the birds that were eating. Blood flew everywhere. One crow pounced on a cake that another had spit out, but yet another gigantic crow latched on to this one and, with a cry of "Sharpies!" ripped the first one's stomach open. From then on it was a total free-for-all, blood calling forth more blood, rage leading to rage. This was all happening over some ridiculous sweets, but to the birds the cakes were everything. Whether a cake was a Sharpie or a non-Sharpie was a matter of life and death to them.

"Now look what you've done!" I said to the director. "You just threw the cakes in front of them like that all of a sudden. The stimulus was too strong."

Then I exited the room by myself, took the elevator down, and left the Sharpie Cakes building. I hated to lose the two million yen in prize money, but I was not going to live the rest of my long life connected with these damned crows.

From now on I would make and eat the food that *I* wanted to eat. The damned Sharpie Crows could peck each other to death for all I cared.

—TRANSLATED BY JAY RUBIN

THE ICE MAN

My husband's an Ice Man.

The first time I met him was at a hotel at a ski resort. It's hard to imagine a more appropriate place to meet an Ice Man. He was in the lobby of the hotel, noisy and crowded with hordes of young people, seated in a corner as far as possible from the fireplace, quietly absorbed in a book. It was nearly noon, but the clear, cold morning light seemed to shine on him alone. *"That's an Ice Man,"* one of my friends whispered. At the time I had no idea what sort of person an Ice Man was, and my friend couldn't help me out. All she knew was that he was the sort of person who went by the name of Ice Man. "They must call him that because he's made out of ice," she added, a serious look on her face. As serious as if the topic wasn't an Ice Man but a ghost, or someone with a contagious disease.

The Ice Man looked young, though that was offset by the white strands, like patches of leftover snow, mixed in among his stiff, wiry head of hair. He was tall, his cheeks were sharply chiseled, like frozen crags, his fingers covered with frost that looked like it would never, ever melt. Other than this, he looked perfectly normal. He wasn't handsome, exactly, though some would find him quite appealing. There was something about him that pierced right through you. Especially his eyes, and that silent, transparent look that gleamed like an icicle on a winter's morning—the sole glint of life in an otherwise provisional body. I stood there for a while, gazing at the Ice Man from across the lobby. He was absorbed in his book, never once moving or looking up, as if trying to convince himself that he was utterly alone.

The next afternoon he was in the same spot, as before, reading his book. When I went to the dining room for lunch, and when I came back with my friends from skiing in the evening, he was always there, seated in the same chair, the same look in his eyes as he scanned the pages of the same book as before. And the next day was exactly the same. Dawn to dusk found him seated alone, quietly reading, for all the world like part of the frozen winter scene outside.

On the afternoon of the fourth day, I made up an excuse and didn't join everyone on the slopes. Instead, I stayed behind in the hotel, wandering around the lobby. With everyone out skiing, the lobby was like an abandoned city. The air there was sticky and hot, filled with a strangely depressing odor—the smell of snow that had clung to the soles of people's boots and had slowly melted in front of the fireplace. I gazed out the windows, leafed through a newspaper. Finally I worked up my courage, went over to the Ice Man, and spoke to him. I'm pretty shy, and hardly ever strike up a conversation with a stranger, but I couldn't help myself. I *had* to talk to him. This was my last night in the hotel and if I let this chance pass I probably would never have another.

You're not skiing? I asked, trying to sound casual. The Ice Man slowly raised his head, looking like he was carefully listening to the wind blowing far away. He gazed intently at me and then quietly shook his head. I don't ski, he said. I'm fine just reading and looking out at the snow. His words floated up in the air, a white comic-book bubble of dialogue, every word visible before me. He gently wiped away some of the frost from his fingers.

I had no idea what to say next. I blushed and stood there, rooted to the spot. The Ice Man gazed into my eyes and gave what looked like a faint smile. Or was it? Had he really smiled? Maybe I was just imagining it. Would you like to sit down? he said. I know you're curious about me, so let's talk for a while. You want to know what an Ice Man is like, right? He chuckled. It's all right, he added. There's nothing to be afraid of. You're not going to catch a cold just talking to me.

We sat on a sofa in a corner of the lobby, hesitantly talking as we watched the swirling snow outside. I ordered a cup of hot cocoa, but the Ice Man didn't drink anything. He was just as shy as I was. On top of which, we had little in common to talk about. We talked about the weather at first, then the hotel. Did you come here alone? I asked him. I did, he responded. Do you like skiing? he asked. Not particularly, I replied. Some of my girlfriends dragged me here. I can barely ski. I was dying to find out more about what an Ice Man was all about. Was he really made out of ice? What did he eat? Where did he live in the summer? Did he have a family? Those sorts of questions. Unfortunately, the Ice Man didn't talk about himself at all, and I didn't dare ask the questions that whirled around in my head. I figured he didn't feel like talking about those things.

Instead he talked about me, who I am. It's hard to believe, but he knew everything there was to know about me. Who was in my family, my age, interests, my health, what school I was attending, my friends. He knew it all. Even things I'd long forgotten, he knew everything about.

I don't get it, I blushed. I felt like I had been stripped naked in front of people. How do you know so much about me? I asked. Are you a mind reader?

No, the Ice Man said, I can't read minds. I just know these things. Like I'm looking deep into a clear block of ice. When I gaze at you like this, I can see everything about you.

Can you see my future? I asked.

No, not the future, he replied blankly, slowly shaking his head. I'm not interested in the future. I have no concept of the future. Ice contains no future, just the past, sealed away. As if they're alive, everything in the world is sealed up inside, clear and distinct. Ice can preserve all kinds of things that way—cleanly, clearly. That's the essence of ice, the role it plays.

I'm glad, I replied, and smiled. I was relieved—there was no way I wanted to hear about my future.

◎

We got together a few times after we returned to Tokyo, eventually dating every weekend. We didn't go on typical dates, to see movies, or spend time in coffee shops. We didn't even go out to eat. The Ice Man hardly ever ate. Instead we'd spend time on a park bench, side by side, talking. We discussed all kinds of subjects, yet not once did the Ice Man talk about himself. Why is this? I asked one day. Why don't you ever talk about yourself? I want to know more about you—where you were born, what kind of parents you had, how you came to be an Ice Man. The Ice Man gazed at me for a while, then slowly shook his head. I don't know the answer to those things, he responded quietly and decisively, exhaling his hard white breath. I have no past. I know the past of everything else, and preserve it. But I have no past myself. I have no idea where I was born. I don't know what my parents looked like, or whether I even had any. I don't know how old I am, or if I even have an age.

The Ice Man was as isolated and alone as an iceberg floating in the darkness.

I fell deeply in love with him, and he came to love me, the present me, apart from any past or future. And I came to love the Ice Man for who he is now, apart from any past or future. It was a wonderful thing. We began to talk about getting married. I had just turned twenty, and the Ice Man was the first person I'd ever truly loved. What loving him really meant was, at the time, beyond me. But that would have been true even if it hadn't been the Ice Man I was in love with then.

My mother and older sister were totally opposed to our marriage. You're too young to get married, they argued. You don't know the man's background—even where or when he was born. How are we supposed to explain that to our relatives? And listen, they went on, he's an Ice Man, so what happens if he melts? You don't seem to understand this, but when you get married you take on certain responsibilities. How can an Ice Man possibly fulfill his duties as a husband?

Their fears were groundless, however. The Ice Man wasn't really made out of ice. He was just as cold as ice. So even if it got hot, he wasn't about to melt. He was cold, all right, but this wasn't the kind of cold that was going to rob someone else of his body heat.

So we got married. No one celebrated our wedding. No one—not my friends, or relatives, or my family—was happy about us getting married. We didn't even have a wedding ceremony. The Ice Man didn't have a family register, so even a civil ceremony was out. The two of us simply decided that we were married. We bought a small cake and ate it, just the two of us. That was our ceremony. We rented a small apartment, and the Ice Man took a job at a refrigerated meat warehouse. The cold never bothered him, of course, and he never got tired, no matter how hard he worked. He never even ate very much. So his boss really liked him, and paid him more than any of his fellow employees. We lived a quiet life, just the two of us, not bothered by anyone else, not troubling anybody.

When we made love, I always pictured a solitary, silent clump of ice off somewhere. Hard ice, as hard as it could possibly be, the largest chunk of ice in the entire world. It was somewhere far away, though the Ice Man must know where that chunk of ice is. What he did was convey a memory of that ice. The first few times we made love, I was confused, but soon I grew used to it. I grew to love it when he took me in his arms. As always, he never said a word about himself, not even why he became an Ice Man, and I never asked him. The two of us simply held each other in the darkness, sharing that enormous ice, inside of which the world's past, millions of years' worth, was preserved.

Our married life was fine. We loved each other, and everyone left us alone. People found it hard at first to get used to the Ice Man, but after a while they started to talk with him. An Ice Man's not so different from anybody else, they concluded. But deep down, I knew they didn't accept him, and they didn't accept me for having married him. We're different people from *them,* they concluded, and the gulf separating them and us will never be filled.

We tried but failed to have a baby, perhaps because of a genetic difference between humans and Ice Men that made having children difficult. Without a baby to keep me busy, I found I had a lot of spare time on my hands. I'd straighten up the house in the morning, but after that had nothing to keep me busy. I didn't have any friends to talk to or go out with, and I didn't know anybody in the neighborhood. My mother and sister were still angry with me over marrying an Ice Man, and refused to get in touch. I was the family black sheep they were embarrassed about. There was no one to talk to, even over the phone. While the Ice Man was working in the warehouse, I stayed alone at home, reading or listening to music. I was a bit of a homebody anyway, and didn't mind being by myself all that much. Still, I was young, and couldn't put up with such a monotonous routine for long. Boredom didn't bother me as much as the sheer repetitiveness of each day. I started to see myself as nothing more than a repetitive shadow within that daily routine.

So, one day I suggested to my husband that we take a trip somewhere to break up the routine. A trip? the Ice Man asked, his eyes narrowing. Why would you want to go on a trip? You're not happy the way we are, just the two of us?

No, that's not it, I replied. I'm perfectly happy. We get along fine. It's just that I'm bored. I'd like to go someplace far away, see things I've never seen before, experience something new. Do you know what I mean? And besides, we never went on a honeymoon. We have enough saved up, plus you have plenty of vacation time. It would be nice to take a leisurely vacation for once.

The Ice Man let out a deep, nearly freezing sigh, which crystallized audibly in the air, then brought his long, frost-covered fingers together on his lap. Well, he said, if you really want to go on a trip that much, I don't see why not. I don't think traveling is all that great, but I'll do whatever it takes to make you happy, go wherever you want. I've worked hard at the warehouse and should be able to take some time off. It shouldn't be a problem. But where would you like to go?

How about the South Pole? I said. I picked the South Pole because I was sure the Ice Man would be interested in going there. And, truth be told, I'd always wanted to go see it. To see the aurora, and the penguins. I had this wonderful mental picture of myself in a hooded parka underneath the aurora, playing with the penguins.

The Ice Man looked deep into my eyes, unblinking. His look was like a sharply pointed icicle piercing deep into my brain. He was silent for a while, thinking, then with a twinkle in his voice he said, All right. If you'd really like to go to the South Pole then let's do it. You're sure that's where you want to go?

I nodded.

I can take a long vacation in a couple of weeks, he said. You should be able to get everything ready for the trip in the meantime. That's all right with you?

I couldn't respond. His icicle stare had frozen my brain and I couldn't think.

As the days passed, though, I started to regret bringing up the idea to my husband of a trip to the South Pole. I'm not sure why. It's like ever since I mentioned the name "South Pole" he changed. His eyes grew more piercing and icicle-like than ever, his breath whiter, his fingers covered with an increasing amount of frost. He was quieter than before, and more stubborn. And he was no longer eating, which had me worried. Five days before we were set to depart I decided I had to say something. Let's not go to the South Pole after all, I said to him. It's too cold, and might not be good for us. It'd be better to go to some ordinary place— Europe or Spain or somewhere. We could drink some wine, eat some paella, watch a bullfight or two. But my husband ignored me. He had this faraway look for a while, then turned to me and looked deep into my eyes. His stare went so deep I felt like my body was about to vanish right then and there. No, my husband the Ice Man said flatly, Spain doesn't interest me. I'm sorry, but it's just too hot and dusty. And the food's too spicy. And I already bought our tickets to the South Pole, and a fur coat and fur-lined boots for you. We can't let those go to waste. We can't just back out now.

To tell you the truth, I was frightened. If we went to the South Pole, I felt sure something terrible was going to happen to us. I had the same awful dream night after night. I'm walking somewhere when I fall into a deep hole. Nobody finds me and I freeze solid. I'm frozen inside the ice, gazing up at the sky. I'm conscious but can't even move a finger. It's such a weird feeling. With each passing moment I'm becoming part of the past. There is no future for me, just the past steadily accumulating. Everybody is watching this happening to me. They're watching the past, watching as I slip further and further away.

Then I wake up and find the Ice Man sleeping beside me. He makes no sound as he sleeps, like something frozen and dead. I love him, though. I start to cry, my tears wetting his cheeks. He awakens and holds me close. I had an awful dream, I tell him. In the darkness he slowly shakes his head. It was only a dream, he says. Dreams come from the past, not from the future. Dreams shouldn't control you—you should control *them*.

You're right, I say—but I'm not at all certain.

So we ended up taking a plane to the South Pole. I couldn't find a reason to call off our trip. The pilots and stewardesses in our plane barely said a word the whole way. I was hoping to enjoy the scenery as we flew, but the clouds were so thick I couldn't see a thing. Before long, the windows were covered with a thick film of ice. All this time, my husband just quietly read a book. I felt none of the usual excitement and happiness you feel as you set out on a trip, merely the feeling that we were fulfilling what we'd set out to do.

As we walked down the ramp and first set foot at the South Pole, I could feel my husband's whole body tremble. It all happened in the blink of an eye, in half an instant, and his expression didn't change a jot, so no one else noticed. But I didn't miss it. Something inside him sent a quiet yet intense jolt through him. I stared at his face. He stood there, looked up at the sky, then at his hands, and then let out a deep breath. He looked over at me and smiled. So this is where you wanted to come? he asked. That's right, I replied.

I knew the South Pole was going to be a lonely place, but it turned out to be lonelier than anything I could have imagined. Hardly anyone lived there. There was just one small featureless town, with one equally featureless hotel. The South Pole isn't much of a tourist destination. There weren't even any penguins, not to mention any aurora. Occasionally I'd stop passersby and ask where the penguins were, but they'd merely shake their head. They couldn't understand my words, so I'd end up sketching a penguin on a piece of paper to show them, but all I got was the same response—a silent shake of the head. I felt so alone. Step outside the town and all you saw was ice. No trees, no flowers, rivers, or ponds. Ice and nothing but—a frozen wasteland as far as the eye could see.

My husband, on the other hand, with his white breath, frosty fingers, and faraway look in his icicle eyes, strode tirelessly here and there. It wasn't long before he learned the language and spoke with the locals in hard, icy tones. They talked for hours, intense looks on their faces, but I didn't have a clue what they could be talking about. My husband was entranced by the whole place. Something about it appealed to him. It upset me at first, and I felt like I was left behind, betrayed and abandoned.

Finally, though, in the midst of this silent, icy world, all strength drained out of me, ebbing away bit by bit. Even, in the end, the strength to feel upset by my situation. My emotional compass had vanished. I lost all sense of direction, of time, of the sense of who I was. I don't know when it began, or when it ended, but before I knew it I was locked away, alone and numb in the endless winter of that world of ice. Even after I'd lost almost all sensation, I still knew this: *The husband here at the South Pole is not the husband I used to know.* I couldn't say how he'd changed, exactly, for he still was always thoughtful, always had kind words for me. And I knew he sincerely meant the things he said. But I also knew that the Ice Man before me now was not the Ice Man I'd first met at the ski resort. But who was I going to complain to? All the South Pole people liked him a lot, and they couldn't understand a word I said. With white breath and frosty faces they talked, joked around, and sang songs in that distinctively spirited language of theirs. I stayed shut up in my hotel room gazing out at the gray skies that wouldn't clear for months, struggling to learn the complicated grammar of the South Pole language, something I knew I'd never master.

There weren't any more airplanes at the airport. After the plane that carried us here departed no more landed. By this time the runway was buried beneath a hard sheet of ice. Just like my heart.

Winter's come, my husband said. A long, long winter. No planes will come, no ships either. Everything's frozen solid, he said. All we can do is wait for spring.

It was three months after we'd come to the South Pole that I realized I was pregnant. And I knew one thing: that the baby I was going to give birth to would be a tiny Ice Man. My womb had frozen over, a thin sheet of ice mixed in with my amniotic fluid. I could feel that chill deep inside my belly. And I knew this, too: my child would have the same icicle eyes as his father, the same frost-covered fingers. And I knew one more thing: our new little family would never step outside the South Pole again. The outrageous weight of the eternal past had grabbed us and wasn't about to let go. We'd never be able to shake free.

My heart is just about gone now. The warmth I used to have has retreated somewhere far away. Sometimes I even forget that warmth ever existed. I'm still able to cry, though. I'm completely alone, in the coldest, loneliest place in the world. When I cry, my husband kisses my cheeks, turning my tears to ice. He peels off those frozen tears and puts them on his tongue. You know I love you, he says. And I know it's true. The Ice Man does love me. But the wind blows his frozen words further and further into the past. And I cry some more, icy tears welling up endlessly in our frozen little home in the far-off South Pole.

—TRANSLATED BY PHILIP GABRIEL

CRABS

They ran across the little restaurant entirely by accident. It was the evening of their first night in Singapore and they were walking near a beach when, on a whim, they ducked into a side street and happened to pass by the place. The restaurant was a one-story building surrounded by a waist-high brick wall, with a garden with low palm trees and five wooden tables. The stucco main building was painted a bright pink. Each table had its own faded umbrella opened over it. It was still early and the place was nearly deserted. Just two old men with short hair, Chinese apparently, sat across from each other, drinking beer and silently eating a variety of snacks. They didn't say a word to each other. On the ground at their feet a large black dog lay there wearily, its eyes half-closed. A ghostly trail of steam streamed out of the kitchen window, and the tempting smell of something cooking. The happy voices of the cooks filtered out as well, along with the clatter of pots and pans. The palm fronds on the trees, trembling in the slight breeze, stood out in the sinking sun.

The woman came to a halt, taking in the scene.

"How about having dinner here?" she asked.

The young man read the name of the restaurant at the entrance and looked around for a menu. But there wasn't a menu posted outside. He gave it some thought. "Hmm. I don't know. You know, eating at some place we're not sure of in a foreign country."

"But I've got a sixth sense about restaurants. I can always sniff out the really good ones. And this one's definitely great. I guarantee it. Why don't we try it?"

The man closed his eyes and took a deep breath. He had no idea what kind of food they made here, but he had to admit it did smell pretty tempting. And the restaurant itself had a certain charm to it. "But do you think it's clean?"

She tugged at his arm. "You're too sensitive. Don't worry. We've flown all this way here, so we should be a little more adventurous. I don't want to eat in the restaurant in the hotel every day. That's boring. Come on, let's give it a try."

Once inside they realized that the place specialized in crab dishes. The menu was written in English and Chinese. Most of the customers were locals, and the prices were quite reasonable. According to the menu Singapore boasts dozens of varieties of crabs, with over a hundred types of crab dishes. The man and the woman ordered Singapore beer, and after looking over what was available, selected several crab dishes and shared them. The portions were generous, the ingredients all fresh, the seasoning just right.

"This really *is* good," the man said, impressed.

"See? What'd I tell you? I told you I have the power to find the best. Now do you believe me?"

"Yep. Have to say I do," the young man admitted.

"This kind of power really comes in handy," the woman said. "You know, eating's much more important than most people think. There comes a time in your life when you've just got to have something super-delicious. And when you're standing at that crossroads your whole life can change, depending on which one you go into—the good restaurant or the awful one. It's like—do you fall on this side of the fence, or the other side."

"Interesting," he said. "Life can be pretty scary, can't it?"

"Exactly," she said, and held up a mischievous finger. "Life is a scary thing. More than you can ever imagine."

The young man nodded. "And we happened to fall on the inside of the fence, didn't we."

"Exactly."

"That's good," the young man said dispassionately. "Do you like crab?"

"Mm, I've always loved it. How about you?"

"I love it. I wouldn't mind eating crab every day."

"A new point we have in common," she beamed.

The man smiled, and the two of them raised their glasses in another toast.

"We've got to come back tomorrow," she said. "There can't be many places like this in the world. I mean, it's so delicious—and look at the prices."

⊚

For the next three days they ate at the little restaurant. In the mornings they'd go to the beach to swim, and sunbathe, then stroll around the town and pick up souvenirs at local handicraft shops. Around the same time each evening they'd go to the little back-street restaurant, try different crab dishes, then return to their hotel room for some leisurely lovemaking, then fall into a dreamless sleep. Every day felt like paradise. The woman was twenty-six, and taught English in a private girls' junior high. The man was twenty-eight and worked as an auditor at a large bank. It was almost a miracle that they were able to take a vacation at the same time, and they wanted to find a place where no one would bother them, where they could simply enjoy themselves. They tried their best to avoid any topic that would spoil the mood and their precious time together.

On the fourth day—the last day of their vacation—they ate crab as always in the evening. As they scooped out meat from the crab legs with metal utensils they talked about how being here, swimming every day at the beach, eating their fill of crab at night, made life back in Tokyo begin to look unreal, and far far away. Mostly they talked about the present. Silence fell on their meal from time to time, each of them lost in their own thoughts. But it wasn't an unpleasant silence. Cold beer and hot crab filled in the gaps nicely.

They left the restaurant and walked back to their hotel, and, as always, ended their day by making love. Quiet, but fulfilling lovemaking. They both took showers and soon fell asleep.

But after a short while the young man woke up, feeling awful. He had a sensation like he'd swallowed a hard cloud. He rushed to the bathroom, and draped over the toilet bowl he spewed out the contents of his stomach. His stomach had been full of white crabmeat. He hadn't had time to switch on the light, but in the light of the moon, which lay floating over the sea, he could make out what was in the toilet. He took a deep breath, closed his eyes, and let time pass. His head was a blank, and he couldn't form a single thought. All he could do was wait. Another wave of nausea hit him and again he hurled up whatever was left in his stomach.

When he opened his eyes he saw a white lump of what he'd vomited floating in the water in the toilet. A huge amount. What a hell of a lot of crab I ate! he thought, half-impressed. Eating this much crab day after day—no wonder I got sick. No matter how you cut it, this was way too much crab. Two or three years' worth of crab in four days.

As he stared he noticed that the lump floating in the toilet looked like it was moving slightly. At first he thought he must be imagining things. The faint moonlight must be producing the illusion. An occasional passing cloud would cover the moon, making everything, for a moment, darker than before. The young man closed his eyes, took a slow deep breath, and opened his eyes again. It was no illusion. The lump of meat was definitely moving. Like wrinkles twisting around, the surface of the meat was wiggling. The young man stood up and flicked on the bathroom light. He leaned closer to the lump of meat and saw that what was trembling on the surface were countless worms. Tiny worms the same color as the crabmeat, millions of them, clinging to the surface of the meat.

Once more he vomited everything in his stomach. But there wasn't anything left, and his stomach clenched into a fist-size lump. Bitter green bile came out, wrung out of his guts. Not content with this, he gulped down mouthwash and spewed it back up. He flushed down the contents of the toilet, flushing over and over to make sure it was all gone. Then he washed his face at the sink, using the fresh white towel to scrub hard around his mouth, and he thoroughly brushed his teeth. He rested his hands against the sink and stared at his reflection in the mirror. His face looked gaunt, wrinkled, his skin the color of dirt. He couldn't believe this was really his face. He looked like some exhausted old man.

He left the bathroom, leaned back against the door, and surveyed the bedroom. His girlfriend was in bed, fast asleep. Face sunk deep in her pillow, she was snoring peacefully, oblivious to what had transpired. Like a delicate fan, her long hair covered her cheeks, her shoulders. Just below her shoulder blades were two small moles, lined up like a pair of twins. Her back revealed a clear swimsuit line. Light from the whitish moon tranquilly filtered in through the blinds, along with the monotonous sound of waves against the shore. On the bedside the green numbers of the alarm clock glowed. Nothing had changed. Except that now, the crab was inside her—that evening they'd shared the same dishes. Only she wasn't aware of it.

The young man sank down in the rattan chair next to the window, closed his eyes, and breathed, slowly and regularly. Breathing fresh air into his lungs, exhaling the old, the stale. Trying to breathe as much air as he could into his body. He wanted all the pores in his body to open wide. Like an antique alarm clock in an empty room, his heart pounded out a hard, dry beat.

Gazing at his sleeping girlfriend, he pictured the countless tiny worms in her stomach. Should he wake her up and tell her about it? Shouldn't they do something? Unsure what to do, he thought for a while, and decided against it. It wouldn't do any good. She hadn't noticed anything. And that was the main problem.

The world felt out of kilter. He could hear as it creaked through this new orbit. Something had happened, he thought, and the world had changed. Everything was out of order, and would never get back to the way it was. Everything had changed, and all it could do was continue in this new direction. Tomorrow I'm going back to Tokyo, he thought. Back to the life I left there. On the surface nothing's changed, but I don't think I'll ever be able to get along with her again. I'll never feel the way I felt about her until yesterday, the young man knew. But that's not all. I don't think I'll ever be able to get along with myself. It's like we fell off a high fence, on the outside. Painlessly, without a sound. *And she never even noticed.*

The young man sat in the rattan chair until dawn, quietly breathing. From time to time a squall came up in the night, the raindrops pounding against the window like some kind of punishment. The rain clouds would pass and the moon showed its face. Again and again. But the woman never woke up. Or even rolled over in bed. Her shoulder shook a little a few times, but that was all. More than anything, he wanted to sleep, to sleep soundly and wake up to find that everything had been solved, that everything was as it had been, operating smoothly as always. The young man wanted nothing more than to fall into a deep sleep. But no matter how much he might stretch his hand out for it, sleep lay out of reach.

The young man remembered that first night, when they passed by that little side-street restaurant. The two old Chinese men silently eating their food, the black dog, eyes closed, at their feet, the faded umbrellas at the tables. How she'd tugged at his arm. It all seemed like years ago. But it was barely three days. Three days in which, through some strange force, he'd changed into one of those ominous, ashen old men. All in the quiet, beautiful seaside city of Singapore.

He brought his hands in front of him and gazed at them intently. He looked at the back of his hands, then the palms. Nothing could hide the fact that his hands were trembling, ever so slightly.

"Mm, I've always loved crab," he could hear her say. "How about you?"

I don't know, he thought.

His heart felt enclosed by something formless, surrounded by a deep, soft mystery. He no longer had the faintest clue where his life was headed, and what might be waiting for him there. But as the eastern sky finally began to lighten he had a sudden thought: One thing I am sure of, he thought. No matter where I go, I'm never going to eat crab again.

—TRANSLATED BY PHILIP GABRIEL

FIREFLY

nce upon a time—more like fifteen years ago, actually—I lived in a privately run dorm for college students in Tokyo. I was eighteen then, a brand-new college freshman, and didn't know the first thing about the city. I'd never lived on my own, either, and my parents were naturally worried; putting me in a dorm seemed the best solution. Money was a factor, too, and the dorm seemed the cheapest way to go. I'd been dreaming of living in my own apartment, having a great old time, but what can you do? My folks were footing the bill for college—tuition and fees, a monthly allowance—so that was that.

The dorm was situated on a generous piece of land on a rise in Bunkyo Ward, and had a fantastic view. The whole place was surrounded by a tall concrete wall, and right inside the main gate stood a huge zelkova tree. Some 150 years old, maybe more. When you stood at its base and looked up, its huge, leafy branches blotted out the sky. The concrete sidewalk detoured around the tree, then ran straight across the courtyard. On either side of the courtyard there were two concrete dorm buildings three stories tall, lined up side by side. Huge buildings. From the open windows somebody's transistor radio was always blasting out some DJ's voice. The curtains in the room were all the same color, cream being the color that fades least in the sunlight.

The two-story main building fronted the sidewalk. A dining hall and communal bath were on the first floor, an auditorium, guest rooms, and meeting rooms on the second. Next to the main building was a third dorm building, also three stories. The courtyard was spacious, and sprin-

klers spun around on the lawn, glinting in the sunlight. Rounding it all
out was a playing field for soccer and rugby behind the main building, as
well as six tennis courts. Who could ask for more?

The only problem with the dorm (not that everybody *was* convinced it
was a problem, though) was who ran it—some mysterious foundation
headed up by a right-wing fanatic. One look at the pamphlet the dorm
put out made this clear. The dorm was founded on a spirit of "achieving
the basic goals of education and cultivating promising talent to serve the
country." And a lot of well-heeled businessmen who agreed with that
philosophy apparently helped underwrite the dorm. At least that was the
official story. What lay beneath the surface was, like many things there,
anybody's guess. Rumor had it the whole place was a tax dodge, or some
sort of land fraud scheme. Not that this made a bit of difference to the
day-to-day life at the dorm. On a practical level, I guess, it didn't matter
who ran it—right-wingers, left-wingers, hypocrites, scoundrels. What
have you. Whatever the real story was, from the spring of 1967 to the fall
of '68, I called this dorm home.

◎

Each day at the dorm began with a solemn flag-raising ceremony. The
platform for the flag raising was in the middle of the courtyard, so you
could see it all from the dorm windows. Of course they played the
national anthem. Just like sports news and marches go together, can't
have one without the other.

The role of flag-raiser was played by the head of the east dorm, the
one I was in. He was fiftyish, an altogether tough-looking customer. He
had bristly hair with a sprinkling of gray, and a long scar on his sun-
burned neck. It was rumored he was a graduate of the Nakano Military
Academy. Next to him was a student who acted as his assistant. The guy
was basically an enigma. He had close-cropped hair and always wore a
school uniform. Nobody had any idea what his name was or which room
he lived in. I'd never run across him in the dining hall or the communal
bath. I wasn't even sure he was a student. But since he wore the uniform,
what else could he have been? Unlike Academy Man, he was short,
chubby, and pasty-looking. Every morning at six the two of them would
hoist the rising sun flag up the flagpole.

I don't know how many times I watched this little scene play out. The six a.m. chime would ring and there they were in the courtyard, Uniform Boy carrying a light wooden box, Academy Man a portable Sony tape recorder. Academy Man placed the tape recorder at the base of the platform and Uniform Boy opened the box. Inside was a neatly folded Japanese flag. Uniform Boy handed it to the boss, who then attached it to the rope. Uniform Boy switched on the tape recorder.

"May thy peaceful reign last long . . . " And the flag glided up the flagpole.

When they got to the part that goes "Until these tiny stones . . . " the flag was halfway up the pole, and it reached the top when they got to the end of the anthem. The two of them snapped to attention and gazed up at the flag. On sunny days when there was a breeze, it was quite a sight.

The evening ceremony was about the same as in the morning, just done in reverse. The flag glided down the pole and was put away in the wooden box. The flag doesn't wave at night.

Why the flag's got to be put away at night I have no idea. The country still exists at night, right? And plenty of people are hard at work. Doesn't seem fair those people can't have the same flag flying over them. Maybe it's a silly thing to worry about—just the kind of thought a person like me is likely to fret over.

In the dorm freshmen and sophomores lived two to a room, while juniors and seniors lived alone. The kind of two-man room I inhabited was cramped and narrow. On the wall furthest from the door was a window with an aluminum frame. The furniture was spartan, but solidly built— two desks and chairs, a bunk bed, two lockers, and built-in shelves. In most of the rooms the shelves were crammed full of the usual stuff: transistor radios, blow-dryers, electric coffeepots, instant-coffee jars, sugar, pots for cooking instant noodles, cups and plates. *Playboy* pinups were taped to the plaster walls, and lined up on the desks were school textbooks, plus the odd popular novel.

With just men living there the rooms were filthy. The bottoms of the trash baskets were lined with moldy orange skins, and the empty tin cans that served as ashtrays contained four-inch-high layers of cigarette butts. Coffee grounds were stuck to the cups, cellophane wrappers from instant-noodle packages and empty beer cans were scattered all over the floor. Whenever the wind blew in, a cloud of dust swirled up from the floor. The rooms stank to high heaven, too, since everyone just stuffed their dirty laundry under their beds. And forget about anyone airing out their bedding, so it all reeked of sweat and BO.

My room, though, was spotless. Not a speck of dirt on the floor, gleaming ashtrays as far as the eye could see. The bedding was aired out once a week, the pencils were lined up neatly in the pencil holders. Instead of a pinup, our room was decked out with a photo of canals in Amsterdam. Why? Simple enough—my roommate was a nut about cleaning. I didn't lift a finger since he did it all—the laundry, too; even *my* laundry, if you can imagine. Say I'd just finished a beer; the instant I set the empty down on the table he'd whisk it away to the trash can.

My roommate was a geography major.

"I'm studying about m-m-maps," he told me.

"So you're into maps, huh?" I asked.

"That's right. I want to get hired by the National Geography Institute and make m-maps."

To each his own, I figured. Up till then I'd never given a thought to what kind of people want to make maps—and why in the world they would. You have to admit, though, that it's a little weird for someone who wanted to work in the Geography Institute to stutter every time he said the word "map." He stuttered only part of the time, sometimes not at all. But when the word "map" came up, so did the stutters.

"What's your major?" he asked me.

"Drama," I replied.

"Drama? You mean you put on plays?"

"No, I don't act in plays. I study the scripts. Racine, Ionesco, Shakespeare, guys like that."

I've heard of Shakespeare but not those others, he said. Actually, I didn't know much about them myself. I was just parroting the course description.

"Anyhow, you like that kind of thing, right?" he asked.

"Not particularly."

That threw him for a loop. When he got flustered he stuttered worse than usual. I felt like I'd done something awful.

"Any subject's fine with me," I hurriedly explained, trying to calm him down. "Indian philosophy, Oriental history, whatever. I just ended up choosing drama. That's all."

"I don't get it," he insisted, still upset. "In m-m-my case I like m-m-maps, so I'm learning how to make them. That's why I came all the way to T-T-Tokyo to go to college and had m-m-my parents foot the bill. But you . . . I don't *g-get* it . . . "

His explanation made more sense than mine. Not worth the effort, I figured, and gave up trying to explain my side of the story. We drew straws to see who'd get the top and bottom bunks. I got the top.

He was tall, with close-cropped hair and prominent cheekbones. He always wore a white shirt and black trousers. When he went to school he invariably wore the school uniform with black shoes, toting a black brief-case. A perfect right-wing student, by the look of it, and certainly the other guys in the dorm tagged him as such. In reality, the guy had zero interest in politics. He just thought it was too much trouble to pick out clothes to wear. The only things that could pique his interest were changes in the shoreline, newly completed tunnels, things like that. Once he got started on those topics he'd go on, stuttering all the while, for a good hour, even two, until you screamed for mercy or fell asleep.

Every morning he was up at six on the dot, the national anthem his alarm clock. So I guess the flag-raising wasn't a complete waste. He dressed and went to wash up, taking an incredibly long time to finish. Made me wonder sometimes if he wasn't taking each tooth out and brushing them individually. Back in the room he smoothed out his towel, hung it on a hanger, and put his toothbrush and soap back on the shelf. Then he'd switch on the radio and start exercising to the morning exercise program.

I was pretty much a night owl, and a heavy sleeper, so when he started up I was usually dead to the world. When he got to the part where he began to leap up and down, I'd bolt out of bed. Every time he jumped up—and believe me he jumped really high—my head would bounce three inches off the pillow. Try sleeping through *that*.

"I'm really sorry," I said on the fourth day of this, "but I wonder if you could do your exercises on the roof or something. It wakes me up."

"I can't," he replied. "If I do it there, the people on the third floor will complain. This is the first floor, so there isn't anyone below us."

"Well, how about doing it in the courtyard?"

"No way. I don't have a transistor radio so I wouldn't be able to hear the music. You can't expect me to do my exercises without music."

His radio was the kind you had to plug in. I could have lent him my transistor, but it only picked up FM stations.

"Well, at least could you turn the music down and stop jumping? The whole room shakes. I don't want to complain or anything, but . . . "

"Jumping?" He seemed surprised. "What do you mean, j-jumping?"

"You know, that part where you bounce up and down."

"What are you talking about?"

I could feel a headache coming on. Go ahead, suit yourself, I thought. But once I'd brought it up I couldn't very well back down. So I started to sing the melody of the NHK radio exercise program, jumping up and down in time to the music.

"See? *This* part. Isn't that part of your routine?"

"Uh—yeah. Guess so. I hadn't noticed."

"So—," I said, "any chance you could skip that part? The rest I can put up with."

"Sorry," he said, brushing the suggestion aside. "I can't leave out one part. I've been doing this for ten years. Once I start I do it w-without th-thinking. If I leave out one part I wouldn't b-be able to d-do any of it."

"Then how about stopping the whole thing?"

"Who do you think you are, bossing me around like that?"

"Come on! I'm not bossing you around. I just want to sleep till eight. If eight's out of the question I still would like to wake up like normal people. You make me feel like I'm waking up in the middle of a pie-eating contest or something. You follow me here?"

"Yeah, I follow," he said.

"So what do you think we should do about it?"

"Hey, I got it! Why don't we get up and exercise together?"

I gave up and went back to sleep. After that he continued his morning routine, never skipping a single day.

◎

She laughed when I told her about my roommate's morning exercises. I hadn't intended it to be funny, but I ended up laughing myself. Her laughter lasted just an instant, and made me realize it'd been a long time since I'd seen her smile.

It was a Sunday afternoon in May. We'd gotten off the train at Yotsuya Station and were walking along the bank beside the railroad tracks in the direction of Ichigaya. The rain had ended around noon, and a southerly breeze had blown away the low-hanging clouds. The leaves on the cherry trees were sharply etched against the sky, and glinted as they shook in the breeze. The sunlight had an early-summer kind of scent. Most of the people we passed had taken off their coats and sweaters and draped them over their shoulders. A young man on a tennis court, dressed only in a pair of shorts, was swinging his racket back and forth. The metal frame sparkled in the afternoon sun. Only two nuns on a bench were still bundled up in winter clothes. Looking at them made me feel maybe summer wasn't just around the corner after all.

Fifteen minutes of walking was all it took for the sweat to start rolling down my back. I yanked off my thick cotton shirt and stripped down to my T-shirt. She rolled the sleeves of her light gray sweatshirt up above her elbows. The sweatshirt was an old one, faded with countless washings. It looked familiar, like I'd seen it sometime, a long time ago.

"Is it fun living with someone?" she asked.

"Hard to say. I haven't been there that long yet."

She stopped in front of the water fountain, sipped a mouthful of water, and wiped her mouth with a handkerchief she took out of her pants pocket. She retied the laces of her tennis shoes.

"I wonder if it'd suit me," she mused.

"You mean living in a dorm?"

"Yes," she said.

"I don't know. It's more trouble than you'd imagine. Lots of rules. Not to mention radio exercises."

"I guess so," she said and was lost in thought for a time. Then looked me straight in the eyes. Her eyes were unnaturally limpid. I'd never noticed. They gave me a kind of strange, transparent feeling, like gazing at the sky.

"But sometimes I feel like I *should*. I mean . . . ," she said, gazing into my eyes. She bit her lip and looked down. "I don't know. Forget it."

End of conversation. She started walking again.

I hadn't seen her for half a year. She'd gotten so thin I almost didn't recognize her. Her plump cheeks had thinned out, as had her neck. Not that she struck me as bony or anything. She looked prettier than ever. I wanted to tell her that, but couldn't figure out how to go about it. So I gave up.

We hadn't come to Yotsuya for any particular reason. We just happened to run across each other in a train on the Chuo Line. Neither of us had any plans. Let's get off, she said, and so we did. Left alone, we didn't have much to talk about. I don't know why she suggested getting off the train. From the beginning we weren't exactly brimming with topics to talk about.

After we got off at the station she headed off without a word. I walked after her, trying my best to keep up. There was always a yard or so between us, and I just kept on walking, staring at her back. Occasionally she'd turn around to say something, and I'd come up with a reply of sorts, though most of the time I couldn't figure out how to respond. I couldn't catch everything she said, but that didn't seem to bother her. She just had her say, then turned around again and walked on in silence.

We turned right at Iidabashi, came out next to the Palace moat, then crossed the intersection at Jimbocho, went up the Ochanomizu slope, and cut across Hongo. Then we followed the railroad tracks to Komagome. Quite a walk. By the time we arrived at Komagome it was already getting dark.

"Where are we?" she suddenly asked.

"Komagome," I said. "We made a big circle."

"How did we end up here?"

"You brought us. I just played Follow the Leader."

We dropped in a soba noodle shop close to the station and had a bite to eat. Neither of us said a word from the beginning to the end of the meal. I was exhausted from the hike and felt like I was about to collapse. She just sat there, lost in thought.

Noodles finished, I turned to her. "You're really in good shape."

"Surprised? I did cross-country in junior high. And my dad liked to hike in the mountains so ever since I was little I went hiking on Sundays. Even now my legs are pretty buff."

"I never would have guessed."

She laughed.

"I'll take you home," I said.

"It's OK. I can get back by myself. Don't bother."

"I don't mind at all," I said.

"It's OK. Really. I'm used to going home alone."

To tell the truth, I was a little relieved she said that. It took more than an hour by train to her apartment, and it'd be a long ride, the two of us sitting there side by side all that time, barely speaking a word to each other. So she ended up going back alone. I felt bad about it, so I paid for our meal.

Just as we were saying goodbye she turned to me and said, "Uh—I wonder, if it isn't too much to ask—if I could see you again? I know there's no real reason for me to ask . . . "

"No need for any special reason," I said, a little taken aback.

She blushed a little. She could probably feel how surprised I was.

"I can't really explain it well," she said. She rolled the sleeves of her sweatshirt up to her elbows, then rolled them down again. The electric lights bathed the fine down on her arms in a beautiful gold. "*Reason*'s the wrong word. I should have used another word."

She rested both elbows on the table and closed her eyes, as if searching for the right words. But the words didn't come.

"It's all right with me," I said.

"I don't know . . . These days I just can't seem to say what I mean," she said. "I just can't. Every time I try to say something, it misses the point. Either that or I end up saying the opposite of what I mean. The more I try to get it right the more mixed up it gets. Sometimes I can't even remember what I was trying to say in the first place. It's like my body's split in two and one of me is chasing the other me around a big pillar. We're running circles around it. The other me has the right words, but I can never catch her."

She put her hands on the table and stared into my eyes.

"Do you know what I'm trying to say?"

"Everybody has that kind of feeling sometimes," I said. "You can't express yourself the way you want to, and it annoys you."

Obviously this wasn't what she wanted to hear.

"No, that isn't what I mean," she said, but stopped there.

"I don't mind seeing you again," I said. "I have a lot of free time, and it'd sure be a lot healthier to go on walks than lie around all day."

We left each other at the station. I said goodbye, she said goodbye.

◎

The first time I met her was in the spring of my sophomore year in high school. We were the same age, and she was attending a well-known

Christian school. One of my best friends, who happened to be her boyfriend, introduced us. They'd known each other since grade school and lived just down the road from each other.

Like many couples who have known each other since they were young, they didn't have any particular desire to be alone. They were always visiting each other's homes and having dinner together with one of their families. We went on a lot of double dates together, but I never seemed to get anywhere with girls so we usually ended up a trio. Which was fine by me. We each had our parts to play. I played the guest, he the able host, she his pleasant assistant and leading lady.

My friend made a great host. He might have seemed a bit standoffish at times, but basically he was a kind person who treated everyone fairly. He used to kid the two of us—her and me—with the same old jokes over and over. If one of us fell silent, he'd restart the conversation, trying to draw us out. His antenna instantly picked up the mood we were in, and the right words just flowed out. And add to that another talent: he could make the world's most boring person sound fascinating. Whenever I talked with him I felt that way—like my ho-hum life was one big adventure.

The minute he stepped out of the room, though, she and I clammed right up. We had zero in common, and no idea what to talk about. We just sat there, toying with the ashtray, sipping water, waiting impatiently for him to return. Soon as he was back the conversation picked up where it left off.

I saw her again just once, three months after his funeral. There was something we had to discuss, so we met in a coffee shop. But as soon as that was finished we had nothing to say. I started to say something a couple of times, but the conversation just petered out. She sounded upset, like she was angry with me, but I couldn't figure out why. We said goodbye.

◎

Maybe she was angry because the last person to see him alive was me, not her. I shouldn't say this, I know, but I can't help it. I wish I could have traded places with her, but it can't be helped. Once something happens, that's all she wrote—you can never change things back to the way they were.

On that afternoon in May, after school—school wasn't out yet but we'd skipped out—he and I stopped inside a pool hall and played four games. I won the first one, he took the last three. As we'd agreed, the loser paid for the games.

That night he died in his garage. He stuck a rubber hose in the exhaust pipe of his N360, got inside, sealed up the windows with tape, and started the engine. I have no idea how long it took him to die. When his parents got back from visiting a sick friend he was already dead. The car radio was still on, a receipt from a gas station still stuck under the wiper.

He didn't leave any note or clue to his motives. I was the last person to see him alive, so the police called me in for questioning. He didn't act any different from usual, I told them. Seemed the same as always. People who are going to kill themselves don't usually win three games of pool in a row, do they? The police thought both of us were a little suspect. The kind of student who skips out of high school classes to hang out in a pool hall might very well be the kind to commit suicide, they seemed to imply. There was a short article on his death in the paper and that was that. His parents got rid of the car, and for a few days there were white flowers on his desk at school.

When I graduated from high school and went to Tokyo, there was only one thing I felt I had to do: try not to think too much. I willed myself to forget all of it—the green-felt-covered pool tables, his red car, the white flowers on the desk, the smoke rising from the tall chimney of the crematorium, the chunky paperweight in the police interrogation room. Everything. At first it seemed like I could forget, but something remained inside me. Like the air, and I couldn't grasp it. As time passed, though, the air formed itself into a simple, clear shape. Into words. And the words were these:

Death is not the opposite of life, but a part of it.

Say it aloud and it sounds trivial. Just plain common sense. But at the time it didn't hit me as words; it was more like air filling my body. Death was in everything around me—inside the paperweight, inside the four balls on the pool table. As we live, we breathe death into our lungs, like fine particles of dust.

Up till then I'd always thought death existed apart, in a separate realm. Sure, I knew death is inevitable. But you can just as easily turn that around and say that until the day it comes, death has nothing to do with us. Here's life, on this side—and over there is death. What could be more logical?

After my friend died, though, I couldn't think of death in such a naïve way. Death is not the opposite of life. Death is already inside me. I couldn't shake that thought. The death that took my seventeen-year-old friend on that May evening grabbed me, too, in its clutches.

That much I understood, but I didn't want to think about it too much. Which was not an easy task. I was still just eighteen, too young to find some safe, neutral ground to stand on.

◎

After that I dated her once, maybe twice a month. I guess you could call it dating. Can't think of any better word for it.

She was going to a women's college just outside Tokyo, a small school but with a pretty good reputation. Her apartment was just a ten-minute walk from the college. Along the road to the school was a beautiful reservoir that we sometimes took walks around. She didn't seem to have any friends. Same as before, she was pretty quiet. There wasn't much to talk about, so I didn't say much either. We just looked at each other and kept on walking and walking.

Not that we weren't getting anywhere. Around the end of summer vacation, in a very natural way, she started walking next to me, not in front. On and on we walked, side by side—up and down slopes, over bridges, across streets. We weren't headed anywhere in particular, no particular plans. We'd walk for a while, drop by a coffee shop for a cup, and off we'd go again. Like slides being changed in a projector, only the seasons changed. Fall came, and the courtyard of my dorm was covered with fallen zelkova leaves. Pulling on a sweater I could catch the scent of the new season. I went out and bought myself a new pair of suede shoes.

At the end of autumn when the wind turned icy, she began to walk closer to me, rubbing up against my arm. Through my thick duffel coat I could feel her breath. But that was all. Hands stuck deep in the pockets of my coat, I continued to walk on and on. Our shoes both had rubber soles, our footsteps were silent. Only when we crunched over the trampled-down sycamore leaves did we make a sound. It wasn't *my* arm she wanted, but someone else's. Not *my* warmth, but the warmth of another. At least that's how it felt at the time.

The guys at the dorm always kidded me whenever she called, or when I went out to see her on Sunday mornings. They thought I'd made a girl-friend. I couldn't explain the situation to them, and there wasn't any reason to, so I just let things stand as they were. Whenever I came back from a date, invariably someone would ask me whether I'd scored. "Can't complain" was my standard reply.

So passed my eighteenth year. The sun rose and set, the flag went up and down. And on Sundays I went on a date with my dead friend's girl-friend. What the hell do you think you're doing? I asked myself. And what comes next? I hadn't the slightest idea. At school I read Claudel's plays, and Racine's, and Eisenstein. I liked their style, but that was it. I made hardly any friends at school, or at the dorm. I was always reading, so people thought I wanted to be a writer. But I didn't. I didn't want to be anything.

I tried to tell her, many times, about these feelings. She of all people should understand. But I could never explain how I felt. It was just like she said—every time I struggled to find the right words, they slipped from my grasp and sank into the murky depths.

On Saturday evenings I sat in the lobby of the dorm where the phones were, waiting for her to call. Sometimes she wouldn't call for three weeks at a stretch, other times two weeks in a row. So I sat on a chair in the lobby, waiting. On Saturday evenings most of the other students went out, and silence descended on the dorm. Gazing at the particles of light in the still space, I struggled to grasp my own feelings. Everyone is looking for something from someone. That much I was sure of. But what comes next, I had no idea. A hazy wall of air rose up before me, just out of reach.

During the winter I had a part-time job at a small record store in Shin-juku. For Christmas I gave her a Henry Mancini record that had one of her favorites on it, the tune "Dear Heart." I wrapped it in paper with a Christmas tree design, and added a pink ribbon. She gave me a pair of woolen mittens she'd knitted. The part for the thumb was a little too short, but they were warm all the same.

She didn't go home for New Year's, and the two of us had dinner over New Year's at her apartment.

A lot of things happened that winter.

At the end of January my roommate was in bed for two days with a temperature of nearly 104. Thanks to which I had to call off a date with her. I couldn't just go out and leave him; he sounded like he was going to die at any minute. And who else would look after him? I bought some ice, wrapped it in a plastic bag to make an ice pack, wiped his sweat away with a cool wet towel, took his temperature every hour. His fever didn't break for a whole day. The second day, though, he leapt out of bed as though nothing had happened. His temperature was back to normal.

"It's weird," he said. "I've never had a fever before in my life."

"Well, you sure had one this time," I told him. I showed him the two free concert tickets that had gone to waste.

"At least they were free," he said.

It snowed a lot in February.

At the end of February I got into a fight with an older guy at the dorm over something stupid, and punched him. He fell over and hit his head on a concrete wall. Fortunately he was OK, but I was called before the dorm head and given a warning. After that, dorm life was never the same.

I turned nineteen and finally became a sophomore. I failed a couple of courses, though. I managed a couple of Bs, the rest Cs and Ds. She was promoted to sophomore, too, but with a much better record— she passed all her classes. The four seasons came and went.

In June she turned twenty. I had trouble picturing her twenty. We always figured the best thing for us was to shuttle back and forth somewhere between eighteen and nineteen. After eighteen comes nineteen, after nineteen comes eighteen—*that* we could understand. But now here she was twenty. And the next winter I'd be twenty, too. Only our dead friend would stay forever as he was—an eternal seventeen.

It rained on her birthday. I bought a cake in Shinjuku and took the train to her place. The train was crowded and bounced around something awful; by the time I reached her apartment the cake was a decaying Roman ruin. But we went ahead and put twenty candles on it and lit them. We closed the curtains and turned off the lights, and suddenly we had a real birthday party on our hands. She opened a bottle of wine and we drank it with the crumbled cake, and had a little something to eat.

"I don't know, but it seems kind of idiotic to be twenty," she said. After dinner we cleared away the dishes and sat on the floor drinking the rest of the wine. While I finished one glass, she helped herself to two.

She'd never talked like she did that night. She told me these long stories about her childhood, her school, her family. Terribly involved stories which started with A, then B would enter the picture, leading on to something about C, going on and on and on. There was no end to it. At first I made all the proper noises to show her I was following along, but soon gave up. I put on a record and when it was over, I lifted up the needle and put on another. After I finished all the records, I put the first one back on. Outside it was still pouring. Time passed slowly as her monologue went on without end.

I didn't worry about it, though, until a while later. Suddenly I realized it was eleven p.m. and she'd been talking nonstop for four hours. If I didn't get a move on, I'd miss the last train home. I didn't know what to do. Should I just let her talk till she dropped? Should I break in and put an end to it? After much hesitation, I decided to interrupt. Four hours should be enough, you'd think.

"Well, I'd better get going," I finally said. "Sorry I stayed so late. I'll see you again real soon, OK?"

I wasn't sure whether my words had gotten through. For a short while she was quiet but soon it was back to the monologue. I gave up and lit a cigarette. At this rate, it looked like I'd better go with Plan B. Let the rest take its course.

Before too long, though, she stopped. With a jolt I realized she was finished. It wasn't that she'd finished wanting to talk: her well of words had just dried up. Scraps of words hung there, suspended in midair. She tried to continue, but nothing came out. Something had been lost. Her lips slightly parted, she looked into my eyes with a vague expression. As if she was trying to make out something through an opaque membrane. I couldn't help feeling guilty.

"I didn't mean to interrupt you," I said slowly, weighing each word. "But it's getting late so I thought I'd better be going . . ."

It took less than a second for the teardrops to run down her cheeks and splash onto one of the record jackets. After the first drops fell, the floodgates burst. Putting her hands on the floor she leaned forward, weeping so much it seemed like she was retching. I gently put my hand out and touched her shoulder; it shook ever so slightly. Almost without thinking, I drew her near me. Head buried in my chest, she sobbed silently, dampening my shirt with her hot breath and tears. Her ten fingers, in search of something, roamed over my back. Cradling her in my left arm, I stroked the fine strands of her hair with my right. For a long while I waited in this pose for her to stop crying. But she didn't stop.

⊚

That night we slept together. That may have been the best response to the situation, maybe not. I don't know what else I should have done.

I hadn't slept with a girl for ages. It was her first time with a man. Stupid me, I asked her why she hadn't slept with *him*. Instead of answering, she pulled away from me, turned to face the opposite direction, and gazed at the rain outside. I stared at the ceiling and smoked a cigarette.

⊚

In the morning the rain had stopped. She was still facing away from me, asleep. Or maybe she was awake all the time, I couldn't tell. Once again she was enveloped by the same silence of a year before. I looked at her pale back for a while, then gave up and climbed out of bed.

Record jackets lay scattered over the floor; half a dilapidated cake graced the table. It felt like time had skidded to a stop. On her desktop there was a dictionary and a chart of French verb conjugations. A calendar was taped to the wall in front of the desk, a pure white calendar without a mark or writing of any kind.

I gathered up the clothes that had fallen on the floor beside the bed. The front of my shirt was still cold and damp from her tears. I put my face to it and breathed in the fragrance of her hair.

I tore off a sheet from the memo pad on her desk and left a note. Call me soon, I wrote. I left the room, closing the door.

⊚

A week passed without a call. She didn't answer her phone, so I wrote her a long letter. I tried to tell her my feelings as honestly as I knew how. There's a lot going on I don't have a clue about, I wrote; I'll try my damnedest to figure it all out, but you've got to understand these things take time. I have no idea where I'm headed—all I know for sure is I don't want to get hung up thinking too deeply about things. The world's too precarious a place for that. Start me mulling over ideas and I'll end up forcing people to do things they hate. I couldn't stand that. I want to see you again very much, but I don't know if that's the right thing to do . . .

That's the kind of letter I wrote.

◎

I got a reply in the beginning of July. A short letter.

◎

For the time being I've decided to take a year off from college. I say for the time being, but I doubt I'll go back. Taking a leave of absence is just a formality. Tomorrow I'll be moving out of my apartment. I know this will seem pretty abrupt to you, but I've been thinking it over for a long time. I wanted to ask your advice, many times I almost did, but for some reason I couldn't. I guess I was afraid to talk about it.

Please don't worry about everything that's happened. No matter what happened, or didn't happen, this is where we end up. I know this might hurt you, and I'm sorry if it does. What I want to say is I don't want you to blame yourself, or anyone else, over me. This is really something I have to handle on my own. This past year I've been putting it off, and I know you've suffered because of me. Perhaps that's all behind us now.

There's a nice sanatorium in the mountains near Kyoto, and I've decided to stay there for a while. It's less a hospital than a place where you're free to do what you want. I'll write you again someday and tell you more about it. Right now I just can't seem to get the words down. This is the tenth time I've rewritten this letter. I can't find the words to tell you how thankful I am to you for being with me this past year. Please believe me when I say this. I can't say anything more than that. I'll always treasure the record you gave me.

Someday, somewhere in this *precarious world,* if we meet again I hope I'll be able to tell you much more than I can right now.

Goodbye.

◎

I must have read her letter over a couple of hundred times at least, and every time I was gripped by a terrible sadness. The same kind of disconcerting sadness I felt when she gazed deep into my eyes. I couldn't shake the feeling. It was like the wind, formless and weightless, and I couldn't wrap it around me. Scenery passed slowly before me. People spoke, but their words didn't reach my ears.

On Saturday nights I still sat in the same chair in the dorm lobby. I knew a phone call wouldn't come, but I had no idea what else to do. I turned on the TV set and pretended to watch baseball. And gazed at the indeterminate space between me and the set. I divided that space into two, and again into two. I did this over and over, until I'd made a space so small it could fit in the palm of my hand.

At ten I turned off the TV, went back to my room, and went to sleep.

◎

At the end of that month my roommate gave me a firefly in an instant-coffee jar. Inside were blades of grass, and bit of water. He'd punched a few tiny air holes in the lid. It was still light out so the firefly looked more like some black bug you'd find at the beach. I peered in the jar and sure enough, a firefly it was. The firefly tried to climb up the slippery side of the glass jar, only to slip back down each time. It'd been a long time since I'd seen one so close up.

"I found it in the courtyard," my roommate told me. "A hotel down the street let a bunch of fireflies out as a publicity stunt, and it must have made its way over here." As he talked, he stuffed clothes and notebooks inside a small suitcase. We were already several weeks into summer vacation. I didn't want to go back home, and he'd had to go out on some fieldwork, so we were just about the only ones left in the dorm. Fieldwork done, though, he was ready to go home.

"Why don't you give it to a girl?" he added. "Girls like those things."

"Thanks, good idea," I said.

After sundown the dorm was silent. The flag was gone, and lights came on in the windows of the cafeteria. There were just a few students left, so only half the lights were lit. The lights on the right were off, the ones on the left were on. You could catch a faint whiff of dinner. Cream stew.

I took the instant-coffee jar with the firefly and went up to the roof. The place was deserted. A white shirt someone had forgotten to take in was pinned to the clothesline, swaying in the evening breeze like a cast-off skin. I climbed the rusty metal ladder in the corner of the roof to the top of the water tower. The cylindrical water tank was still warm from the heat it had absorbed during the day. I sat down in the cramped space, leaned against the railing, and looked down at the moon before me, just a day or two short of full. On the right, I could see the streets of Shinjuku, on the left, Ikebukuro. The headlights of the cars were a brilliant stream of light flowing from one part of the city to another. Like a cloud hanging over the streets, the city was a mix of sounds, a soft, low hum.

The firefly glowed faintly in the bottom of the jar. But its light was too weak, the color too faint. The way I remembered it, fireflies were supposed to give off a crisp, bright light that cuts through the summer darkness. This firefly might be growing weak, might be dying, I figured. Holding the jar by its mouth, I shook it a couple of times to see. The firefly flew for a second and bumped against the glass. But its light was still dim.

Maybe the problem wasn't with the light, but with my memory. Maybe fireflies' light wasn't that bright after all. Was I just imagining it was? Or maybe, when I was a child, the darkness that surrounded me was deeper. I couldn't remember. I couldn't even recall when I had last seen a firefly.

What I could remember was the sound of water running in the night. An old brick sluice gate, with a handle you could turn around to open or close it. A narrow stream, with plants covering the surface. All around was pitch black, and hundreds of fireflies flew above the still water. A powdery clump of yellow light blazed above the stream, and shone in the water.

When was that, anyway? And where was it?

I had no idea.

Everything was mixed up, and confused.

I closed my eyes and took a few deep breaths to calm myself. If I kept my eyes shut tight, at any moment my body would be sucked into the summer darkness. It was the first time I'd climbed the water tower after dark. The sound of the wind was clearer than it had ever been. The wind wasn't blowing hard, yet strangely left a clear-cut trace as it rushed by me. Taking its time, night slowly enveloped the earth. The city lights might shine their brightest, but slowly, ever so slowly, night was winning out.

I opened the lid of the jar, took out the firefly, and put it on the edge of the water tower that stuck out an inch or two. It seemed like the firefly couldn't grasp where it was. After making one bumbling circuit of a bolt, it stretched out one leg on top of a scab of loose paint. It tried to go to the right but, finding a dead end, went back to the left. It slowly clambered on top of the bolt and crouched there for a time, motionless, more dead than alive.

Leaning against the railing, I gazed at the firefly. For a long time the two of us sat there without moving. Only the wind, like a stream, brushed past us. In the dark the countless leaves of the zelkova rustled, rubbing against each other.

◎

I waited forever.

◎

A long time later, the firefly took off. As if remembering something, it suddenly spread its wings and in the next instant floated up over the railing and into the gathering dark. Trying to win back lost time, perhaps, it quickly traced an arc beside the water tower. It stopped for a moment, just long enough for its trail of light to blur, then flew off toward the east.

Long after the firefly disappeared, the traces of its light remained within me. In the thick dark behind my closed eyes that faint light, like some lost wandering spirit, continued to roam.

Again and again I stretched my hand out toward that darkness. But my fingers felt nothing. That tiny glow was always just out of reach.

—TRANSLATED BY PHILIP GABRIEL

CHANCE TRAVELER

The "I" here, you should know, means me, Haruki Murakami, the author of the story. Mostly this is a third-person narrative, but here at the beginning the narrator does make an appearance. Just like in an old-fashioned play where the narrator stands before the curtain, delivers a prologue, then bows out. I appreciate your patience, and promise I won't keep you long.

The reason I've turned up here is I thought it best to relate directly several so-called strange events that have happened to me. Actually, events of this kind happen quite often. Some of them are significant, and have affected my life in one way or another. Others are insignificant incidents that have no impact at all. At least I think so.

Whenever I bring up these incidents, say, in a group discussion, I never get much of a reaction. Most people just make some noncommittal comment, and it never goes anywhere. It never jump-starts the conversation, never spurs someone else to bring up something similar that's happened to him. The topic I bring up is like so much water flowing down the wrong channel and being sucked up in a nameless stretch of sand. No one says anything for a while, then invariably someone changes the subject.

At first I thought I was telling the story wrong, so one time I tried writing it down as an essay. I figured if I did that maybe people would take it more seriously. But no one seemed to believe what I'd written. "You've made it all up, right?" I don't know how many times I've heard that. Since I'm a novelist people assume that anything I say or write must have a touch of make-believe. Granted, my fiction contains more than its share of invention, but when I'm not writing fiction I don't go out of my way to make up meaningless stories.

As a kind of preface to a tale, then, I'd like to briefly relate some strange experiences I've had. I'll stick to the trifling, insignificant ones. If I started in on the life-changing experiences, I'd use up most of my allotted space.

◎

From 1993 to 1995 I lived in Cambridge, Massachusetts. I was a sort of writer-in-residence at a college, and was working on a novel entitled *The Wind-Up Bird Chronicle.* In Harvard Square there was a jazz club called the Regattabar Jazz Club where they had lots of live performances. It was a comfortable, relaxed, cozy place. Famous jazz musicians played there, and the cover charge was reasonable.

One evening the pianist Tommy Flanagan appeared with his trio. My wife had something else to do so I went by myself. Tommy Flanagan is one of my favorite jazz pianists. He usually appears as an accompanist; his performances are invariably warm and deep, and marvelously steady. His solos are fantastic. Full of anticipation, then, I sat down at a table near the stage and enjoyed a glass of California Merlot. To tell the truth, though, his performance was a bit of a letdown. Maybe he wasn't feeling well. Or else it was still too early for him to get in the swing of things. His performance wasn't bad, it was just missing that extra element that sends us flying to another world. It lacked that special magical glow, I guess you could say. Tommy Flanagan's better than this, I thought as I listened—just wait till he gets up to speed.

But time didn't improve things. As their set was drawing to a close I started to get almost panicky, hoping that it wouldn't end like this. I wanted something to remember his performance by. If things ended like this, all I'd take home would be lukewarm memories. Or maybe no memories at all. And I may never have a chance to see Tommy Flanagan play live again. (In fact I never did.) Suddenly a thought struck me: what if I were given a chance to request two songs by him right now—which ones would I choose? I mulled it over for a while before picking "Barbados" and "Star-Crossed Lovers."

The first piece is by Charlie Parker, the second a Duke Ellington tune. I add this for people who aren't into jazz, but neither one is very popular, or performed much. You might occasionally hear "Barbados," though it's one of the less flashy numbers Charlie Parker wrote, and I bet most people have never heard "Star-Crossed Lovers" even once. My point being, these weren't typical choices.

I had my reasons, of course, for choosing these unlikely pieces for my fantasy requests—namely that Tommy Flanagan had made memorable recordings of both. "Barbados" appeared on the 1957 album *Dial JJ 5* where he was pianist with the J. J. Johnson Quintet, while he recorded "Star-Crossed Lovers" on the 1968 album *Encounter!* with Pepper Adams and Zoot Sims. Over his long career Tommy Flanagan has played and recorded countless pieces as a sideman in various groups, but it was the crisp, smart solos, short though they were, in these two particular pieces that I've always loved. That's why I was thinking if only he would play those two numbers right now it'd be perfect. I was watching him closely, picturing him coming over to my table and asking, "Hey, I've had my eye on you. Do you have any requests? Why don't you give me the titles of two numbers you'd like me to play?" Knowing all the time, of course, that the chances of that happening were nil.

And then, without a word, and without so much as a glance in my direction, Tommy Flanagan launched into the last two numbers of his set—the very ones I'd been thinking of. He started off with the ballad "Star-Crossed Lovers," then went into an up-tempo version of "Barbados." I sat there, wineglass in hand, speechless. Jazz fans will understand that the chance of his picking these two pieces from the millions of jazz numbers out there was astronomical. And also—and this is the main point here—his performances of both numbers were amazing.

The second incident took place around the same time, and also had to do with jazz. I was in a used-record store near the Berklee School of Music one afternoon, checking out the records. Rummaging around in old shelves of LPs is one of the few things that makes life worth living, as far as I'm concerned. On that particular day I'd located a used copy of Pepper Adams's recording for Riverside called *10 to 4 at the 5 Spot*. It was a live recording of the Pepper Adams Quintet, with Donald Byrd on trumpet, recorded in New York at the Five Spot jazz club. "10 to 4," of course, meant ten minutes till four o'clock, meaning that they played such a hot set they went on till dawn. This copy of the album was a first pressing, in mint condition, and was going for only seven or eight dollars. I owned the Japanese version of the record and had listened to it so much it was all scratched. Finding an original recording in this good shape and at this price seemed, to exaggerate a little, like a minor miracle. I was overjoyed as I bought the record, and just as I was exiting the shop a young man passed me and asked, "Hey, do you have the time?" I glanced at my watch and automatically answered, "Yeah, it's ten to four."

After I said this I noticed the coincidence and gulped. What in the world is going on? I wondered. Was the god of jazz hovering in the sky above Boston, giving me a wink and a smile and saying, "Yo, you dig it?"

Neither one of these incidents was anything special. It wasn't like my life turned in a new direction. I was simply struck by the strange coincidences—that things like this actually do happen.

Don't misunderstand me—I'm not the sort of person who's into occult phenomena. Fortune-telling doesn't do a thing for me. Instead of going to the trouble of having a fortune-teller read my palm, I think I'm better off trying to rack my brain for a solution to whatever problem I have. Not that I have a brilliant mind or anything, just that this seems a quicker way to find a solution. I'm not into paranormal powers either. Transmigration, the soul, premonitions, telepathy, the end times—I'll pass. I'm not saying I don't believe in any of these. No problem with me if they really do exist. I'm just personally not interested. Still, a significant number of strange, out-of-left-field kinds of things have colored my otherwise humdrum life.

The story I'm about to tell is one a friend of mine told me. I happened to tell him once about my own two episodes, and afterward he sat there for a time with a serious look on his face and finally said, "You know, something like that happened to me, too. Something that coincidence led me to. It wasn't something totally weird, but I can't really explain it. At any rate, a series of coincidences took me somewhere I never expected to be."

I've changed some of the facts to protect people's identities, but other than that the story is just as he related it.

⊙

My friend works as a piano tuner. He lives in the western part of Tokyo, near the Tama River. He's forty-one, and gay. He doesn't especially hide the fact that he's gay. He has a boyfriend three years younger than he is. The boyfriend works in real estate and because of his job isn't able to come out, so they live apart. My friend might be a lowly piano tuner but he graduated from the piano department of a music college and is an impressive pianist himself. His forte is modern French composers—Debussy, Ravel, and Erik Satie—and he plays them with a deep expressiveness. But Francis Poulenc is his favorite.

"Poulenc was gay," he explained to me one day. "And he made no attempt to hide it. Which was a pretty hard thing to do in those days. He said this once: 'If you took away my being homosexual my music never would have come about.' I know exactly what he means. He had to be as true to his homosexuality as he was to his music. That's music, and that's life."

I've always liked Poulenc's music, too. When my friend comes over to tune my old piano I sometimes have him run through a few short Poulenc pieces when he's finished. The "French Suite," the "Pastoral," and so on.

He "discovered" he was gay after entering music college. Before then he never once considered the possibility. He was handsome, well brought up, had a calm demeanor, and was popular with the girls in his high school. He never had a steady girlfriend, but he did go out on dates. He loved walking with a girl, gazing at her hairdo close-up, the fragrance of her neck, holding her delicate hand in his. But he never experienced sex. After several dates with a girl he'd start to sense that she was hoping he'd take the initiative and do *something,* but he never was able to take the next step. He never felt anything inside driving him to do so. Without exception the other guys around him wrestled with their own sexual demons, some of them struggling with them, others plunging ahead and giving in, but he never felt the same kind of urges. Maybe I'm just a late bloomer, he figured. Or maybe I just haven't met the right girl yet.

In college he went out with a girl in the same year in the percussion department. They enjoyed talking, and whenever they were together they felt close. Not long after they met they had sex in her room. She was the one who led him on. They'd had a few drinks. The sex went off smoothly, though it wasn't as thrilling and satisfying as everybody said. In fact he found the act rough, grotesque even. And the faint odor the girl gave off when she got sexually aroused turned him off. He much preferred just talking with her, playing music together, sharing a meal. As time passed, having sex with her became a burden.

Still, he just thought he was indifferent to sex. But one day . . . No, I think I'll skip this part. It'll take too long, and really isn't connected to the story I want to tell. Let's just say that something took place and he discovered that he was, unmistakably, gay. He didn't want to make up some excuse so he came right out and told her. Within a week the news had spread to all his friends. He lost a few of them, and things grew difficult between him and his parents, but in the final analysis it was good it all came out. He wasn't the type who could have hid who he really was.

What hurt the most, though, was how this affected his relationship with the person he was closest to in his family, his sister, who was two years older. When her fiancé's family heard about his coming out it looked like the marriage might be canceled, and though they were able to persuade the man's parents and finally get married, the whole thing nearly gave his sister a nervous breakdown, and she got incensed at her brother. Why did you have to pick this time in my life to make waves? she yelled at him. Her brother naturally defended himself, but after this they grew apart, and he even passed on attending her wedding.

He mostly enjoyed his life as a gay man living alone. Other than those who had a physical revulsion to gays, most people liked him—he was, after all, always well dressed, kind, and courteous, with a nice sense of humor and winning smile. He was good at his job, so he had a large list of clients and a steady income. Several famous pianists insisted on having him tune their instruments. He purchased a two-bedroom apartment near a university and had nearly paid off the mortgage. He owned an expensive stereo system, was a skilled organic chef, and kept himself in shape by working out five days a week at a gym. After going out with a number of men, he met his present partner and had been enjoying a settled sexual relationship with him for nearly a decade.

On Tuesdays he'd cross over the Tama River in his green, stick-shift Honda convertible sports car and go to an outlet mall in Kanagawa Prefecture. The mall had all the typical big-box stores—the Gap, Toys R Us, the Body Shop. On weekends the place was packed and you could barely find a parking spot, but on weekday mornings the mall was nearly deserted. He'd head to a large bookstore at the mall, buy a book that caught his eye, then spend a pleasant few hours sipping coffee and reading in a café. That was the way he spent his Tuesdays.

"The mall's hideous," he told me, "but that café is the exception—a very comfortable little place. I just happened to run across it. They don't play any music, it's all nonsmoking, and the chairs are perfect for reading. Not too hard, not too soft. And there's never anybody there. I don't imagine on a Tuesday morning you'd find many people heading for a café. Even if they were, they'd probably go to the nearby Starbucks."

So Tuesday mornings find him in that café, lost in a book, from just past ten till one. At one he heads to a nearby restaurant, has a lunch of tuna salad and Perrier, then goes to the gym to work out. That's a typical Tuesday.

On that particular Tuesday morning he was reading, as usual, in the nearly empty café. Charles Dickens's *Bleak House*. He'd read it many years ago, and when he spied it on a bookshelf decided to try it again. He had a clear memory of it as an interesting read, though he couldn't for the life of him remember the plot. Dickens had always been one of his favorite writers. Reading Dickens made the world fade away. From the first page he found himself completely absorbed by the story.

After an hour's concentrated reading, though, he felt tired. He closed his book, put it on top of his table, signaled the waitress for a refill, and went to the restroom outside the café. When he returned to his seat, a woman at the next table, who was also reading, spoke to him.

"I'm sorry, but do you mind if I ask you a question?" she said.

A somewhat ambiguous smile came to him as he returned her gaze. She was about the same age as he was. "Of course," he replied.

"I know it's forward of me to speak like this, but there's something I've been wondering about," she said, blushing slightly.

"It's fine. I'm in no hurry, go right ahead."

"By any chance is that book you're reading by Dickens?"

"It is," he said, picking up the book and showing it to her. *"Bleak House."*

"I thought so," she said, clearly relieved. "I glanced at the cover and thought it might be that book."

"Are you a fan of *Bleak House,* too?"

"I am. What I mean is, I've been reading the same book. Right next to you, just by coincidence." She took the plain paper wrapping off the book, the kind bookstores put on if you like, and showed him the cover.

It was definitely a surprising coincidence. Imagine—on a weekday morning, in a deserted café in a deserted shopping mall two people happen to be sitting right next to each other, reading the same exact book. And this wasn't some worldwide best seller but Charles Dickens. And not even one of his better-known works. This strange and startling chance meeting took both of them by surprise, but it also helped them overcome the awkwardness of a first encounter.

The woman lived in a new housing development not far from the mall. She'd purchased *Bleak House* five days ago at the very same bookstore, and when she first sat down at this café to order a cup of tea and opened the book she found she couldn't stop reading. Before she knew it two hours had passed. She hadn't been so absorbed in reading since she was in college.

She was petite and, although not overweight, was starting to put on a bit of extra flesh in all the typical places. She had a large bust and an attractive face. Her clothes were tasteful, and looked a little on the expensive side. The two of them chatted for a while. The woman was in a book club and their book of the month happened to be *Bleak House.* One of the women in the club was a great fan of Dickens and had suggested that novel as their next reading. The woman in the café had two children (two girls, a third grader and a first grader) and normally found it hard to find any time to read. Though sometimes she was able to get out of the house like this and carve out some time. Most of the people she dealt with every day were the mothers of her children's classmates, and their topics of conversation were limited to TV dramas and gossip about their children's teachers, so she had joined a local book club. Her husband used to be quite a reader himself, though now work kept him so busy that he was lucky to have time to glance through a few business books now and then.

He told her a little about himself. That he worked as a piano tuner, lived across the Tama River, and was single. He liked this little café so much he drove all the way here once a week just to sit and read. He didn't mention being gay. He didn't intentionally hide it, but it wasn't the sort of thing you tell just anybody.

They had lunch together in a restaurant in the mall. The woman was a very open, honest sort of person. Once she relaxed she laughed a lot—a natural, quiet laugh. Without her putting it into words, he could well imagine the kind of life she'd led till then. She was a pampered daughter of a well-to-do family in Setagaya, attended a decent college, where she got good grades and was popular (more with other girls than with boys, perhaps), married a man three years older than her who was pulling in a good salary, and had two daughters. The girls were attending private school. Her twelve years of marriage hadn't exactly been all roses, but she had no particular complaints. The two of them had a light lunch and talked about books they'd read recently, music they liked. They talked for about an hour.

"I enjoyed this," the woman said after they'd finished, and she blushed. "I don't have anybody I can really talk to."

"I enjoyed it, too," he said. And that was the truth.

◎

The next Tuesday, as he sat in the café reading, she showed up again. They greeted each other with a smile and sat at separate tables, both silently delving into their copies of *Bleak House*. Just before noon she came over to his table and spoke to him, and like the week before they went off to have lunch. I know a cozy little French place nearby, she said, and I was wondering if you'd like to go. There aren't any decent restaurants in the mall. Sounds good, he agreed, let's go. They drove to the restaurant in her blue, automatic Peugeot 306, and had watercress salad and grilled sea bass, a glass of white wine. And discussed Dickens's novel as they ate.

After lunch, as they were driving back to the mall, she stopped the car in a park and took his hand in hers. She wanted to go someplace nice and quiet with him, she said. He was a little surprised at how fast things had developed.

"I've never done this kind of thing after I got married. Not even once," she explained. "But you're all I've thought about this past week. I promise I won't make any demands, or cause you any trouble. Of course if you don't find me attractive . . ."

He gently squeezed her hand, and quietly explained things. If I were an ordinary guy, he said, I'm sure I'd be happy to go with you to someplace nice and quiet. You're an attractive woman and I know spending time like that with you would be wonderful. But the thing is, I'm gay. So I can't manage sex with women. Some gay men are able to, but not me. I hope you'll understand. I can be your friend, but not your lover, I'm afraid.

It took quite a while for her to truly comprehend what he was trying to convey (he was the first homosexual she'd ever met), and after she finally grasped it, she began to cry. Pressing her face against the piano tuner's shoulder, she cried for a long time. It must have been a shock for her. The poor woman, he thought, then he put his arms around her and caressed her hair.

"Forgive me," she finally said. "I made you talk about something you didn't want to talk about."

"That's all right. I'm not trying to hide who I am. I guess I should have picked up on where we were headed so there wouldn't be any misunderstanding. I'm afraid *I'm* the one who made *you* feel bad."

His long, slim fingers gently stroked her hair for a long time, and that gradually had a calming effect. There was a single mole, he noticed, on her right earlobe. The mole called up a childhood memory. His older sister had a mole about the same size, in the same spot. When he was little, he used to playfully rub his sister's mole when she was asleep, trying to rub it off. His sister would wake up, angry.

"I've been excited every day since I met you," she said. "I haven't felt this way in a long time. It was great—I felt like a teenager again. So I don't mind. I went to the beauty salon, went on a quick diet, bought some Italian lingerie . . ."

"Sounds like I made you waste your money," he laughed.

"But I think I needed that right now."

"Needed what?"

"I had to do something to express what I'm feeling."

"By buying sexy Italian lingerie?"

She blushed to her ears. "It wasn't sexy. Not at all. Just very beautiful."

He beamed and looked in her eyes. He indicated he'd just been joking and that broke the tension. She smiled back, and for a time they gazed deep into each other's eyes.

He took out his handkerchief and wiped away her tears. She sat up and redid her makeup, checking herself in the sun visor mirror.

"The day after tomorrow I have to go to a hospital in town to get a second examination for breast cancer." She'd just pulled into the parking lot at the mall and had set the parking brake. "They found a suspicious shadow on my annual X-ray and told me to come in so they can run some more tests. If it really turns out to be cancer I might have to have an operation right away. Maybe that's why I acted the way I did today. What I mean is . . ."

She didn't say anything for a while, and then shook her head vigorously.

"I don't understand it myself."

The piano tuner measured her silence for a time. Listening carefully, as if to pick up a faint sound within.

"Almost every Tuesday morning I'll be here," he said. "Right here, reading. There's not much I can do to help, but I'm here if you need somebody to talk to. If you don't mind talking to somebody like me, that is."

"I haven't told anybody about this. Not even my husband."

He rested his hand on top of hers, on top of the parking brake.

"I'm scared," she said. "Sometimes so scared I can't think."

A blue minivan pulled into the space beside them, an unhappy middle-aged couple emerging. They were arguing about something pointless. Once they had gone, silence returned. Her eyes were closed.

"I'm in no position to hand down any advice," he said, "but there's a rule I always follow when I don't know what to do."

"A rule?"

"If you have to choose between something that has form and something that doesn't, go for the one without form. That's my rule. Whenever I run into a wall I follow that rule, and it always works out. Even if it's hard going at the time."

"You made up that rule yourself?"

"I did," he replied, looking at the Peugeot's odometer. "From my own experience."

"If you have to choose between something that has form and something that doesn't, choose the one without form," she repeated.

"That's right."

She considered this. "But if I had to do that right now I don't know if I could tell the difference. Between what has form and what doesn't."

"Maybe not, but somewhere down the line I'm sure you'll have to make that kind of choice."

"How do you know that?"

He nodded quietly. "An experienced gay guy like me has all kinds of special powers."

She laughed. "Thank you."

A long silence followed. But it wasn't as thick and stifling as before.

"Goodbye," the woman said. "I really want to thank you. I'm happy I could meet you, and talk. I feel a little more able to face up to things now."

He smiled and shook her hand. "Take care of yourself."

He stood there, watching as her blue Peugeot drove away. He gave a final wave toward her rearview mirror, and then slowly walked back toward where his Honda was parked.

◎

The next Tuesday it was raining and the woman didn't show up at the café. He silently read until one and then left.

On this day the piano tuner decided not to go to the gym. He just didn't feel like exercising. Instead he went straight home without stopping for lunch and lay there on his couch, listening to Arthur Rubinstein playing Chopin ballads. Eyes closed, he could picture the woman's face, the touch of her hair. The shape of the mole on her earlobe came back clearly to him. After a while her face and the Peugeot faded from his mind, but that mole remained. Whether he kept his eyes opened or closed, that small black dot remained, like a forgotten period.

Around two thirty in the afternoon he decided to phone his sister. It had been a long time since they'd spoken. How long, he wondered. Ten years? They were that estranged from each other. One reason was that back when her engagement got messed up, the two of them had gotten worked up and said some things they shouldn't have. Another reason was that he didn't like her husband. He was arrogant and crude, and treated the piano tuner's sexual orientation like it was a contagious disease.

Unless he absolutely had to, the piano tuner didn't want to come within a hundred yards of the guy.

He hesitated several times before picking up the phone, but finally punched in the number. The phone rang over ten times and he was about to give up—with a certain sense of relief, actually—when his sister picked up. Her familiar voice. When she realized it was him, there was a deep silence for a moment on the other end of the line.

"Why are you calling me?" she said, in a flat tone.

"I don't know," he admitted. "I just thought I'd better call you. I was worried about you."

Silence once more. A long silence. Maybe she's still mad at me, he thought.

"There's no particular reason I called. I just wanted to check that everything's okay."

"Hold on a second," his sister said. He could tell that she had been weeping. "I'm sorry, but could you give me a moment?"

Silence continued for a time. He kept the receiver held to his ear the whole time. He couldn't hear anything, or sense anything. "Are you busy now?" she finally asked.

"No, I'm free," he replied.

"Can I come over to see you?"

"Of course. I'll pick you up at the station."

An hour later he picked up his sister at the train station and took her back to his apartment. It had been ten years since they'd seen each other, and they had to admit that they'd each aged. They were each like a mirror for the other, reflecting the changes in themselves. His sister was still slim and stylish, and looked five years younger than her real age. Still, her hollow cheeks had a severity to them he'd never seen before, and her impressive dark eyes had lost their usual luster. He himself looked younger than his years, too, though it was hard to hide the fact that his hair was thinning out. In the car they hesitantly talked about typical things: work, her children, news about mutual friends, the state of their parents' health.

Inside his apartment he went into the kitchen to boil some water.

"Are you still playing piano?" she asked as she eyed the upright piano in his living room.

"Just for my own amusement. And only simple pieces. I can't get my hands around the harder ones anymore."

His sister opened the lid of the piano and rested her fingers on the yellowed, well-used keys. "I was sure you were going to be a famous concert pianist one day."

"The music world is where child prodigies go to die," he said as he ground some coffee beans. "Having to give up the idea of being a professional pianist was a major disappointment. It was like everything I'd done up till then was a complete waste. I just wanted to disappear. But it turned out my ears are superior to my hands. There are a lot of people more talented than me, but nobody has as good an ear. I realized that not long after I started college. And that being a first-class piano tuner was a lot better than being a second-rate pianist."

He took out a container of cream from the refrigerator and poured it into a ceramic pitcher.

"It's funny, but after I switched to a major in piano tuning I began to enjoy playing the piano much more. Ever since I was little I'd practiced piano like crazy. It was fun to see myself improve, but I never once enjoyed playing. Playing piano was just a way of solving certain problems. Trying to avoid fingering mistakes or letting my fingers get all tangled up—all just to impress other people. It wasn't until I gave up the idea of becoming a pianist that I finally understood how enjoyable playing the piano can be. And how wonderful music really is. It was like a weight was lifted off my shoulders, a weight I never realized I was lugging around until I got rid of it."

"You never told me about this."

"I didn't?"

His sister shook her head.

"It was the same when I realized I'm gay," he went on. "Issues I could never understand were suddenly resolved. Life was much easier after that, like the clouds had parted and I could finally see. When I gave up being a pianist, and came out as a homosexual, I'm sure it upset a lot of people. But I want you to understand that that's the only way I could get back to who I really am. The real me."

He placed a coffee cup down in front of his sister, then took his own mug and sat down next to her on the sofa.

"I probably should have made more of an effort to understand you better," his sister said. "But before you took those steps you should have explained things to us. Told us what was on your mind, let us in on what you were thinking and—"

"I didn't want to explain things," he said, cutting her off. "I wanted people to understand me, without having to put it into words. *You*, especially."

She didn't say anything.

"Back then I just couldn't consider others' feelings. I couldn't afford to think about that."

His voice shook a little as he recalled that time of his life. He felt like bursting out crying but somehow held himself in check and went on.

"My life completely changed back then, in a short space of time. It was all I could do to hang on and not get thrown off. I was so scared, so very frightened. At the time I couldn't explain things to anybody. I felt like I was about to slip off the face of the earth. I just wanted you to *understand* me. And hold me. Without any logic or explanations. But nobody ever—"

His sister covered her face with her hands. Her shoulders shook as she silently wept. He gently laid his hand on her shoulder.

"I'm sorry," she said.

"It's all right," he replied. He poured some cream into his coffee, stirred it, and took a slow sip, trying to calm himself. "No need to cry about it. It was my fault, too."

"Tell me," she said, raising her face to look straight at him, "why *today* of all days did you call me?"

"Today?"

"You haven't called for ten years, and I just wanted to know why you picked—today?"

"Something happened," he said, "and it made me think of you. I just wondered how you're doing. I wanted to hear your voice. That's all."

"No one told you anything?"

There was something different about her voice, and he tensed up. "No, I haven't heard anything from anybody. Did something happen?"

His sister was silent for a while, gathering her feelings. He waited patiently for her to explain.

"I'm going into the hospital tomorrow," she said.

"The hospital?"

"I'm having an operation for breast cancer tomorrow. They're going to remove my right breast. The whole thing. Nobody knows, though, if that will stop the cancer from spreading. They won't know till they've taken it off."

He couldn't say a thing for a while. His hand still on her shoulder, he gazed around meaninglessly from one object to another in the room. The clock, an ornament, the calendar, the remote control for the stereo. Familiar objects in a familiar room, but he somehow couldn't grasp the distance that separated one object from the other.

"For the longest time I wondered whether I should get in touch with you," his sister said. "I ended up thinking I shouldn't, so I never said anything. But I wanted to see you so much. I thought we should have at least one good talk. There were things I had to apologize for. But . . . I didn't want to see you like this. Do you know what I'm saying?"

"I do," her brother said.

"If we were going to meet, I wanted it to be under happier circumstances, where I could be more optimistic about things. So I decided not to get in touch with you. Right when I'd made up my mind, though, you called me—"

Wordlessly, he put both arms around her and drew her close. He could feel her breasts pressing against his chest. His sister rested her face on his shoulder and cried. Brother and sister stayed that way for a long while.

Finally she spoke up. "You said something happened and you thought of me. What was it? If you don't mind telling me."

"I don't know how to put it. It's hard to explain. It was just something that happened. A series of coincidences. One coincidence after another and then I—"

He shook his head. The sense of distance was still off. Several light-years separated the ornament from the remote control.

"I just can't explain it," he said.

"That's okay," she said. "But I'm glad it happened. Very glad."

He touched her right earlobe and lightly rubbed the mole. And then, like sending a wordless whisper into some very special place, he leaned forward and kissed it.

◉

"My sister's right breast was removed in the operation, but fortunately the cancer hadn't spread and she was able to get by with mild chemotherapy. Her hair didn't even fall out. She's completely fine now. I went almost every day to see her in the hospital. It must be awful for a woman to lose a breast that way. After she went home, I started to visit them pretty often. I've grown close to my nephew and niece. I've even been teaching my niece piano. Not to brag or anything, but there's a lot of promise there. And my brother-in-law's not as bad as I thought, now that I've gotten to know him. Sure, he's still full of himself and a bit crude, but he works hard and he's good to my sister. And he's finally gotten it through his head that being gay isn't a contagious disease I'm going to give his children. A small but significant step."

He laughed. "Getting back together with my sister, I feel like I've moved on in life. Like I can live the way I'm supposed to now, more than ever before . . . It was something I had to face up to. I think deep down I was always hoping my sister and I would make up, and be able to hug each other one more time."

"But something had to happen before you could?" I asked.

"That's right," he said, and nodded several times. "That's the key. And you know, this thought crossed my mind at the time: maybe chance is a pretty common thing after all. Those kinds of coincidences are happening all around us, all the time, but most of them don't catch our attention and we just let them go by. It's like fireworks in the daytime. You might hear a faint sound, but even if you look up at the sky you can't see a thing. But if we're really hoping something may come true, it may become visible, like a message rising to the surface. Then we're able to make it out clearly, decipher what it means. And seeing it before us we're surprised and wonder at how strange things like this can happen. Even though there's nothing strange about it. I just can't help thinking that. What do you think? Is this forcing things?"

I thought about what he'd said. You know, you may be right, I managed to reply. But I wasn't at all sure that things could be neatly wrapped up like that.

"I'd rather believe in something simpler, like in a god of jazz," I said.

He laughed. "I like that. It'd be nice if there was a god of gays, too."

I have no idea whatever happened to that petite woman he met in the bookstore café. I haven't had my piano tuned for over half a year, and haven't had a chance to talk with him. But I imagine on Tuesdays he's still driving across the Tama River and going to that café. Who knows—maybe he ran into her again. But I haven't heard anything, which means that this is where the story ends.

I don't care if it's the god of jazz, the god of gays, or some other type of god, but I hope that, somewhere, unobtrusively, as if it were all coincidence, someone up there is watching over that woman. I hope this from the bottom of my heart. A very simple hope.

— TRANSLATED BY PHILIP GABRIEL

HANALEI BAY

Sachi lost her nineteen-year-old son to a big shark that attacked him when he was surfing in Hanalei Bay. Properly speaking, it was not the shark that killed him. Alone far from shore when the animal ripped his right leg off, he panicked and drowned. Drowning, therefore, was the official cause of death. The shark nearly tore his surfboard in half as well. Sharks are not fond of human flesh. Most often their first bite disappoints them and they swim away. Which is why there are many cases in which the person loses a leg or an arm but survives as long as he doesn't panic. Sachi's son, though, suffered a kind of cardiac arrest, swallowed massive amounts of ocean water, and drowned.

When notice came from the Japanese consulate in Honolulu, Sachi sank to the floor in shock. Her head emptied out, and she found it impossible to think. All she could do was sit there staring at a spot on the wall. How long this went on, she had no idea. But eventually she regained her senses enough to look up the number of an airline and make a reservation for a flight to Hawaii. The consulate staff person had urged her to come as soon as possible in order to identify the victim. There was still some chance it might not be her son.

Because of the holiday season, all seats were booked on that day's flight and the next day's as well. Every airline she called told her the same thing, but when she explained her situation, the United reservationist said, "Just get to the airport as soon as you can. We'll find you a seat." She packed a few things in a small bag and went out to Narita Airport, where the woman in charge handed her a business-class ticket.

"This is all we have today, but we'll only charge you economy fare," she said. "This must be terrible for you. Try to bear up." Sachi thanked her for being so helpful.

When she arrived at Honolulu Airport, Sachi realized she had been so upset that she had forgotten to inform the Japanese consulate of her arrival time. A member of the consulate staff was supposed to be accompanying her to Kauai. She decided to continue on to Kauai alone rather than deal with the complications of making belated arrangements. She assumed that things would work out once she got there. It was still before noon when her second flight arrived at Lihue Airport in Kauai. She rented a car at the Avis counter and went straight to the police station nearby. There, she told them she had just come from Tokyo after having received word that her son was killed by a shark in Hanalei Bay. A graying police officer with glasses took her to the morgue, which was like a cold-storage warehouse, and showed her the body of her son with one leg torn off. Everything from just above the right knee was gone, and a ghastly white bone protruded from the stump. This was her son—there could no longer be any doubt. His face carried no hint of an expression; he looked as he always did when sound asleep. She could hardly believe he was dead. Someone must have arranged his features like this. He looked as though, if you gave his shoulder a hard shake, he would wake up complaining the way he always did in the morning.

In another room, Sachi signed a document certifying that the body was that of her son. The policeman asked her what she planned to do with it. "I don't know," she said. "What do people normally do?" They most often cremate it and take the ashes home, he told her. She could also transport the body to Japan, but this required some difficult arrangements and would be far more expensive. Another possibility would be to bury her son on Kauai.

"Please cremate him," she said. "I'll take the ashes with me to Tokyo." Her son was dead, after all. There was no hope of bringing him back to life. What difference did it make whether he was ashes or bones or a corpse? She signed the document authorizing cremation and paid the necessary fee.

"I only have American Express," she said.

"That will be fine," the officer said.

Here I am, paying the fee to have my son cremated with an American Express card, Sachi thought. It felt unreal to her, as unreal as her son's having been killed by a shark. The cremation would take place the next morning, the policeman told her.

"Your English is very good," the officer said as he put the documents in order. He was a Japanese American by the name of Sakata.

"I lived in the States for a while when I was young," Sachi said.

"No wonder," the officer said. Then he gave Sachi her son's belongings: clothes, passport, return ticket, wallet, Walkman, magazines, sunglasses, shaving kit. They all fit into a small Boston bag. Sachi had to sign a receipt listing these meager possessions.

"Do you have any other children?" the officer asked.

"No, he was my only child," Sachi replied.

"Your husband couldn't make the trip?"

"My husband died a long time ago."

The policeman released a deep sigh. "I'm sorry to hear that. Please let us know if there is anything we can do for you."

"I'd appreciate it if you could tell me how to get to the place where my son died. And where he was staying. I suppose there'll be a hotel bill to pay. And I need to get in touch with the Japanese consulate in Honolulu. Could I use your phone?"

He brought her a map and used a felt-tip marker to indicate where her son had been surfing and the location of the hotel where he had been staying. She slept that night in a little hotel in Lihue that the policeman recommended.

As Sachi was leaving the police station, the middle-aged Officer Sakata said to her, "I have a personal favor to ask of you. Nature takes a human life every now and then here on Kauai. You see how beautiful it is on this island, but sometimes, too, it can be wild and deadly. We live here with that potential. I'm very sorry about your son. I really feel for you. But I hope you won't let this make you hate our island. This may sound self-serving to you after everything you've been through, but I really mean it. From the heart."

Sachi nodded to him.

"You know, ma'am, my brother died in the war in 1944. In Belgium, near the German border. He was a member of the 442nd Regimental Combat Team made up of all Japanese American volunteers. They were there to rescue a Texas battalion surrounded by the Nazis when they took a direct hit and he was killed. There was nothing left but his dog tags and a few chunks of flesh scattered in the snow. My mother loved him so much, they tell me she was like a different person after that. I was just a little kid, so I only knew my mother after the change. It's painful to think about."

Officer Sakata shook his head and went on:

"Whatever the 'noble causes' involved, people die in war from the anger and hatred on both sides. But Nature doesn't have 'sides.' I know this is a painful experience for you, but try to think of it like this: your son returned to the cycle of Nature; it had nothing to do with any 'causes' or anger or hatred."

◎

Sachi had the cremation performed the next day and took the ashes with her in a small aluminum urn when she drove to Hanalei Bay on the north shore of the island. The trip from the Lihue police station took just over an hour. Virtually all the trees on the island had been deformed by a giant storm that struck a few years earlier. Sachi noticed the remains of several wooden houses with their roofs blown off. Even some of the mountains showed signs of having been reshaped by the storm. Nature could be harsh in this environment.

She continued on through the sleepy little town of Hanalei to the surfing area where her son had been attacked by the shark. Parking in a nearby lot, she went to sit on the beach and watched a few surfers— maybe five in all—riding the waves. They would float far offshore, hanging on to their surfboards, until a powerful wave came through. Then they would catch the wave, push off, and mount their boards, riding almost to the shore. As the force of the waves gave out, they would lose their balance and fall in. Then they would retrieve their boards and slip under the incoming waves as they paddled back out to the open sea, where the whole thing would start over again. Sachi could hardly understand them. Weren't they afraid of sharks? Or had they not heard that her son had been killed by a shark in this very place a few days earlier?

Sachi went on sitting there, vacantly watching this scene for a good hour. Her mind could not fasten onto any single thing. The weighty past had simply vanished, and the future lay somewhere in the distant gloom. Neither tense had any connection with her now. She sat in the continually shifting present, her eyes mechanically tracing the monotonously repeating scene of waves and surfers. At one point the thought dawned on her: *What I need now most of all is time.*

Then Sachi went to the hotel where her son had been staying, a shabby little place with an unkempt garden. Two shirtless, long-haired white men sat there in canvas deck chairs, drinking beer. Several empty green Rolling Rock bottles lay among the weeds at their feet. One of the men was blond, the other had black hair. Otherwise, they had the same kind of faces and builds and wore the same kind of florid tattoos on both arms. There was a hint of marijuana in the air, mixed with a whiff of dog shit. As she approached, the two men eyed her suspiciously.

"My son was staying here," she said. "He was killed by a shark three days ago."

The men looked at each other. "You mean Takashi?"

"Yes," Sachi said. "Takashi."

"He was a cool dude," the blond man said. "It's too bad."

The black-haired man explained in flaccid tones, "That morning, there was, uh, lots of turtles in the bay. The sharks come in lookin' for the turtles. But, y'know, those guys usually leave the surfers alone. We get along with 'em fine. But, I don't know, I guess there's all kinds of sharks. . . ."

Sachi said she had come to pay Takashi's hotel bill. She assumed there was an outstanding balance on his room.

The blond man frowned and waved his bottle in the air. "No, lady, you don't get it. Surfers are the only ones who stay in this hotel, and they ain't got no money. You gotta pay in advance to stay here. We don't have no 'outstanding balances.' "

Then the black-haired man said, "Say, lady, you want to take Takashi's surfboard with you? Damn shark ripped it in two, kinda shredded it. It's an old Dick Brewer. The cops didn't take it. I think it's, uh, somewhere over there . . ."

Sachi shook her head. She did not want to see the board.

"It's really too bad," the blond man said again as if that was the only expression he could think of.

"He was a cool dude," the black-haired fellow said. "Really OK. Damn good surfer, too. Come to think of it, he was with us the night before, drinkin' tequila. Yeah."

Sachi ended up staying in Hanalei for a week. She rented the most decent-looking cottage she could find and cooked her own simple meals. One way or another, she had to get her old self back again before returning to Japan. She bought a vinyl chair, sunglasses, a hat and sunscreen, and sat on the beach every day, watching the surfers. It rained a few times each day—violently, as if someone were tipping a huge bowl of water out of the sky. Autumn weather on the north shore of Kauai was unstable. When a downpour started, she would sit in her car, watching the rain. And when the rain let up, she would go out to sit on the beach again, watching the sea.

Sachi started visiting Hanalei at this season every year. She would arrive a few days before the anniversary of her son's death and stay three weeks, watching the surfers from a vinyl chair on the beach. That was all she would do each day, every day. It went on like this for ten years. She would stay in the same cottage and eat in the same restaurant, reading a book. As her trips became an established pattern, she found a few people with whom she could speak about personal matters. Many residents of the small town knew her by sight. She became known as the Japanese mom whose son was killed by a shark nearby.

One day, on the way back from Lihue Airport, where she had gone to exchange a balky rental car, Sachi spotted two young Japanese hitchhikers in the town of Kapaa. They were standing outside the Ono Family Restaurant with big sports equipment bags hanging over their shoulders, facing traffic with their thumbs stuck out but looking far from confident. One was tall and lanky, the other short and stocky. Both had shoulder-length hair dyed a rusty red and wore faded T-shirts, baggy shorts, and sandals. Sachi passed them by, but soon changed her mind and turned around.

Opening her window, she asked them in Japanese, "How far are you going?"

"Hey, you can speak Japanese!" the tall one said.

"Well, of course, I *am* Japanese. How far are you going?"

"A place called Hanalei," the tall one said.

"Want a ride? I'm on the way back there myself."

"Great! Just what we were hoping for!" the stocky one said.

They put their bags in the trunk and started to climb into the backseat of Sachi's Neon.

"Wait just a minute there," she said. "I'm not going to have you both in back. This is no cab, after all. One of you sit in front. It's plain good manners."

They decided the tall one would sit in front, and he timidly got in next to Sachi, wrenching his long legs into the available space. "What kind of car is this?" he asked.

"It's a Dodge Neon. A Chrysler car," Sachi answered.

"Hmm, so America has these cramped little cars, too, huh? My sister's Corolla maybe has more room than this."

"Well, it's not as if all Americans ride around in big Cadillacs."

"Yeah, but this is really *little.*"

"You can get out right here if you don't like it," Sachi said.

"Whoa, I didn't mean it that way!" he said. "I was just kinda surprised how small this is, that's all. I thought all American cars were on the big side."

"So anyway, what're you going to Hanalei for?" Sachi asked as she drove along.

"Well, surfing, for one thing."

"Where're your boards?"

"We'll get 'em there," the stocky boy said.

"Yeah, it's a pain to lug 'em all the way from Japan. And we heard you could get used ones cheap there," the tall one added.

"How about you, lady? Are you here on vacation, too?"

"Uh-huh."

"Alone?"

"Alone," Sachi said lightly.

"I don't suppose you're one of them legendary surfers?"

"Don't be crazy!" Sachi said. "Anyway, have you got a place to stay in Hanalei?"

"Nah, we figured it'd work out once we got there," the tall one said.

"Yeah, we figured we can always sleep on the beach if we have to," the stocky one said. "Besides, we ain't got much money."

Sachi shook her head. "It gets *cold* at night on the north shore this time of year—cold enough for a sweater indoors. Sleep outside and you'll make yourselves sick."

"It's not always summer in Hawaii?" the tall one asked.

"Hawaii's right up there in the northern hemisphere, you know. It's got four seasons. The summers are hot, and winters can be cold."

"So we'd better get a roof over our heads," the stocky boy said.

"Say, lady, do you think you could help us find a place?" the tall one asked. "Our English is, like, nonexistent."

"Yeah," said the stocky boy. "We heard you can use Japanese anywhere in Hawaii, but so far it hasn't worked at all."

"Of course not!" Sachi said, exasperated. "The only place you can get by with Japanese is Oahu, and just one part of Waikiki at that. They get all these Japanese tourists wanting Louis Vuitton bags and Chanel No. 5, so they hire clerks who can speak Japanese. The same with Hyatt and Sheraton. But outside the hotels, English is the only thing that works. I mean, it's America, after all. You came all the way to Kauai without knowing that?"

"I had no idea. My mom said everybody in Hawaii speaks Japanese."

Sachi groaned.

"Anyhow, we can stay at the cheapest hotel in town," the stocky boy said. "Like I said, we ain't got any money."

"Newcomers do *not* want to stay at the cheapest hotel in Hanalei," Sachi cautioned them. "It can be dangerous."

"How's that?" asked the tall boy.

"Drugs, mainly," Sachi answered. "Some of those surfers are bad guys. Marijuana might be OK, but watch out for ice."

" 'Ice'? What's that?"

"Never heard of it," said the tall boy.

"You two don't know anything, do you? You'd make perfect pigeons for those guys. Ice is a hard drug, and it's everywhere in Hawaii. I don't know exactly, but it's some kind of crystallized upper. It's cheap, and easy to use, and it makes you feel good, but once you get hooked on it you might as well be dead."

"Scary," said the tall one.

"You mean it's OK to do marijuana?" asked the stocky one.

"I don't know if it's OK, but at least it won't kill you. Not like tobacco. It might mess your brain up a little, but you guys wouldn't know the difference."

"Hey, that's harsh!" said the stocky boy.

The tall one asked Sachi, "Are you one of those boomer types?"

"You mean . . ."

"Yeah, a member of the baby boom generation."

"I'm not a 'member' of any generation. I'm just me. Don't start lumping me in with any groups, please."

"That's it! You *are* a boomer!" said the stocky boy. "You get so serious about everything right away. Just like my mom."

"And don't lump me together with your precious 'mom,' either," Sachi said. "Anyhow, for your own good, you'd better stay in a decent place in Hanalei. Things happen . . . even murder sometimes."

"Not exactly the peaceful paradise it's supposed to be," the stocky boy said.

"No," agreed Sachi. "The age of Elvis is long gone."

"I'm not sure what that's all about," said the tall boy, "but I know Elvis Costello is an old guy already."

Sachi drove without talking for a while after that.

Sachi spoke to the manager of her cottage, who found the boys a room. Her introduction got them a reduced weekly rate, but still it was more than they had budgeted for.

"No way," said the tall one. "We haven't got that much money."

"Yeah, next to nothin'," said the stocky one.

"You must have something for emergencies," Sachi insisted.

The tall boy scratched his earlobe and said, "Well, I do have a Diners Club family card, but my dad said absolutely not to use it except for a real, honest-to-goodness emergency. He's afraid once I start I won't stop. If I use it for anything but an emergency, I'll catch hell when I get back to Japan."

"Don't be stupid," Sachi said. "This *is* an emergency. If you want to stay alive, get that card out right now. The last thing you want is for the police to throw you in jail and have some big Hawaiian make you his girl-friend for the night. Of course, if you *like* that kind of thing that's another story, but it *hurts*."

The tall boy dug the card out of his wallet and handed it to the manager. Sachi asked for the name of a store where they could buy cheap used surfboards. The manager told her, adding, "And when you leave, they'll buy them back from you." The boys left their packs in the room and hurried off to the store.

Sachi was sitting on the beach, looking at the ocean as usual the next morning, when the two young Japanese boys showed up and started surfing. Their surfing skills were solid, in contrast to their helplessness on land. They would spot a strong wave, mount it nimbly, and guide their boards toward shore with grace and sure control. They kept this up for hours without a break. They looked truly alive when they were riding the waves: their eyes shone, they were full of confidence. There was no sign of yesterday's timidity. Back home, they probably spent their days on the water, never studying—just like her dead son.

Sachi had begun playing the piano in high school—a late start for a pianist. She had never touched the instrument before. She started fooling around with the one in the music room after classes, and before long she had taught herself to play well. It turned out she had absolute pitch, and an ear that was far above ordinary. She could hear a melody once and turn it into patterns on the keyboard. She could find the right chords for the melody. Without being taught by anyone, she learned how to move her fingers smoothly. She obviously had a natural, inborn gift for the piano.

The young music teacher heard her playing one day, liked what he heard, and helped her correct some basic fingering errors. "You *can* play it that way, but you can speed it up if you do it like this," he said, and demonstrated for her. She got it immediately. A great jazz fan, this teacher instructed her in the mysteries of jazz theory after school: chord formation and progression, use of the pedal, the concept of improvisation. She greedily absorbed everything. He lent her records: Red Garland, Bill Evans, Wynton Kelly. She would listen to them over and over until she could copy them perfectly. Once she got the hang of it, such imitation became easy for her. She could reproduce the music's sound and flow directly through her fingers without transcribing anything. "You've got real talent," the teacher said to her. "If you work hard, you can be a pro."

But Sachi didn't believe him. All she could do was produce accurate imitations, not music of her own. When urged to ad-lib, she didn't know what to play. She would start out improvising and end up copying someone else's original solo. Reading music was another of her stumbling blocks. With the detailed notation of a score in front of her, she found it hard to breathe. It was far easier for her to transfer what she heard directly to the keyboard. No, she thought: there was no way she could become a pro.

She decided instead to study cooking after high school. Not that she had a special interest in the subject, but her father owned a restaurant, and since she had nothing else she particularly wanted to do, she thought she would carry the business on after him. She went to Chicago to attend a professional cooking school. Chicago was not a city known for its sophisticated cuisine, but the family had relatives there who agreed to sponsor her.

A classmate at the cooking school introduced her to a small piano bar downtown, and soon she was playing there. At first she thought of it as part-time work to earn some spending money. Barely managing to scrape by on what little they sent her from home, she was glad for the extra cash. The owner of the bar loved the way she could play any tune at all. Once she heard a song, she would never forget it, and even with a song she had never heard before, if someone hummed it for her, she could play it on the spot. She was no beauty, but she had attractive features, and her presence started bringing more and more people to the bar. The tips they left her also began to mount up. She eventually stopped going to school. Sitting in front of the piano was so much easier—and so much more fun—than dressing a bloody chunk of pork, grating a rock-hard cheese, or washing the scum from a heavy frying pan.

And so, when her son became a virtual high school dropout to spend all his time surfing, Sachi resigned herself to it. *I did the same kind of thing when I was young. I can't blame him. It's probably in the blood.*

She played in the bar for a year and a half. Her English improved, she put away a fair amount of money, and she got herself a boyfriend—a handsome African American aspiring actor. (Sachi would later spot him in a supporting role in *Diehard 2*.) One day, however, an immigration officer with a badge on his chest showed up at the bar. She had apparently made too big a splash. The officer asked for her passport and arrested her on the spot for working illegally. A few days later she found herself on a jumbo jet bound for Narita—with a ticket she had to pay for from her savings. So ended Sachi's life in America.

Back in Tokyo, Sachi thought about the possibilities open to her for the rest of her life, but playing the piano was the only way she could think of to make a go of it. Her opportunities were limited by her handicap with written music, but there were places where her talent for playing by ear was appreciated—hotel lounges, nightclubs, and piano bars. She could play in any style demanded by the atmosphere of the place, the types of customer, or the requests that came in. She might be a genuine "musical chameleon," but she never had trouble making a living.

She married at the age of twenty-four, and two years later gave birth to a son. The man was a jazz guitarist one year younger than Sachi. His income was virtually nonexistent. He was addicted to drugs, and he fooled around with women. He stayed out much of the time, and when he did come home, he was often violent. Everyone opposed the marriage, and afterward everyone urged Sachi to divorce him. Unpolished though he was, Sachi's husband possessed an original talent, and in the jazz world he was gaining attention as an upcoming star. This was probably what attracted Sachi to him in the first place. But the marriage lasted only five years. He suffered a heart seizure one night in another woman's room, and died stark naked as they were rushing him to the hospital. It was probably a drug overdose.

Soon after her husband died, Sachi opened her own small piano bar in the fashionable Roppongi neighborhood. She had some savings, and she collected on an insurance policy she had secretly taken out on her husband's life. She also managed to get a bank loan. It helped that a regular customer at the bar where Sachi had been playing was the head of a branch. She installed a used grand piano in the place, and built a counter that followed the shape of the instrument. To run the business, she paid a high salary to a capable bartender-manager she had decided to hire away from another bar. She played every night, taking requests from customers and accompanying them when they sang. A fishbowl sat on the piano for tips. Musicians appearing at jazz clubs in the neighborhood would stop by now and then to play a quick tune or two. The bar soon had its regular customers, and business was better than Sachi had hoped for. She was able to repay her loan on schedule. Quite fed up with married life as she had known it, she did not remarry, but she had men friends every now and then. Most of them were married, which made it all the easier for her. As time went by, her son grew up, became a surfer, and announced that he was going to go to Hanalei in Kauai. She didn't like the idea, but she tired of arguing with him and reluctantly paid his fare. Long verbal battles were not her specialty. And so, while he was waiting for a good wave to come in, her son was attacked by a shark that entered the bay in pursuit of turtles, and ended his short life of nineteen years.

Sachi worked harder than ever once her son was dead. She played and played and played that first year, almost without letup. And when autumn was coming to an end, she took a three-week break, bought a business-class ticket on United Airlines, and went to Kauai. Another pianist took her place while she was gone.

⊙

Sachi sometimes played in Hanalei, too. One restaurant had a baby grand that was played on weekends by a string bean of a pianist in his midfifties. He would perform mostly harmless little tunes such as "Bali Hai" and "Blue Hawaii." He was nothing special as a pianist, but his warm personality came through in his playing. Sachi got friendly with him and sat in for him now and then. She did it for fun, so of course the restaurant didn't pay her anything, but the owner would treat her to wine and a plate of pasta. It just felt good to get her hands on the keys: it opened her up. This was not a question of talent or whether the activity was of any use. Sachi imagined that her son must have felt the same way when he was riding the waves.

In all honesty, however, Sachi had never really *liked* her son. Of course she loved him—he was the most important person in the world to her—but as an individual human being, she had had trouble liking him, which was a realization that it took her a very long time to reach. She probably would have had nothing to do with him had they not shared the same blood. He was self-centered, could never concentrate on anything, could never bring anything to fruition. She could never talk to him seriously about anything; he would immediately make up some phony excuse to avoid such talk. He hardly ever studied, which meant his grades were miserable. The only thing he ever lent some effort to was surfing, and there was no telling how long he would have kept that up. A sweet-faced boy, he never had a shortage of girlfriends, but after he had gotten what fun he could out of a girl, he would cast her off like an old toy. *Maybe I'm the one who spoiled him,* Sachi thought. *Maybe I gave him too much spending money. Maybe I should have been stricter with him.* But she had no concrete idea what she could have done so as to *be* stricter with him. Work had kept her too busy, and she knew nothing about boys—their psyches or their bodies.

Sachi was playing at the restaurant one evening when the two young surfers came in for a meal. It was the sixth day since they had arrived in Hanalei. They were thoroughly tanned, and they seemed to have a sturdier look about them now as well.

"Hey, you play the piano!" the stocky one exclaimed.

"And you're good, too—a real pro," chimed in the tall one.

"I do it for fun," she said.

"Know any songs by the B'z?"

"No J-pop for me, thanks!" Sachi said. "But wait a minute, I thought you guys were broke. Can you afford to eat in a place like this?"

"Sure, I got my Diners Card!" the tall one announced.

"Yes, *for emergencies . . .*"

"Oh, I'm not worried. My old man was right, though. Use it once and it becomes a habit."

"True, so now you can take it easy," Sachi said.

"We were thinking we ought to buy you dinner," the stocky boy said. "To thank you. You helped us a *lot.* And we're goin' home the day after tomorrow."

"Yeah," said the tall one. "How about right now? We can order wine, too. Our treat!"

"I've already had my dinner," Sachi said, lifting her glass of red wine. "And this was on the house. I'll accept your thanks, though. I appreciate the sentiment."

Just then a large white man approached their table and stood near Sachi with a glass of whiskey in his hand. He was around forty and wore his hair short. His arms were like slender telephone poles, and one bore a large dragon tattoo above the letters "USMC." Judging from its fading colors, the tattoo had been applied some years before.

"Hey, little lady, I like your piano playing," he said.

Sachi glanced up at him and said, "Thanks."

"You Japanese?"

"Sure am."

"I was in Japan once. A long time ago. Stationed two years in Iwakuni. A long time ago."

"Well, what do you know? I was in Chicago once for two years. A long time ago. That makes us even."

The man thought about this for a moment, seemed to decide that she was joking, and smiled.

"Play something for me. Something upbeat. You know Bobby Darin's 'Beyond the Sea'? I wanna sing it."

"I don't work here, you know," she said. "And right now I'm having a conversation with these two boys. See that skinny gentleman with the thinning hair sitting at the piano? He's the pianist here. Maybe you ought to give your request to him. And don't forget to leave him a tip."

The man shook his head. "That fruitcake can't play anything but wishy-washy queer stuff. I wanna hear *you* play—something snappy. There's ten bucks in it for you."

"I wouldn't do it for five hundred."

"So that's the way it is, huh?" the man said.

"Yes, that's the way it is," Sachi said.

"Tell me something, then, will you? Why aren't you Japanese willing to fight to protect your own country? Why do *we* have to drag our asses to Iwakuni to keep you guys safe?"

"And because of that I'm supposed to shut up and play?"

"You got it," the man said. He glanced across the table at the two boys. "And lookit you two—a coupla Jap surf bums. Come all the way to Hawaii—for what? In Iraq, we—"

"Let me ask you a question," Sachi interjected. "Something I've been wondering about ever since you came over here."

"Sure. Ask away."

Twisting her neck, Sachi looked straight up at the man. "I've been wondering this whole time," she said, "how somebody gets to be like you. Were you born that way, or did something terrible happen to make you the way you are? Which do you think it is?"

The man gave this a moment's thought and then slammed his whiskey glass down on the table. "Look, lady—"

The owner of the restaurant heard the man's raised voice and hurried over. He was a small man, but he took the ex-marine's thick arm and led him away. They were friends apparently, and the ex-marine offered no resistance other than a parting shot or two.

The owner came back shortly afterward and apologized to Sachi. "He's usually not a bad guy, but liquor changes him. Don't worry, I'll set him straight. Meanwhile, let me buy you something. Forget this ever happened."

"That's okay," Sachi said. "I'm used to this kind of thing."

The stocky boy asked Sachi, "What was that guy saying?"

"Yeah, I couldn't catch a thing," the tall boy added, "except 'Jap.'"

"It's just as well," Sachi said. "Never mind. Have you guys had a good time here in Hanalei? Surfing your brains out, I suppose."

"Faaantastic!" said the stocky boy.

"Just super," said the tall one. "It changed my life. No kiddin'."

"That's wonderful," Sachi said. "Get all the fun you can out of life while you're still able. They'll serve you the bill soon enough."

"No problem," said the tall boy. "I've got my card."

"That's the way," Sachi said, shaking her head. "Nice and easy."

Then the stocky boy said, "I've been meaning to ask you something, if you don't mind."

"About what?"

"I was just wondering if you had ever seen the one-legged Japanese surfer."

"One-legged Japanese surfer?" Sachi looked straight at him with narrowed eyes. "No, I never have."

"We saw him twice. He was on the beach, staring at us. He had a red Dick Brewer surfboard, and his leg was gone from here down." The stocky boy drew a line with his finger a few inches above his knee. "Like it was chopped off. He was gone when we came out of the water. Just disappeared. We wanted to talk to him, so we tried hard to find him, but he wasn't anywhere. I guess he musta been about our age."

"Which leg was gone? The right one or the left one?" Sachi asked.

The stocky boy thought for a moment and said, "I'm pretty sure it was the right one. Right?"

"Yeah, definitely. The right one," the tall boy said.

"Hmm," Sachi said and moistened her mouth with a sip of wine. She could hear the sharp, hard beating of her heart. "You're sure he was Japanese? Not Japanese American?"

"No way," the tall boy said. "You can tell the difference right away. No, this guy was a surfer from Japan. Like us."

Sachi bit hard into her lower lip, and stared at them for some moments. Then, her voice dry, she said, "Strange, though. This is such a small town, you couldn't miss seeing somebody like that even if you wanted to: a one-legged Japanese surfer."

"Yeah," said the stocky boy. "I *know* it's strange. A guy like that'd stick out like a sore thumb. But he was there, I'm sure of it. We both saw him."

The tall boy looked at Sachi and said, "You're always sitting there on the beach, right? He was standing there on one leg, a little ways away from where you always sit. And he was looking right at us, kind of like leaning against a tree trunk. He was under that clump of iron trees on the other side of the picnic tables."

Sachi took a silent swallow of her wine.

The stocky boy went on: "I wonder how he can stand on his surfboard with one leg? It's tough enough with two."

Every day after that, from morning to evening, Sachi walked back and forth along the full length of Hanalei's long beach, but there was never any sign of the one-legged surfer. She asked the local surfers, "Have you seen a one-legged Japanese surfer?" but they all gave her strange looks and shook their heads. A one-legged Japanese surfer? Never seen such a thing. If I had, I'd be sure to remember. He'd stand out. But how can anybody surf with one leg?

The night before she went back to Japan, Sachi finished packing and got into bed. The cries of the geckos mingled with the sound of the surf. Before long, she realized that her pillow was damp: she was crying. Why can't I see him? she wondered. Why did he appear to those two surfers—who were nothing to him—and not to me? It was so unfair! She brought back the image of her son's corpse in the morgue. If only it were possible, she would shake his shoulder until he woke up, and she would shout at him—Tell me why! How could you do such a thing?

Sachi buried her face in her damp pillow for a long time, muffling her sobs. Am I simply not *qualified* to see him? she asked herself, but she did not know the answer to her own question. All she knew for sure was that, whatever else she might do, she had to accept this island. As that gentle-spoken Japanese American police officer had suggested to her, she had to accept the things on this island as they were. *As they were:* fair or unfair, qualified or unqualified, it didn't matter. Sachi woke up the next morning as a healthy middle-aged woman. She loaded her suitcase into the backseat of her Dodge and left Hanalei Bay.

◎

She had been back in Japan for some eight months when she bumped into the stocky boy in Tokyo. Taking refuge from the rain, she was drinking a cup of coffee in a Starbucks near the Roppongi subway station. He was sitting at a nearby table. He was nattily dressed, in a well-pressed Ralph Lauren shirt and new chinos, and he was with a petite, pleasant-featured girl.

"What a coincidence!" he exclaimed as he approached her table with a big smile.

"How've you been?" she asked. "Look how short your hair is!"

"Well, I'm just about to graduate from college," he said.

"I don't believe it! *You*?"

"Uh-huh. I've got at least that much under control," he said, slipping into the chair across from her.

"Have you quit surfing?"

"I do some on weekends once in a while, but not much longer: it's hiring season now."

"How about beanpole?"

"Oh, he's got it easy. No job-hunting worries for him. His father's got a big Western pastry shop in Akasaka, says they'll buy him a BMW if he takes over the business. He's so lucky!"

Sachi glanced outside. The passing summer shower had turned the streets black. Traffic was at a standstill, and an impatient taxi driver was honking his horn.

"Is she your girlfriend?" Sachi asked.

"Uh-huh . . . I guess. I'm workin' on it," he said, scratching his head.

"She's cute. Too cute for you. Probably not giving you what you want."

His eyes went up to the ceiling. "Whoa! I see you still say exactly what you think. You're right, though. Got any good advice for me? To make things happen, I mean . . ."

"There are only three ways to get along with a girl: one, shut up and listen to what she has to say; two, tell her you like what she's wearing; and three, treat her to really good food. Easy, huh? If you do all that and still don't get the results you want, better give up."

"Sounds good: simple and practical. Mind if I write it down in my notebook?"

"Of course not. But you mean to say you can't remember that much?"

"Nah, I'm like a chicken: three steps, and my mind's a blank. So I write everything down. I heard Einstein used to do that."

"Oh, sure, Einstein."

"I don't mind being forgetful," he said. "It's actually *forgetting* stuff that I don't like."

"Do as you please," Sachi said.

Stocky pulled out his notebook and wrote down what she had said.

"You always give me good advice. Thanks again."

"I hope it works."

"I'll give it my best shot," he said, and stood up to go back to his own table. After a moment's thought, he held out his hand. "You, too," he said. "Give it your best shot."

Sachi took his hand. "I'm glad the sharks didn't eat you in Hanalei Bay," she said.

"You mean, there are sharks there? Seriously?"

"Uh-huh," she said. "Seriously."

Sachi sits at the keyboard every night, moving her fingers almost auto-matically, and thinking of nothing else. Only the sounds of the piano pass through her mind—in one door and out the other. When she is not play-ing, she thinks about the three weeks she spends in Hanalei at the end of autumn. She thinks about the sound of the incoming waves and the sigh-ing of the iron trees. The clouds carried along by the trade winds, the albatrosses sailing across the sky, their huge wings spread wide. And she thinks about what surely must await her there. That is all there is for her to think about now. Hanalei Bay.

—TRANSLATED BY JAY RUBIN

WHERE I'M LIKELY TO FIND IT

My husband's father was run over by a streetcar three years ago and died," the woman said, and paused.

I didn't say a word, just looked her right in the eyes and nodded twice. During the pause, I glanced at the half-dozen pencils in the pen tray, checking to see how sharp they were. Like a golfer carefully selecting the right club, I deliberated over which one to use, finally picking one that wasn't too sharp, or too worn, but just right.

"The whole thing's a little embarrassing," the woman said.

Keeping my opinion to myself, I laid a memo pad in front of me and tested the pencil by writing down the date and the woman's name.

"There aren't many streetcars left in Tokyo," she went on. "They've switched to buses most everywhere. The few that are left are kind of a memento of the past, I guess. And it was one of those that killed my father-in-law." She gave a silent sigh. "This was the night of October first, three years ago. It was pouring that night."

I noted down the basics of her story. *Father-in-law, three years ago, streetcar, heavy rain, October 1, night.* I like to take great care when I write, so it took a while to note all this down.

"My father-in-law was completely drunk at the time. Otherwise, he obviously wouldn't have fallen asleep on a rainy night on the streetcar tracks."

She fell silent again, lips closed, her eyes steadily gazing at me. She was probably wanting me to agree with her.

"He must have been pretty drunk," I said.

"So drunk he passed out."

"Did your father-in-law often drink that much?"

"You mean did he often drink so much that he passed out?"

I nodded.

"He did get drunk every once in a while," she admitted. "But not all the time, and never so drunk that he'd fall asleep on the streetcar tracks."

How drunk would you have to be to fall asleep on the rails of a streetcar line? I wondered. Was the amount a person drank the main issue? Or did it have more to do with why he was getting drunk in the first place?

"What you're saying is that he got drunk sometimes, but usually not falling-down drunk?" I asked.

"That's the way I see it," she replied.

"May I ask your age, if you don't mind?"

"You want to know how old I am?"

"You don't have to answer if you don't want to."

The woman rubbed the bridge of her nose with her index finger. It was a lovely, perfectly straight nose. My guess was she had recently had plastic surgery. I used to go out with a woman who had the same habit. She'd had a nose job, and whenever she was thinking about something she rubbed the bridge with her index finger. As if she were making sure her brand-new nose was still there. Looking at this woman in front of me now brought on a mild case of déjà vu. Which, in turn, conjured up vague memories of oral sex.

"I'm not trying to hide my age or anything," the woman said. "I'm thirty-five."

"And how old was your father-in-law when he died?"

"Sixty-eight."

"What did he do? His job, I mean."

"He was a priest."

"By priest you mean a Buddhist priest?"

"That's right. A Buddhist priest. Of the Jodo sect. He was head of a temple in the Toshima Ward."

"That must have been a real shock," I said.

"That my father-in-law was run over by a streetcar?"

"Yes."

"Of course it was a shock. Especially for my husband," the woman said.

I noted some more things down on my memo pad. *Priest, Jodo sect, 68.*

The woman was sitting at one end of my love seat. I was in my swivel chair behind my desk. Two yards separated us. She had on a sharp-looking sage green suit. Her legs were beautiful, and her stockings matched her black high-heeled shoes. The stilettos looked like some kind of deadly weapon.

"So what you've come to ask me," I said, "concerns your husband's late father?"

"No. It's not about him," she said. She shook her head slightly a couple of times to emphasize the negative. "It's about my husband."

"Is he also a priest?"

"No, he works at Merrill Lynch."

"The investment firm?"

"That's right," she replied, clearly a little irritated. What other Merrill Lynch *is* there? her tone implied. "He's a stockbroker."

I checked the tip of my pencil to see how worn it was, then waited for her to continue.

"My husband is an only son, and he was more interested in stock-trading than Buddhism, so he didn't succeed his father as head priest of the temple."

Which all makes perfect sense, don't you think? her eyes said, but since I didn't have an opinion one way or the other regarding Buddhism or stock-trading, I didn't respond. Instead, I adopted a neutral expression that indicated that I was absorbing every word.

"After my father-in-law passed away, my mother-in-law moved into an apartment in our condo, in Shinagawa. A different unit in the same building. My husband and I live on the twenty-sixth floor, and she's on the twenty-fourth. She lives alone. She'd lived in the temple with her husband, but after another priest came to take over she had to move. She's sixty-three. And my husband, I should add, is forty. He'll be forty-one next month, if nothing's happened to him, that is."

I made a memo of it all. *Mother-in-law 24th floor, 63. Husband, 40, Merrill Lynch, 26th floor, Shinagawa.* The woman waited patiently for me to finish.

"After my father-in-law died, my mother-in-law started having panic attacks. They seem to be worse when it's raining, probably because her husband died on a rainy night. A fairly common thing, I imagine."

I nodded.

"When the symptoms are bad, it's like a screw's come loose in her head. She calls us and my husband goes down the two floors to her place to take care of her. He tries to calm her down, to convince her that everything's going to be all right. If my husband's not at home, then I go."

She paused, waiting for my reaction. I kept quiet.

"My mother-in-law's not a bad person. I don't have any negative feelings toward her. It's just that she's the nervous type, and has always relied too much on other people. Do you understand the situation?"

"I think so," I said.

She crossed her legs, waiting for me to write something new on my pad. But I didn't write anything down.

"She called us at ten one Sunday morning. Two Sundays—ten days—ago."

I glanced at my desk calendar. "Sunday the third of September?"

"That's right, the third. My mother-in-law called us at ten that morning," the woman said. She closed her eyes as if recalling it. If we were in a Hitchcock movie, the screen would have started to ripple at this point and we'd have segued into a flashback. But this was no movie, and no flashback was forthcoming. She opened her eyes and went on. "My husband answered the phone. He'd been planning to play golf, but it had been raining hard since dawn, so he canceled. If only it hadn't been raining, this never would have happened. I know I'm just second-guessing myself."

September 3rd, golf, rain, canceled, mother-in-law—phoned. I wrote it all down.

"My mother-in-law said that she was having trouble breathing. She felt dizzy and couldn't stand up. So my husband got dressed, and without even shaving he went down to her apartment. He told me that it wouldn't take long and asked me to get breakfast ready."

"What was he wearing?" I asked.

She rubbed her nose again lightly. "Chinos and a short-sleeved polo shirt. His shirt was dark gray. The trousers were cream-colored. Both items we'd bought from the J.Crew catalogue. My husband's nearsighted and always wears glasses. Metal-framed Armanis. His shoes were gray New Balance. He didn't have any socks on."

I noted down all the details.

"Do you want to know his height and weight?"

"That would help," I said.

"He's five-eight, and weighs about one fifty-eight. Before we got married, he weighed about one thirty-five, but he's put on some weight."

I wrote down this information. I checked the tip of my pencil and exchanged it for another. I held the new pencil for a while, getting used to the feel.

"Do you mind if I go on?" she asked.

"Not at all," I said.

She uncrossed and recrossed her legs. "I was getting ready to make pancakes when his mother called. I always make pancakes on Sunday morning. If he doesn't play golf on Sundays, my husband eats a lot of pancakes. He loves them, with some crisp bacon on the side."

No wonder the guy put on twenty pounds, I thought.

"Twenty-five minutes later my husband called me. He said his mother had settled down and he was on his way upstairs. 'I'm starving,' he told me. 'Get breakfast ready so I can eat as soon as I get there.' So I heated up the frying pan and started cooking the pancakes and bacon. I heated up the maple syrup as well. Pancakes aren't difficult to make— it's all a matter of timing and doing everything in the right order. I waited and waited, but he didn't come home. The stack of pancakes on his plate was getting cold. I phoned my mother-in-law and asked her if my husband was still there. She said he'd left a long time ago."

She brushed off an imaginary, metaphysical piece of lint on her skirt, just above the knee.

"My husband disappeared. He vanished into thin air. And I haven't heard from him since. He disappeared somewhere between the twenty-fourth and twenty-sixth floors."

"You contacted the police?"

"Of course I did," she said, her lips curling a little in irritation. "When he wasn't back by one o'clock, I phoned the police. But they didn't put much effort into looking for him. A patrolman from the local police station came over, but when he saw there was no sign of a violent crime he couldn't be bothered. 'If he isn't back in two days,' he said, 'go to the precinct and file a missing-persons report.' The police seem to think that my husband wandered off somewhere on the spur of the moment, as if he were fed up with his life and just took off. But that's ridiculous. I mean, think about it. My husband went down to his mother's completely empty-handed—no wallet, driver's license, credit cards, no watch. He hadn't even shaved, for God's sake. And he'd just phoned me and told me to get the pancakes ready. Somebody who's running away from home wouldn't call and ask you to make pancakes, would he?"

"You're absolutely right," I agreed. "But, tell me, when your husband went down to the twenty-fourth floor, did he take the stairs?"

"He never uses the elevator. He hates elevators. Says he can't stand being cooped up in a confined place like that."

"Still, you chose to live on the twenty-sixth floor of a high-rise?"

"We did. But he always uses the stairs. He doesn't seem to mind—he says it's good exercise and helps him to keep his weight down. Of course, it does take time."

Pancakes, twenty pounds, stairs, ~~elevator~~, I noted on my pad.

"So that's the situation," she said. "Will you take the case?"

No need to think about it. This was exactly the kind of case I'd been hoping for. I went through the motions of checking my schedule, though, and pretended to be shuffling a few things around. If you instantly agree to take a case, the client might suspect some ulterior motive.

"Luckily I'm free until later this afternoon," I said, shooting my watch a glance. It was eleven thirty-five. "If you don't mind, could you take me over to your building now? I'd like to see the last place you saw your husband."

"I'd be happy to," the woman said. She gave a small frown. "Does this mean you're taking the case?"

"It does," I replied.

"But we haven't talked about the fee yet."

"I don't need any money."

"I'm sorry?" she said, looking steadily at me.

"I don't charge anything," I explained, and smiled.

"But isn't this your job?"

"No, it isn't. This isn't my profession. I'm just a volunteer, so I don't get paid."

"A volunteer?"

"Correct."

"Still, you'll need something for expenses . . ."

"No expenses needed. I'm totally a volunteer, so I can't accept payment of any kind."

The woman still looked perplexed.

"Fortunately, I have another source of income that provides enough to live on," I explained. "I'm not doing this for the money. I'm just very interested in locating people who've disappeared. Or more precisely, people who've disappeared in a *certain way*. I won't go into that—it'll only complicate things. But I am pretty good at this sort of thing."

"Tell me, is there some kind of religion or New Age thing behind all this?" she asked.

"Neither one. I don't have a connection with any religion or New Age group."

The woman glanced down at her shoes, perhaps contemplating how—if things got really weird—she might have to use the stiletto heels against me.

"My husband always told me not to trust anything that's free," the woman said. "I know this is rude to say, but he insisted there's always a catch."

"In most cases, I'd agree with him," I said. "In our late-stage capitalist world, it's hard to trust anything that's free. Still, I hope you'll trust me. You have to, if we're going to get anywhere."

She reached over for her Louis Vuitton purse, opened it with a refined click, and took out a thick sealed envelope. I couldn't tell how much money was inside, but it looked like a lot.

"I brought something for expenses," she said.

I shook my head. "I don't accept any fee, gift, or payment of any kind. That's the rule. If I did accept a fee or a gift, the actions I'll be engaged in would be meaningless. If you have extra money and feel uncomfortable with not paying a fee, I suggest you make a donation to a charity—the Humane Society, the Fund for Traffic Victims' Orphans, whichever group you like. If doing so makes you feel better."

The woman frowned, took a deep breath, and returned the envelope to her purse. She placed the purse, once more fat and happy, back where it had been. She rubbed her nose again and looked at me, much like a retriever ready to spring forward and fetch a stick.

"The actions you'll be engaged in," she said in a somewhat dry tone.

I nodded and returned my worn pencil to the tray.

The woman with the sharp high heels took me to her building. She pointed out the door to her apartment (number 2609) and the door to her mother-in-law's (number 2417). A broad staircase connected the two floors, and I could see that even a casual stroll between them would take no more than five minutes.

"One of the reasons my husband bought this condo was that the stairs are wide and well lit," she said. "Most high-rise apartments skimp on the stairs. Wide staircases take up too much space, and, besides, most residents prefer the elevator. Condo developers like to spend their money on places that attract attention—a library, a marble lobby. My husband, though, insisted that the stairs were the critical element—the backbone of a building, he liked to say."

I have to admit, it really was a memorable staircase. On the landing between the twenty-fifth and twenty-sixth floors, next to a picture window, there was a sofa, a wall-length mirror, a standing ashtray, and a potted plant. Through the window you could see the bright sky and a couple of clouds drifting by. The window was sealed and couldn't be opened.

"Is there a space like this on every floor?" I asked.

"No. There's a little lounge on every fifth floor, not on every floor," she said. "Would you like to see our apartment and my mother-in-law's?"

"Not right now."

"Since my husband disappeared, my mother-in-law's nerves have taken a turn for the worse," she said. She fluttered her hand. "It was quite a shock for her, as I'm sure you can imagine."

"Of course," I agreed. "I don't think I'll have to bother her."

"I really appreciate that. And I'd like it if you would keep this from the neighbors, too. I haven't told anyone that my husband has vanished."

"Understood," I said. "Do you usually use these stairs yourself?"

"No," she said, raising her eyebrows slightly, as if she'd been unreasonably criticized. "*Normally* I take the elevator. When my husband and I are going out together, he leaves first and then I take the elevator and we meet up in the lobby. And when we come home, I take the elevator by myself and he comes up on foot. It'd be dangerous to attempt all these stairs in heels, and it's hard on you physically."

"I imagine so."

I wanted to investigate things on my own, so I asked her to go have a word with the building super. "Tell him that the guy wandering around between the twenty-fourth and twenty-sixth floors is doing an insurance investigation," I instructed her. "If someone thinks I'm a thief casing the place and calls the police, that would put me in a bit of a spot. I don't have any real reason to be loitering here, after all."

"I'll tell him," the woman said. She disappeared up the stairs. The sound of her heels rang out like the pounding of nails to post some ominous proclamation, then gradually faded into silence. I was left alone.

The first thing I did was walk the stairs from the twenty-sixth floor down to the twenty-fourth and back a total of three times. The first time, I walked at a normal pace, the next two times much more slowly, carefully observing everything around me. I focused so as not to miss any detail. I concentrated so hard I barely blinked. Every event leaves traces behind, and my job was to tease these out. The problem was that the staircase had been thoroughly scrubbed. There wasn't a scrap of litter to be found. Not a single stain or dent, no butts in the ashtray. Nothing.

Going up and down the steps without a break had tired me out, so I rested for a minute on the sofa. It was covered in vinyl, and was not what you'd call high quality. But you had to admire the building management for having had the foresight to put a sofa there, where probably few people were likely ever to use it. Across from the sofa was the mirror. Its surface was spotless, and it was set at the perfect angle for the light shining in the window. I sat there for a time, gazing at my own reflection. Maybe on that Sunday that woman's husband, the stockbroker, had taken a break here, too, and looked at his own reflection. At his own unshaven face.

I had shaved, of course, but my hair was getting a bit long. The hair behind my ears curled up like the fur of a long-haired hunting dog that had just paddled his way across a river. I made a mental note to go to a barber. I noticed that the color of my trousers didn't match my shoes. I'd had no luck in coming up with a pair of socks that matched my outfit, either. Nobody would think it strange if I finally got my act together and did a little laundry. Otherwise, though, my reflection was just that—the same old me. A forty-five-year-old bachelor who couldn't care less about stocks or Buddhism.

Come to think of it, Paul Gauguin had been a stockbroker, too. But he wanted to devote himself to painting, so one day he left his wife and kids for Tahiti. Wait a sec . . . I thought for a minute. No, Gauguin couldn't have left his wallet behind, and if they'd had American Express cards back then I bet he would have taken one along. He was going all the way to Tahiti, after all. I can't picture him saying to his wife, "Hey, honey, I'll be back in a minute—make sure the pancakes are ready" before he vanished. If you're planning to disappear, you have to go about it in a systematic way.

I stood up from the sofa, and as I made my way up the stairs again I started to mull over the notion of freshly made pancakes. I concentrated as fiercely as I could and tried to picture the scene: you're a forty-year-old stockbroker, it's Sunday morning, raining hard outside, and you're on your way home to a stack of piping hot pancakes. The more I thought about it, the more it whetted my appetite. I'd had only one small apple since morning.

Maybe I should zip over to Denny's and dig into some pancakes, I thought. I'd passed a sign for Denny's on the drive here. It was probably even close enough to walk. Not that Denny's made great pancakes—the butter and the syrup weren't up to my standards—but they would do. Truth be told, I'm a huge pancake fan. Saliva began to well up in my mouth. But I shook my head and tried to banish all pancake thoughts for the time being. I blew away all the clouds of illusion. Save the pancakes for later, I cautioned myself. You've still got work to do.

"I should have asked her if her husband had any hobbies," I said to myself. "Maybe he actually *was* into painting."

But that didn't make sense—any guy who was so into painting he'd abandon his family wouldn't be the type to play golf every Sunday. Can you imagine Gauguin or van Gogh or Picasso decked out in golf shoes, kneeling down on the tenth green, trying to read the putt? I couldn't.

I sat down on the sofa again and looked at my watch. It was one thirty-two. I shut my eyes and focused on a spot in my head. My mind a total blank, I gave myself up to the sands of time and let the flow take me wherever it wanted. Then I opened my eyes and looked at my watch. It was one fifty-seven. Twenty-five minutes had vanished somewhere. Not bad, I told myself. A pointless way of whittling away time. Not bad at all.

I looked at the mirror again and saw my usual self there. I raised my right hand, and my reflection raised its left. I raised my left hand and it raised its right. I made as if to lower my right hand, then quickly lowered the left; my reflection made as if to lower its left hand, then quickly lowered its right. The way it should be. I got up from the sofa and walked the twenty-five flights down to the lobby.

◎

I visited the staircase every day around eleven a.m. The building super and I got pretty friendly (the boxes of chocolates I brought him didn't hurt), and I was allowed to wander the building at will. All told, I made about two hundred round-trips between the twenty-fourth and twenty-sixth floors. When I got tired, I took a rest on the sofa, gazed out the window at the sky, checked my reflection in the mirror. I'd gone to the barber and got a good trim, done all my laundry, and was able to wear trousers and socks that actually matched, vastly reducing the chances that people would be whispering about me behind my back.

No matter how hard I looked, I couldn't find a single clue, but I wasn't discouraged. Locating a key clue was a lot like training an uncooperative animal. It requires patience and focus. Not to mention intuition.

As I went to the apartment building every day, I discovered that there were other people who used the staircase. I'd find candy wrappers on the floor, a Marlboro butt in the ashtray, a discarded newspaper.

One Sunday afternoon, I passed a man who was running up the stairs. A short guy in his thirties, with a serious look, in a green jogging outfit and Asics running shoes. He was wearing a large Casio watch.

"Hi there," I said. "Do you have a minute?"

"Sure," the man said, and pushed a button on his watch. He took a couple of deep breaths. His Nike tank top was sweaty at the chest.

"Do you always run up and down these stairs?" I asked.

"I do. Up to the thirty-second floor. Going down, though, I take the elevator. It's dangerous to run down stairs."

"You do this every day?"

"No, work keeps me too busy. I do a few round-trips on the weekends. If I get off work early, I sometimes run during the week."

"You live in this building?"

"Sure," the runner said. "On the seventeenth floor."

"I was wondering if you know Mr. Kurumizawa, who lives on the twenty-sixth floor?"

"Mr. Kurumizawa?"

"He's a stockbroker, wears metal-framed Armani glasses, and always uses the stairs. Five feet eight, forty years old."

The runner gave it some thought. "Yeah, I do know that guy. I talked with him once. I pass him on the staircase sometimes when I'm running. I've seen him sitting on the sofa. He's one of those guys who use the stairs because they hate the elevator, right?"

"That's the guy," I replied. "Besides him, are there a lot of people who use the stairs every day?"

"Yeah, there are," he said. "Not that many, maybe, but there are a few you might call regulars. People who don't like to take elevators. And there are two other people I've seen who run up the stairs like me. There's no good jogging course around here, so we use the stairs. There're also a few people who walk up the stairs for exercise. I think more people use these stairs than in most apartment buildings—they're so well lit, spacious, and clean."

"Do you happen to know any of these people's names?"

"I'm afraid I don't," the runner said. "I just know their faces. We say hi as we pass each other, but I don't know their names. This is a huge building."

"I see. Well, thanks for your time," I said. "Sorry to keep you. And good luck with the jogging."

The man pressed the button on his stopwatch and resumed his jog.

◎

On Tuesday, as I was sitting on the sofa, an old man came down the stairs. Midseventies, I'd say, with gray hair and glasses. He was wearing sandals, gray slacks, and a long-sleeved shirt. His clothes were spotless and neatly ironed. The old man was tall and had good posture. He looked to me like a recently retired elementary-school principal.

"Hello," he said.

"Hello," I replied.

"Do you mind if I smoke here?"

"Not at all," I said. "Go right ahead."

The old man sat down beside me and pulled a pack of Seven Stars from a trouser pocket. He struck a match, lit his cigarette, then blew out the match and placed it in the ashtray.

"I live on the twenty-sixth floor," he said, slowly exhaling smoke.

"With my son and his wife. They say the place gets all smoky, so I always come here when I want to have a cigarette. Do you smoke?"

"I quit twelve years ago," I told him.

"I should quit, too," the old man said. "I smoke only a couple of cigarettes a day, so it shouldn't be too hard. But, you know, going to the store to buy cigarettes, coming down here for a smoke—it helps pass the time. Gets me up and moving and keeps me from thinking too much."

"You keep smoking for your health is what you're saying," I said.

"Exactly," the old man said with a serious look.

"You said you live on the twenty-sixth floor?"

"Yes."

"Do you know Mr. Kurumizawa in 2609?"

"I do. He wears glasses and works at Salomon Brothers, I believe?"

"Merrill Lynch," I corrected him.

"That's right—Merrill Lynch," the old man said. "I've talked with him here. He uses this sofa sometimes."

"What does he do here?"

"I don't really know. He sort of just sits here, staring off into space. I don't believe he smokes."

"He looks like he's thinking about something?"

"I'm not sure if I could tell the difference—between just staring into space and thinking. We're usually thinking all the time, aren't we? Not that we live in order to think, but the opposite isn't true, either— that we think in order to live. I believe, contrary to Descartes, that we sometimes think in order *not* to be. Staring into space might unintentionally actually have the opposite effect. At any rate, it's a difficult question."

The old man took a deep drag on his cigarette.

"Did Mr. Kurumizawa ever mention any problems at work or at home?" I asked.

The old man shook his head and dropped his cigarette into the ashtray. "As I'm sure you know, water always picks the shortest route to flow down. Sometimes, though, the shortest route is actually formed *by* the water. The human thought process is a lot like that. At least, that's my impression. But I haven't answered your question. Mr. Kurumizawa and I never once talked about such deep things. We just chatted—about the weather, the apartment association's regulations, things of that nature."

"I understand. Sorry to have taken up your time," I said.

"Sometimes we don't need words," the old man said, as if he hadn't heard me. "Rather, it's words that need *us*. If we were no longer here, words would lose their whole function. Don't you think so? They would end up as words that are never spoken, and words that aren't spoken are no longer words."

"Exactly," I said. "It's sort of like a Zen koan."

"That's right," the old man said, nodding, and stood up to go back to his apartment. "Take care now," he said.

"Goodbye," I replied.

⊙

After two the following Friday afternoon, as I made my way to the landing between the twenty-fifth and twenty-sixth floors, I found a little girl sitting on the sofa, gazing at herself in the mirror as she sang a song. She looked just old enough to have started elementary school. She was wearing a pink T-shirt and denim shorts, with a green daypack on her back and a hat in her lap.

"Hi there," I said.

"Hi," she said, and stopped singing.

I wanted to sit down on the sofa beside her, but if anybody passed by and saw us they might think something strange was going on, so instead I leaned against the windowsill, keeping a distance between us.

"Is school over?" I asked.

"Don't want to talk 'bout school," she said in no uncertain terms.

"Well, then, we won't," I said. "Do you live in this building?"

"Yes," she said. "On the twenty-seventh floor."

"You don't walk all the way up, do you?"

"The elevator's stinky," the girl said. "The elevator's stinky, so I'm walking up to the twenty-seventh floor." She looked at herself in the mirror and gave a big nod. "Not always, but sometimes."

"Don't you get tired?"

She didn't answer. "You know something? Of all the mirrors in the staircase, this one reflects the best. It's not at all like the mirror in our apartment."

"How do you mean?"

"Take a look yourself," the little girl said.

I took a step forward, faced the mirror, and looked for a while at my reflection. And, sure enough, the image of me reflected in the mirror was a few degrees removed from what I was used to seeing. The me in the mirror looked plumper and happier. As if I'd just polished off a stack of hot pancakes.

"Do you have a dog?" the little girl asked.

"No, I don't. I do have some tropical fish."

"Hmm," she said. Her interest in tropical fish seemed nonexistent.

"Do you like dogs?" I asked.

She didn't respond, but asked a different question. "Do you have any children?"

"No, I don't," I answered.

She eyed me suspiciously. "Mom says never talk to men who don't have children. Mom says there's a *likely-hood* they're weird."

"Not necessarily," I said, "though I do agree with your mom that you have to be careful when you talk to men you don't know."

"But I don't think *you're* weird."

"I don't either."

"You're not going to show me your weenie, are you?"

"No."

"And you don't collect little girls' underpants?"

"No way."

"Do you collect anything?"

I had to think about it. I did collect first editions of modern poetry, but bringing that up here wouldn't get us anywhere. "No, I don't really collect anything. How about you?"

The girl gave it some thought, and shook her head a couple of times. "I don't collect anything, either."

We were silent for a moment.

"Hey, at Mister Donut which doughnut do you like the best?"

"Old-fashioned," I said right away.

"I don't know that one," the girl said. "You know which ones I like? I like full moons and bunny whips."

"I've never heard of those."

"They're the ones with fruit or sweet bean paste inside. They're great. But Mom says if you eat sweets all the time you end up dumb, so she doesn't buy them for me much."

"They sound delicious," I said.

"What are you doing here? I saw you yesterday," the girl said.

"I'm looking for something."

"What is it?"

"I have no idea," I admitted. "I imagine it's like a door."

"A door?" the little girl repeated. "What kind of door? There are all shapes and colors of doors."

I thought about this. What sort of shape and color? Come to think of it, I'd never once thought about the shape and color of doors. "I don't know. I wonder what shape and color it might be. Maybe it isn't even a door."

"You mean maybe it's an umbrella or something?"

"An umbrella?" I said. "Hmm. No reason it can't be an umbrella, I suppose."

"But umbrellas and doors are different shapes and sizes, and what they do is different."

"That's right. But I'm sure I'll recognize it when I see it. Like, 'Hey! This is it!' Whether it's an umbrella, a door, or even a doughnut."

"Hmm," the little girl said. "Have you been looking for a long time?"

"For a long time. Since before you were born."

"Is that right?" the little girl said, staring at her palm for a while. "How 'bout I help you find it?"

"I'd really like that," I said.

"So I should look for something, I don't know what it is but it might be a door or an umbrella or a doughnut or an elephant?"

"Exactly," I said. "But when you see it you'll know that's it."

"Sounds like fun," she said. "But I have to go home now. I have a ballet lesson."

"See you later," I said. "Thanks for talking with me."

"Tell me again the name of the doughnut you like?"

"Old-fashioned."

Frowning, the girl repeated the words "old-fashioned" over and over. Then she stood and vanished up the stairs, singing all the while. I closed my eyes, gave myself up once more to the flow, letting time be pointlessly whittled away.

◎

One Saturday morning I got a call from my client.

"My husband's been found," she began, skipping a greeting. "I was contacted by the police around noon yesterday. They found him sleeping on a bench in a waiting room in Sendai Station. He didn't have any money on him, or ID, but after a while he remembered his name, address, and phone number. I flew to Sendai right away. It's my husband, all right."

"But why would he be in Sendai?" I asked her.

"He has no idea how he got there. He just woke up on a bench in Sendai Station with a railroad employee shaking his shoulder. How he got all the way to Sendai without any money, how he ate the last twenty days—he doesn't remember a thing."

"How was he dressed?"

"He had on the same clothes as when he left our apartment. He had a beard and he'd lost more than twenty pounds. He'd also lost his glasses somewhere. I'm calling from a hospital in Sendai right now. They're running some tests. CAT scan, X-rays, neurological exams. But his mind seems entirely fine, and nothing is physically wrong with him. But his memory's gone. He remembers leaving his mother's place and walking up the stairs, but, after that, nothing. Anyway, we should be able to come back to Tokyo tomorrow."

"That's great news."

"I really appreciate all you've done trying to find him, I really do. But now that things have turned out this way I don't need you to continue the investigation."

"I guess not," I said.

"The whole thing's been so crazy and incomprehensible, but at least I have my husband back safe and sound, and that's all that matters."

"Of course," I said. "That's what's important."

"Are you sure, now, that you won't accept anything for your services?"

"As I told you the first time we met, I can't accept any kind of payment whatsoever. So please don't trouble yourself over that. I do appreciate the sentiment, though."

Silence. A refreshing silence that implied we'd come to a mutual understanding. I played my own role in supporting this, appreciating the calm.

"Take care of yourself, then," the woman finally said and hung up, her tone carrying with it a hint of sympathy.

I put down the phone. For a while I sat there, slowly twirling a brand-new pencil, staring at the blank memo pad in front of me. The white pad reminded me of a freshly washed sheet just back from the laundry. The sheet made me think of a calico cat stretched out on it for a pleasant nap. That image—of a napping cat on a freshly laundered sheet—helped me relax. I started to search my memory, and I carefully wrote down on my memo pad, one by one, all the salient points the woman had made: *Sendai Station, Friday around noon, telephone, lost twenty pounds, same clothes, lost his glasses, memory of twenty days gone.*

Memory of twenty days gone.

I laid the pencil on the desk, leaned back in my chair, and stared up at the ceiling. The ceiling boards had some irregular spots here and there, and if I squinted it looked like a celestial chart. I gazed up at this imaginary starry night and wondered if maybe I should start smoking again—for my health. My head was filled with the click of the woman's high heels on the stairway.

"Mr. Kurumizawa," I said aloud to a corner of the ceiling. "Welcome back to the real world. Back to the three sides of your beautiful triangular world—your panic-attack-prone mother, your wife, with her ice-pick heels, and good old Merrill Lynch."

I imagine my search will continue—somewhere. A search for something that could very well be shaped like a door. Or maybe something closer to an umbrella, or a doughnut. Or an elephant. A search that, I hope, will take me where I'm likely to find it.

—TRANSLATED BY PHILIP GABRIEL

THE KIDNEY-SHAPED STONE
THAT MOVES EVERY DAY

Junpei was sixteen years old when his father made the following pronouncement. True, they were father and son; the same blood flowed in their veins. But they were not so close that they could open their hearts to each other, and it was extremely rare for Junpei's father to offer him views of life that might (perhaps) be called philosophical. And so that day's exchange remained with him as a vivid memory long after he had forgotten what prompted it.

"Among the women a man meets in his life, there are only three that have real meaning for him. No more, no less," his father said—or, rather, declared. He spoke coolly but with utter certainty, as he might have in noting that the earth takes a year to revolve around the sun. Junpei listened in silence, partly because his father's declaration was so unexpected; he could think of nothing to say on the spur of the moment.

"You will probably become involved with many women in the future," his father continued, "but you will be wasting your time if a woman is the wrong one for you. I want you to remember that."

Later, several questions formed in Junpei's young mind: *Has my father already met his three women? Is my mother one of them? And if so, what happened with the other two?* But he was not able to ask his father these questions. As noted earlier, the two were not on such close terms that they could speak with each other heart-to-heart.

Junpei left the house at eighteen when he went to college in Tokyo, and he became involved with several women, one of whom "had real meaning" for him. He knew this with absolute certainty at the time, and he is just as certain of it now. Before he could express his feelings in concrete form, however (by nature, it took him longer than most people to put things into concrete form), she married his best friend, and since then she has become a mother. For the time being, therefore, she had to be eliminated from the list of possibilities that life had to offer Junpei. He had to harden his heart and sweep her from his mind, as a result of which the number of women remaining who could have "real meaning" in his life—if he was going to accept his father's theory at face value— was reduced to two.

Whenever Junpei met a new woman after that, he would ask himself, *Is this a woman who has real meaning for me?* and the question would call forth a dilemma. For even as he continued to hope (as who does not?) that he would meet someone who had "real meaning" for him, he was afraid of playing his few remaining cards too early. Having failed to join with the very first important Other he encountered, Junpei lost confidence in his ability—the exceedingly important ability—to give outward expression to love at the appropriate time and in the appropriate manner. *I may be the type who manages to grab all the pointless things in life but lets the really important things slip away.* Whenever this thought crossed his mind—which was often—his heart would sink down to a place devoid of light and warmth.

And so, after he had been with a new woman for some months, if he should begin to notice something about her character or behavior, however trivial, that displeased him or touched a nerve, somewhere in a recess of his heart he would feel a twinge of relief. As a result, it became a life pattern for him to maintain pale, indecisive relationships with one woman after another. He would stay with a woman as if taking stock of the situation until, at some point, the relationship would dissolve on its own. The breakups never entailed any discord or shouting matches because he never became involved with women who seemed as if they might be difficult to get rid of. Before he knew it, he had developed a kind of nose for convenient partners.

Junpei himself was unsure whether this power stemmed from his own innate character or had been formed by his environment. If the latter, it could well have been the fruit of his father's curse. Around the time he graduated from college, he had a violent argument with his father and cut off all contact with him, but his father's "three-women" theory, its

basis never fully explained, became a kind of obsession that clung tena-
ciously to his life. At one time he even half-jokingly considered moving
on to homosexuality: maybe then he could free himself from this stupid
countdown. For better or worse, though, women were the only objects
of Junpei's sexual interest.

The next woman Junpei met, he soon discovered, was older than he
was. Thirty-six. Junpei was thirty-one. An acquaintance of his was opening a little French restaurant on a street leading out of central Tokyo,
and Junpei was invited to the party. He wore a Perry Ellis shirt of deep
blue silk with matching summer sport coat. He had planned to meet a
close friend at the party, but the friend cancelled at the last minute,
which left Junpei with time to kill. He nursed a large glass of Bordeaux
alone at the bar. When he was ready to leave and beginning to scan the
crowd to say goodbye to the owner, a tall woman approached him holding some kind of purple cocktail. Junpei's first thought on seeing her was,
Here is a woman with excellent posture.

"Somebody over there told me you're a writer. Is that true?" she
asked, resting an elbow on the bar.

"I suppose so, in a way," Junpei answered.

"A writer *in a way.*"

Junpei nodded.

"How many books have you published?"

"Two volumes of short stories, and one book I translated. None of
them sold much."

She gave him a quick head-to-toe inspection and smiled with apparent satisfaction.

"Well, anyhow, you're the first real writer I've met."

"It might be a little disappointing," Junpei said. "Writers don't have
any talents to offer. A pianist could play you a tune. A painter could draw
you a sketch. A magician could perform a trick or two. There's not much
a writer can do."

"Oh, I don't know, maybe I can just enjoy your artistic aura or
something."

"Artistic aura?" Junpei said.

"A special radiance, something you don't find in ordinary people?"

"I see my face in the mirror every morning when I'm shaving, but I've
never noticed anything like that."

She smiled warmly and asked, "What type of stories do you write?"

"People ask me that a lot, but it's hard to talk about my stories as 'types.' They don't fit into any particular genre."

She ran a finger around the lip of her cocktail glass. "I suppose that means you write *literary* fiction?"

"I suppose it does. But you say that the way you might say '*chain letters.*'"

She smiled again. "Could I have heard your name?"

"Do you read the literary magazines?"

She gave her head a small, sharp shake.

"Then you probably haven't. I'm not that well known."

"Ever been nominated for the Akutagawa Prize?"

"Twice in five years."

"But you didn't win?"

Junpei smiled but said nothing. Without asking his permission, she sat on the bar stool next to his and sipped what was left of her cocktail.

"Oh, what's the difference?" she said. "Those prizes are just an industry gimmick."

"I'd be more convinced if I could hear that from somebody who's actually won a prize."

She told him her name: Kirie.

"How unusual," he said. "Sounds like 'Kyrie' from a mass."

Junpei thought she might be an inch or more taller than he was. She wore her hair short, had a deep tan, and her head was beautifully shaped. She wore a pale green linen jacket and a knee-length flared skirt. The sleeves of the jacket were rolled up to the elbow. Under the jacket she had on a simple cotton blouse with a small turquoise brooch on the collar. The swell of her breasts was neither large nor small. She dressed with style, and while there was nothing affected about it, her entire outfit reflected strongly individualistic principles. Her lips were full, and they would mark the ends of her sentences by spreading or pursing. This gave everything about her a strange liveliness and freshness. Three parallel creases would form across her broad forehead whenever she stopped to think about something, and when she finished thinking, they would disappear.

Junpei noticed himself being attracted to her. Some indefinable but persistent something about her was exciting him, pumping adrenaline to his heart, which began sending out secret signals in the form of tiny sounds. Suddenly aware that his throat was dry, Junpei ordered a Perrier from a passing waiter, and as always he began to ask himself, *Is she someone with real meaning for me? Is she one of the remaining two? Or will she be my second strike? Should I let her go, or take a swing?*

"Did you always want to be a writer?" Kirie asked.

"Hmm, let's just say I could never think of anything else I wanted to be."

"So, your dream came true."

"I wonder. I wanted to be a *superior* writer." Junpei spread his hands about a foot apart. "There's a pretty big distance between the two, I think."

"Everybody has to start somewhere. You have your whole future ahead of you. Perfection doesn't happen right away." Then she asked, "How old are you?"

This was when they told each other their ages. Being older didn't seem to bother her in the least. It didn't bother Junpei. He preferred mature women to young girls. In most cases, it was easier to break up with an older woman.

"What kind of work do you do?" he asked.

Her lips formed a perfectly straight line, and her expression became earnest for the first time.

"What kind of work do you *think* I do?"

Junpei jogged his glass, swirling the red wine inside it exactly once. "Can I have a hint?"

"No hints. Is it so hard to tell? Observation and judgment are your business."

"Not really," he said. "What a writer is *supposed* to do is observe and observe and observe again, and put off making judgments to the last possible moment."

"Of course," she said. "All right, then, observe and observe and observe again, and then use your imagination. That wouldn't clash with your professional ethics, would it?"

Junpei raised his eyes and studied Kirie's face with new concentration, hoping to find a secret sign there. She looked straight into his eyes, and he looked straight into hers.

After a short pause, he said, "All right, this is what I imagine, based on nothing much: you're a professional of some sort. Not just anyone can do your job. It requires some kind of special expertise."

"Bull's-eye! You're right: not just anyone can do what I do. But try to narrow it down a little."

"Something to do with music?"

"No."

"Fashion design?"

"No."

"Tennis?"

"No," she said.

Junpei shook his head. "Well, you've got a deep tan, you're solidly built, your arms have a good bit of muscle. Maybe you do a lot of outdoor sports. I *don't* think you're an outdoor laborer. You don't have that vibe."

Kirie lifted her sleeves, rested her bare arms on the counter, and turned them over, inspecting them. "You seem to be getting there."

"But I still can't give you the right answer."

"It's important to keep a few little secrets," Kirie said. "I don't want to deprive you of your professional pleasure—observing and imagining. . . . I *will* give you one hint, though. It's the same for me as for you."

"The same how?"

"I mean, my profession is exactly what I always wanted to do, ever since I was a little girl. Like you. Getting to where I am, though, was not an easy trip."

"Good," Junpei said. "That's important. Your work should be an act of love, not a marriage of convenience."

"An act of love," Kirie said. The words seemed to have made an impression on her. "That's a wonderful metaphor."

"Meanwhile, do you think I might have heard your name some-where?" Junpei asked.

"Probably not," she answered, shaking her head. "I'm not that well known."

"Oh, well, everybody has to start somewhere."

"Exactly," Kirie said with a smile. Then she turned serious. "My case is different from yours in one way. I'm expected to attain perfection right from the start. No mistakes allowed. Perfection or nothing. No in-between. No second chances."

"I suppose that's another hint."

"Probably."

A waiter circulating with a tray of champagne approached them. She took two glasses from him and handed one to Junpei.

"Cheers," she said.

"To our respective areas of expertise," Junpei said.

They clinked glasses with a light, secretive sound.

"By the way," she said, "are you married?"

Junpei shook his head.

"Neither am I," Kirie said.

◎

She spent that night in Junpei's room. They drank wine—a gift from the restaurant—had sex, and went to sleep. When Junpei woke at ten o'clock the next morning, she was gone, leaving only an indentation like a missing memory in the pillow next to his, and a note: "I have to go to work. Get in touch with me if you like." She included her cell phone number.

He called her, and they had dinner at a restaurant the following Saturday. They drank a little wine, had sex in Junpei's room, and went to sleep. Again the next morning, she was gone. It was Sunday, but she left another simple note: "I have to work, am disappearing." Junpei still had no idea what kind of work Kirie did, but it certainly started early in the morning. And—on occasion at least—she worked on Sundays.

The two were never at a loss for things to talk about. She had a sharp mind and was knowledgeable on a broad range of topics. She enjoyed reading, but generally favored books other than fiction—biography, history, psychology, and popular science—and she retained an amazing amount of information. One time, Junpei was astounded at her detailed knowledge of the history of prefabricated housing.

"Prefabricated housing? Your work must have something to do with construction or architecture."

"No," she said. "I just tend to be attracted to highly practical topics. That's all."

She did, however, read the two story collections that Junpei had published, and found them "wonderful—far more enjoyable than I had imagined. To tell you the truth, I was worried. What would I do if I read your work and didn't like it? What could I say? But there was nothing to worry about. I enjoyed them thoroughly."

"I'm glad to hear that," said Junpei, relieved. He had had the same worry when, at her request, he gave her the books.

"I'm not just saying this to make you feel good," Kirie said, "but you've got something special—that special something it takes to become an outstanding writer. Your stories have a quiet mood, but several of them are quite lively, and the style is beautiful, but mainly your writing is so *balanced*. For me, that is always the most important thing—in music, in fiction, in painting. Whenever I encounter a work or a performance that lacks that balance—which is to say, whenever I encounter a poor, unfinished work—it makes me sick. Like motion sickness. That's probably why I don't go to concerts and hardly read any fiction."

"Because you don't want to encounter unbalanced things?"

"Exactly."

"And in order to avoid that risk, you don't read novels and you don't go to concerts?"

"That's right."

"Sounds a little far out to me."

"I'm a Libra. I just can't stand it when things are out of balance. No, it's not so much that I can't stand it as—"

She closed her mouth in search of the right words, but she wasn't able to find them, releasing instead a few tentative sighs. "Oh, well, never mind," she went on. "I just wanted to say that I believe someday you are going to write full-length novels. And when you do that, you will become a more important writer. It may take a while, but that's what I feel."

"No, I'm a born short story writer," Junpei said dryly. "I'm not suited to writing novels."

"Even so," she said.

Junpei offered nothing more on the subject. He remained quiet and listened to the breeze from the air conditioner. In fact, he had tried several times to write novels, but always bogged down partway through. He simply could not maintain the concentration it took to write a story over a long period of time. He would start out convinced that he was going to write something wonderful. The style would be lively, and his future seemed assured. The story would flow out almost by itself. But the farther he went with it, the more its energy and brilliance would fade— gradually at first, but undeniably until, like an engine losing speed and coming to a halt, it would peter out entirely.

The two of them were in bed. It was autumn. They were naked after long, warm lovemaking. Kirie's shoulder pressed against Junpei, whose arms were around her. Two glasses of white wine stood on the nightstand.

"Junpei?"

"Uh-huh."

"You're in love with another woman, aren't you? Somebody you can't forget?"

"It's true," Junpei admitted. "You can tell?"

"Of course," she said. "Women are very sensitive about such things."

"Not all women, I'm sure."

"I don't mean *all* women."

"No, of course not," Junpei said.

"But you can't see her?"

"There are problems."

"And no possibility those 'problems' could be solved?"

"None," Junpei said with a quick shake of the head.

"They go pretty deep, huh?"

"I don't know how deep they are, but they're there."

Kirie drank a little wine. "I don't have anybody like that," she said almost under her breath. "I like you a lot, Junpei. You really move me. When we're together like this, I feel tremendously happy and calm. But that doesn't mean I want to have a serious relationship with you. How does that make you feel? Relieved?"

Junpei ran his fingers through her hair. Instead of answering her question, he asked one of his own. "Why is that?"

"Why don't I want to be with you?"

"Uh-huh."

"Does it bother you?"

"A little."

"I can't have a serious everyday relationship with anybody. Not just you: anybody," she said. "I want to concentrate completely on what I'm doing now. If I were living with somebody—if I had a deep emotional involvement with somebody—I might not be able to do that. So I want to keep things the way they are."

Junpei thought about that for a moment. "You mean you don't want to be distracted?"

"That's right."

"If you were distracted, you could lose your balance, and that might prove to be an obstacle to your career."

"Exactly."

"And so to avoid any risk of that, you don't want to live with anybody."

She nodded. "Not as long as I'm involved in my current profession."

"But you won't tell me what that is."

"Guess."

"You're a burglar."

"No," Kirie answered with a grave expression that quickly gave way to amusement. "What a sexy guess! But a burglar doesn't go to work early in the morning."

"You're a hit man."

"Hit *person*," she corrected him. "But no. Why are you coming up with these awful ideas?"

"So, what you do is perfectly legal?"

"Perfectly."

"Undercover agent?"

"No. OK, let's stop for today. I'd rather talk about your work. Tell me about what you're writing now. You *are* writing something now?"

"Yes, a short story."

"What kind of story?"

"I haven't finished it yet. I'm taking a break."

"So tell me what happens up to the break."

Junpei fell silent. He had a policy of not talking to anyone about works in progress. That could jinx the story. If he put it into words and those words left his mouth, some important something would evaporate like morning dew. Delicate shades of meaning would be flattened into a shallow backdrop. Secrets would no longer be secrets. But here in bed, running his fingers through Kirie's short hair, Junpei felt that it might be all right to tell her. After all, he had been experiencing a block. He hadn't been able to move forward with the story for some days now.

"It's in the third person, and the protagonist is a woman," he began. "She's in her early thirties, a skilled internist who practices at a big hospital. She's single, but she's having an affair with a surgeon at the same hospital. He's in his late forties and has a wife and kids."

Kirie took a moment to imagine the heroine. "Is she attractive?"

"I think so. Quite attractive," Junpei said. "But not as attractive as you."

Kirie smiled and kissed Junpei on the neck. "That's the right answer," she said.

"I make it a point to give right answers when necessary."

"Especially in bed, I suppose."

"Especially in bed," he replied. "So anyway, she has a vacation and goes off on a trip by herself. The season is autumn: the same as this. She's staying at a little hot-spring resort in the mountains and she goes for a walk by a stream in the hills. She's a bird-watcher, and she especially enjoys seeing kingfishers. She steps down into the dry streambed and notices an odd stone. It's black with a tinge of red, it's smooth, and it has a familiar shape. She realizes right away that it's shaped like a kidney. I mean, she's a doctor, after all. Everything about it is just like a real kidney—the size, the coloration, the thickness."

"So she picks it up and takes it home."

"Right," Junpei said. "She brings it to her office at the hospital and uses it as a paperweight. It's just the right size and weight."

"And it's the perfect shape for a hospital."

"Exactly," Junpei said. "But a few days later, she notices something strange."

Kirie waited silently for him to continue with his story. Junpei paused as if deliberately teasing his listener, but in fact this was not deliberate at all. He had not yet written the rest of the story. This was the point at which it had come to a stop. Standing at this unmarked intersection, he surveyed his surroundings and worked his brain as hard as he could. Then he thought of how the story should go.

"Every morning, she finds the stone in a different place. She leaves it on her desk when she goes home at night. She's a very methodical person, so she always leaves it in exactly the same spot, but in the morning she finds it on the seat of her swivel chair, or next to the vase, or on the floor. Her first thought is that she must be wrong about where she left it. Then she begins to wonder if her memory is playing tricks on her. The door is locked, and no one else should be able to get in. Of course the night watchman has a key, but he has been working at the hospital for years, and he would never take it upon himself to enter anyone's office. Besides, what would be the point of his barging into her office every night just to change the position of a stone she's using as a paperweight? Nothing else in her office has changed, nothing is missing, and nothing has been tampered with. The position of the rock is the only thing that changes. She's totally stumped. What do *you* think is going on? Why do *you* think the stone moves during the night?"

"The kidney-shaped stone has its own reasons for doing what it does," Kirie said with simple assurance.

"What kind of *reasons* can a kidney-shaped stone have?"

"It wants to shake her up. Little by little. Over a long period of time."

"All right, then, why does it want to shake her up?"

"I don't know," she said. Then with a giggle she added, "Maybe it just wants to *rock* her world."

"That's the worst pun I've ever heard," Junpei groaned.

"Well *you're* the writer. Aren't *you* the one who decides? I'm just a listener."

Junpei scowled. He felt a slight throbbing behind his temples from having concentrated so hard. Maybe he had drunk too much wine. "The ideas aren't coming together," he said. "My plots don't move unless I'm actually sitting at my desk and moving my hands, making sentences. Do you mind waiting a bit? Talking about it like this, I'm beginning to feel as if the rest of the story is going to work itself out."

"I don't mind," Kirie said. She reached over for her glass and took a sip of wine. "I can wait. But the story is really getting interesting. I want to know what happens with the kidney-shaped stone."

She turned toward him and pressed her shapely breasts against his side. Then quietly, as if sharing a secret, she said, "You know, Junpei, everything in the world has its reasons for doing what it does." Junpei was falling asleep and could not answer. In the night air, her sentences lost their shape as grammatical constructions and blended with the faint aroma of the wine before reaching the hidden recesses of his consciousness. "For example, the wind has its reasons. We just don't notice as we go about our lives. But then, at some point, we are made to notice. The wind envelops you with a certain purpose in mind, and it rocks you. The wind knows everything that's inside you. And not just the wind. Everything, including a stone. They all know us very well. From top to bottom. It only occurs to us at certain times. And all we can do is go with those things. As we take them in, we survive, and deepen."

For the next five days, Junpei hardly left the house; he stayed at his desk, writing the rest of the story of the kidney-shaped stone. As Kirie predicted, the stone continues quietly to shake the lady doctor—little by little, over time, but decisively. She is engaged in hurried coupling with her lover one evening in an anonymous hotel room when she stealthily reaches around to his back and feels for the shape of a kidney. She knows that her kidney-shaped stone is lurking in there. The kidney is a secret informer that she herself has buried in her lover's body. Beneath her fingers, it squirms like an insect, sending her kidney-type messages. She converses with the kidney, exchanging intelligence. She can feel its sliminess against the palm of her hand.

The lady doctor grows gradually more used to the existence of the heavy, kidney-shaped stone that shifts position every night. She comes to accept it as natural. She is no longer surprised when she finds that it has moved during the night. When she arrives at the hospital each morning, she finds the stone somewhere in her office, picks it up, and returns it to her desk. This has simply become part of her normal routine. As long as she remains in the room, the stone does not move. It stays quietly in one place, like a cat napping in the sun. It awakes and begins to move only after she has left and locked the door.

Whenever she has a spare moment, she reaches out and caresses the stone's smooth, dark surface. After a while, it becomes increasingly difficult for her to take her eyes off the stone, as if she has been hypnotized. She gradually loses interest in anything else. She can no longer read books. She stops going to the gym. She maintains just enough of her powers of concentration to see patients, but she carries on all other thought through sheer force of habit and improvisation. She loses interest in talking to her colleagues. She becomes indifferent to her own grooming. She loses her appetite. Even the embrace of her lover becomes a source of annoyance. When there is no one else around, she speaks to the stone in a lowered voice, and she listens to the wordless words the stone speaks to her, the way lonely people converse with a dog or a cat. The dark, kidney-shaped stone now controls the greater part of her life.

Surely the stone is not an object that has come to her from without: Junpei becomes aware of this as his story progresses. The main point is something inside herself. That something inside herself is activating the dark, kidney-shaped stone and urging her to take some kind of concrete action. It keeps sending her signals for that purpose—signals in the form of the stone's nightly moves.

While he writes, Junpei thinks about Kirie. He senses that she (or something inside her) is propelling the story; it was never his intention to write something so divorced from reality. What Junpei had imagined vaguely beforehand was a more tranquil, psychological story line. In *that* story line, rocks did not take it upon themselves to move around.

Junpei imagined that the lady doctor would cut her emotional ties to her married surgeon. She might even come to hate him. This was probably what she was seeking all along, unconsciously.

Once the rest of the story had become visible to him, writing it out was relatively easy. Listening repeatedly to songs of Mahler at low volume, Junpei sat at his computer and wrote the conclusion at what was, for him, top speed. The doctor makes her decision to part with her surgeon lover. "I can't see you anymore," she tells him. "Can't we at least talk this over?" he asks. "No," she tells him firmly, "that is impossible." On her next free day she boards a Tokyo Harbor ferry, and from the deck she throws the kidney-shaped stone into the sea. The stone sinks down to the bottom of the deep, dark ocean toward the core of the earth. She resolves to start her life over. Having cast away the stone, she feels a new sense of lightness.

The next day, however, when she goes to the hospital, the stone is on her desk, waiting for her. It sits exactly where it is supposed to be, as dark and kidney-shaped as ever.

As soon as he finished writing the story, Junpei telephoned Kirie. She would probably want to read the finished work, which she, in a sense, had inspired him to write. His call, however, did not go through. "Your call cannot be completed as dialed," said a recorded voice. "Please check the number and try again." Junpei tried it again—and again. But the result was always the same. She was probably having some kind of technical problem with her phone, he thought.

Junpei stuck close to home, waiting for word from Kirie, but nothing ever came. A month went by. One month became two, and two became three. The season changed to winter, and a new year began. His story came out in the February issue of a literary magazine. A newspaper ad for the magazine listed Junpei's name and the title, "The Kidney-Shaped Stone That Moves Every Day." Kirie might see the ad, buy the magazine, read the story, and call him to share her impressions—or so he hoped. But all that reached him were new layers of silence.

The pain Junpei felt when Kirie vanished from his life was far more intense than he had imagined. She left behind a void that truly shook him. In the course of a day he would think to himself any number of times, "If only she were here!" He missed her smile, he missed the words shaped by her lips, he missed the touch of her skin as they held each other close. He gained no comfort from his favorite music or from the arrival of new books by authors that he liked. Everything felt distant, divorced from him. Kirie may have been woman number two, Junpei thought.

◎

Junpei's next encounter with Kirie occurred after noon one day in early spring—though you couldn't really call it an "encounter." He heard her voice.

He was in a taxi stuck in traffic. The young driver was listening to an FM broadcast. Kirie's voice emerged from the radio. Junpei was not sure at first that he was hearing Kirie. He simply thought the voice was similar to hers. The more he listened, though, the more it sounded like Kirie, her manner of speaking—the same smooth intonation, the same relaxed style, the special way she had of pausing now and then.

Junpei asked the driver to turn up the volume.

"Sure thing," the driver said.

It was an interview being held at the broadcast studio. The female announcer was asking her a question: "—and so you liked high places from the time you were a little girl?"

"That is true," answered Kirie—or a woman with exactly the same voice. "Ever since I can remember, I liked going up high. The higher I went, the more peaceful I felt. I was always nagging my parents to take me to tall buildings. I was a very strange little creature," the voice said with a laugh.

"Which is how you got started in your present line of work, I suppose."

"First I worked as an analyst at a securities firm. But I knew right away it wasn't right for me. I left the company after three years, and the first thing I did was get a job washing windows in tall buildings. What I really wanted to be was a steeplejack, but that's such a macho world, they don't let women in very easily. So for the time being, I took part-time work as a window washer."

"From securities analyst to window washer—that's quite a change!"

"To tell you the truth, washing windows was much less stressful for me: if anything falls, it's just you, not stock prices." Again the laugh.

"Now, by 'window washer' you mean one of those people who get lowered down the side of a building on a platform."

"Right. Of course, they give you a lifeline, but some spots you can't reach without taking the lifeline off. That didn't bother me at all. No matter how high we went, I was never scared. Which made me a very valuable worker."

"I suppose you like to go mountain climbing?"

"I have almost no interest in mountains. I've tried climbing a few times, but it does nothing for me. I can't get excited climbing mountains, no matter how high I go. The only things that interest me are man-made multistory structures that rise straight up from the ground. Don't ask me why."

"So now you run a window-washing company that specializes in high-rise buildings in the Tokyo metropolitan area."

"Correct," she said. "I saved up and started my own little company about six years ago. Of course I go out with my crews, but basically I'm an owner now. I don't have to take orders from anybody, and I can make up my own rules: it's very handy."

"Meaning, you can take the lifeline off whenever you like?"

"In a word." (Laughter.)

"You really don't like to put one on, do you?"

"It's true. It makes me feel I'm not myself. It's as if I'm wearing a stiff corset." (Laughter.)

"You really *do* like high places, don't you?"

"I do. I feel it's my calling to be up high. I can't imagine doing any other kind of work. Your work should be an act of love, not a marriage of convenience."

"It's time for a song now," said the announcer. "James Taylor's 'Up on the Roof.' We'll talk more about tightrope walking after this."

While the music played, Junpei leaned over the front seat and asked the driver, "*What* does this woman do?"

"She says she puts up ropes between high-rise buildings and walks across them," the driver explained. "With a long pole in her hands for balance. She's some kind of performer. *I* get scared just riding in a glassed-in elevator. I guess she gets her kicks that way. She's gotta be a little weird. She's probably not all that young, either."

"It's her *profession*?" Junpei asked. He noticed that his voice was dry and the weight had gone out of it. It sounded like someone else's voice coming through a gap in the taxi's ceiling.

"Yeah. I guess she gets a bunch of sponsors together and puts on a performance. She just did one at some famous cathedral in Germany. She says she wants to do it on higher buildings but can't get permission.

'Cause if you go that high a safety net won't help. She wants to keep adding to her record, and challenging herself with buildings that are a little higher every time. Of course, she can't make a living that way, so— well, you heard her say she's got this window-cleaning company. She wouldn't work for a circus even if she could do tightrope walking that way. The only thing she's interested in is high-rise buildings. Weird chick."

⊚

"The most wonderful thing about it is, when you're up there you change yourself as a human being," Kirie declared to the interviewer. "You change yourself, or rather, you *have* to change yourself or you can't survive. When I come out to a high place, it's just me and the wind. Nothing else. The wind envelops me, rocks me. It understands who I am. At the same time, I understand the wind. We accept each other and we decide to go on living together. Just me and the wind: there's no room for anybody else. It's that moment that I love. No, I'm not afraid. Once I set foot onto that high place and enter completely into that state of concentration, all fear vanishes. We are there, inside our own warm void. It's that moment that I love more than anything."

Kirie spoke with cool assurance. Junpei could not tell whether the interviewer understood her. When the interview ended, Junpei stopped the cab and got out, walking the rest of the way to his destination. Now and then he would look up at a tall building and at the clouds flowing past. No one could come between her and the wind, he realized, and he felt a violent rush of jealousy. But jealousy toward what? The wind? Who could possibly be jealous of the wind?

Junpei waited several months after that for Kirie to contact him. He wanted to see her and talk to her about lots of things, including the kidney-shaped stone. But the call never came, and his calls to her could never be "completed as dialed." When summer came, he gave up what little hope he had left. She obviously had no intention of seeing him again. And so the relationship ended calmly, without discord or shouting matches—exactly the way he had ended relationships with so many other women. At some point the calls stop coming, and everything ends quietly, naturally.

Should I add her to the countdown? Was she one of my three women with real meaning? Junpei agonized over the question for some time without reaching a conclusion. *I'll wait another six months,* he thought. *Then I'll decide.*

During that six months, he wrote with great concentration and produced a large number of short stories. As he sat at his desk polishing the style, he would think, *Kirie is probably in some high place with the wind right now. Here I am, alone at my desk writing stories, while she's all alone somewhere, up higher than anyone else—without a lifeline. Once she enters that state of concentration, all fear is gone: "Just me and the wind."* Junpei would often recall those words of hers and realize that he had come to feel something special for Kirie, something that he had never felt for another woman. It was a deep emotion, with clear outlines and real weight in the hands. Junpei was still unsure what to call this emotion. It was, at least, a feeling that could not be exchanged for anything else. Even if he never saw Kirie again, this feeling would stay with him forever. Somewhere in his body—perhaps in the marrow of his bones—he would continue to feel her absence.

As the year came to an end, Junpei made up his mind. He would count her as number two. She was one of the women who "had real meaning" for him. Strike two. Only one left. But he was no longer afraid. *Numbers aren't the important thing. The countdown has no meaning.* Now he knew: *What matters is deciding in your heart to accept another person completely. And it always has to be the first time and the last.*

One morning, the doctor notices that the dark kidney-shaped stone has disappeared from her desk. And she knows: it will not be coming back.

—TRANSLATED BY JAY RUBIN

A SHINAGAWA MONKEY

ecently she'd had trouble remembering her own name. Mostly this happened when someone unexpectedly asked her name. She'd be at a boutique, getting the sleeves of a dress altered, and the clerk would say, "And your name, ma'am?" Or she'd be at work, on the phone, and the person would ask her name, and she'd totally blank out. The only way she could remember was to pull out her driver's license, which was bound to make the person she was talking with feel a little weird. If she happened to be on the phone, the awkward moment of silence as she rummaged through her purse inevitably made the person on the other end wonder what was going on.

When *she* was the one who brought up her name, she never had trouble remembering it. As long as she knew in advance what was coming, she had no trouble with her memory. But when she was in a hurry, or someone suddenly asked her name, it was like a breaker had shut down and her mind was a complete blank. The more she struggled to recall, the more that featureless blank took over and she couldn't for the life of her remember what she was called.

She could remember everything else. She never forgot the name of people around her. And her address, phone number, birthday, passport number were no trouble at all. She could rattle off from memory her friend's phone numbers, and the phone numbers of important clients. She'd always had a decent memory—it was just her own name that escaped her. The problem had started about a year before, the first time anything like this had ever happened to her.

Her married name was Mizuki Ando, her maiden name Ozawa. Neither one was a very unique or dramatic name, which isn't to say that this explained why, in the course of her busy schedule, her name should vanish from her memory.

She'd become Mizuki Ando in the spring three years earlier, when she married a man named Takashi Ando. At first she couldn't get used to her new name. The way it looked and sounded just didn't seem right to her. But after repeating her new name, and signing it a number of times, she gradually came to think it wasn't so bad after all. Compared to other possibilities—Mizuki Mizuki or Mizuki Miki or something (she'd actually dated a guy named Miki for a while)—Mizuki Ando wasn't so bad. It took time, yet gradually she began to feel comfortable with her new, married name.

A year ago, however, that name started to slip away from her. At first this happened just once a month or so, but over time it became more frequent. Now it was happening at least once a week. Once "Mizuki Ando" had escaped, she was left alone in the world, a nobody, a woman without a name. As long as she had her purse with her she was fine—she could just pull out her license and remember who she was. If she ever lost her purse, though, she wouldn't have a clue. She wouldn't become a complete nonentity, of course—losing her name for a time didn't negate the fact that she still existed, and she still remembered her address and phone number. This wasn't like those cases of total amnesia in movies. Still, the fact remained that forgetting her own name was upsetting. A life without a name, she felt, was like a dream you never wake up from.

Mizuki went to a jewelry shop, bought a thin simple bracelet, and had her name engraved on it: *Mizuki (Ozawa) Ando*. Not her address or phone number, just her name. Makes me feel like I'm a cat or a dog, she sighed. She made sure to wear the bracelet every time she left home, so if she forgot her name all she had to do was glance at it. No more yanking out her license, no more weird looks from people.

She didn't let on about her problem to her husband. She knew he'd only say it proved she was unhappy with their life together. He was overly logical about everything. He didn't mean any harm; that's just the way he was, always theorizing about everything under the sun. That way of looking at the world was not her forte, however. Her husband was also quite a talker, and wouldn't easily back down once he started on a topic. So she kept quiet about the whole thing.

"I'm looking for something."

"What is it?"

"I have no idea," I admitted. "I imagine it's like a door."

"A door?" the little girl repeated. "What kind of door? There are all shapes and colors of doors."

I thought about this. What sort of shape and color? Come to think of it, I'd never once thought about the shape and color of doors. "I don't know. I wonder what shape and color it might be. Maybe it isn't even a door."

"You mean maybe it's an umbrella or something?"

"An umbrella?" I said. "Hmm. No reason it can't be an umbrella, I suppose."

"But umbrellas and doors are different shapes and sizes, and what they do is different."

"That's right. But I'm sure I'll recognize it when I see it. Like, 'Hey! This is it!' Whether it's an umbrella, a door, or even a doughnut."

"Hmm," the little girl said. "Have you been looking for a long time?"

"For a long time. Since before you were born."

"Is that right?" the little girl said, staring at her palm for a while. "How 'bout I help you find it?"

"I'd really like that," I said.

"So I should look for something, I don't know what it is but it might be a door or an umbrella or a doughnut or an elephant?"

"Exactly," I said. "But when you see it you'll know that's it."

"Sounds like fun," she said. "But I have to go home now. I have a ballet lesson."

"See you later," I said. "Thanks for talking with me."

"Tell me again the name of the doughnut you like?"

"Old-fashioned."

Frowning, the girl repeated the words "old-fashioned" over and over. Then she stood and vanished up the stairs, singing all the while. I closed my eyes, gave myself up once more to the flow, letting time be pointlessly whittled away.

One Saturday morning I got a call from my client.

"My husband's been found," she began, skipping a greeting. "I was reflection. And, sure enough, the image of me reflected in the mirror was a few degrees removed from what I was used to seeing. The me in the mirror looked plumper and happier. As if I'd just polished off a stack of hot pancakes.

"Do you have a dog?" the little girl asked.

"No, I don't. I do have some tropical fish."

"Hmm," she said. Her interest in tropical fish seemed nonexistent.

"Do you like dogs?" I asked.

She didn't respond, but asked a different question. "Do you have any children?"

"No, I don't," I answered.

She eyed me suspiciously. "Mom says never talk to men who don't have children. Mom says there's a *likely-hood* they're weird."

"Not necessarily," I said, "though I do agree with your mom that you have to be careful when you talk to men you don't know."

"But I don't think *you're* weird."

"I don't either."

"You're not going to show me your weenie, are you?"

"No."

"And you don't collect little girls' underpants?"

"No way."

"Do you collect anything?"

I had to think about it. I did collect first editions of modern poetry, but bringing that up here wouldn't get us anywhere. "No, I don't really collect anything. How about you?"

The girl gave it some thought, and shook her head a couple of times. "I don't collect anything, either."

We were silent for a moment.

"Hey, at Mister Donut which doughnut do you like the best?"

"Old-fashioned," I said right away.

"I don't know that one," the girl said. "You know which ones I like? I like full moons and bunny whips."

"I've never heard of those."

"They're the ones with fruit or sweet bean paste inside. They're great. But Mom says if you eat sweets all the time you end up dumb, so she doesn't buy them for me much."

"They sound delicious," I said.

"What are you doing here? I saw you yesterday," the girl said.

Still, she thought, what her husband said—or would likely have said if he only knew—was off the mark. She wasn't worried or dissatisfied with their marriage. Apart from his sometimes excessive logicality, she had no complaints about her husband, and no real negative feelings about her in-laws, either. Her father-in-law was a doctor who operated a small clinic in Sakata City, in the far north prefecture of Yamagata. Her in-laws were definitely conservative, but her husband was a second son so they generally kept out of Mizuki's and her husband's lives. Mizuki was from Nagoya, and so was at first overwhelmed by the frigid winters in Sakata, but during their one or two annual trips there she started to like the place. Two years after she and her husband married, they took out a mortgage and bought a condo in a new building in Shinagawa. Her husband, now thirty, worked in a lab in a pharmaceutical company. Mizuki was twenty-six and worked at a Honda dealership. She answered the phone, showed customers to the lounge, brought coffee, made copies when necessary, took care of files and updating their computerized customer list.

Mizuki's uncle, an executive at Honda, had found the job for her after she graduated from a women's junior college in Tokyo. It wasn't the most thrilling job imaginable, but they did give her some responsibility and overall it wasn't so bad. Her duties didn't include car sales, but whenever the salesmen were out she took over, always doing a decent job of answering the customers' questions. She learned by watching the salesmen, and quickly grasped the necessary technical information, and the knack of selling cars. She'd memorized the mileage ratings of all the models in the showroom, and could convince anyone, for instance, how the Odyssey handled less like a minivan and more like an ordinary sedan. Mizuki was a good conversationalist herself, and that and her winning smile always put customers at ease. She also knew how to subtly change her tack based on her reading of each customer's personality. Unfortunately, however, she didn't have the authority to give discounts, negotiate prices of trade-ins, or throw in options for free, so even if she had the customer ready to sign on the dotted line, in the end she had to turn over negotiations to the sales staff. She might have done most of the work, but one of the salesmen would take over and get the commission. The only reward she could expect was the occasional free dinner from one of the salesmen sharing his windfall.

Occasionally the thought crossed her mind that if they'd let her do sales they'd sell more cars and the dealership's overall record would improve. If these young salesmen, fresh out of college, only put their minds to it, they could sell twice as many cars. Nobody told her, though, that she was too good at sales to be wasting her time in clerical work, that she should be transferred to the sales division. That's the way a company operates. The sales division is one thing, the clerical staff another, and except in very rare cases, these were unbreachable boundaries. Besides, she wasn't ambitious enough to want to try to boost her career that way. She much preferred putting in her eight hours, nine to five, taking all the vacation time she had coming, and enjoying her time off.

At work Mizuki continued to use her maiden name. If she officially changed her name, then all the data concerning her in their computer system would have to be changed, a job she'd have to do herself. It was too much trouble and she kept putting it off, and finally she just decided to go by her maiden name. For tax purposes she was listed as married, but her name was unchanged. She knew it wasn't right to do that, but nobody at work said anything (they were all far too busy to worry about details), so she still went by Mizuki Ozawa. That was still the name on her business cards, her name tag, her time card. Everybody called her either Ozawa-san, Ozawa-kun, Mizuki-san, or even the familiar Mizuki-chan. She wasn't trying to avoid using her married name. It was just too much paperwork to change it, so she managed to slip by without ever making the changes. If somebody else would input all the changes for her, she thought, she'd be happy to go by Mizuki Ando.

Her husband knew she was going by her maiden name at work (he called her occasionally), but didn't have a problem with it. He seemed to feel that whatever name she used at work was just a matter of convenience. As long as he was convinced of the logic, he didn't complain. In that sense he was pretty easygoing.

◎

Mizuki began to worry that forgetting her name so completely might be a symptom of some awful disease, perhaps an early sign of Alzheimer's. The world was full of unexpected, fatal diseases. She'd never known, until recently, that there were diseases such as myasthenia and Huntington's disease. There must be countless others she'd never heard of. And with most of these illnesses the early symptoms were quite slight. Unusual, but slight symptoms such as—forgetting your own name? Once she started thinking this way, she grew worried that an unknown disease was silently spreading throughout her body.

Mizuki went to a large hospital and explained the symptoms. The young doctor in charge, however—who was so pale and exhausted he looked more like a patient than a physician—didn't take her seriously. "Do you forget anything else besides your name?" he asked. No, she said. Right now it's just my name. "Hmm. This sounds more like a psychiatric case," he said, his voice devoid of any interest or sympathy. "If you start to forget things other than your name, please check back with us. We can run some tests then." We've got our hands full with a lot more seriously ill people than you, he seemed to imply. Forgetting your own name every once in a while is no big deal.

One day, in the local ward newsletter that came in the mail, she came across an article announcing that the ward office would be opening a counseling center. It was just a tiny article, something she'd normally have overlooked. The center would be open twice a month and feature a professional counselor who, at a greatly reduced rate, would advise people one-on-one. Any resident of Shinagawa Ward over eighteen was free to make use of its services, the article said, with everything held in the strictest confidence. Mizuki had her doubts about whether a ward-sponsored counseling center would do any good, but decided to give it a try. It couldn't hurt, she concluded. The dealership she worked at was busy on the weekends, but getting a day off during the week wasn't difficult and she was able to adjust her schedule to fit the schedule of the counseling center, which was an unrealistic one for ordinary working people. The center required an appointment, so she phoned ahead. One thirty-minute session cost two thousand yen, not an excessive amount for her to pay. She made an appointment for one p.m. the following Wednesday.

When she arrived at the counseling center on the third floor of the ward office, Mizuki found she was the only client. "They started this program rather suddenly," the woman receptionist explained, "and most people don't know about it yet. Once people find out, I'm sure we'll get more people coming by. But now we're pretty open, so you're lucky."

The counselor, whose name was Tetsuko Sakaki, was a pleasant, short, heavyset woman in her late forties. Her short hair was dyed a light brown, her broad face wreathed in an amiable smile. She wore a light-colored summer-weight suit, a shiny silk blouse, a necklace of artificial pearls, and low heels. She looked less like a counselor than some friendly, helpful neighborhood housewife.

"My husband works in the ward office here, you see. He's section chief of the Public Works Department," she said by way of friendly intro-duction. "That's how we were able to get support from the ward and open this counseling center. Actually, you're our first client, and we're very happy to have you. I don't have any other appointments today, so let's just take our time and have a good heart-to-heart talk." The woman spoke extremely slowly, everything about her slow and deliberate.

It's very nice to meet you, Mizuki said. Inside, though, she wondered whether this sort of person would be of any help.

"You can rest assured that I have a degree in counseling and lots of experience. So just leave everything up to me," the woman added, sounding like she'd read Mizuki's mind.

Mrs. Sakaki was seated behind a plain metal office desk. Mizuki sat on a small, ancient sofa that looked like something they'd just dragged out of storage. The springs were about to go, and the musty smell made her nose twitch.

"I was really hoping to get one of those nice couches so it looks more like a counselor's office, but that's all we could come up with at the moment. We're dealing with a town hall here, so you can always count on a lot of red tape. An awful place. I promise next time we'll have some-thing better for you to sit on, but I hope today you won't mind."

Mizuki sank back into the flimsy old sofa and began to explain how she'd come to forget her name so often. All the while Mrs. Sakaki just nodded along. She didn't ask any questions, never showed any surprise. She hardly even made any appropriate sounds to show she was follow-ing Mizuki. She just listened carefully to Mizuki's story, and except for the occasional frown as if she were considering something, her face remained unchanged, her faint smile, like a spring moon at dusk, never wavered.

"That was a wonderful idea to put your name on a bracelet," she com-mented after Mizuki had finished. "I like the way you dealt with it. The first thing is to come up with a practical solution, to minimize any incon-venience. Much better to deal with the issue in a realistic way than be tormented by a sense of guilt, brood over it, or get all flustered. I can see you're quite clever. And it's a gorgeous bracelet. It looks wonderful on you."

"Do you think forgetting one's name might be connected with a more serious disease? Are there cases of this?" Mizuki asked.

"I don't believe there are any diseases that have that sort of defined early symptom," Mrs. Sakaki said. "I am a little concerned, though, that the symptoms have gotten worse over the past year. I suppose it's possible this might lead to other symptoms, or that your memory loss could spread to other areas. So let's take it one step at a time and determine where this all started. I would imagine that since you work outside the home, forgetting your name must lead to all sorts of problems."

Mrs. Sakaki began by asking several basic questions about Mizuki's present life. How long have you been married? What kind of work do you do? How is your health? She went on to question her about her childhood, about her family, her schooling. Things she enjoyed, things she didn't. Things she was good at, things she wasn't. Mizuki tried to answer each and every question as honestly, as quickly, and as accurately as she could.

Mizuki was raised in a quite ordinary family, with her parents and older sister. Her father worked for a large insurance company, and though they weren't affluent by any means, she never remembered them hurting for money. Her father was a serious person, while her mother was on the delicate side and a bit of a nag. Her sister was always at the top of her class, though according to Mizuki she was a little shallow and sneaky. Still, Mizuki had no special problems with her family and got along with them all right. They'd never had any major fights. Mizuki herself had been the sort of child who didn't stand out. She was always healthy, never got sick, which doesn't mean that she was particularly athletic—she wasn't. She didn't have any hang-ups about her looks, though nobody ever told her she was pretty, either. Mizuki saw herself as fairly intelligent, but didn't excel in any one area. Her grades were all right—if you were looking for her name on the grade roster, it was faster to count from the top of the ranked list than from the bottom. She'd had some good friends in school, but they'd all moved to other places after getting married and now they seldom kept in touch.

She didn't have any particular complaints about married life. In the beginning she and her husband made the usual, predictable mistakes young marrieds make, but over time they'd cobbled together a decent enough life. Her husband wasn't perfect by any means (besides his argumentative nature, his sense of fashion was nonexistent), but he had a lot of good points—he was kind, responsible, clean, would eat anything, and never complained. He seemed to get along fine with everyone at work, both his colleagues and his bosses. Of course there were times when unpleasant things did arise at work, an unavoidable consequence of working closely with the same people day after day, but still he didn't seem to get too stressed out by it.

As she responded to all these questions, Mizuki was struck by what an uninspired life she'd led. Nothing approaching the dramatic had ever touched her. If her life were a movie, it would be one of those low-budget environmental documentaries guaranteed to put you to sleep. Washed-out scenery stretching out endlessly to the horizon. No changes of scene, no close-ups, nothing exciting, just a flatline experience with nothing whatsoever to draw you in. Nothing ominous, nothing suggestive. Occasionally the camera angle would shift ever so slightly as if nudged out of its complacency. Mizuki knew it was a counselor's job to listen to her clients, but she started to feel sorry for the woman who was having to listen so intently to such a tedious life story. Surely she couldn't suppress a yawn forever. If it were me and I had to listen to endless tales of stale lives like mine, Mizuki thought, at some point I'd keel over from sheer boredom.

Tetsuko Sakaki, though, listened intently to Mizuki, taking down a few concise notes. Occasionally she'd ask a quick question, but for the most part she was silent, as if focusing entirely on the process of listening to Mizuki's story. The few times when she did speak, her voice revealed no hint of boredom, rather a warmth that showed her genuine concern. Listening to Tetsuko's distinctive drawl, Mizuki found herself strangely calmed. No one's ever listened so patiently to me before, she realized. When their meeting, just over an hour, wound up, Mizuki felt a burden lifted from her.

"Mrs. Ando, can you come at the same time next Wednesday?" Mrs. Sakaki asked, smiling broadly.

"Yes, I can," Mizuki replied. "You don't mind if I do?"

"Of course not. As long as you're all right with it. Counseling takes many sessions before you see any progress. This isn't like one of those radio call-in shows where you can easily wrap up things and just advise the caller to 'Hang in there!' It might take time, but we're like neighbors, both from Shinagawa, so let's take our time and do a good job."

◎

"I wonder if there's any event you can recall that had to do with names?" Mrs. Sakaki asked during their second session. "Your name, somebody else's name, the name of a pet, name of a place you've visited, a nickname, perhaps? Anything having to do with a name. If you have any memory at all concerning a name, I'd like you to tell me about it."

"Something to do with names?"

"Names, naming, signatures, roll calls . . . It can be something trivial, as long as it has to do with a name. Try to remember."

Mizuki thought about it for a long while.

"I don't think I have any particular memory about a name," she finally said. "At least nothing's coming to me right now. Oh . . . I do have a memory about a name tag."

"A name tag. Very good."

"But it wasn't *my* name tag," Mizuki said. "It was somebody else's."

"That doesn't matter. Tell me about it," Mrs. Sakaki said.

"As I mentioned last week, I went to a private girls' school for both junior and senior high," Mizuki began. "I was from Nagoya and the school was in Yokohama so I lived in a dorm at school and went home on the weekends. I'd take the Shinkansen train home every Friday night and be back on Sunday night. It was only two hours to Nagoya, so I didn't feel particularly lonely."

Mrs. Sakaki nodded. "But weren't there a lot of good private girls' schools in Nagoya? Why did you have to leave your home and go all the way to Yokohama?"

"My mother graduated from there and wanted one of her daughters to go. And I thought it might be nice to live apart from my parents. The school was a missionary school but was fairly liberal. I made some good friends there. All of them were like me, from other places, with mothers who'd graduated from the school. I was there for six years and generally enjoyed it. The food was pretty bad, however."

Mrs. Sakaki smiled. "You said you have an older sister?"

"That's right. She's two years older than me."

"Why didn't she go to that school?"

"She's more of a homebody. She's been sort of sickly, too, since she was little. So she went to a local school, and lived at home. That's why my mother wanted me to attend that school. I've always been healthy and a lot more independent than my sister. When I graduated from elementary school and they asked me if I'd go to the school in Yokohama, I said OK. The idea of riding the Shinkansen every weekend to come home was kind of exciting, too."

"Excuse me for interrupting," Mrs. Sakaki said, smiling. "Please go on."

"Most people had a roommate in the dorm, but when you got to be a senior you were given your own room. I was living in one of those single rooms when this all happened. Since I was a senior they made me student representative for the dorm. There was a board at the entrance of the dorm with name tags hanging there for each of the students in the dorm. The front of the name tag had your name in black, the back in red. Whenever you went out you had to turn the name tag over, and turn it back when you returned. So when the person's name was in black they were in the dorm; if it was red it meant they'd gone out. If you were staying overnight somewhere or were going to be on leave for a while, your name tag was taken off the board. Students took turns manning the front desk and when you got a phone call for one of the students it was easy to tell their status just by glancing at the board. It was a very convenient system."

Mrs. Sakaki gave a word of encouragement for her to go on.

"Anyway, this happened in October. It was before dinnertime and I was in my room, doing homework, when a junior named Yuko Matsunaka came to see me. She was by far the prettiest girl in the whole dorm—fair skin, long hair, beautiful, doll-like features. Her parents ran a well-known Japanese inn in Kanazawa and were pretty well-off. She wasn't in my class so I'm not sure, but I heard her grades were very good. In other words, she stood out in a lot of ways. There were lots of younger students who practically worshipped her. But Yuko was friendly and wasn't stuck up at all. She was a quiet girl who didn't show her feelings much. A nice girl, but I sometimes couldn't figure out what she was thinking. The younger girls might have looked up to her but I doubt she had any close friends."

Mizuki was at her desk, listening to the radio in her room when she heard a faint knock at her door. She opened it to find Yuko Matsunaka standing there, dressed in a tight turtleneck sweater and jeans. I'd like to talk with you, Yuko said, if you have time. "Fine," Mizuki said, frankly taken aback. "I'm not doing anything special right now." Mizuki had never once had a private conversation with Yuko, just the two of them, and she'd never imagined Yuko would come to her room to ask her advice about anything personal. Mizuki motioned for her to sit down, and made some tea with the hot water in her thermos.

"Mizuki, have you ever felt jealous?" Yuko said all of a sudden.

Mizuki was surprised by this sudden question, but gave it serious thought.

"No, I guess I never have," she replied.

"Not even once?"

Mizuki shook her head. "At least, when you ask me out of the blue like that I can't remember any times. Jealousy . . . What kind do you mean?"

"Like you love somebody but he loves somebody else. Like there's something you want very badly but somebody else just grabs it. Or there's something you want to be able to do, and somebody else is able to do it with no effort . . . Those sorts of things."

"I don't think I've ever felt that way," Mizuki said. "Have you?"

"A lot."

Mizuki didn't know what to say. How could a girl like this want anything more in life? She was gorgeous, rich, did well in school, and was popular. Her parents doted on her. Mizuki had heard rumors that on weekends she went on dates with a handsome college student. So how on earth could she want anything more?

"Like what, for instance?" Mizuki asked.

"I'd rather not say," Yuko said, choosing her words carefully. "Besides, listing all the details here is pointless. I've wanted to ask you that for a while—whether you've ever felt jealous."

"Really?"

"Yes."

Mizuki had no idea what this was all about, but made up her mind to answer as honestly as she could. "I don't think I've ever had that sort of experience," she began. "I don't know why, and maybe it's a little strange if you think about it. I mean, it's not like I have tons of confidence, or get everything I want. Actually there're lots of things I should feel frustrated about, but for whatever reason, that hasn't made me feel jealous of other people. I wonder why."

Yuko Matsunaka smiled faintly. "I don't think jealousy has much of a connection with real, objective conditions. Like if you're fortunate you're not jealous, but if life hasn't blessed you, you are jealous. Jealousy doesn't work that way. It's more like a tumor secretly growing inside us that gets bigger and bigger, beyond all reason. Even if you find out it's there, there's nothing you can do to stop it. It's like saying people who are fortunate don't get tumors, while people who're unhappy get them more easily—that isn't true, right? It's the same thing."

Mizuki listened without saying anything. Yuko hardly ever had so much to say at one time.

"It's hard to explain what jealousy is to someone who's never felt it. One thing I do know is it's not easy living with it. It's like carrying around your own small version of hell, day after day. You should be thankful you've never felt that way."

Yuko stopped speaking and looked straight at Mizuki with what might pass for a smile on her face. She really is lovely, Mizuki thought again. Nice clothes, a wonderful bust. What would it feel like to be like her— such a beauty you stop traffic wherever you go? Is it something you can simply be proud of? Or is it more of a burden?

Despite these thoughts, Mizuki never once felt envious of Yuko.

"I'm going back home now," Yuko said, staring at her hands in her lap. "One of my relatives died and I have to go to the funeral. I already got permission from our dorm master. I should be back by Monday morning, but while I'm gone I was wondering if you would take care of my name tag."

She extracted her name tag from her pocket and handed it to Mizuki. Mizuki didn't understand what was going on.

"I don't mind keeping it for you," Mizuki said. "But why go to the bother of asking me? Couldn't you just stick it in a desk drawer?"

Yuko looked even deeper into Mizuki's eyes, which made her uncomfortable.

"I just want you to hold on to it for me this time," Yuko said, point-blank. "There's something that's bothering me, and I don't want to keep it in my room."

"I don't mind," Mizuki said.

"I don't want a monkey running off with it while I'm away," Yuko said.

"I doubt there're any monkeys here," Mizuki said brightly. It wasn't like Yuko to make jokes. And then Yuko left the room, leaving behind the name tag, the untouched cup of tea, and a strange blank space where she had been.

◎

"On Monday Yuko still hadn't returned to the dorm," Mizuki told her counselor, Mrs. Sakaki. "The teacher in charge of her class was worried, so he phoned her parents. She'd never gone home. No one in her family had passed away, and there had never been any funeral for her to attend. She'd lied about the whole thing and then vanished. They found her body the following week, on the weekend. I heard about it after I came back from spending the weekend at home in Nagoya. She'd killed herself in a woods somewhere, slitting her wrists. When they found her she was dead, covered with blood. Nobody knew why she did it. She didn't leave behind a note, and there wasn't any clear motive. Her roommate said she'd seemed the same as always. She hadn't seemed troubled by anything. Yuko had killed herself without saying a word to anybody."

"But wasn't this Miss Matsunaka trying to tell *you* something?" Mrs. Sakaki asked. "That's why she came to your room, left her name tag with you. And talked about her jealousy."

"It's true she talked about jealousy with me. I didn't make much of it at the time, though later I realized she must have wanted to tell someone about it before she died."

"Did you tell anybody that she'd come to your room just before she died?"

"No, I never did."

"Why not?"

Mizuki inclined her head and gave it some thought. "If I told people about it, it would only cause more confusion. No one would understand, and it wouldn't do any good."

"You mean that jealousy might have been the reason for her suicide?"

"Right. If I told people that, they might start thinking something's wrong with me. Who in the world would a girl like Yuko be envious of?

Everybody was pretty confused then, and worked up, so I decided the best thing was just to keep quiet. You can imagine the atmosphere in a girls' school dorm—if I'd said anything it would have been like lighting a match in a gas-filled room."

"What happened to the name tag?"

"I still have it. It's in a box in the back of my closet. Along with my own name tag."

"Why do you still keep it with you?"

"Things were in such an uproar at school then and I lost my chance to return it. And the longer I waited, the harder it became to just casually return it. But I couldn't bring myself to throw it away, either. Besides, I started to think that maybe Yuko wanted me to keep that name tag. That's why she came to my room just before she died and left it with me. Why she picked me, I have no idea."

"It is sort of strange. You and Yuko weren't very close, were you."

"Living in a small dorm, naturally we ran across each other," Mizuki said. "We exchanged a few words every once in a while. But we were in different grades, and we'd never once talked about anything personal. Maybe she came to see me because I was the student representative in the dorm. I can't think of any other reason."

"Perhaps Yuko was interested in you for some reason. Maybe she was attracted to you. Maybe she saw something in you she was drawn toward."

"I wouldn't know about that," Mizuki said.

Mrs. Sakaki was silent, gazing for a time at Mizuki as if trying to make sure of something.

"All that aside, you honestly have never felt jealous? Not even once in your life?"

Mizuki didn't reply right away. "I don't think so. Not even once."

"Which means that you can't comprehend what jealousy is?"

"In general I think I can—at least what might cause it. But I don't know what it actually *feels* like. How overpowering it is, how long it lasts, how much you suffer because of it."

"You're right," Mrs. Sakaki said. "Jealousy goes through many stages. All human emotions are like that. When it's not so serious, people call it fretting or envy. There are differences in intensity, but most people experience those less intense emotions as a matter of course. Like say one of your co-workers is promoted ahead of you, or a student in your class becomes the teacher's pet. Or a neighbor wins the lottery. That's just envy. It seems unfair, and you get a little mad. An entirely natural reaction. Are you sure you've never felt that? You've never even envied someone else?"

Mizuki gave it some thought. "I don't think I have. Of course there're plenty of people more fortunate than I am. But that doesn't mean I've ever felt envious of them. I figure everybody's life is different."

"Since everybody's different it's hard to compare them?"

"I suppose so."

"An interesting point of view . . . ," Mrs. Sakaki said, hands folded together on top of the desk, her relaxed voice betraying amusement. "Anyway, those are just mild cases, envy as we've said. In cases of intense jealousy, things aren't so simple. With jealousy a parasite takes root in your heart, and as your friend said, it becomes like a cancer that eats away at your soul. In some cases it may even lead the person to death. They can't control it, and their life does indeed become a living hell."

◎

After Mizuki got back home, she took out an old cardboard box wrapped in tape from the back of her closet. She'd put Yuko's name tag in there along with her own, inside an envelope, so they should still be there. All sorts of memorabilia of Mizuki's life were stuffed inside the box—old letters from grade school, diaries, photo albums, report cards. She'd been meaning to get rid of it, but had always been too busy, so she'd dragged it along every time she moved. But the envelope was nowhere to be found. She dumped out the contents of the box and sorted through them carefully, but came up empty-handed. She was bewildered. When she moved into the condo she'd done a quick check of the box's contents and distinctly remembered seeing the envelope. So I still have it, she'd thought then, impressed. She'd sealed the name tags back inside the envelope and hadn't opened the box once since then. So the envelope *had* to be here. Where could it have disappeared to?

◎

Since she started going to the ward counseling office once a week and talking with Mrs. Sakaki, Mizuki didn't worry as much about forgetting her name. She still forgot it about as often as before, but the symptoms seemed to have stabilized, and nothing else had slipped from her memory. Thanks to her bracelet, she'd avoided any embarrassment. She'd even begun to feel, occasionally, that forgetting her name was just a natural part of life.

Mizuki kept her counseling sessions a secret from her husband. She hadn't intended to hide it from him, but explaining the whole thing just seemed like more trouble than it was worth. Knowing him, her husband would demand a detailed explanation. And besides, forgetting her name and going once a week to a ward-sponsored counselor weren't bothering him in any way. The fees were minimal.

Two months passed. Every Wednesday Mizuki made her way to the office on the third floor of the ward office for her counseling. The number of clients had increased a little, so they had to scale back their one-hour sessions to thirty minutes. The reduced time didn't matter, though, since they were already on the same wavelength and made the best use of their time together. Sometimes Mizuki wished they could talk longer, but with the absurdly low fees, she couldn't complain.

"This is our ninth session together," Mrs. Sakaki said, five minutes before the end of one session. "You aren't forgetting your name less often, but it hasn't gotten worse, has it?"

"No, it hasn't," Mizuki said. "The symptoms are holding steady."

"That's wonderful," Mrs. Sakaki said. She put her black-barreled ballpoint pen back in her pocket and tightly clasped her hands on the desktop. She paused for a moment. "Perhaps—just perhaps—when you come here next week we might make great progress concerning the issue we've been discussing."

"You mean about me forgetting my name?"

"Exactly. If things go well, we should be able to determine a definite cause and even be able to show it to you."

"The reason why I'm forgetting my name?"

"Precisely."

Mizuki couldn't quite grasp what she was getting at. "When you say a definite cause . . . you mean it's something visible?"

"Of course it's visible," Mrs. Sakaki said, rubbing her hands together in satisfaction. "Something we can set down on a platter and say, here you go! I can't go into details until next week. At this point, I'm still not sure whether it will work out or not. I'm just hoping that it will. And if it does, don't worry; I'll explain the whole thing to you."

Mizuki nodded.

"At any rate, what I'm trying to say is, we've gone up and down with this but things are finally heading toward a solution. You know what they say—about life being three steps forward and two steps back? So don't worry. Just trust good old Mrs. Sakaki. I'll see you next week, then. And don't forget to make an appointment on your way out."

Mrs. Sakaki punctuated all this with a wink.

The following week at one p.m. when Mizuki entered the counseling office, Mrs. Sakaki sat there behind her desk with the biggest smile Mizuki had ever seen on her.

"I've discovered the reason why you've been forgetting your name," she announced proudly. "And we've found a solution."

"So I won't be forgetting my name anymore?" Mizuki asked.

"Correct. You won't forget your name anymore. We've solved the problem and taken care of it."

"What in the world was the cause of it?" Mizuki asked doubtfully.

From a black enamel handbag beside her Mrs. Sakaki took out something and laid it on the desk.

"I believe this is yours."

Mizuki got up from the sofa and walked over to the desk. On the desk were two name tags. Mizuki Ozawa was written on one of them, Yuko Matsunaka on the other. Mizuki paled. She went back to the sofa and sank down, speechless for a time. She held both palms pressed against her mouth as if preventing the words from spilling out.

"It's no wonder you're surprised," Mrs. Sakaki said. "But not to worry, I'll explain everything. Relax. There's nothing to be frightened of."

"But how did you—?" Mizuki said.

"How did I happen to have your high school name tags?"

"Yes. I just don't—"

"Don't understand?"

Mizuki nodded.

"I recovered them for you," Mrs. Sakaki said. "Those name tags were stolen from you and that's why you have trouble remembering your name. So we had to get the name tags back so you could recover your name."

"But who would—?"

"Who would break into your house and steal these two name tags? And for what possible purpose?" Mrs. Sakaki said. "Rather than having me respond to that, I think it's best if you ask the individual responsible directly."

"The person who did it is *here*?" Mizuki asked in astonishment.

"Of course. We captured him and took back the name tags. I didn't nab him myself, mind you. My husband and one of the men under him did it. Remember I told you my husband is section head of the Shinagawa Public Works Department?"

Mizuki nodded without thinking.

"So what do you say we go meet the culprit? Then you can give him a piece of your mind face-to-face."

Mizuki followed Mrs. Sakaki out of the counseling office, down the hallway, and into the elevator. They got off at the basement, walked down a long deserted corridor, came up to a door at the very end. Mrs. Sakaki knocked, a man's voice told them to come in, and she opened the door.

Inside were a tall, thin man around fifty, and a larger man in his midtwenties, both dressed in light khaki work clothes. The older man had a name tag on his chest that read "Sakaki," the younger man one that read "Sakurada." Sakurada was holding a black nightstick in his hands.

"Mrs. Mizuki Ando, I presume?" Mr. Sakaki asked. "My name's Yoshio Sakaki, Tetsuko's husband. I'm section chief of the Public Works Department here. And this is Mr. Sakurada, who works with me."

"Nice to meet you," Mizuki said.

"Is he giving you any trouble?" Mrs. Sakaki asked her husband.

"No, he's sort of resigned himself to the situation, I think," Mr. Sakaki said. "Sakurada here has been keeping an eye on him all morning, and apparently he's been behaving himself."

"He's been quiet," Mr. Sakurada said, sounding disappointed. "If he started to get violent I was all set to teach him a lesson, but nothing like that's happened."

"Sakurada was captain of the karate team at Meiji University, and is one of our up-and-coming young men," Mr. Sakaki said.

"So—who in the world broke into my place and stole those name tags?" Mizuki asked.

"Well, why don't we introduce you to him?" Mrs. Sakaki said.

There was another door at the rear of the room. Mr. Sakurada opened it, and switched on the light. He made a quick sweep of the room with his eyes and turned to the others. "Looks OK. Please come on in."

Mr. Sakaki went in first, followed by his wife, with Mizuki bringing up the rear.

The room looked like a small storage room of some kind. There was no furniture, just one chair, on which a monkey was sitting. He was large for a monkey—smaller than an adult human, but bigger than an elementary-school student. His hair was a shade longer than is usual for monkeys and was dotted with gray. It was hard to tell his age, but he was definitely no longer young. The monkey's arms and legs were tightly tied by a thin cord to the wooden chair, and his long tail drooped on the floor. As Mizuki entered the monkey shot her a glance, then stared back down at the ground.

"A *monkey*?" Mizuki asked in surprise.

"That's right," Mrs. Sakaki replied. "A monkey stole the name tags from your apartment."

I don't want a monkey running off with it, Yuko had said. So that wasn't a joke after all, Mizuki realized. Yuko had known all about this. A chill shot up Mizuki's spine.

"But how could you—?"

"How could I know about this?" Mrs. Sakaki said. "As I told you when we first met, I'm a professional. A licensed practitioner, with lots of experience. Don't judge people by appearances. Don't think somebody providing inexpensive counseling in a ward office is any less skilled than someone working in some fancy building."

"No, of course not. It's just that I was so surprised, and I—"

"Don't worry. I'm just kidding!" Mrs. Sakaki laughed. "To tell the truth, I know I'm a bit of an oddball. That's why organizations and academia and I don't exactly get along. I much prefer going my own way in a place like this. Since, as you've observed, my way of doing things is pretty unique."

"But very effective," her husband added.

"So this monkey stole the name tags?" Mizuki asked.

"Yes, he sneaked into your apartment and stole the name tags from your closet. Right around the time you began forgetting your name, about a year ago, I believe?"

"Yes, it was around then."

"I'm very sorry," the monkey said, speaking for the first time, his voice low but spirited, with almost a musical quality to it.

"He can talk!" Mizuki exclaimed, dumbfounded.

"Yes, I can," the monkey replied, his expression unchanged. "There's one other thing I need to apologize for. When I broke into your place to steal the name tags, I helped myself to a couple of bananas. I hadn't planned to take anything besides the name tags, but I was so hungry, and though I knew I shouldn't, I ended up snatching two bananas that were on the table. They just looked too good to pass up."

"The nerve of this guy," Mr. Sakurada said, slapping the black nightstick in his hands a couple of times. "Who knows what else he swiped. Want me to grill him a little to find out?"

"Take it easy," Mr. Sakaki told him. "He confessed about the bananas himself, and besides, he doesn't strike me as such a brutal sort. Let's not do anything drastic until we hear more facts. If they find out we mistreated an animal inside the ward office we could be in deep trouble."

"Why did you steal the name tags?" Mizuki asked the monkey.

"It's what I do. I'm a monkey who takes people's names," the monkey answered. "It's a sickness I suffer from. Once I spot a name I can't help myself. Not just any name, mind you. I'll see a name that attracts me, especially a person's name, and then I have to have it. I sneak inside people's homes and steal those kinds of names. I know it's wrong, but I can't control myself."

"Were you the one who was trying to break into our dorm and steal Yuko's name tag?"

"That's correct. I was head over heels in love with Miss Matsunaka. I've never been so attracted to somebody in my life. But I wasn't able to make her mine. I found this too much to handle, being a monkey, so I decided that no matter what, at least I had to have her name for myself. If I could possess her name, then I'd be satisfied. What more could a monkey ask for? But before I could carry out my plan, she passed away."

"Did you have anything to do with her suicide?"

"No, I didn't," the monkey said, shaking his head emphatically. "I had nothing to do with that. She was overwhelmed by an inner darkness, and nobody could have saved her."

"But how did you know, after all these years, that Yuko's name tag was at my place?"

"It took a long time to trace it. Soon after Miss Matsunaka died, I tried to get hold of her name tag, before they took it away, but it had already vanished. Nobody had any idea where. I worked my butt off trying to track it down, but no matter what I did, I couldn't locate it. I didn't imagine at the time that Miss Matsunaka had left her name tag with you, since you weren't particularly close."

"True," Mizuki said.

"But one day I had a flash of inspiration, that maybe—just *maybe*—she'd left her name tag with you. This was in the spring of last year. It took a long time to track you down—to find out that you'd gotten married, that your name was now Mizuki Ando, that you were living in a condo in Shinagawa. Being a monkey slows down an investigation like that, as you might imagine. At any rate, that's how I came to sneak into your apartment to steal it."

"But why did you steal my name tag too? Why not just Yuko's? I suffered a lot because of what you did. I couldn't remember my name!"

"I'm very, very sorry," the monkey said, hanging his head in shame. "When I see a name I like, I end up snatching it. This is kind of embarrassing, but your name really moved my poor little heart. As I said before, it's a kind of illness. I'm overcome by urges I can't control. I know it's wrong, but I do it anyway. I deeply apologize for all the problems I caused you."

"This monkey was hiding in the sewers in Shinagawa," Mrs. Sakaki said, "so I asked my husband to have some of his young colleagues catch him. It worked out well, since he's section chief of Public Works and they're in charge of the sewers."

"Young Sakurada here did most of the work," Mr. Sakaki added.

"Public Works has to sit up and take notice when a dubious character like this is hiding out in our sewers," Sakurada said proudly. "The monkey apparently had a hideout underneath Takanawa that he used as a base for foraging operations all over Tokyo."

"There's no place for us to live in the city," the monkey said. "There aren't many trees, few shady places in the daytime. If we go aboveground, people gang up on us and try to catch us. Children throw things at us or shoot at us with BB guns. Huge dogs tear after us. If we take a rest up in a tree, TV crews pop up and shine a bright spotlight on us. We never get any rest, so we have to hide underground. Please forgive me."

"But how on earth did you know this monkey was hiding in the sewer?" Mizuki asked Mrs. Sakaki.

"As we've talked over the past two months, many things have gradually become clear to me, like the fog lifting," Mrs. Sakaki said. "I realized there had to be *something* that was stealing names, and that whatever it was it must be hiding underground somewhere around here. And if you're talking about under a city, that sort of limits the possibilities—it's got to be either the subway or the sewers. So I told my husband I thought there was some creature, not a human, living in the sewers and asked him to look into it. And sure enough, they came up with this monkey."

Mizuki was at a loss for words for a while. "But—how did just listening to me make you think that?"

"Maybe it's not my place, as her husband, to say this," Mr. Sakaki said with a serious look, "but my wife is a special person, with unusual powers. Many times during our twenty-two years of marriage I've witnessed strange events take place. That's why I worked so hard to help her open the counseling center here in the ward office. I knew that as long as she had a place where she could put her powers to good use, the residents of Shinagawa would benefit. But I'm really glad we've solved the mystery. I must admit I'm relieved."

"What are you going to do with the monkey?" Mizuki asked.

"Can't let him live," Sakurada said casually. "No matter what he tells you, once they acquire a bad habit like this they'll be up to their old tricks again in no time, you can count on it. Let's destroy him. That's the best thing to do. Give him a shot of disinfectant and that's all she wrote."

"Hold on, now," Mr. Sakaki said. "No matter what reasons we might have, if some animal rights group found out about us killing a monkey, they'd lodge a complaint and you can bet there'd be hell to pay. You remember when we killed all those crows, the big stink about that? I'd like to avoid a repeat of that."

"I beg you, please don't kill me," the bound monkey said, bowing its head deeply. "What I've done is wrong. I understand that. I've caused humans a lot of trouble. I'm not trying to argue with you, but there's also some good that comes from my actions."

"What possible good could come from stealing people's names? Explain yourself," Mr. Sakaki said sharply.

"I do steal people's names, no doubt about that. In doing so, though, I'm also able to remove some of the negative elements that stick to those names. I don't mean to brag, but if I'd been able to steal Yuko Matsunaka's name back then, she may very well not have taken her life."

"Why do you say that?" Mizuki asked.

"If I had succeeded in stealing her name, I might have taken away some of the darkness that was hidden inside her," the monkey said. "Take her darkness, along with her name, back to the world underground."

"That's too convenient. I don't buy it," Sakurada said. "This monkey's life is on the line, so of course he's going to use any tricks he can to explain away his actions."

"Maybe not," Mrs. Sakaki said, arms folded, after she'd given it some thought. "He might have a point after all." She turned to the monkey. "When you steal names you take on both the good and the bad?"

"Yes, that's right," the monkey said. "I have no choice. If there are evil things included in them, we monkeys have to accept those, too. We take on the whole package, as it were. I beg you—don't kill me. I'm a monkey with an awful habit, I know that, but I may be performing a useful service."

"Well—what sort of bad things were included in *my* name?" Mizuki asked the monkey.

"I'd rather not say in front of you," the monkey said.

"Please tell me," Mizuki insisted. "If you tell me that, I'll forgive you. And I'll ask all those present to forgive you."

"Do you mean it?"

"If this monkey tells me the truth, will you forgive him?" Mizuki asked Mr. Sakaki. "He's not evil by nature. He's already suffered, so let's hear what he has to say and then you can take him to Mount Takao or somewhere and release him. If you do that, I don't think he'll bother anyone again. What do you think?"

"I have no objection as long as it's all right with you," Mr. Sakaki said. He turned to the monkey. "How 'bout it? You swear if we release you in the mountains you won't come back to the Tokyo city limits?"

"Yes, sir. I swear I won't come back," the monkey promised, a meek look on his face. "I will never cause any trouble for you again. Never again will I wander around the sewers. I'm not young anymore, so this will be a good chance for a fresh start in life."

"Just to make sure, why don't we brand him on the butt so we'll recognize him again," Sakurada said. "I think we have a soldering iron around here that brands in the official seal of Shinagawa Ward."

"Please, sir—don't do that!" the monkey pleaded, eyes welling up. "If you put a strange brand on my butt the other monkeys will never let me join them. I'll tell you everything you want to know, but just don't brand me!"

"Well, let's forget about the branding iron, then," Mr. Sakaki said, trying to smooth things over. "If we used the official Shinagawa seal, we'd have to take responsibility for it later on."

"I'm afraid you're right," Sakurada said, disappointed.

"All right, then, why don't you tell me what evil things have *stuck* to my name?" Mizuki said, staring right into the monkey's small red eyes.

"If I tell you it might hurt you."

"I don't care. Go ahead."

For a time the monkey thought about this, deep frown lines on his forehead. "I think it's better that you don't hear this."

"I told you it's all right. I really want to know."

"All right," the monkey said. "Then I'll tell you. Your mother doesn't love you. She's never loved you, even once, since you were little. I don't know why, but it's true. Your older sister's the same. She doesn't like you. Your mother sent you away to school in Yokohama because she wanted to get rid of you. Your mother and sister wanted to drive you away as far as possible. Your father isn't a bad person, but he isn't what you'd call a forceful personality, and he couldn't stand up for you. For these reasons, then, ever since you were small you've never gotten enough love. I think you've had an inkling of this, but you've intentionally turned your eyes away from it, shut this painful reality up in a small dark place deep in your heart and closed the lid, trying not to think about it. Trying to suppress any negative feelings. This defensive stance has become part of who you are. Because of all this, you've never been able to deeply, unconditionally love anybody else."

Mizuki was silent.

"Your married life seems happy and problem-free. And perhaps it is. But you don't truly love your husband. Am I right? Even if you were to have a child, if things don't change it would just be more of the same."

Mizuki didn't say a thing. She sank down onto the floor and closed her eyes. Her whole body felt like it was unraveling. Her skin, her insides, her bones felt like they were about to fall to pieces. All she heard was the sound of her own breathing.

"Pretty outrageous thing for a monkey to say," Sakurada said, shaking his head. "Chief, I can't stand it anymore. Let's beat the crap out of him!"

"Hold on," Mizuki said. "What this monkey's saying is true. I've known it for a long time, but I've always tried to avoid it. I always closed my eyes to it, shut my ears. This monkey's telling the truth, so please forgive him. Just take him to the mountains and let him go."

Mrs. Sakaki gently rested a hand on Mizuki's shoulder. "Are you sure you're OK with that?"

"I don't mind, as long as I get my name back. From now on I'm going to live with what's out there. That's my name, and that's my life."

Mrs. Sakaki turned to her husband. "Honey, next weekend why don't we drive out to Mount Takao and let the monkey go. What do you say?"

"I have no problem with that," Mr. Sakaki said. "We just bought a new car and it'd make for a nice little test run."

"I'm so grateful. I don't know how to thank you," the monkey said.

"You don't get carsick, do you?" Mrs. Sakaki asked the monkey.

"No, I'll be fine," the monkey replied. "I promise I won't throw up or pee on your new car seats. I'll behave myself the whole way. I won't be a bother at all."

As Mizuki was saying goodbye to the monkey she handed him Yuko Matsunaka's name tag.

"You should have this, not me," she said. "You liked Yuko, didn't you?"

"I did. I really did like her."

"Take good care of her name. And don't steal anybody else's."

"I'll take very good care of it. And I'm not going to ever steal again, I promise," the monkey said, a serious look on his face.

"But why did Yuko leave this name tag with me just before she died? Why would she pick *me*?"

"I don't know the answer," the monkey said. "But because she did, at least you and I have been able to meet and talk with each other. A twist of fate, I suppose."

"You must be right," Mizuki said.

"Did what I told you hurt you?"

"It did," Mizuki said. "It hurt a lot."

"I'm very sorry. I didn't want to tell you."

"It's all right. Deep down, I think I knew all this already. It's something I had to confront—someday."

"I'm relieved to hear that," the monkey said.

"Goodbye," Mizuki said. "I don't imagine we'll meet again."

"Take care of yourself," the monkey said. "And thank you for saving the life of the likes of me."

"You better not show your face round Shinagawa anymore," Sakurada warned, slapping his palm with the nightstick. "We're giving you a break this time since the chief says so, but if I ever catch you here again, you aren't going to get out of here alive."

The monkey knew this was no empty threat.

◉

"Well, so what should we do about next week?" Mrs. Sakaki asked after they returned to the counseling center. "Do you still have things you'd like to discuss with me?"

Mizuki shook her head. "No. Thanks to you, I think my problem's solved. I'm so grateful for everything you've done for me."

"You don't need to talk over the things the monkey told you?"

"No, I should be able to handle that by myself. It's something I have to think over on my own for a while."

Mrs. Sakaki nodded. "You should be able to handle it. If you put your mind to it, I know you can grow stronger."

"But if I can't, can I still come to see you?" Mizuki asked.

"Of course!" Mrs. Sakaki said. Her supple face broke into a broad smile. "We can catch something else together."

The two of them shook hands and said goodbye.

◉

After she got home Mizuki took the name tag with "Mizuki Ozawa" and the bracelet with *Mizuki (Ozawa) Ando* engraved on it, put them in a plain brown business envelope, and placed that inside the cardboard box in her closet. She finally had her name back, and could resume a normal life. Things might work out. And then again they might not. But at least she had her own name now, a name that was hers, and hers alone.

—TRANSLATED BY PHILIP GABRIEL